Chasing the *Music*

People are Talking about
Mark Alan Leslie

True North: Tice's Story

"Leslie vividly describes the plight of runaway slaves ... Tice exhibits a deep religious confidence that will endear him to readers of inspirational literature. While the main plot is a work of fiction, the well-researched historical elements make it believable and even, at times, educational."

—*Publishers Weekly*

Midnight Rider for the Morning Star:
From the Life and Times of Francis Asbury

"In a world of namby-pamby Christianity, along comes a story of a man who played no games with God. The life and exploits of Francis Asbury read like the biblical Book of Acts. Mark Alan Leslie did not write 'just another book.' I couldn't put *Midnight Rider for the Morning Star* down. Neither will you. This one is a 'must read.'"

—*Frank Eiklor, President, Shalom International Outreach*

"... engaging, entertaining, informative and *convicting*. We spend so little time in God's Word, and have so little passion for souls! I am inspired by Asbury's life and example. Although I am one of our congregation's main evangelists, Bishop Asbury puts me to shame and challenges me to be more passionate, saltier, wiser, more effective at redeeming the time, and certainly more willing to suffer for the sake of the gospel."

—*Jamie Lash, Jewish Jewels, Fort Lauderdale, Fla.*

"*Midnight Rider* is an exciting, exhilarating story that challenges the reader in an intense way."

"Again and again, it spoke to my heart."

[It] is a stimulating and imagination-provoking book."

"An exhilarating historical novel, helping readers experience the heart and mind of this 'saint.'"

"This is a fast-paced ride and read through the new Republic with America's most influential religious leader."

"If the life of Francis Asbury ever inspires a movie, the script may resemble Mark Alan Leslie's historical novel, *Midnight Rider for the Morning Star.*

"A delightful, enriching and inspiring read. The Church needs to read this and regain Asbury's passion and zeal. As a Christian and pastor, I've used this book for a witness several times."

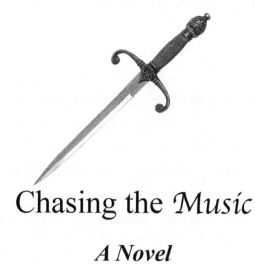

Chasing the *Music*

A Novel

Mark Alan Leslie

Elk Lake Publishing

Chasing the Music: A Novel

Copyright © 2016 by Mark Alan Leslie

Requests for information should be addressed to:

Elk Lake Publishing, Atlanta, GA 30024

ISBN-13 Number: 978-1-944430-01-6

Graphics Design: Anna M. O'Brien

Editor: Deb Haggerty

Published in association with Les Stobbe Literary Agency

Dedication:

To Jesus Christ, our Lord and Savior,
the ultimate inspiration to King David when he wrote,
played and sang his Psalms.
And all the saints who lift their voices in praise to the heavens.

Acknowledgements

Besides my chief encourager and wife, Loy,
I want to extend special gratitude to my agent,
Les Stobbe *(a wonderful and talented gentleman),*
Editor Deb Haggerty *(an exhaustless lady),*
and designer Anna O'Brien
(who did a marvelous job depicting the core of this book).

Also a thanks to special friends Sherwood and Jennifer Burton
of Jerusalem, who acted as our personal tour guides
through God's country.

In my research, I found increasingly evident how crucial music is to
worship, whether sung by a Jewish cantor,
or the voices of a Christian chorus.

"*Uni* means 'one' and *verse* means 'song,' so the entire creation is created as a song in God's heart because He is a musical God."

—Pastor Ray Hughes of Selah Ministries

Chapter One

Atop Dragot, seemingly in the clouds just north of Masada and with a magnificent view of Dead Sea to the east, Danny Arens knelt and bent over the ancient tablet with curiosity, his face close to the ground. The writing on the tablet was ancient Aramaic, his specialty. He rubbed his hands on his khakis to dry the perspiration of anxiety, then picked up the tools of his trade—a small whisk broom and a pocket magnifying loupe.

Danny himself had discovered the tablet as the previous night settled in. He'd told his five-person team of volunteer archeologists about the find before sending them off for the weekend. All they knew was everything he knew at the time; he wanted this moment alone, to share the discovery with the memory of his dead wife, who had so patiently supported him in his digs.

The hair on his neck rose in anticipation. But then, out of utter silence, he heard vehicles approaching up the nearly vertical, twisting road.

Tourists! His team was all in Jerusalem or other parts unknown. This was the first writing they had uncovered in two weeks working the site, so he pushed aside the sound and bent to lightly dust off the tablet, then blew away microscopic powder.

He leaned in to read the markings, and gasped "Oh, my!" He read aloud, "For the director of music. To the tune of 'The Doe of the Morning.' A psalm of David."

My G-d, My G-d, why have you forsaken me?

Behind him, the roar of engines became louder and closer.

"They must be tourists—or partiers!" Danny said in exasperation, "That's all I need."

He turned to look and, driving over the hill came two beat-up black Volvo sedans, covered with dirt and probably unfit for such a treacherous journey back downhill. After all, this was a road with dead-man curves so frightening that the "Caution-Curve" signs contained exclamation marks!

Danny shook his head in disgust and pushed himself to a standing position. Slipping his brush in one back pocket and the loupe in the other, he prepared himself to inform these people that a dig was in progress and off-limits except to his team and officials of the Israeli Department of Antiquities.

But instead of tourists pouring out of the cars, a half dozen men carrying rifles jumped out of the doors.

Fear soaring up his spine, Danny spun around. Before him, his archeological dig was cordoned off in grids by strings of twine and vinyl flagging, each encompassing an area being meticulously "dug." Some had barely scratched the surface; others were deeper.

Birds flying around the hill below him, combined with the steepness of the precipice, planted the idea he could use this spot to his advantage.

Gulping a breath, he leaped over the square before him, then over a foot-deep hole and sprinted toward the nearby fall to the south side of the hill. Gunfire erupted behind him and bullets spit up dirt in the air on both sides.

There were no trees at this height on this hill, no protection. He had run track through high school and college, but outrunning a bullet was

14

another matter. A bullet whizzed by, close enough to hear, and he ducked and leaped forward, over the edge of the hill, tumbling down the steep slope. Head over heels he fell, any concern for being hurt overridden by fear of death by bullet.

The south side of this hill was out of the sight of anyone anywhere. He was on his own. He faintly heard voices shrieking behind him and guessed the leader was telling the others to spread out left and right and pursue him. "Kill the infidel," were three Arabic words that sent terror-induced adrenaline into his veins.

Danny didn't resist the tumble, hoping, in fact, the fall would carry him free of immediate danger. His rolling felt like minutes but probably was only ten or fifteen seconds, when finally, he barreled into some low bushes.

Danny rose up on his haunches and pulled twigs out of his shirt around his neck. He shook his head and took stock of his body. All felt okay, no broken bones for sure. He stood and looked behind him. He spotted three or four men halfway down the steep incline, probably forty yards away. Two of them saw him and raised their rifles to fire.

He lurched to his right, which would eventually connect him to the Dead Sea Highway—if he could get that far. Dragot was south of Qumran and halfway to Ein Gedi, so there was plenty of traffic along the roadway—if only he could get there before being killed.

When he took his second step, a pain shot up from his right ankle. *Oh, there's the injury. No way could I fall that far without one.*

A spray of bullets pelted the ground and bushes around him but, miraculously, he was not hit. He bent low to shrink their target area and hurried as fast as he could, aiming for the treeline just fifty feet away.

More orders erupted on the hillside. "Hurry! Hurry!" Again the words were Arabic. "He's heading toward the highway!"

"You three, head him off!" demanded the obvious commander of the group.

15

Danny scrambled further down the slope, hoping to disappear from their sight. Adrenaline filled his veins, helping to mask the pain.

"Dear God, protect me!" he said aloud. "Protect me from my enemies—whoever they are!"

Again, he flung himself forward onto the ground, this time into a sideways roll, praying he wouldn't further damage his ankle.

Rocks cut into his arms and legs and brush impeded his speed, but he continued to roll. Finally, he smacked into the base of a wild date palm. He tried to muffle a screech from pain in his ribs, thinking that indeed now he had a broken rib as well as a sprained ankle.

He sat up and put a hand to his right ribcage. Breathing was difficult. Could a broken rib puncture a lung?

Danny grunted, grabbed hold of the tree and pulled himself to his feet.

There was an odd silence and, for a moment, he wondered if he had clambered far enough away to be safe. His answer came with two bullets, one ricocheting off the tree trunk and another planting itself no more than two inches from his nose.

He looked at the back end of the slug and spun around to the backside of the tree. More bullets pelted the tree and surroundings.

Getting his bearings, Danny guessed he was one mile, perhaps a mile and a half, from the Dead Sea Highway. He pulled his cell phone from a cargo pocket in his khakis. He was a bit startled to see the device hadn't been destroyed. But there was no tower signal.

He cursed his new enemies and speculated who they were. ISIS? Hamas? Hezbollah? Martyrs for Allah? And why? Perhaps the clue about the original music to the Psalms?

No. That couldn't be the answer. How would they know?

Danny thought of a fifteen-hundred-meter race against Ben Gurion University. He had run through pain that day and won by nearly two seconds. He could run through the pain again. He was only thirty-seven and still ran three, six-and-a-half-minute miles a day.

He grimaced, then, determined not to feel the pain in his ankle or ribs, took a deep breath, heard the starter's pistol in his head and raced eastward. Bullets followed him, splitting branches and kicking up dead leaves and dirt.

Trees and bushes became a blur. He scrambled over a knoll and then down another slope, staying in the tree-cover. Again, there was silence except for his breathing. The knoll had served as a barrier to the shooters. He glanced at his watch, figuring he could gauge the distance by the time he was running. This was good; he knew he had enough oxygen if his mind could work on equations.

But he called himself a petty name for wearing work boots. *If only I'd worn running sneakers.* He hadn't had to wear work boots today. *Meshuggeneh! Crazy!*

Through the forest he ran, slapping aside branches of trees, using his arms as protection when running through brush. Once he stumbled on a rock, but caught his balance and rushed on. The ache in his chest, the throbbing in his ankle became dull memories. *Adrenaline. Gotta love it.*

Four-and-a-half minutes into the pursuit, with sweat sticking his shirt to his chest, he spun around a huge baobab tree and stumbled over a root partly above the ground. He broke his fall with his right arm and felt searing pain in his chest. Looking up from the ground, he scrutinized the tree, broad and naked at the bottom with a large cap of foliage at the top. He realized this was the baobab he and a crewmate had noticed while driving along the Dead Sea Highway. The tree was unusually big, its canopy probably spanning twenty yards. They had joked about contacting the *Guinness Book of World Records* and reporting discovery of the world's largest baobab tree. They'd called it "The Silly Tree" because they were in a strictly juvenile mood at the time.

He recalled the moment and then looked ahead. There was Route 90—the Dead Sea Highway! Only a hundred yards away.

He'd get to the road, stop a car, any car, and get away. He hadn't heard a gunshot for minutes. Those guys were trudging their way through the woods, weighted down by rifles, probably not an athlete among them.

Danny scrambled to his feet and headed for the highway. Suddenly he heard a single gunshot and, a split second later, felt the impact of lead in his leg below his knee followed by excruciating pain. A second shot rang out, and he felt a piercing pain in his right shoulder, which knocked him to the ground. He tried to stand but couldn't.

But, I'm oh, so close! He realized the race was over, and he had lost. *But they had to drive to get ahead of me*, he mused wryly. On this spot, he would die. Forget all his PhDs and famous digs—his legacy was incomplete.

Then the thought of his cell phone came to him. He pulled the device out of his pocket. A three-bar signal. *Yes!*

He looked up and didn't see the shooter, but figured they were hurrying to get to him.

He didn't know how to call the IDF or police. His option: Dr. Katherine Cardova, his consultant on the dig and his friend who had named this "The Silly Tree."

He punched the key, and Katherine picked up on the first ring.

"Kat!" he said.

"Hi, Danny." Her voice was soft, winsome. She sounded relaxed. Perhaps she was in Masada, just a few minutes away, or down at the Dead Sea spa—even closer!

"Where are you?" he asked.

"Tiberias."

"Oh, no!" he cried.

"Why?" Her voice was suddenly anxious.

"Kat, I've been shot. They're trying to kill me!"

"Who!?" Now it was alarmed.

"I don't know. They speak Arabic, though. They came to the dig and started shooting."

"Danny, where are you?"

"Remember the baobab tree? The Silly Tree? Right there."

"I'll call the police. I'm on my way."

"You'll never make it in time. Kat, wait. Late yesterday I discovered a tablet in the dig. There's a unique symbol—"

"Yes?" Kat asked as his voice tailed off amidst the crackle of a lost connection.

Having pulled his Land Rover into a parking space at the outdoor restaurant in Tiberias, Max Braxton stood for a moment, watching three Jesus Boats near shore on the Sea of Galilee. He remembered the last time he was here, the memory almost causing the taste of the St. Peter's fish that awaited him.

Suddenly, a beautiful redhead slammed open the restaurant door and rushed to the sedan parked next to him. Max watched as she opened the door and hurriedly turned the ignition. The starter spit out a whir, nothing else. Again. A faint sound like a metal whistle blown by a child. The lady put her head to the steering wheel and grabbed the wheel, her knuckles turning white. She was frantic.

Max tapped on the passenger window and asked, "May I help you, miss?"

Her face lifted and she turned to look at him, her green eyes glistening with tears. She pushed a button, the window rolled down and she leaned toward him.

"A friend of mine is in danger, being shot at by killers. I have to get there!"

The hairs on Max's neck bristled. "Pop the hood," he said and hustled to the front of the car as she did.

"Turn the ignition," he said.

She did. He looked and listened.

"I'm afraid it's your starter."

"Oh, no! Oh, God!" she said and tears that had welled around her eyes began to roll down her cheeks.

"Listen," Max said, "I'll take you. Where's your friend?"

"At the bottom of Dragot, just off the highway. A ways north of Masada," she said.

"Wow! That's hours away. If he's being shot at, we need to call the police. Hop in with me and I'll take you there."

The lady slid out of the car, opened the back door and pulled out a duffle bag, then pulled herself up abruptly. "With all due respect, sir," she said over the roof of the sedan, "I can't jump into a car with a stranger."

"You can trust me," he said.It was a statement.

"I don't even know you."

"My name's Max Braxton."

"I'm Katherine Cardova—Kat. But I still don't know you."

"Let's fix the trust issue first." Max pulled a cell phone from a pocket on his cargo pants. "Will you trust me if I get us a police escort?"

She stammered as he scrolled through his contacts.

Max spoke into the phone, "Call Dudi Danino."

"Who's he?" Kat asked.

"Israel's police commissioner." Max pushed the SPEAKER button so Kat could hear the conversation.

"He's an old friend. The Israeli police, or Mishteret Yisrael, handle crime, public security, traffic and—counter-terrorism. Dudi and I taught a hostage rescue course together for his Yaman—that's their Special Police Unit—and their MAGAV—that's the combat arm or Border Police."

Kat began to speak at the same time Danino's secretary answered the phone. Max held up a staying hand and said: "Martha, this is Max Braxton calling the commissioner. Tell him this is an extreme emergency—bullets in the air."

"Certainly, Colonel."

A moment later, Danino answered, "Max, what is it?"

"We need your men on the ground where a fellow's being shot at off Highway 90 immediately south of Dragot. And, Dudi, I need a police escort from Tiberias down there."

"Just a moment," Danino said.

A few seconds later, he was back on the line. "My men will be at Dragot in ten minutes and Chief Inspector Moshe Halevi is at Hammat Tiberias, about six miles south of you. He's one of my best officers, Max. He'll give you an escort. What are you driving?"

"A white Land Rover with gear on the racks."

"Hold on a moment while I tell Halevi what vehicle to look for."

Max looked at Kat and motioned for her to get into the Rover. She hustled around to the other side of the Rover, tossed her gear into the back seat and jumped into the front just as he angled into the driver's seat.

A few seconds later, Danino was back on the line. "You're all set. But exactly what's happening, Max?"

Screeching out of the parking lot, Max floored the accelerator and veered around a car whose driver decided to stop in the middle of the road for no apparent reason.

"I'll let this young lady tell you, Dudi. I'm kind of busy."

Max handed the cell phone to Kat and swerved to avoid yet another crazy Israeli driver who was pulling out of a side street in front of him. "Actually most all of them are crazy," he muttered to himself.

21

Chapter Two

With her right hand, Kat gripped the grab handle over her side window and, with her left hand, grasped the cell phone Max handed her.

She was too frightened by what had happened to Danny to be scared by what would surely be a hell-bent-on-speed ride down a usually busy Highway 90—police escort or not.

"Commissioner Danino," she said, "I'm certain that Doctor Danny Arens, who is heading up an archeological dig on the top of Dragot, has been shot, perhaps killed by now."

"Why would someone want to kill him?" Danino asked.

"He may have just discovered something that got him killed," she said.

"Hamas," Danino said.

"Maybe. Perhaps others," Kat replied.

"I'm heading out of the door and will copter to Dragot. I'll meet you there."

Kat passed Max the phone. He took the cell, then glanced at his watch.

"Eleven-forty-two," he said. "I'll get us there by one-ten."

"And kill us, too?" she raised an eyebrow. "That's over one hundred and thirty miles."

Max simply looked at her and smiled.

Danny Arens awoke. He had passed out while on the phone with Kat, but how long was he out? The gunmen must be close by. Fighting intense pain in his shoulder and guessing the bullet had shattered his collar bone, he peeled off his belt and tightened the strap around his leg just above the gun wound.

Spotting his cell phone on the ground beside him, he picked it up and, in excruciating discomfort, began to hobble southward, parallel to the highway but, hopefully, away from his pursuers.

A half-minute later, noises broke through the silence, probably two or more people crashing through the trees and brush.

"Hear my cry, O God," fell from Danny's lips in Hebrew. Suddenly he stumbled and fell down an embankment, finding himself lying beside a thick, low-growing bush. Putting his left hand hard against his shoulder wound, he dove behind the bush and curled himself into a ball as best he could.

Arabic curse words spoken in harsh tones met his ears. They had found the spot where he had been shot.

"Spread out," came the order in Arabic. So, there were more than two people. Oh, if only he had come prepared. He did have a weapons permit and, as an ex-IDF officer knew how to use his sidearm. But the gun was at home, locked away.

"Stop!" The leader's voice, obviously. "He left a trail."

Yea, though I walk through the valley of the shadow of death … Danny repeated the twenty-third Psalm to himself, knowing God had miraculously saved his life more than once in battle, but certain that, indeed, only another miracle could save him this time.

"He's going this way," the leader said, and Danny could tell they were only a dozen or so yards away. He wondered what having his head sliced off with a dull blade would feel like—and flinched.

I shall fear no evil, for You are with me.

"Circle out," came the command. Obviously, there were four, maybe more of them.

You prepare a table before me in the presence of my enemies.

Danny heard footsteps approaching the very bush he lay behind.

You anoint my head with oil; my cup overflows.

I'm on the verge of the discovery of a lifetime, and here I am—about to die.

Suddenly he had the urge—a sort of spiritual nudge—to look behind him. He craned his neck and noticed there was a hollow beneath the roots of the bush. With his good leg, he hurried to push himself backward into the burrow, battling the urge to cry out in pain.

"Find him and bring him to me!" the command went out. "I, myself will cut off the head of this infidel—with a dull knife!"

Exactly what Danny had imagined. He cringed at the thought and thanked whatever groundhog, gopher, or other animal had dug this particular hollow in the ground. He took the chance to reach out and pull a large handful of dead grass in front of him.

Just then, one foot followed by a second were planted on the ground not more than three feet away.

Just before drifting into unconsciousness, Danny raised his thoughts to the heavens and finished the psalm, *And I will dwell in the house of the Lord forever.*

Mumim Maloof stood in front of the bush and surveyed the woods around him. This wretch could not have gotten far. Shot twice, he should be dead. He hefted his AK-47 in his hands and smiled crookedly. The smile transformed into a snarl when his men, one after another, reported failure at finding Arens.

Suddenly, distant police sirens broke the relative silence.

Maloof cursed and pulled a cell phone out of a pocket. Seconds later, he said, "Have you destroyed it all?" After a moment's hesitation, he ordered, "Then get off the hilltop now. Police are coming."

Maloof then called to his men, "Let the Jew rot in the ground and the vultures eat his flesh. For now, let's get to the vehicle and leave."

Maloof scrambled back up the knoll and hustled off toward the highway. Yes, he would have many Jewish heads before long. What was one less?

For now, he and most of his men would return to the Gaza Strip, a job well done, while two would stay behind and watch the dig site from a distance. Twenty minutes ago, before they had started their trek up the hillside, they had placed a "Road Under Construction" sign in the middle of the road. The result—no witnesses, no collateral damage. This was a good sign from Allah. No music. No Third Temple. No problem.

Chapter Three

Max and Kat sped southward, the Rover's emergency lights flashing, and Max honking the horn every now and then to prevent drivers from pulling out in front of them or to warn a vehicle they were about to pass.

Max took a couple of opportunities to assess his passenger. She was obviously a lady of class, of elegance—a refined woman who didn't need to gussy up to look absolutely tantalizing. Green eyes. Short-cut, curly red hair. Lanky, athletic, about five-foot-eight, thirty-five-ish. No wedding band. Wearing khaki shorts very well indeed.

If she was available, he was interested. He had no romantic ties, no children, just a thousand-dollar-a-month alimony payment and a train wreck of bad memories. This was as good a time as ever to find out about her.

"So you're an archeologist?" he asked.

"Yes," she said. "And I teach. Anthropology and linguistics. At Yale." The tension of the moment retreating, her voice was now a breeze high in the pines, mellow and inviting.

"Yale," he repeated. "Impressive."

She shrugged, then added, "My specialty is semiology."

"Semi—?"

"Semiology, the study of sign processes."

He was perplexed and showed his bafflement.

"There are three branches in the study of semiology," she said. "My specialty is semantics: the relation between symbols and the things to which they refer, their *denotata*."

"A-huh." Obviously, Max still stood in the midst of a cloud on the matter. He hesitated. "That's so … foreign … to me; I'd like to learn more."

"I could always tutor you." She coughed out a half-laugh, then started to weep.

They had reached Hammat Tiberias, and an Israeli police vehicle, the familiar wavy two-tone blue stripe down the side and "Police" markings in both English and Hebrew, peeled out of a parking lot in front of them, reaching seventy-miles-per-hour in a couple of seconds—Max knew because that was his speed.

With overhead lights flashing and siren wailing, Chief Inspector Moshe Halevi quickly pushed their speed to eighty, then ninety miles per hour on the nearly straight highway that ran parallel to the Jordan River. Several times they had to veer one way or another to avoid and pass cars whose drivers didn't pull to the side of the road, who didn't hear the siren screaming in their ears as Halevi approached.

Max thought wryly that the military's tactics-driving course, for which he was a top-tier driver, was coming in handy.

He caught a glimpse of Kat apparently praying and concentrated on his driving for a while.

When she straightened herself, he said, "By the sounds of what your friend discovered in the dig, perhaps you with your semi—"

"Semiology," she finished.

"Right. Are the best person to decipher the fragment."

"Perhaps."

Suddenly, a dark sedan heading out of a parking lot tried to squeeze in behind Halevi and in front of them. Max, fast on the cruiser's rear end, blasted the horn and veered sharply toward the center stripe, wheels squealing. Kat was slammed against the side door and gasped in pain.

Coming directly at them was an eighteen-wheeler, its grill a frightening few feet ahead. Max flung the steering wheel to the right, fishtailing the Land Rover back toward the travel lane. The truck driver responded at the same time, steering to his right. Max shot a quick look in his side-view mirror as the truck flew by, its left-front grill missing the Rover by inches. Maybe an inch. Maybe less.

Max brought the Rover back under control, releasing a breath. He stole a look at Kat.

"You all right?" he asked.

She grimaced and put her hand on her rib cage, then forced a smile and nodded.

"Israeli drivers," he spit out with a shake of his head, masterfully bringing the vehicle back under control. "I mean, I love the Israelis, but their performance on the highways could fill books of bad driving jokes."

Kat laughed, then grabbed her side.

During the next half hour, Max discovered that Kat was a Midwest girl, born and raised outside Omaha, Nebraska. Her parents were Oral Roberts University alumnae and owned a landscaping business in addition to raising Jacob sheep. ("Because they're beautiful and mild-tempered," she said.)

She had earned a bachelor's degree in archeology from Bryn Mawr College in Pennsylvania, which boasted the nation's first Department of Classical and Near Eastern Archaeology. Her master's and doctoral degrees were from the University of Chicago. Her doctoral thesis, a massive treatise entitled *The Semiotics of Anthropology*, was published as a book by Oxford University Press.

She had been involved in archeological digs from Kansas to Israel and had the calluses to show. (She showed him her palms in proof.)

Max related as much of his life as he lawfully could.

His father died when Max was fourteen. His widowed mother, Clair, lived in Dallas.

Max's younger sister, Maise, was married with two children and taught high school English in nearby Arlington, Texas.

Max and his ex-wife, Nancy, had no children which, he said, was probably a good thing.

After graduating from The Citadel in Charleston, South Carolina, he had majored in modern languages, especially Hebrew, Arabic, and Mandarin, with a minor in history. He also learned French and Spanish and had received his master's degree at the United States Naval War College in Newport, Rhode Island. His curriculum focused on joint military operations, and he later trained in shared wargaming with the SEALs and Rangers.

Kat asked, "How have you transferred this 'gaming' to 'real life'?"

"I'm sorry. That's something I can't divulge," Max replied.

"Top secret?"

"Most all of it."

"My students would think you're 'way cool'," Kat said.

He laughed. "Cool? Not me. *Cool* is Steve McQueen. Look at the 'cool' movie stars, singers and athletes today. Any of them really, indeed, cool? No, McQueen was the epitome of cool. He didn't need tats all over his body or weird facial hair or a fashion consultant. No, and he didn't need any props or groupies. Or to pose for photo ops. No tough-guy talk, no bragging, no nothing. He just was. And that was *cool*. Period." He chuckled, "Me, cool? Admittedly not."

Kat turned to better observe this man beside her. Six-foot-two-ish, forty-two-ish, short, curly black hair with streaks of premature gray. *He kind of looks like Jeff Chandler—now he was a cool movie star!* Square-jawed with a square face. If the SEALs had wanted a poster boy, this guy would be the choice.

In her mind, she could visualize Max in Steve McQueen's place on top of the motorcycle in *The Great Escape* or behind the wheel of the Mustang in *Bullitt* or putting a bad guy in cuffs as bounty hunter, Doc, or—and she grinned—flying off with Faye Dunaway in *The Thomas Crown Affair*. In her vision, *she* was Faye Dunaway. Why was she smiling?

Finally, she asked, "Why are you in Israel now?"

"Big decisions and a project."

She gave him a questioning look.

"I can re-up for another four years or take a standing offer to teach at either the Naval War College or The Citadel. But before that, I'm writing a book. And I figured the best way to clear my head was to be alone, hike the Israel National Trail—"

"Ha! Spoiled that, haven't I?" Kat said.

He glanced at her. "I wouldn't say you could spoil anything, Doctor Cardova."

She smiled, knowing she was blushing, then asked, "What's the book about?"

"My working title is *The Eye of Evil*. The book's about the perils of war without strong political leadership," he said, suddenly swerving and following Helavi's lead around another driver stubbornly staying in the travel lane.

31

Kat was impressed he didn't curse at some of these people.

Straightening out the Rover, Max flashed her a firm look. "When politics gets tangled up with war, soldiers die," he said, "and yet the people who send those soldiers to die are the very ones deeply involved in politics. Too often, they make decisions based on their self-interests or those of their political party, not those of the soldiers and, sometimes, the country."

"Historically, anecdotally, and in other countries down through history, you have a sound argument," Kat said, "but don't you think we need the President and Congress involved?"

"Yes, I think it's probably important to have a non-military person in charge of the military in any country, even a republic like ours. But at the same time, that person must realize his or her limitations in that regard. Besides, I've too often seen a military decision made by a politician with his eye on the all-important election cycle. That, Doctor, is a recipe for disaster."

Kat nodded. What he said was often all too obvious.

"Our military leaders," Max said, "know how to fight a battle and win and then get out. Failure to do so is nearly always the fault of some politician who, simply because he has the title of commander-in-chief, fancies himself knowledgeable in the art and science of war. Too often his confidence is greater than his insight and his arrogance is greater than his understanding."

He glanced at her. "Let me ask you, Kat. If you were going into major surgery, would you hand over the instruments of the operating room to the hospital's chief financial officer?"

She laughed, "No."

They continued high-flying down the highway, and she marveled at how Max could converse in the midst of such a race. She fought back the fear of the speed and her lack of control over the car. She liked to be

32

in control—she had come to realize her biggest fear was loss of control in any area of her life. If she were in a vehicle, she wanted to drive. If she were on a dig, she wanted to map the location out. If she were teaching, she had to have complete control of the curriculum.

This fear of lack of control was often obsessive. Besides that, she bordered on being a perfectionist. And those two traits—control freak and perfectionist—were ingredients for conflagration. If you were not in control and could not affect perfection, pow!

Her mom always told her, "Katherine, be a perfectionist, but don't expect perfection from everyone else."

And her dad would say, "Kat, thy middle name is Perfection."

Setting these thoughts aside, Kat asked, "What do your colleagues think of you writing the book?"

Max shrugged. "As with any black-ops material—"

"Black ops?" she interjected with tension in her voice. *Oh, Lord.*

She noticed Max stealing a glance at her and nodding assent. "I've trained with the Rangers and SEALs as well as special operations units in Great Britain, Germany, Australia, France, and Israel."

"Uh-huh."

"That bothers you."

She hesitated. She'd have to think this through. Finally, she said, "We'll see. I'm undecided."

Max smiled, "I can live with that."

After a couple of minutes of silence, Kat again turned to him. "So you were saying about clearing your book with your, uh, comrades."

Max nodded. "As I said, because the book involves black ops, I've had to run the thesis past many of these guys I've fought with. They've given me a unanimous thumbs-up."

Suddenly, Max pointed ahead. "Homestretch coming up."

They approached the Highway 1 intersection, with the Dead Sea in view in the distance to the southwest. Halevi slowed in front of them, but not much, changed the tone of his siren to a herky-jerky sound, then floored the accelerator again. Max and Kat closed in on the police cruiser's rear end until they were stuck like glue. They were so close that, with the siren howling, conversation was difficult.

Max checked his wristwatch—two minutes past one o'clock.

He glanced at Kat and spoke loud enough for her to hear over the din. "I told you we'd be there at one-ten. It'll be more like one-fifteen."

Kat cut a crooked smile. Drawing close to Dragot suddenly returned her thoughts to Danny and wondering what exactly they would find.

Past the Qumran Caves they flew, with the Dead Sea to their left and the caves snuggled high in the cliffside to their right. They sailed past pull-offs that led to the sea. Finally, they reached the turnoff to Dragot. There, Halevi slowed and just a quarter mile later, they pulled to the side of the highway. A helicopter, with police markings, sat silent across the highway, the pilot standing beside his aircraft with a military rifle strapped to his back.

Max and Kat bailed out of the Land Rover and hustled forward.

"Kol hakavod, Chief Inspector," Max said to Halevi in thanks and shook his hand. "Todah raba!"

"Al lo davar," Halevi said and pointed toward the woods, to one very tall tree in particular. "The commissioner says to head for that tree. It's a—"

"Baobab tree," Kat finished, already sprinting in that direction.

For a brief moment, Max admired her form in the khaki shorts and noticed an oddity he hadn't seen—she wore mismatched socks, the left striped purple and white, the right yellow polka dots on blue. He wondered at that, but the question would have to wait. If he lagged behind, he'd lose her.

Cutting through the woods was not easy, but when Max, Kat, and Halevi got to the baobab tree, they were met by two Israeli officers—young, serious. One of them stepped forward. He nodded to Halevi, then turned his eyes to Max and Kat and asked, "Colonel Braxton? Doctor Cardova?"

"Yes," they replied.

"We think we just now found your friend, Doctor Cardova."

"And?" Kat's face was flush with anxiety.

"He's alive but unconscious. He's been shot in the leg and shoulder and has lost a lot of blood. An ambulance should be here any minute."

The officers led them down a small embankment.

"Max!"

Max looked up and saw Dudi Danino rise out of a crouch over a man's prone body, which looked like he'd taken a shower in dirt and twigs. Large circles of blood stained the man's shirt and pants.

Max offered a faint smile and acknowledged the head of the Israeli police.

Danino, a short man in his sixties with close-cropped gray hair, offered a hand to Kat. "Doctor Cardova, I'm Dudi Danino. Is this Doctor Arens?"

"Yes. Yes, it is," Kat said between sobs. "Is he going to live?"

"I don't know. We can't do much for him here. We might do more harm than good if we move him to the highway for the ambulance. So, we're waiting." Dudi pointed to a hollow beneath a bush and said, "By the grace of G-d, he found that spot to hide from his pursuers. Almost too good a spot—we couldn't find him either. We thought the terrorists had taken him away, but then Corporal Goldberg here discovered him."

35

"Has he spoken at all?" Max asked.

Dudi shook his head. "Unconscious from the moment Goldberg pulled him from the hollow."

"Thank you for responding, Commissioner," Kat said, "and for your personal attention. Danny's a wonderful man, a true teacher for his students. A masterful archeologist."

"Does he have family?"

"Most of his family died when his sister's wedding was bombed a couple years ago. Since then he has dedicated his life to his work."

Danino nodded.

"I hear from my men up on top of Dragot that the dig's pretty messed up."

"Can we go up to see?" Max asked.

"Of course. You'll want to take a look now because I'll be closing down the site."

Kat's face erupted with disagreement. "No! Why?"

"The site's a crime scene now," Danino said, shaking his head. "Besides that, the Minister of Antiquities will want to deliberate about the whys and wherefores of reopening a dig that inspired someone to destruction and attempted murder of the head of the project."

"It can't be stopped," Kat objected. "It just can't—"

She was interrupted by the rapid "caw-caw-caw" of an ambulance siren drawing near. All heads turned toward the highway, and they waited as a four-man forensics team arrived.

Minutes later, Danino let the team take charge of the area around the baobab tree and a three-man emergency medical unit efficiently hurried about Danny with an oxygen mask, fluid drip, bandages, and tourniquet.

As they slipped Danny onto a stretcher, Kat asked, "Where are you taking him?"

"Hadassah Medical Center," one of the technicians replied.

Kat bent down to his ear and whispered to him.

When the EMTs had left, Danino offered to escort Max and Kat to the dig.

Walking to the highway and their vehicles, Max said to Kat, "May I ask what you said to Doctor Arens?"

"I told him I would handle his search until he recovers."

Normally, Kat loved being on top of Dragot simply for the panoramic view. From north to southwest, you could see two-hundred-and-seventy degrees and from one end of the Dead Sea to the other. Due south was Masada, and along the southeastern shore of the sea were the hardened dunes that looked so much like they could be have been the streets of Sodom and Gomorrah, with homes dug into eight- and ten-foot-high columns of salt; but, that was for another archeologist to prove.

Today, there was no sightseeing, no camaraderie between professionals and students eager to unearth history, to discover something previously only dreamed about, to perhaps write a new chapter in the textbooks of tomorrow.

A breeze from the east made the temperature cooler here compared to the eighty or eighty-five degrees Fahrenheit at the bottom of the hill.

The Land Rover turned abrupt curves and steep inclines for several minutes and finally rose over the edge of the hill, exposing the dig site. Kat gasped. As soon as Max settled in behind the police cruiser they had followed and parked, she flung open the door and jumped out.

Devastation! Who had done this? Whoever had, had used shovels to push dirt back into the excavation; smashed all the team's pup tents to the ground; shredded the "office tent," and generally turned order into chaos. Just yesterday, the camp was the epitome of order—an Arens specialty.

Rope, vinyl flagging, and PVC stakes were strewn everywhere. Kat spotted soil probes, whisk brooms, metric open reels, rock picks, a hand auger—all broken or ground into the earth, some simply thrown a distance away. The sight of the destruction caused what felt like a blow to her stomach. *Horrid. Unforgivable! Oh, my God, it's despicable!* She wiped a tear from her cheek.

Danino and Haveli had stepped out of the chief inspector's cruiser ahead of them and were speaking with two other officers.

Danino turned to Kat and Max. He held up a poster-sized paper. "Inspector Yechimovich and Sub-Inspector Pollard found this propped up on a stake in front of the dig," he said.

On the paper, words written in Arabic declared "ONLY DEATH WILL REIGN ON THIS SITE. KEEP OUT!"

"Arabic," Max said. "Gives us a clue, doesn't it?"

Danino nodded.

Kat put her hands on her hips and shook her head. When she consulted Danny about this dig, she suggested he hire security. He said he didn't have the finances for that and, besides, this was not a high-profile project; he hoped to unearth information about the Israelites who had been massacred at Masada. If only—

She walked over to what they jokingly called "the office," which served as headquarters, mess hall, and general get-out-of-the-sun oasis.

The canvas lay in shreds, strewn over the ground. She picked up a corner of the tent and started tugging at the material to see if anything remained underneath.

"Let me help you," said Max, and together they pulled aside the tent.

Kat bent to the ground and picked up crumpled papers. "The site map, Danny's excavation notes, they're probably destroyed," Kat said. She paused and wiped another tear from her cheek.

"Here, what's this?" Max held up a small black spiral notebook.

Kat shrugged and held out a hand.

Max passed the book to her, which Kat opened. Her eyes widened. "Eureka!

"What is it?"

"You ever watch Star Trek?"

Max nodded.

"This is like Captain Kirk's starlog, chronicling the voyage."

Kat leafed through the notebook until she came to the previous day's entry.

Danino and the others stepped closer.

Kat looked at them all and read, "July 8th. Whisking my way through Grid 5A, I discovered what may be the find of my life! It's too dark to continue today, but ..."

She leafed through a couple more pages, "That was his final entry. But when he called me, he said he'd discovered a symbol—"

"Yes, and?" Danino asked.

"Well, I don't know. But from the sound of his voice, whatever he found was unusual. Even so, how would these people who murdered him know about the discovery?"

"Where are the members of the dig team?" Max asked.

"I don't know," Kat said.

She snapped a finger. "I'll call Lois Knowles. She's on the team."

She pulled her cell phone out of a pocket and announced, "Two bars."

She scrolled through her contacts and clicked on Lois Knowles' name. A few seconds later, the woman answered.

"Lois, this is Kat Cardova."

She broke the news of the attempted murder, watching as Max and Danino searched the ruins of the pup tents.

After several minutes consoling the woman, Kat signaled for the men to join her. When they had, she put the cell phone on SPEAKER and asked, "Lois, what did Danny discover last night?"

Lois hesitated, then said, "He asked us not to tell anyone."

"Lois, I know," Kat said soothingly, "but Danny called me while he was being chased and tried to tell me about his discovery. It must be important."

"Danny was excited about a possible clue to where the original music to the Psalms is."

"The music of the Psalms?" Kat responded.

"Yes."

"That's the find of a lifetime—a millennium!" Kat said.

"It would be. And all of us would be part of it."

"But how would anyone else find out?"

"Only if one of us had talked," Lois said. "We were all here in Jerusalem last night. All but Sam Livingston. He drove on to Tel Aviv for the night life."

Danino broke in, asking Kat if he could take over the conversation.

She handed him the phone. "Please do, Commissioner. I'd like to investigate Grid 5A."

As Danino spoke to Lois Knowles, Kat turned to the front page of the logbook.

"What are you looking for?" Max asked.

"The grid map—and here …," she said, detaching the map from a paperclip and spreading the paper open for him to see. She scrutinized the layout, turned to survey the site, then pointed to a spot and declared, "5A is the corner grid and should be over at the edge of where the dirt has been shoveled."

She picked up a half-buried whisk broom and small hand-held vacuum out of the rubble and walked straight to a spot. Max grabbed a flat-bladed shovel and following close behind.

"Be careful, very careful," Kat said.

Kat and Max spent the next couple of hours in meticulous search for Danny Arens' tablet.

A forensics crew had arrived and was scrutinizing the dig site, making clay impressions of vehicle tracks, dusting for prints and searching for other clues about the perpetrators.

Meanwhile, Danino was glued to a police radio, directing a search for Sam Livingston, and Haveli oversaw the operation atop and alongside the hill. He and his two officers were now somewhere down the side, looking for bullet casings and other evidence and trying to reconstruct the terrorists' pursuit of Danny.

Shortly after five o'clock, Kat flashed Max a look.

"What is it?" he asked.

Kat put her whiskbroom in a rear pocket and ran the vacuum over a small spot. Light dust disappeared up the vacuum's tube, exposing a flat tablet, about six-by-eight inches, with etchings on it.

One look and Kat said, "This is it!"

She smiled broadly at Max, then stood and waved to Danino. "We found it, commissioner."

As Danino hurried over, she leaned toward the rock and Max hovered above her.

"It's Aramaic," she said. "It says, 'For the director of music. To the tune of 'The Doe of the Morning.' A psalm of David.'"

"What's this?" Max asked, pointing.

She looked more closely. Below the script were three faint etchings. The one on top was a symbol that looked like a "z" beneath and connected to a backward "z."

✦   ∕   ⌐   <   ∧   ∣   ⊢   ∖   ⌡   ∨   ⚐

Kat pointed to the symbol and said, "The first we saw this mark was in the eighth century when the Masorites used the mark to preserve the

41

Hebrew text denoting a vocal shake. But I've never seen the symbol dated to the time of Christ, which the sentence structure points to.

"A few years ago, some folks discovered what they called the Davidic Cipher, showing musical *tones* hidden within the words of the Psalms, and this was one of ten ciphers."

"Then people already know the music?" Danino asked.

"In a sense. They have sharps and flats in what they call a cycle of fifths, but not what we think of as a musical script like Brahms or Beethoven wrote. Certainly not the actual tune of *Doe in the Morning* or anything like that."

Kat turned her attention back to the tablet. Below the vocal-shake was a crown of royalty atop the Aramaic letter "D" which was shaped like two walls and a roof, with a curl at the left-hand side of the roof and a fat bottom of the left-hand wall.

"This denotes the Davidic kingship," Kat said, pointing.

"It looks like the H—Heth—in Hebrew," Max said.

"True." Kat nodded agreement and looked back at the tablet. Next to the "D" was another etching.

"The Lion of Judah," Kat exclaimed, pointing to the mark, "It symbolized King David's family, the Tribe of Judah."

Below the two symbols was Aramaic writing.

Kat translated, "Two Temples will be built and destroyed. Hold this sacred music until a Third Temple is built, then release the music to the world."

She looked up at Max, her eyes wide. "The timing of this find is astonishing."

"An amazing coincidence," Max said in a low voice.

"Coincidence? God-incidence," she corrected.

She turned her attention back to the tablet.

Below the writing was a design with red hues. "Amazing," Kat said, looking up. "I've never seen color in these symbols before."

Kat pulled a magnifying loupe out of a shirt pocket and peered at the etching, which depicted a cave high up in a wall. "Aha!" she exclaimed.

"What is it?" Max asked.

She looked at him with a sparkle in her eyes. "This, soldier, is a clue!"

"A clue to what?"

"To where to find the music." Her voice rose an octave and her eyes went wide. "Max, I know where to start the search. I can do this for Danny."

"You alone?" he asked.

"Who else?"

"After your friend's attack, I'd say you shouldn't be unprotected."

She shrugged. "Do you know anyone I could hire for protection?"

He smiled. "Me—and I come free of charge."

"I can't ask you to—"

Max put a forefinger to her lips.

"It's a done deal, Doctor Cardova. Max Braxton at your service." He bowed and, with a flourish, spread his arms wide.

She flashed him a wide grin and breathed a sigh of relief she wouldn't be alone.

Max turned to the commissioner. "We're hunting this down, Dudi."

"Whoa!" Danino said. "If they tried to kill Doctor Arens because of this knowledge, then your life would be in danger as well." He straightened up. "What would the meaning be, anyhow?"

Kat looked at him, astonished. "Commissioner, can't you imagine the importance of this?"

Danino stared at her, frowned, and then glanced at Max and simply shrugged.

Max smiled. "You up for a lecture from one of the world's great archeologists, Dudi?"

"Sure," he said.

"You know King David was an accomplished musician," Kat started.

Danino nodded.

"The songs he'd play soothed King Saul. And many of the Psalms he wrote, ones that fill the pages of the Old Testament, were to be sung to specific music. Some of King David's writings he described as 'a psalm; a song,' and many were to be given to 'the director of music.' And many were called 'songs of ascent.'

"In particular, something called 'The Lily of the Covenant' was to be the music of Psalm 60. Tunes called 'Doe of the Morning,' 'Do Not Destroy,' and 'Lilies' were to be used for a couple of different Psalms.

"And throughout the Psalms, the psalmists mention musical terms like maskil, sheminith, miktam, and shiggaion. But we don't know what these terms meant. Where do you think all this music is?"

"I don't know," Danino said.

Kat looked at Max.

"Don't ask me," he said, with an exaggerated rise of his shoulders.

"The fact is, no one knows," Kat said. "The music's lost in the shadows of history and folklore. But, believe me, Jews and Christians alike would absolutely love to have the music. The value is priceless."

"But, again, why would people kill for it?" Danino asked. "Why would Muslims care? David wasn't *their* king."

Kat put her hands on her hips and thought intensely. *Just what would be the problem?* As she whirled the question around in her mind, a flash of discernment occurred and her eyes widened.

"The Muslims do *not* want a Third Temple!" she said.

"You're talking about the synagogue that Jewish group wants to build?" Max asked.

"Not just a group. A lot of people," Kat said, "from Israel and around the world—even supporters in America. But, yes, The Temple Faithful are at the forefront."

Max shrugged. "So the music is critical for a Third Temple?"

"Maybe, maybe not. But that is when David wanted the tunes to be revealed. Listen." She looked at Max and then Danino. "They want to build the synagogue on the Temple Mount near the Muslims' Dome of the Rock and Al-Aqsa Mosque.

"The Temple Faithful have made all the things they need for construction—from veils to lavers to the musical instruments. In early 2015, they even finished building a massive outdoor temple altar, sixteen feet tall, fifty-two feet wide, complete with four 'horns' and a ramp. All in anticipation of actually building the Third Temple on the Temple Mount.

"They even have a herd of red heifers, which is vital to renewing Jewish ceremonies. They say the Temple is in accordance with the Word of God and all the Hebrew prophets. When Israel liberated the Temple Mount from Arab occupation in 1967, The Temple Faithful said the place could now, again, be consecrated to the Name of God."

Danino interrupted. "You must remember, the battle here in the Middle East is the battle for Jerusalem, and the battle for Jerusalem is the battle for the Temple Mount and who will be worshiped there. The reconsecration would have been immeasurably easier for them if Moshe Dayan, as defense minister in 1967, had *not* made the terrible decision of turning control of the Temple Mount over to the Muslim authorities. We spend immense resources keeping peace in and around the Temple Mount. There are contentions every day, and tourists constantly complain about being mishandled and frightened by the Palestinian authorities there."

"I know," Kat said. "But, from the Muslims' viewpoint, a Third Temple is unthinkable, unbearable."

"Good reason, then, for them to destroy a dig that might lead to finding the original music," Max said. "But how in the world would they find out about this if Danny only discovered the tablet last night?"

At that moment, Danino's police phone rang.

Before answering his cell, he looked at them, "We may have the solution to that question right here. This is a call from Jacob Ayalon, our chief inspector for the Tel Aviv-Yafo District. He's been checking on Sam Livingston."

He clicked on the unit. "Danino."

He listened, nodding. And then his eyes shot up to meet Kat's and Max's.

"Where?" he asked in Hebrew. Then, "Any leads to the killer or killers?" A moment later, "No?" Again, he nodded. "I see." He ran his fingers through his graying hair. "Moshe, I need you to keep this investigation quiet. We have a highly flammable situation."

A few seconds later, Danino spoke in English. "Jacob said Livingston's been found dead. He was stuffed in a trash bin outside a bar, his neck slit from ear to ear."

Kat gasped and Max wrapped an arm around her. Looking down at her, he asked, "Did you know him?"

Between sobs into Max's chest, she managed to say, "Only to say 'hello.' But what a death!"

The sight of Livingston being killed like that flashed in her mind. *Poor man. What terror he must have felt. Here he was, on an archeological dig of all things, and then to find his very life in peril? To see a knife at his throat! To know he was going to die a horrible death. Never mind not to be able to say goodbye to his wife and children. Inhuman!*

Kat looked up at Max and quoted, *Their portion will be in the lake that burns with fire and sulfur, which is the second death.*

"You know these people?" he asked.

"Whoever they are, the Book of Revelation numbers them among *the cowardly, the faithless, the detestable, as for murderers.*"

Max whistled a breath.

Danino cut in. "Doctor Cardova, would it have been unusual for Livingston to leave his colleagues?"

"I don't know," Kat said.

"Well, it sure looks like he may have been the leak," Max said. "Do your men have any clues what happened leading to his death?"

"He was in Kiryat Hamelacha, a harsh, seedy part of the south side of Tel Aviv. All we know so far is that he'd been in a bar frequented by foreign workers, locals—a mixed crowd."

"Maybe he got drunk and spilled the beans," Max said.

"Spilled the beans?" Danino looked at him, puzzled.

"Told people about Danny Arens' tablet," Max explained.

"Oh." Danino nodded. "Perhaps he did—as much as he knew."

"If so, they had plenty of time to get here and kill Danny, or try to," Kat said. Apprehension swept over her. "Then, are the others in the dig in fear of their lives?"

Danino shrugged. "I'd say whoever might seek after this forgotten, ancient music should beware."

A shiver played down Kat's back. She'd never been this close to death, to this type of tragedy, to a possible threat to her own life. As close as she'd ever come was probably when her Dad was "fired" as pastor of his church and how that threatened her family's way of life. But this? This was real life-and-death. How did it feel to be told you might have cancer or some other deadly disease that endangered your life? This was probably a similar emotion.

Kat stepped back from Max and locked his eyes with her own. "Are you sure you want to go with me, be my protector?"

"Yes," he said. No hesitation. A man of action. Turning to peer at the tablet, Max asked, "So what's your clue, doctor? I'm at your command."

47

Kat thought of her last boyfriend and how he, a professor of physics, would have responded. Not so much a man of action.

Kat pulled up her shoulders and straightened her back. "We need to get to Petra. But, first, to Jerusalem to see a man."

"A man?"

"Gershon Zoref," she said. "The executive director of The Temple Faithful. That's where we ought to start."

As they headed to Max's Land Rover, Kat turned to Danino. "Commissioner, will you ask the doctors at Hadassah to inform us of any changes in Danny's condition?"

Danino nodded.

"Especially when he wakes up."

"You have faith, doctor."

"Yes, I do."

Chapter Four

"So, you get a free room here whenever you're in Jerusalem?" Max asked as he drove into the front entrance to the King David Hotel an hour later. "Why?"

"The corporation that owns the King David backed a dig of mine up in the territory of Dan," Kat said. "It was very successful, so now they let me stay at any of their hotels when I'm around—Haifa, Tel Aviv, Eilat, Ashkelon, Caesarea. Not bad."

"Not bad?" Max coughed out the words.

Max glanced at this unusual woman beside him. He figured her smile would light up the Texas Rangers' Glove Life Park.

He'd seen stunning women the world over, but Kat? The whole package was disarming. He forced himself to take his eyes off her just so he could function.

And add to that, she was witty, humble and, oh, yes, brilliant to boot. The only anomaly? Those mismatched socks. Still, a question for another time.

Kat broke up his thoughts, tossing him an offended look and saying, "Now I discover you'll be my guardian because of my accommodations."

"Young lady," he said, "your connections are the least of your attractions."

The smile she flashed made his spine shiver.

He pulled the Land Rover up next to a doorman and valet and stepped out to look around. Sitting on an elevated site just two blocks from the Jaffa Gate, the King David overlooked the Old City and Mount Zion. Its pink-quartz exterior transformed what otherwise might be a quite ordinary broad, eight-story building into a stunning sight. In the dusk, beams from ground-level lights made the hotel look almost magical, giving Max a chill almost equal to gazing at the white Jerusalem stone walls of the Old City.

"It's magnificent, isn't it?" Kat asked.

"Sure is." Max walked to the back of the vehicle, collected his suitcase and Kate's duffle, handed them to the doorman and tossed his car keys to the valet.

"It's historic, too," Kat said, walking around beside him. "Built in the 1930s by Cairo Jews and served as a stronghold for Israel during the war of independence in 1948."

"Well," Max said with a grin, "Certainly is a far cry from tenting out along the Israeli National Trail."

They walked inside into an elegant and luxurious reception area. He was able to check into a room adjacent to Kat's and an hour later— minus the dust of the day and wearing light casual clothes—they sat on the patio of King's Garden Restaurant, munching on pita bread and biscuits dipped in humus.

Wearing a serious expression, Kat said, "My research and my classes are important to me. What's important to you?"

Max straightened up and thought a moment before answering, "My country. My family. Certain friends." He shrugged.

"That's it?"

"Basically. Except for a brief, and bad, marriage I've had no life outside defending my country and loving my family."

Straight to the heart of the matter. "Many people would mention God among their top two or three priorities. I mention this because He'll be at the center of our search. He is the One this music worships. His Name is what the music uplifts and calls on for deliverance."

Max intertwined his fingers, trying to hide his discomfort. "I don't mind a conversation about God—not really."

"But He's not all that important to you."

He could read disappointment in her manner.

"I may not be a semiologist," he said, "but I can discern the signals—the drooping and sloping forward of the shoulders. You're upset."

"True."

"Disheartened."

"True again."

"That's good. It means you care." He flashed a crooked half-smile.

Her right eye narrowed. He was correct.

"Kat, I don't open up to people like this," he said, "but I must say, you're—different."

Max stared down at his hands, his thoughts shrouded in a past secret to all but a few—and those few were seated in the furthest clandestine reaches of the American government, the military hierarchy and a very select few in a handful of friendly countries.

He looked back at her. "You do realize you're going for the jugular."

"The jugular?"

He nodded. A deep frown furrowed his forehead. *This is not me. I do not talk about these things. To anyone. Ever!*

He looked again at her eyes—startling green, searching, accessible, hopeful. Finally, he opened his hands, palms up, and broke the silence.

"Two things about me and God," he said. "First, my father died when I was fourteen. He died because of his exposure to Agent Orange. He died having saved many, many men. He died an awful death far, far before his time. I loved and admired my Pop. My relationship with God? When Pop died, that relationship took a hit that has never been fully recovered."

Kat started to speak, but he motioned for her to wait, then continued: "Second, doing the, ah, tasks I've had to do to protect my country— well, let's just say I've avoided confronting God about them. Not that I'm afraid of the consequences of, um, dealing harshly with bad guys; I just haven't wanted to weigh the pluses and minuses of my actions."

Kat nodded.

Max guessed his words confirmed her thoughts. Nevertheless, he plowed on.

"I was a hard-drinking, bad husband in a poor marriage. I've let relationships die of drought and have sabotaged friendships. And the debris doesn't stop there—not by a long shot."

Again, Kat began to speak and again he flagged her to wait.

Wagging his head, like a fighter shaking away mental cobwebs after absorbing a severe blow, he said, "The result is, I've walked a distance away from God—much to my mother's chagrin."

Noticing the look of anxiety in her face—no, no, the look was hurt and, perhaps, pity—he again held up a hand. "Not directly *away* from God, but more like a parallel road, Kat. I see Him there but I'm not yet ready for a one-on-one with Him. Not just now. Know what I mean?"

Kat nodded.

Drawing a deep breath, she said, "I'm guessing you were fourteen about twenty-five years ago or so. You know, Max, God has never walked away from you—in any direction. He's there at the door, waiting for you to let Him in. No pressure. And a lot less pain than what you're experiencing now."

"Well, He'd have a lot to forgive—"

"Doesn't matter."

"There's a lot you don't know—"

"Doesn't matter."

"But people have di—"

"Max, that doesn't matter." In obvious frustration, Kat's voice raised an octave, but she caught herself. Lowering her voice, she continued, "Max, God only wants a heart that's repentant. The apostle Paul allowed the murder of Stephen before his Damascus Road experience with Christ. John Newton was captain of a slave ship before being saved and writing "Amazing Grace." Many people over the ages have been transformed by His power, from murderers to believers. If you believe. If you proclaim Jesus as Lord of the universe, and Lord of your life, that's all that's required for forgiveness. Jesus dying on the cross, shedding His pure blood for your sins, accomplished everything else."

"But that's too easy—"

"You're right. It's too easy. But that's so that you'll never be able to boast about your salvation. Salvation is completely a work of the Lord—not you, not me, not any law, creed or Bible. Nothing and nobody—except God."

Max peered at Kat. He had come as close to baring his soul to this lady as he had anyone in the world, even his mom and his old buddies, Al and Julius. Here he had been with her for what—he glanced at his watch—a total of ten hours and she had led him to the brink. The brink of what?

A tear tried to force its way out of the corner of his eye. That had never happened before—well, not except when his Pop or a buddy had died. He turned away from Kat and surreptitiously dried the tear with a forefinger.

She reached her hand toward him and he quickly laid his upon it. A warm hand. A firm hand. A strong hand.

The wounded expression on his face, Kat thought, seemed totally alien, like a painting on leather. He was so strong in body, and, obviously, in willpower and self-control.

But she remembered her own moment of realization of what God had done for her; drenched in tears of thanksgiving, she had lost control.

Max suddenly sat straight and firm.

"This is important," he said. "I know that. You've given me much to think about, but I need to do the thinking alone right now."

She nodded acceptance and, just then, dinner arrived.

Chapter Five

The next morning, Max and Kat sat drinking coffee poolside.

The sun shone brightly, a spattering of clouds cluttered the sky and the heat of the day lay a couple hours in the future.

The setting and the day would have constituted a perfect time—but the cloud of Danny's assault still hung over Kat.

She called Hadassah Medical Center but could only discover Danny was still unconscious and in serious condition.

She pushed aside the fear, looked across the patio table at Max and a smile curled at her lips. Here was this man's man, probably with heroes' ribbons stashed away in a closet somewhere, with muscles in places most men didn't have places, and yet wearing humility like a cloak. A man who had struggled with overcoming self-condemnation for dark deeds done to wipe away evil and maintain liberty for his country. A man who was now writing a book which, she considered, might move the powers that be in the United States to reset how they conduct wars and conflicts. A man still shaken by the untimely death of his father and apparently trying to win the dead man's favor, or even find a place atop the mantle with his hero father. A man who was, in one day seemingly, wrestling her heart away from her scientific work.

Max broke her reverie, saying, "So, on our way here from Dragot, you said the colored etching depicted Petra—"

"Yes. Have you been there?"

Max shook his head.

"You'll be amazed," she said. "But first, we talk with Gershon Zoref."

"What's his organization again?

"The Temple Faithful."

"Well, they've got to have a lot of faith if they think they're ever going to build a Jewish synagogue on the Temple Mount, with the Muslims in control there."

Kat shrugged. "They're adamant and they're committed. I'd like a dime for every man-hour they've put into recreating everything for the temple to the exact dimensions God set forth."

"Kat, are you really unafraid to start this hunt? Remember what Dudi said."

"Afraid or not, I must." Despite her tears of shock and loss, she appeared fearless, especially at a time when she had the most reason to be afraid.

Suddenly, the face of her four-year-old border collie sprang to Kat's mind and she blurted out, "I miss Tuck."

"Tuck who?" Max asked.

"My dog. He's the smartest and coolest dog in either hemisphere. He usually serves the role as my protector."

"So you want to send for him rather than me?" Max grinned.

Kat shrugged. "I just suddenly miss him. He's always at my side—in the classroom, in my apartment, out and about everywhere."

"But not here."

"The quarantine period's too long."

56

"Of course."

"He's smarter than some people I know."

Max smiled.

"I do not jest. He *is*," she said.

"You're saying Tuck could be a librarian?"

Kat reached over and smacked his hand. "Easily—and I miss him."

"So, if he's as smart as you say, phone him up." Max chuckled. "Where is he?"

"He's staying with a friend, Alice, back in the States."

"So call Alice, find out how Tuck's doing and ask to speak to him."

He was joshing with her now, so, she'd show him a thing or two about Tuck.

Kat checked her watch. "Okay. It's three o'clock there. She'll be up and about, getting ready for work in a few minutes. She hosts an early-morning radio talk show. Let's head for The Temple Faithful headquarters and I'll call Alice afterward."

Max had to chuckle as he drove to Jerusalem's Aliash Street and the Temple Faithful headquarters. What he heard was Kat's end of the phone conversation.

"Alice?"

"Yes, it's Kat."

"Well, I'm fine, but my friend Danny Arens was shot yesterday morning and is in the hospital unconscious and fighting for his life."

"Yes, right at his dig site."

"We're pretty sure it was Islamic terrorists."

"No, I'm okay. We weren't there."

"Oh—*we* because I'm with a new friend. Max."

"Not sure, but we think because Danny stumbled onto something they don't want known."

"I'll write you an email filling you in. I just wanted to see how Tuck is doing."

"Yeah?"

"Really? To their school?"

She laughed.

"No. No, I don't think he's ever been a 'show-and-tell' before."

"He did?"

"Well, I'm not surprised. I think he knows half of what I say. I have to spell some words and he's figured them out, so I go to the Thesaurus and find another word to spell—"

"You, too? I should have mentioned."

"Yes, you, Bill and the kids will figure him out."

"Right."

"Can I speak to him?

"Yes, Tuck."

Kat looked at Max and said, "You remember that old TV show 'Are You Smarter than a Fifth Grader?' Well, I think Tuck is."

Max laughed. "Of course."

Kat held up her hand for silence. "Tuck?"

No response.

"Tuck, it's Mommy."

A bark. Two barks.

"I'm sorry, but I'll be gone longer than expected."

Silence.

"I'll bring you a gift."

A low growl.

"You don't want a gift?"

Another growl.

"Then I'll just bring me."

Bark-bark-bark.

Kat looked at Max. "That's my boy."

Max chuckled. "And a lucky boy at that."

Kat slapped his arm.

"Tuck, I love you. Be a good boy."

A bark.

"Bye-bye."

Bark-bark.

A moment later, clearly Alice was back on the line.

"I think I'll be awhile longer than I expected," Kat said.

"No. I'll fill you in on everything in the email. Thanks again, Alice. You're the best friend."

"Mm-hm. You, too. Give Bill and the boys my love."

"Bye."

Max glanced at Kat. He could tell she had relaxed by the tilt of her shoulders and the loosening of those tight lines along her jaw. She had been so stressed yesterday and last night.

Now? He read her mixed feelings. She was obviously struggling with the idea that her friend had been shot, yet determined—in the face of daring those killers to target her also—to unearth the mystery Danny had happened upon.

"Ah!" Kat exclaimed, pointing to their right, to a wide, two-story building of white Jerusalem stone. "It's right over there."

"We're not that far from the Knesset," Max said.

"You've been there?"

"I testified there."

"Testified? About what?"

Max hesitated. "Well, I testified behind closed doors and, even today, I can't speak of the subject in public. Sorry."

"Black-ops days." A statement, not a question.

"Black-ops days," he agreed.

Max pulled the Land Rover into a parking slot in front of the building, turned to Kat and asked, "So, how well do you know this guy who heads up The Temple Faithful?"

"We met when I consulted on a dig near the southwestern corner of the Holy Temple Mount where Eli Shukron and Professor Ronnie Reich of the University of Haifa discovered a Second Temple Era seal, used by the High Priest in Temple worship."

"Wow!" Max exclaimed.

"Yeah, the seal was dated to the first century and was the first discovery of such an item. The seal is the size of a shekel and bears the inscription 'pure to the G-d of Israel.' Products for service in the Temple—like oil, wine, and grains—had to be checked by the high priest to confirm they were kosher. When he determined the items were kosher, he stamped them with the seal.

"Together with the golden bell of the high priest and other discoveries from the Temple, the seal is direct archeological evidence of Jewish activity on the Temple Mount during the Second Temple Era."

"So that disproves the Palestinians' claim that the Jews have no historic claim on the land," Max said.

"Precisely. Which angers them, no end. Nevertheless, they continue to teach the lie in their schools."

"Of course."

"Well," Kat checked her watch, "we're right on time for our appointment."

That Gershon Zoref was Jewish was unmistakable. Curly black hair, noble nose, dark eyes. He wore his eyeglasses atop his graying head as often as before his eyes. He stepped out of his office, right hand outstretched, to greet them.

"Doctor Cardova! Kat! What a surprise."

Kat took his hand and introduced Max.

"What brings you here? Another dig?" Zoref asked Kat.

The sting of her friend's assault oddly struck her again and Kat responded, "An assault *because* of a dig, I'm sad to say."

"Oh, my! Come in. Come in." Zoref waved them into his expansive office, asking them to sit on a sofa while he took a chair opposite them. "An assault, you say—?" He spoke in English but with a thick Jewish accent.

"Danny Arens."

Zoref gasped, "Danny? Oh, no!"

Zoref took a deep breath and said, "I know him well. My Lord, what happened?"

Warning Zoref the incident was hush-hush for the moment, Kat retold the story and felt like she was reliving those moments, flinching as she did so. When she spoke of the missing music, Zoref leaned forward on the edge of his chair.

When she mentioned Petra, he nodded, as if accepting the location as a possibility.

At that moment, a lady entered the office with a large tray containing coffee, cream, and sugar. She set the tray on the coffee table between Zoref and his visitors.

"Thank you, Sarah," Zoref said, and she left the room as the three took their mugs of the hot brew.

"I have two questions," Kat said. "First, who would you put at the top of the list of those who would want to kill Danny to prevent the discovery of the music? And, second, have you ever heard any clues to the music's whereabouts?"

61

Zoref chuckled darkly. "Who would desire to kill our friend?" he asked himself and drank from his mug.

Max chimed in, "Particularly, who would actually hunt him down like an animal, try to murder him, and then destroy the dig site, leaving behind the message that death awaited anyone who dared continue the dig?"

"Mr. Braxton, for nearly two thousand years the land of Israel waited for the return of her Jewish sons and daughters. She waited through occupations of the Roman, Byzantine, Sassanid and Seljuk empires as well as the Caliphate. She endured the Crusades, the Saladin and Ottoman empires and European colonization.

"Then in 1948, the dream became true. Problem is, it was not a dream for some, but a nightmare. All those who hate the Jew—from the Nazis to the Arabs, many in Great Britain and Europe—even America where they turned back our ship loaded with people escaping the gas chambers."

"I know of your struggles—and your enemies. I've fought with your IDF Special Forces and trained with the Yehidat Shaldag and the Sayeret Matkal," Max said.

"Then you know about the Muslim terrorists, ISIS, Hamas and Hezbollah and any number of others," Zoref said. "They would be my number-one guess as to who would try to kill Danny. They don't want us to worship to our fullest. And, from a personal standpoint, I would consider having the original music to be the crowning jewel to the Third Temple. Imagine our cantor singing 'Lilies of the Covenant'? Imagine that at synagogues all over the world!"

"And churches," Kat added.

"Yes, and churches," Zoref agreed.

"You say some Islamic group would be your first guess," Max said. "Do you have a second?"

Zoref leaned forward, his elbows on his knees and rubbed his chin. "Yes, but before I tell you, I must give you this preface: Until we Jews returned from the Diaspora and were granted statehood, the God of Israel protected our biblical past, hiding treasure buried safely beneath the ground of the Holy City of Jerusalem. Until now. Until this prophetic end-time era we live in today. Many discoveries were found by the Israeli archeologists after the Six-Day War and in the last few years, seemingly more and more are unearthed each week.

"With these discoveries, a bit at a time we are restoring our historical biblical chain and reconnecting with the link our enemies severed when they destroyed the kingdom of Israel nearly two millennia ago."

He tilted a hand toward Kat and continued, "Kat herself, and others, have unearthed biblical finds connected to the Holy Temple and, specifically, to sacred temple worship. In fact, I'm surprised the music itself has remained undiscovered all this time."

Zoref looked at Kat for confirmation and she shrugged a "yeah-I-guess-so."

"Some of the discoveries have been around the Temple Mount, others in the City of David that lies just to the south.

"I feel strongly they are clear messages from the Lord to His people the Jews to rebuild His Holy Temple on the Temple Mount, on the very place He appointed King Solomon to build His house and to renew the days of Israel as in the biblical times and to continue a prophetic chain as was prophesied by God in His end-time prophecies."

Kat leaned forward. "I agree with you, Gershon."

Zoref smiled at Kat and turned his eyes again on Max. "But here's my other answer to Kat's first question about who might be the killers. Every time Kat, or one of her archeology colleagues, discovers an important artifact, especially if the find is here in Jerusalem, there are rumbles from within the Jewish community."

"Really?" Max asked.

"Well, from a certain tiny fraction of the community. The ultra-orthodox. Those who consider that Israel, as it stands today, is illegitimate. That Israel will *only* be legitimate if the Messiah appears and ushers our people home to Israel."

"Are you talking about the Neturei Karta?" Kat asked.

"Yes, them or an offshoot of them," Zoref said.

"What's their angle?" Max asked.

"Traditionally, religious Jews believe the return of Jewish sovereignty to the historic land of Israel is integral to humanity's redemption and Messiah's coming," Zoref said. "But they say our sovereignty is supposed to be under God's ultimate kingship, operating according to the Torah. Some believe the arrival of the Messiah is a prerequisite for this; and since Messiah has not arrived, establishing Jewish sovereignty over Israel was and is actually sinful."

"Some groups within Neturei Karta," Kat said, "actually endorsed Yasser Arafat and his successors and say they're the rightful rulers of the land."

"Ouch!" Max said. "Even though those people want to kill Jews? And even though Arafat was an Egyptian?"

"Even though ..." Zoref said.

"Embracing people who want you dead," Max said, "that's outright suicidal."

"More than that," Zoref said. "They're really serving the purposes of the anti-Semitic propaganda enemy. They're tiny in number but they get a lot of press because they're the ones attending Holocaust denial conferences and smooching Jew-haters for the cameras.

"There have even been reports showing that Neurei Karta has been on the PLO payroll."

"So these Israelis wouldn't allow Jewish believers in Jesus to become citizens, but they'd allow these anti-Zionists to live here?" Max asked.

Zoref shrugged and nodded yes, then added, "Israel does have its flaws. But despite them all, we think the worldwide aliyah, or return of the Jewish people to their homeland, is nothing short of miraculous—an astonishing achievement that must have been orchestrated by God."

"But would these anti-Zionist Jews kill their own people?" Kat asked.

Zoref shrugged. "I wouldn't think so, but ..." He raised his hands questioningly.

"I've heard the ultra-orthodox will stone your car if you drive through their neighborhood, Mea Shearim, on the Sabbath," Kat said.

"What can I say? They do. So would the Lubavitchers and some other ultra-orthodox Jews."

Zoref took a drink of his coffee and leaned back in his chair, seeming to relax.

Kat and Max followed suit.

After a moment, Kat asked, "In all your contacts with people, have you ever heard any reports or rumors of whether the music still exists and, if so, where?"

"I heard the story of a famous archeologist who happened upon a vault of music during an excavation in the Negev Desert in the late 1800s. The story goes that he wrote home to England, thrilled about his discovery and the impact the music would have on the Jewish and Christian religions. He said he was going to stop in Rome en route home, but he was never heard from again. Was he aboard a ship that sank, was he murdered by marauders, or what might have happened to him?"

"I've heard that story, too," Kat said, "but never saw any corroboration."

"Does the story say he was headed to the Vatican?" Max asked.

"The Vatican says they never set eyes upon him there ... but, we can never trust the Vatican."

"Why not?"

Zoref carefully interlaced the fingers of his two hands, flexed them and locked his eyes on Max's.

"When the Romans destroyed the Second Temple in 70 AD, they stole away the temple menorah, the vessels, and various temple treasures and took them to Rome. We've petitioned the Pope to return them to their rightful owners so the priests of Israel can use them in the Holy Third Temple. No response."

"Are you sure the Vatican has them?" Kat asked.

"We believe so. And if there was music, they may have that, also."

"But if so, why withhold the music from the world?" Max asked.

Zoref threw up his hands. "That's what we ask. Why not return the menorah? Why not return the vessels?"

He leaned forward and, with a twinkle in his eye, said, "I've also heard a story that the family of Yeshua protected the music for a time."

"Jesus' family?" Kat asked in surprise.

Zoref nodded.

"But how? Why?"

"I doubt there is proof. We know that Jesus though he was poor, was of the family of King David. Again, the family possessing the music makes sense. We know that Jesus' family members were prominent in the early Christian movement. His brother, James, and his descendants—Jude, Elzasus, and Nascien—were leaders in the church. And his brother, Jude, and his descendants—Menahem, James, and Zoker—were, also."

"But if they had kept the music, they surely would have released the melodies to the world," Max said.

Zoref shrugged. "I only pass on the story."

When they climbed back into the Land Rover, Max turned to Kat. "So where do we stand now?" he asked.

"Are you still sure you want 'in' on this with me?" she responded.

Max smiled broadly. "I'm all yours."

"Then off to Petra we go."

"As in 'put the pedal to the medal, Harry'?"

"Remember, their traffic lights have cameras to catch speeders."

"Yeah, yeah. My kingdom for a stealth vehicle."

"My kingdom for the Star Trek machine that beamed people to places."

Max laughed as he stopped at a streetlight. "I'd settle for a computer that could make streetlights change to green when you approach."

"You're buds with Commissioner Danino. I'll bet he could do it for you."

"I think I'll keep my string-pulling for more important matters."

"Like getting to murder scenes?"

"Like that." Max stepped on the gas as the light turned green.

"Well, soldier, what else would you give your kingdom for?"

"The look on your face when you find what you're looking for. What about you?"

Kat smiled. "For me? My kingdom for a piece of my Mom's cherry-nut cake."

"For someone who probably weighs a mere one-twenty, you like your desserts, don't you, Doctor Cardova?"

"It's one-fifteen, mister." She looked at him with mock disgust. "Just drive to the King David Hotel at the Eilat crossing into Jordan. I'll keep my eye out for pie stands."

"Another free room?"

Kat grinned.

"This is getting a bit pricier than my tenting experience," Max said.

"Oh, I'm sorry, Max. Let's tent out."

"No way."

"Yes, way. I'd love to do that. I live great portions of my life in tents. No problem."

"Then tenting we shall go," he said.

"What do you say we drive east on Route 1 to the Dead Sea, then south on Route 90, past Dragot and the scene of the crime, to the Eilat crossing?" Kat said. "That way we can check out the dig and see what they've uncovered."

"Good idea."

Chapter Six

When they reached Dragot, Max drove up the steep incline, twisting and turning to the top.

The area was cordoned off with yellow police tape like that used in America and a police officer greeted them in Hebrew. "Please turn around. This is a crime site."

"I know," Max said through the driver's window. "We reported the murder."

Just then, Inspector Yechimovich stepped over the rise of the hill behind the dig site.

"Let them pass," he called to the officer.

Max hopped out of the vehicle, watching as Kat did the same, and Yechimovich approached them.

"Colonel," Yechimovich said.

"Inspector," Max acknowledged. "Any news?"

Yechimovich, broad-shouldered and even taller than Max's six-foot-two, held up a plastic bag with gunshot shells.

Max took the bag, examined the contents and said, "Looks like AK-47 shells."

"Normal for our friends the Palestinians," Yechimovich said.

Max nodded.

"We found them all over the hillside." He looked at Kat and said, "It looks like they took a lot of shots at your friend, Doctor Cardova."

"He was fast," Kat said. "A runner. At least five miles a day."

"The AK-47's not very accurate, but given that the rifle fires a bullet at two thousand feet per second or faster, Danny stood little chance," Max said.

Kat hung her head.

"Any other evidence?" Max asked.

"The people on the dig are being questioned at headquarters in Jerusalem," he said. "Here, the forensics team has gotten fingerprints on various things. We've identified the tire tread of two vehicles and have molds of half a dozen footprints. We'll take everything back to the lab, do some comparisons to attacks of the past and see where the investigation takes us. That's all I can say right now."

"Did you contact Danny's family?" Kat asked.

"His sister and her family are the only immediate family alive. The rest were killed in that wedding bombing."

Suddenly, Kat held up a hand as if asking for silence. Then she looked quickly to Yechimovich.

"Inspector, have you scrutinized that tent yet?" She pointed to one of the pup tents that had been driven to the ground.

Max watched as Yechimovich followed her finger, hesitated for a moment, then replied, "No, Miss, we have not."

"That, I believe, is the tent used by Sam Livingston, the team member they found dead in Tel Aviv."

"Really?" Yechimovich said. "That's good to know."

"May we take a look, Inspector?"

"You shouldn't even be on the site," he said.

When Max started to object, Yechimovich stepped back with a hand to his chin. Finally, he said, "Okay. You're familiar with the dig and its operation. You may have eyes to see what we would not see. But only with a forensics technician and me or Sub-Inspector Pollard accompanying you."

"Sure," Max said.

Yechimovich signaled a member of the forensics team who was fingerprinting items from the main tent to join them, and they walked together to Livingston's tent site. The nylon tent, fiberglass aluminum poles, polyester fly, guy ropes, and stakes—all were strewn in a pile. The four of them pulled the tent debris aside, revealing a cot, several stacked books, a battery-operated lamp, duffel bag, electric razor, mirror, calf-high working boots and assorted other items.

Kat gingerly stepped up beside the cot, leaned over and picked up a cell phone.

"Funny he'd leave this behind," she said.

"Anxious for the weekend to start, perhaps," Max said. "If he were heading for the seedy part of Tel Aviv, he'd have no need for a phone or the desire to be bothered with a phone call."

Yechimovich nodded. "A man, a bar, a foreign country. Right, Colonel, no need for a phone."

"Then perhaps there's something to glean from it," Kat said. "Recent calls. Apps. Memos to himself."

She handed the phone to Yechimovich.

"We'll check it out," he said.

Suddenly Max spotted a glint, a flash of reflected sunlight. He looked in its direction. There was the light again, coming from an adjacent, although lower, hilltop.

He reached into a cargo pocket and pulled out palm-sized surveillance zoom binoculars.

"What is it?" Kat asked.

"Hold on," he said. "I saw a flash of light from that hill over there."

"That's odd," Yechimovich said. "There's nothing over there but a dirt road that dead-ends."

"I'll just take a look-see," Max said.

"But that's a mile and a half away," Yechimovich said.

"It's tiny but this baby has eighty magnification, Inspector. If that's a person, I'll tell you the color of their eyes."

Max saw the flash of light again and moved to focus there. "Zooming in. Zooming in," he said.

He found the glare. He located the cause of the glare.

"It's a man," he said. "Looking up here at the site. He's got tourists' field glasses. He's lucky if we're as big as specks to him."

"He's just watching the site?" Kat asked.

"Wait. There's another man beside him," Max said. "And that guy has a rifle.

"Zooming in. Zooming in," he said. "An AK-47."

"I wouldn't say he's hunting deer," Yechimovich said.

Max moved his sights to the man with the field glasses.

"I lied," he said. "I can't tell you the color of the watcher's eyes because he's glued to the binoculars. But he's wearing a New York Yankees T-shirt, baggy brown pants and, ah, LL Bean hiking boots."

"What about his face?" Yechimovich asked.

"Black hair. Wide forehead. Large nose. Big hands. But his face is hidden behind the field—ah-ha!" Max pulled the glasses away. "Brown eyes. A beard. Definitely Arabic. I could ID this guy in a line-up if you can catch him."

Max moved the glasses slightly left. "The other fellow could be his brother. Maybe a couple inches taller. Wearing all black—pants, shirt. White sneakers."

He passed the binoculars to Yechimovich, who peered through them. After a moment, he said, "I don't recognize either of them."

Returning binoculars to Max, he turned away and hustled toward several police vehicles.

"Pollard!" he called, and the sub-inspector appeared.

"There are two men watching us from that hill. I want them in handcuffs. Let's go!"

Max interjected. "Give me one of your radios, and I'll watch the men from here and keep in contact with you to let you know their movements."

"Good idea." Yechimovich tossed him his handheld radio.

With that, the two men raced to Yechimovich's vehicle, joined by an officer who was standing guard.

Max looked at Kat. "You never know what you'll run into on a trip to Petra, do you?"

"Appears that way." Kat chuckled and shook her head. "In the midst of all of this, you're calmer than ever."

"Hey, we're a distance away from any danger. The guy with the AK-47 couldn't hit anything four-hundred yards away. Probably even three-hundred yards. No need for anxiety, professor."

They stood so close he could smell the sweet aroma of her hair.

"What can I do?" Kat asked.

"Pray the police catch them and no one gets hurt," Max said. "Otherwise, perhaps you should wander the dig site and pretend you don't know those men are there watching."

Several minutes later, Kat was busying herself in the square where Danny had discovered the stone, and Max spotted Yechimovich's vehicle churning up dust speeding up the hill. The road was rugged, with twists and turns, but not as steep as Dragot. Closer they got. Closer until they stopped at what appeared to be the end of the road.

Max put his binoculars to his eyes. Where they stopped sat another vehicle, an old beat-up black Volvo.

Max got on the police phone. "They're about a hundred yards due west and at the same height, Inspector."

"Okay, Colonel."

Max kept his eyes glued to the scene playing out before him. He heard Yechimovich command his two men in Hebrew: "We'll stay together until we reach them, then, Shani, you go to the right; Pollard, you go uphill to the left."

The three, all with rifles strapped to their backs, closed quickly on the two Arabs.

"They're just fifty yards away," Max said into the police radio.

"Gotcha," replied Yechimovich.

"Thirty yards."

"Twenty."

Just then, the Arab with the gun turned toward the policemen.

"I think they've heard you," Max said.

Yechimovich held up his hand to slow his comrades.

Max watched as the gunman spoke, then took a step, then another in the direction of the Israelis. The man with the field glasses also turned and said something.

"The gunman's coming your way," Max whispered.

Yechimovich and the others all hunched down low.

Suddenly, the gunman lifted his rifle and took aim.

"Take cover!" Max hollered.

Yechimovich dove behind a tree as did his officers.

Gunfire erupted from the Arab's AK-47. Bullets sprayed the tree Yechimovich lay behind, sending splinters of bark flying.

74

Kat had heard Max holler and ran to his side. "What is it?" she asked.

"There's trouble. There's shooting."

"Anyone hit?"

Max looked back into his binoculars and spotted the Israelis. "Not yet. But I'm calling in the cavalry." He pulled his cell phone to his mouth and called the only police number he had, that of the commissioner.

When the secretary answered, he told her to send help and gave her the location.

After a few moments, she returned to the line. "They're dispatched, sir. ETA, twenty minutes."

"Twenty minutes!" Max exclaimed.

"Sorry, sir. Yes."

Max hung up and turned his attention to the scene on the next hillside.

Yechimovich was calling out something, probably something like, "Israeli police. Put down your weapons."

The answer was more gunfire but the gunman then hustled in the other direction. He approached the man with field glasses, who pointed westward and they hurried in that direction. But before they did, the man with field glasses grabbed a rifle that was leaning against a tree.

"They're both armed," Max said into the radio. "Looks like one of them has a magazine pouch, but I can't tell how full. I'll call the one who shot at you Abu and the other Mohammed."

"Gotcha, Colonel," Yechimovich responded. "Abu and Mohammed."

"Deeper into the forest you go, pals," Max whispered.

"What?" Kat asked.

Max turned to Kat. "Abu and Mohammed. The Arabs are running away, going deeper into the woods. Keep going and they'll actually hit desert—not their ally."

Kat prayed, "Oh, Lord, protect the inspector and his men."

75

Yechimovich and the others came out from their cover, with guns raised. Yechimovich fired several shots with what looked like an M16 assault rifle. Pollard and Shani fired away with M1 carbines, the .30-caliber semi-automatics Max knew were the standard-issue weapons of the Civil Guard.

Max spotted the Arabs.

"Inspector," he said, "they're heading due west of you, straight back into the woods."

Back to Yechimovich, Max watched him spread his men out and rush off in pursuit.

For a moment, Max couldn't spot the Arabs, then saw them hunkered down behind a large boulder. They were speaking furiously with each other and readying their weapons.

"Inspector, beware. They're behind a large boulder about forty yards directly ahead of you."

"Is there a large bush next to the boulder?"

Max checked. "Yes."

Yechimovich signaled Pollard and Shani to go further left and right, sprinted for cover behind the next tree in front of him, then the next, until he was about twenty yards away.

With Kat gripping his elbow, Max turned his attention to the Arabs. They were taking positions on each side of the boulder.

As Yechimovich raced to his next cover, the two Arabs rose from their positions. One of them spotted Yechimovich and fired a burst of bullets. The slugs sprayed dirt around the inspector's feet and he dove behind a bush.

At the same time Pollard, from higher ground, fired on the other Arab. His bullets ricocheted off the boulder, barely missing the Arab. For a full five seconds, they exchanged gunfire, but neither was hit.

Max was getting anxious. This was a new experience. He'd rather be in the thick of the action. He thought about having Kat take over the lookout while he gunned the Land Rover over there to help out. He felt the familiar heft of his Glock 23 at his hip, then thought, *Don't bring a handgun to an AK-47 fight. Good reasoning, that.*

Back to the action, Max noticed Yechimovich holding his thigh, then removing his belt and tightening the strap like a tourniquet just below his hip.

He got on the radio, "Are you bad hit, Inspector?"

Yechimovich was wincing in pain. "I'll survive," he said grimly. "Afraid I won't be able to run if they try to get away, though."

Another burst of gunfire sprayed the branches above his head. Max thought Yechimovich must be wishing, probably for the first time in his life, that he were shorter. Yechimovich cursed in Russian.

"I haven't heard that phrase for awhile," Max said.

"Sorry, Colonel. My Russian temper rising up."

So Yechimovich was a Russian Jew. Must have come here in the last ten years or so, like so many others coming back to their homeland.

Max noticed movement by the boulder and moved his binoculars to check. The two Arabs had abandoned the spot and were running.

"They're on the go, but heading more in this direction—I'd say northwesterly," he said.

"Spasee'ba," Yechimovich said. He pushed himself from the ground and limped forward. Max couldn't spot Pollard or Shani, but guessed they were in chase.

"Watch out, Shani," he said. "They could be coming nearer to you."

Max glanced to Kat. "They're all rushing through the woods." He pointed to their location. "Not quite there but heading that way." He pointed southwest from the spot he was standing on.

Kat nodded. "How long before more help arrives?"

77

"Fifteen minutes."

"Oh, no."

"Don't worry. These Israelis are the best fighters in the world."

"Except for *your* guys," she said.

Max smiled. "Well, of course."

The sounds of more gunfire crackled through the air and Max noticed that the forensics team—all four of them—had gathered near him, drawn to the drama though they could not see.

"Are the inspector and the others okay?" one of them asked in Hebrew.

"The inspector's wounded but not badly," Max replied. "They're in pursuit of two armed men."

The team members moved even closer and he wondered if they thought his proximity would provide protection. *Don't bring a handgun to an AK-47 fight.*

He returned to his binoculars and saw nothing for several minutes. Suddenly, the two Arabs appeared out of the canopy of the trees, then disappeared again.

Max detected Yechimovich hobbling along the hillside.

"Inspector, you can't keep up with those men," he said.

"I have to try," Yechimovich said, almost breathless.

"You'll just cause more bleeding and weaken yourself until you can't run anymore. I think you best get back to your vehicle. They may try to get back to theirs," he said.

Max watched as Yechimovich stopped and breathed deeply. After a few seconds, he relented. "Good idea," he said. "I'll be there waiting if they do."

"That's right, sir." Max identified the voice, speaking Hebrew, as that of Pollard. "We can get these two."

"Right," Shani added.

Max looked down the hill and discovered that Pollard was nearly flying down the incline.

"Sub-Inspector Pollard," Max said. "You're no more than sixty yards or so away from the two gunmen."

Pollard grunted acknowledgment.

"And," Max said, "Shani, I don't know your exact location, but Abu and Mohammed are nearing a bunch of very tall trees at the very base of the hill."

Shani got on the phone. "I'm there. I don't see them."

Gunfire then exploded in the forest below Max and Kat. The fury made Kat jump backward.

"I hit one of them!" Shani reported, his voice high-pitched.

"He's down!" Pollard said and added, "I'll handcuff him to a tree."

More gunfire.

"AK-47s' standard magazines carry thirty rounds," Max said to Kat. "How many magazines do you think these two jokers have used?"

Kat shrugged. "I can't tell the difference between gunshots from one rifle to another. What do *you* think?"

"One of them carried a magazine pouch with extra magazines. The other one didn't. But which one's wounded and which one is still on the run?"

"Ask Pollard if the guy he's got down has a pouch," Kat said.

"Brilliant, professor." He smiled, trying to lighten the situation. "If ever I were in a trench, I'd want to be with you."

"'Brilliant' can't pull a trigger," she said.

A couple of the forensics team members snickered.

More gunfire—and closer—sounded in the valley below.

"Pollard, does that man have a pouch?"

Through grunts and heavy breathing, Pollard answered, "No."

79

Max clicked on the radio. "Inspector," he said, "are you at your vehicle yet?"

"Affirmative."

"I think you ought to get back over here to the dig. Pollard and either Abu or Mohammed appear heading this way."

Max turned to the forensics team and spoke in Hebrew, "I think you should all get into your vehicle and flee. Wait at the highway for an all-clear."

They all started hustling toward the forensics van.

Max looked at Kat.

"I'm not leaving you," she said firmly.

"You are."

"I'm not."

"Please, Kat."

"I won't leave your side, Max."

"For my sake."

"You just said if you were ever in a trench you'd want me there with you."

"That was figurative."

"So I'm figurative?"

"No, Kat, you're *too* real. I've had friends die in my arms. I don't want that to happen to the woman I'm supposed to be protecting."

Max turned to look back down the hill. About a quarter mile away, the Arab gunman was headed directly at them.

He looked back at Kat and read her face just as irritation and frustration seeped in to rob just a bit of her determination.

"Then you come, too," she said.

"I'm the watchman here," he said. "I can't abandon my post."

Kat lowered her eyes and her head moved back and forth. He knew she was formulating an argument.

She looked up. "I'll get in the Land Rover and be ready to go if the gunman gets up here."

"Kat, get in the Rover and head down the hill. Please!"

The frown on her forehead deepened. She looked at him with pleading green eyes.

"Don't worry. I'll be fine. I just want you to be safe," he said firmly.

He turned back and spotted Shani, now at the valley floor, looking up. The Israeli was close enough to the Arab he could shoot him.

"Fire away!" Max said into the radio.

Just then, the Arab turned, saw Shani and opened fire on him. A flurry of gunfire landed all about the officer, then one or two hit. His legs flew up, he fell to the ground and rolled backward. The Arab continued to fire. Shani dove behind a tree, screaming in pain.

"Where are you, Inspector?" Max said.

"At the bottom of Dragot, heading up right now," he responded.

"Shani's been wounded. Pollard isn't anywhere in sight—probably because he was cuffing the other one to a tree back there."

"How bad is Shani?"

"Looks like he got hit in the foot." Max heard a sigh of relief, then added, "Watch out for the forensics team coming down the hill," he said.

"Right."

"Either Abu or Mohammed is heading up the hill. I'm sending Kat down in the Land Rover."

At that, Max set steely eyes on Kat, and she wilted to the pressure. She started to jog toward the vehicle.

"Quickly," Max urged, and she picked up the pace.

Max took a deep breath and turned back to the hillside. The Arab had made remarkable progress for someone who had run a mile and a half through the woods with an AK-47 in his arms. Max thought briefly the fellow had probably trained at one of the terrorist camps in North

81

Africa. Then his thoughts turned to self-defense.

He pulled his Glock 23 from its hip holster. *Don't take a handgun to an AK-47 fight!*

The thought played taps on his spine. He'd been asked more than once if he felt fear going into a black-ops mission. His standard response was, "If you're not afraid, be afraid."

His buddy from Louisiana, JoeJoe Deloit, feared nothing and what did he get? Dead.

Max looked down the slope. The Arab—ah, Abu—had climbed the steepest part of the hill and was now only fifty yards away, well within range for an AK-47. In fact, if Max had an AK-47 right now, he could put a neat little pattern of a heart in Abu's chest, with an exclamation point in the middle. But, he looked at his Glock. He had a handgun in— right—an AK-47 fight.

Abu stopped and raised his weapon. Max looked for cover and there was none. He dove to the ground while bullets whizzed over his head. The slope of the hill was his only protection. In front of him was the two-foot-deep spot Danny Arens had dug when he found the stone. Max snaked forward and slithered into the depression.

Kat's words came to him: "You just said if you were ever in a trench you'd want me there with you."

Her beautiful face flashed before him and he wondered if hers would be the last words he'd ever hear.

Gunfire spit up dirt across the top of Arens' 5A square and Max hugged the ground. He counted one second, two. Then looked up, pushed himself up onto his elbows and used his elbows as a tripod. He held his Glock in his right hand, steadied by his left. Abu came over the edge of the hill, close enough so Max could read rage and ferocity in his dark eyes.

Max took aim and, right then, the noise of the Land Rover's engine whined behind him; the whine and not a roar told Max the vehicle was coming in reverse. Kat was coming back, driving the vehicle in reverse!

Distracted, Abu pulled the trigger and a 39mm shell sliced through Max's flesh at his left shoulder. Max pointed his Glock to return fire and noticed Abu was pulling the trigger but the AK-47 was out of ammunition.

Instead of shooting—and killing Abu in front of Kat—Max gauged the distance to the gunman and the time the Arab would take to reload. Max scrambled to his feet.

Frantic, Abu started expelling the used magazine. He *does* have another in his pouch, Max thought.

Hands trembling, Abu dropped the spent magazine to the ground and reached into the pouch for a spare. Max closed on him quickly—twenty yards, fifteen, ten.

Abu pushed the magazine into the AK-47. Time slowed for Max in that next second. He admired the weapon, the cherry wood shoulder stock and hand grip, the sleek black barrel to avoid glinting in the sun, the curve of the magazine, the sights that perfected the accuracy. At the same moment, he knew of the AK-47's famed deftness at killing. His best friend's face flashed before him. Killed by an Afghan Taliban with just this same weapon. The extra adrenaline surged through his body—two yards, one— and as Abu raised the rifle to fire, Max slammed into him.

The gunman landed on his back, the weapon clattering to the ground over his head. Max landed on top of him. Max didn't feel the pain from his wound nor the impact of the fall. What happened next was all skilled reaction from thousands of hours of combat training.

A powerful elbow to Abu's jaw knocked him senseless, Max sat into a squat, spun Abu around and onto his stomach. Using his knee on the man's lower back as leverage, Max pulled Abu's arms behind him. He held the Arab's arms with one hand and removed his belt with another, then wrapped the belt tightly around Abu's wrists.

"I saw a rodeo once." At the sound, Max looked behind him to see Yechimovich, a hand on his wounded leg.

"Yeah," the inspector continued, "the rodeo came all the way from America to Israel. I saw a cowboy tie up a young bull just like that. I wish I had a time watch."

Max grinned. Standing up, he pulled the Arab to his feet. "A calf is actually harder to tie up than this guy."

Stepping in front of Abu, he said in English, "Time for you to face the piper, Abu."

The Arab looked at him questioningly.

Max said in Arabic, "What's your name?"

"Abu," he answered.

Max laughed, then grimaced at the pain in his shoulder. *I'm too used to this.*

Kat stepped out from behind Yechimovich and looked at him in concern.

"You're shot!" she exclaimed.

"Ah, it's nothing," he said, trying to calm her.

Just then, Shani climbed over the hill, winded, perspiring and limping. Blood soaked the bottom of his pants legs. He looked down at the gunman. "Thank God," he said in Hebrew.

"You can also thank Colonel Braxton," Yechimovich said.

"No, I think he was right, Inspector," Max said. "The rule is never, ever take a handgun to an AK-47 fight and that's all I had."

He held up his Glock. "No match for that man's weapon. There may have been a higher power on my side." He looked at Kat and said, "If you hadn't come back—and I mean exactly when you did—I might be the one on the ground right now."

I know I didn't want to kill someone right in front of you.

The wrinkle in her brow asked the question.

"The sound of the Land Rover distracted him at the moment he pulled the trigger."

Chapter Seven

Two hours later, Israeli ambulances had transported Yechimovich and Shani as well as the wounded Mohammed to Hadassah Medical Center in Jerusalem, where Danny Arens was being treated. A police medic had dressed Max's wound, and Pollard and another officer had taken Abu to headquarters in Jerusalem.

Before being carted away, Yechimovich had checked in with Commissioner Danino.

News crews, Danino informed him, had somehow picked up the police chatter and reportedly were on their way to Dragot.

Because Yechimovich was being hospitalized, another inspector, Stas Halevi, would take over the case. Max and Kat had helped Halevi put together a report on the incident. And the forensics team had compared the tire tracks of the Volvo left behind by the two gunmen to the tracks left from Danny Arens' flight. They matched.

Danino told Halevi, who had his radio on SPEAKER, "Do not reveal Colonel Braxton's part in this to the media. He holds our highest military honor, the Medal of Valor. He saved three of our Yehidat Shaldag guys in a firefight on the Lebanese border and has a standing invitation to stay with the Prime Minister. Keep his name only in your report. And let him and Doctor Cardova get out of there as quickly as possible."

As Max and Kat drove down the precipitous incline from Dragot, she turned to him. "The Medal of Valor, huh?"

He shrugged.

"Saved three lives?"

He shrugged again.

"A standing invitation from the Prime Minister?"

Another shrug.

"And you make a deal out of me being able to stay at the King David?"

Max smiled. "Hey, let me tell you: the King David's better digs than the Prime Minister's house. Have you seen it?"

Kat simply shook her head. *What more is there to learn about this man?*

At the bottom of Dragot, they turned south onto Route 91.

Kat looked to her right, spotted the baobab tree and thought of Danny in disbelief. Young, fun and brilliant, he didn't deserve this fate. But this discovery could still change his life, as well as her own if she could follow it through.

Her own life? Whoa! It would change the worship lives of two billion believers and Jews around the world.

She pulled out her Bible, which she had stuck in the pocket of her door and turned to Psalm 45.

"For the director of music," it read. "To the tune of '*Lilies*.' Of the Sons of Korah. A *maskil*. A wedding song." A superscription implied that it was composed and sung by a member of the Levitical temple choir.

Imagine having this song at your wedding ceremony, she thought as she read from verse 9 on:

88

"Daughters and kings are among your honored women; at your right hand is the royal bride in gold of Ophir.

Listen, O daughter, consider and give ear; forget your people and your father's house. The king is enthralled by your beauty; honor him, for he is your lord.

The Daughter of Tyre will come with a gift, men of wealth will seek your favor.

All glorious is the princess within her chamber; her gown is interwoven with gold. In embroidered garments she is led to the king; her virgin companions follow her and are brought to you.

They are led in joy and gladness; they enter the palace of the king..."

Noticing that she had opened the Bible and that a smile played across her face, Max asked, "What are you reading?"

"A wedding song."

"Ah."

"If we find the music, you'd better believe young women the world over will use this song on their wedding days."

"Ah."

"And listen to this," she said, "Psalm 61 verse 2:

"Lead me to the rock that is higher than I. For You have been my refuge, a strong tower against the foe.

I long to dwell in Your tent forever and take refuge in the shelter of Your wings."

"That's beautiful," Max said.

"Imagine it sung with stringed instruments to David's original music," she said.

"I'm learning the guitar. I could give it a try," Max said and chuckled.

"Well, then, we'll try to make that happen." Her tone was serious.

They stopped for a meal at a Burger Ranch at Hatzeva, a pleasant spot just south of the Dead Sea, then drove down the Arava through the Negev Desert—flat, hot and uninviting—toward Eilat. They made one more stop at Yotvata for an ice cream, made at the famous Yotvata Kibbutz.

As they enjoyed the ice cream in dishes, Max looked at Kat and wondered what she was thinking.

His answer came with a question from her lips: "Back at Dragot—"

"Um-hm."

"When that terrorist—"

"Abu," he interjected.

"Right, Abu."

He watched as she tried to suppress a smile.

"When Abu was coming over the mountaintop—" she hesitated, thought for a moment, then continued, "were you afraid for your life?"

He nodded.

"You've been there before."

"More times than you can guess."

"So you're used to it." It was a statement—one that had to be refuted.

"That never happens," Max said. "My Pop told me that and it's true."

"Your father?"

"A helicopter pilot in the Vietnam Conflict. He flew rescue missions to get men out of the jungle who were in peril. He was a hero."

Kat beamed. "Then that's two of you. His son's a hero, too."

"No, Pop was a *certified* hero."

"Certified?" Kat looked bewildered. "Max, you've been presented the Medal of Valor from the IDF."

"Kat, my father put his life in danger every single day, sometimes several times a day, over two tours in Vietnam—the second tour voluntary. It's a miracle he survived. At his funeral, more than two dozen ex-soldiers flew into Dallas from all over the world and testified how he had changed their lives, how they would not have lived, let alone had families if it weren't for my Pop."

"But, they said you saved three Israeli soldiers—" Exasperation had crept into her voice.

Max cut her off and raised a hand. "Pop saved that many in an ordinary morning. One of those men Pop saved was governor of Montana. Another was a heart surgeon. Imagine how many lives he saved. So you could actually say, Pop had a hand in all those people's lives as well."

Kat put her elbows on her knees and bent in toward Max, catching his eyes in hers.

"Am I hearing that you've been keeping score, trying to live up to your father's heroism?"

Max thought about this. It made him uncomfortable. Did he, could he compare his exploits to his Pop's? No way. Was he trying, subconsciously, to do so? This question had flitted at the outskirts of his mind for years, too intimidating to delve into with seriousness. After a few moments, he still had no answer. That area of his mind was a blank, muddled, dark as a dungeon. Finally, he simply shrugged and gave her a crooked smile.

It appeared Kat took his response as a no-fly zone.

Then, she looked at him coyly and said, "I know a place."

"A place?"

"A quiet place."

He simply smiled.

"For a cup of coffee or tea," she said. "They have everything and anything."

"Really? Then I'm there with you."

They only had to walk to a café nearby.

In a few minutes, they sat outdoors, enjoying the cooling temperatures.

"You are such a man of mystery, Colonel Max Braxton."

Kat was startled. She had thought the words but didn't mean to speak them. In her mind the thought exuded dark humor; she only hoped he wasn't offended.

She smiled enigmatically, then waved her hand as if pointing to a cartoon bubble, "Secretive special-ops, super-hero with a super medal— from Israel of all places. I'll bet you have one or two of those from America, too."

He shrugged.

Her green eyes locked onto his, smile lines crinkled ever so slightly, and she added, "The inscrutable always intrigues scientists."

"And you?"

"Are you asking if the inscrutable intrigues me, too?"

He nodded.

She placed her chin on her fist and made an elaborate display of contemplating an answer. Finally, "Me, too."

"Good."

"Maybe. We'll see."

Kat took a moment and buttered a cinnamon scone. She sipped her second cup of green tea and winced as Max downed his second double espresso con panna from a demitasse cup, then wiped the foam from his upper lip with a finger. She had watched John Wayne do that to a shot of whiskey in *The Quiet Man*.

The thought of it somehow hurt her esophagus. *Who is this man? What drives him? Why on earth is he taking all this time to help a stranger? To help me? Oh, well, that last one's an easy read!*

Misreading her expression as a question about his choice of drink, Max said, "Espresso, in its various forms, is my favorite drink since I swore off hard liquor. Café con leche with steamed milk (sometimes on the side), café Romano (with a twist of lemon), café crème (with an ounce of heavy cream). I'll drink them all. Can't seem to get café Ristretto anywhere in the States, or even here."

"What's café Ristretto?"

"A very strong, restricted shot with only about half the water."

"Very informative." She spoke dryly, but Max spotted a twinkle in her eye. She's toying with me, he thought.

"How did you become a connoisseur of espresso?" she asked.

Max shrugged. "Here and there. Italy, Austria, Spain, France, Latin America, Cuba, a place or two I can't mention."

Ahh, Cuba, she thought. And what was he doing there?

"I have to admit," Max said, "at one time, before I swore off alcohol, my favorite was café corretto."

"Corretto?" Kat said. "In Italian, that means 'corrected.'"

"That's right. It's 'corrected' with a shot of brandy or, in my case, cognac. I got acquainted with it in a little café in Melbourne."

"Oh, my. You not only have a strong taste bud, you get around—Bud." Kat put a fingertip to her full lips. Her eyes twinkled merrily. She was thrilled to hear liquor was "in the past." There was a lot to this man she wanted to discover. But was the time investment worth it?

She leaned forward, forgetting the scone, the tea, the people scuffling around them. She noticed that women, more often than not, sneaked a look at the striking man across from her.

Suddenly, Max looked at his watch. "Hey, we'd better get to the campground so we can set up the tents before dark. Are you sure you don't want to stay at the hotel there?"

"Surer than Jerusalem sits on a hill." She smiled.

An hour later they had settled into a campsite at the Eilat Field School, across from the Coral Reef Nature Preserve, with mountains rising behind them. The whole time Kat considered the ease with which she and Max had been in each other's presence. He was calm, assured, friendly—not at all what a girl would think of in a special-ops warrior type of man.

Sitting on a picnic table next to the two tents, they watched sunset arrive and depart, with hues of red and orange filling the western horizon and low-lying clouds painted purple. Then, as evening turned quickly to night, they planned out the next day.

"The border crossing into Jordan doesn't open until eight o'clock," Kat said.

Max shook his head in disbelief and asked, "And how long to get through—say we get there an hour or so early and are first in line?"

"Probably two hours, if we're lucky."

Max again shook his head. "My kingdom for 24/7 hours and American promptness."

Kat smiled. "But just think. Once on the other side, we can explore Petra for clues to the music."

"What do you know about Petra?" Max asked.

"I've been there several times and it's stunning—and enormous— much larger than I first thought going in," Kat said.

"Well, give me a square-mile estimate."

Kat hesitated, then said, "I'd say a few square miles, but some say it's thirty-six square miles and some even say it's four hundred. But that's like calling New York City four hundred square miles when you're only talking about Manhattan. Petra's spread out, but its city proper isn't huge."

"Its residents had to get around the city, so short distances must have been encouraged," Max said.

Kat shrugged. "We're guessing their intent. In fact, no one in the West knew anything about it until a couple hundred years ago when a Swiss archeologist discovered it. His jaw must have hit the ground!"

Max smiled in acknowledgment.

She continued: "Archeologists say the Nabataeans built it around the 6th century BC, carving homes into the red rock. (Everything's carved not 'built,' by the way.) Seven hundred years later, about 106 AD, this whole region was absorbed into the Roman Empire. It was a flourishing, splendid place at the time, but then some calamity happened—we're not sure what. An invasion, or some such thing. Traders started using other travel routes. Then an earthquake devastated Petra sometime around 360 AD.

"Christians found their way to Petra in the 4th century AD, just after this devastation. St. Athanasius the Great, a bishop of the Coptic Orthodox Church in Alexandria, mentions a Catholic bishop of Petra named Asterius; and that was before 373 because that's when Athanasius died. There was another bishop, named Jason, in the mid-400s.

"So, here's what I'm theorizing. Somehow, these Christians got their hands on the music of the Psalms. How? We can only guess at this point. Maybe Zoref's idea that Jesus' family protected it for some time is true. But Christians indeed did and, since they were being terrorized all over the known world, they decided the best place for safe keeping was in Petra.

"At least one of the tombs was used as a church. But then the Islamists conquered Petra in 632 AD and left the city abandoned."

She looked at Max, and added, "I may be off a few years because I'm recalling this off the top of my head."

"And a pretty head it is," he said. "I'm impressed."

Kat planted a serious look across her face and folded her arms in a show of consternation but she figured he would read that the expression was, indeed, a show.

"You're interrupting my train of thought," Kat said. "I'm telling this for my own good as well as yours."

Max shrugged and said, "Well then, go on."

Kat smiled. "Islam ruled here until the First Crusade when the Catholic Church regained Petra and Baldwin the First took charge of the Kingdom of Jerusalem, including Petra. A handful of Christian monks still inhabited the Monastery of Saint Aaron on Jebal Haroun here—that's the burial site of Moses' brother, Aaron. My guess is, those monks could very well have been the guardians of the music. They asked Baldwin to protect them from Saracen raiders. Who in the world would have thought they held such a treasure?"

"Probably no one," Max said, then hesitated and added, "or was that a rhetorical question?"

"Sorry," Kat said, "I use rhetorical questions all the time when I'm teaching. They can actually be useful when I look out over the classroom and see who's paying attention. But, as I was saying, probably realizing Petra's strategic importance, Baldwin indeed did build three Crusader castles—the one we're going to investigate tomorrow morning. One is al-Habis, which will be to our left once we enter the city; al-Wu'ayra, which is one kilometer north of the Wadi Musa, the Valley of Moses, which will be to our right; and Montreal, which is some twenty miles away.

"They're all built on high points of land—" she added.

"So that the Crusaders could signal each other with messages from one castle tower to the other," Max said.

Kat cocked her head. "Correct, soldier."

"No radios or telephones," Max said with a shrug.

"You're a history buff in your own right, aren't you?" Kat said with a grin.

"Just trying to add my two cents, which is probably more than my information is worth."

"I've got a widow's mite back home in the States. I'll give the coin to you in payment." She raised an eyebrow, awaiting his retort.

Instead, he changed tact, simply catching her eyes in his. After a few moments, with a smile, Max said, "Your beauty is only matched by your wisdom."

"Is your forwardness a part of your military training, Colonel, or were you born that way?" she asked.

Max flashed a smile and his brown eyes sparkled at her. Oh, he's enjoying this, she thought, and look at me, I'm a mess.

"We Marines are nothing if not forward because to do otherwise would be to retreat... But with courtesy and aplomb," he said, circling his right arm three times downward as if he were bowing to a queen.

She decided to play along.

"Sir knight," she said, straightening her back, "thinkest thou it good fortune thou hast saved a damsel in distress?"

He chuckled, then said, "I believeth such noble stock as thou wouldest made a way unaided if need be, my lady. My appearance was nothing but fortunate, for me."

She nodded, maintained an emotionless expression, and didn't respond for a few moments, thinking that, in fact, this man had dropped his plans for her, a stranger; and, also, in fact, she could not have found

97

another way to Dragot the morning Danny was attacked—at least not for hours. And she certainly would not have been able to connect with Israel's top police officer.

She looked up and examined his handsome face. Brad Pitt, move over, she thought.

He smiled back at her, obviously oblivious to her thoughts.

Just then an idea did occur to her. An eyebrow went up and she raised her right index finger.

"What is it?" Max asked.

"You know I said we should check El Dier, the Monastery—"

"Yes and—"

"I'm having another thought." Kat hesitated. "I'm thinking those might be too easy. What I mean is that the monks would have realized their weakness compared to the Crusaders' strength and known Baldwin was in much better position to protect it. They would have also recognized the Crusaders as principled, honorable Christians."

"Therefore," Max said, "instead of hiding music in an obvious place like a monastery, they'd hide it in a castle—Al-Habis! But if there have been excavations and hunts the last two hundred years, wouldn't someone have discovered it?"

"You'd think so," Kat said. "Every bit of earth has been brushed down to the original, and you'd think every possibility of hidden nooks has been investigated. But we might get lucky."

"So where else would you check?" Max asked.

"Al-Wu'ayra."

"That's the one you said was a kilometer north of the Wadi Musa?

"Yes," she said. "But, listen, we can check out Al-Habis first. It's dead center in the city. It's a steep climb up that most tourists don't make. But you can't get to the castle proper anymore.

98

"*Can't* is not in a Marine's language," Max said. "What do you say we check it out anyhow?"

Kat agreed, snapping off a crisp salute. "Count me in, general."

"And if we can't find it there—"

"Al-Wu'ayra, here we come," Kat said.

Chapter Eight

The next morning, Max and Kat rose early, reached the crossing and parked the Land Rover on the Israeli side of the border because foreign vehicles were not allowed in Jordan. Halfway through their two-hour wait, Max turned to Kat and said, "One reason I went special operations—"

"What was that?" she asked.

"Fewer people means shorter lines, less waiting."

Kat shook her head and smiled.

Max decided to shake his backpack off his shoulders. He figured he had everything in it that he would need from beef jerky and water for both of them to rope, ultra-light power cams, and crampons. He could only hope his Glock 23, which he left in the Rover, would not be needed.

Kat turned her back to him so he could remove her backpack as well.

"Whoa!" he said as he set the backpack on the ground. "What have you got in here anyhow?"

Kat's green eyes sparkled and she answered lightheartedly. "Wouldn't you like to know, mister?"

He chuckled.

She raised and lowered her shoulders. "You know, the comforts of home. Hair dryer, hair brushes, makeup, chess board—"

"No, really," he said.

"It's not that heavy, Mr. Ranger, SEAL, et cetera. I have a few etceteras in there, too."

"Well, then, it's your 'etceteras' that concern me."

"Okay, I've got a frying pan in there, all right? It's the one thing from home, from my Mom, that I take with me on every dig."

Max held up his hands as if for protection. "All right, professor. All right. I'm more impressed with your strength than I was before. I'm more of a drink-wild-cactus-juice kind of hiker, but I respect all types."

"Cactus juice." She spit the words out with a chuckle.

"Bitter but thirst-quenching," Max said it with all the TV-ad-channel voice-over he could muster.

"I'm sure I can trust that you're right on both counts."

"You can trust me in *all* counts," Max said and caught her eyes in his.

After a few earnest moments, during which she obviously caught his drift, she turned away and looked up the line of tourists. Max looked her over including one blue sock with yellow stars and another black-and-white-striped sock and figured this lady didn't have one bad angle, mismatches or not. She could adorn the cover of any magazine—from *Outdoor Life* to *Cosmopolitan*.

Finally, they showed their passports and crossed the border, then rented a Chevrolet Tahoe at a Hertz and followed buses and assorted others. By 10:30 they reached Petra.

"Amazing, they buy American," Max said as he pulled the SUV into a parking space.

"Or simply steal Israeli cars and drive them across the border."

"Yeah, I've heard the stories. But I'd say Hertz is innocent."

"True."

102

A few minutes later, as a crowd of people poured past them, their faces filled with awe, Max and Kat stood looking up at Al-Siq, the famous rose-red, walled-in gorge separating the outside world from the protected old-world city of Petra.

Max knew his mouth was agape, but he was truly astounded. What he saw was a deep split in a red sandstone gorge that rose straight up as high as a New York City skyscraper—probably higher than any of those back in Dallas.

"Phew!" he exhaled.

"And think," Kat said, "when we go through the gorge it gets as narrow as nine or ten feet. You look up and can't see the top."

"Well, then, I won't strain my neck."

They set off on foot and soon the gorge opened up into an astonishing little city carved into cliffs.

"That's Al Khazneh, the Treasury," Kat said, pointing straight ahead.

"Looks Greek," Max said.

"If you saw *Indiana Jones and the Last Crusade* you saw Al Khazneh."

"Really?"

"It represented the entrance where Indy found the Holy Grail."

Max nodded. "Oh yeah."

"Probably built somewhere between 100 BC and 200 AD," Kat said. "One legend has it that bandits or pirates hid their loot in a stone urn up on the second level."

"Gone by now."

Kat nodded. "It also could have been the treasury of an Egyptian Pharaoh since so much in it has to do with the afterlife."

Max looked to the top of the edifice. Four stone eagles stood watch.

Apparently noticing where his eyes went, Kat said, "The eagles were said to carry away men's souls."

103

Max shivered.

"See the two figures flanking the entrance?" Kat asked.

Max squinted and instinctively stepped forward for a better look at the two busts.

Kat walked up beside him and he felt a shiver of a different kind. Much better.

"They're the twins Castor and Pollux," she said.

Castor and Pollux. Castor and Pollux. Knowing this lady was taxing his brain.

He flashed her a puzzled look.

"Greek and Roman mythology," she said. "Castor was a real person, the son of a king. Pollux was the divine son of Zeus. They were said to live partly on Olympus and partly in the underworld."

"Appropriate that they're here," Max said. "This has kind of an other-world feel to it."

Kat's eyebrow raised when she looked up at him.

Those green eyes! Another good shiver.

"True," she said. It was a simple word. One syllable. Said in firmness. But the utterance drew his attention to her lips. Full and perfect.

She took a step back from his gaze and smiled. Perfect teeth, too, he thought. Then he figuratively slapped himself. He had a real-or-Memorex moment. This wasn't a Texas livestock sale where you evaluate head carriage, muscle development and body length. Geez. This was a woman and a very intelligent, astonishingly beautiful, inordinately intriguing one at that.

Take hold of yourself, boy-o. The words of his old black-ops mentor returned to him as if spoken in his ear. *Distraction endangers the mission.*

Max came out of his conversation with Captain Jake Gibson and briefly recalled how this great man had died, largely because one of his colleagues had been distracted by a beautiful woman on a mission in Sarajevo.

He shook his head to get out of the reverie. What was he looking at? Oh, Castor and Pollux. Al Khazneh, the Treasury. And a gorgeous archeologist who now rested a hand on his shoulder and pointed to their left with her other hand.

"That's where I think we should start," she said. "Past those buildings and over those cliffs. Jebal Al-Habis.

Several minutes later, with people of all different colors milling about them—oohing and aahing and snapping photographs—Max and Kat walked a colonnaded street.

Kat pointed. "A modern wonder of the world."

"The Nymphaeum?" Max asked.

"Yes, the public fountain—a miracle of running water in the desert."

Max nodded.

"The Romans dedicated the fountain to water nymphs."

Max laughed. "I have a hard time reconciling armed Roman soldiers and nymphs.

Kat grinned.

They walked past a soda shop and an old Arab man stepped out, pointed to the precipice before them and asked in heavily accented English, "Do you see the camel?"

Max looked closely and answered in Arabic. "Yes, at the north end. Looks like a camel's head!"

Kat chuckled. "You're the perfect tourist, Max."

"Thank you."

They continued the walk to the Crusader castle Jebal al-Habis.

"On the lower slopes are a visitors' center and a museum," Kat said.

"Let's skip straight to the castle, especially if we'll need to get to Al-Wu'ayra today," Max said.

Kat nodded agreement, then sped up and Max followed as they hustled past a suite of tombs known as the Hermitage and ascended a stone staircase in remarkably good condition. Less than half an hour later they reached the top.

"We're the only ones here," Max marveled.

"Easier hikes to make," Kat said.

Before them a wall ran between two cliffs, seemingly blocking the way up the mountain.

"Around here," Kat gestured, leading the way to a demolished gateway, which enabled them to climb higher.

Looks like Beirut, Max thought, observing ruins of walls, towers and buildings all around them as they clambered higher. His mind got inside those of the Crusaders who built this castle, constructing walls across every gully by which an enemy might access the castle. A couple of gullies had eroded so badly the walls hung over nothing at all.

"Ready your swords, men. The enemy's afoot," Max said softly.

"What's that?" Kat turned to him.

"Oh, just talking to myself—and a few of my predecessors." Max stepped over a large boulder.

Finally, they reached a small plateau and a nearly sheer slope confronted them. Max and Kat walked to the edge of the plateau. A breeze arose as they peered down a drop several hundred feet to the base of Al-Habis. A hundred feet away, a path running up the mountainside to the castle proper had nearly completely eroded.

"This is as far as you can go now," Kat said and swept an arm around her. "I've been in the castle before, but it's not reachable any longer. Except for mountain goats."

"Mountain goats and Rangers," Max said with a grin.

"I think of you as a Marine."

"A hybrid, actually. I'm a Marine, who's trained and fought with

106

Rangers, SEALs and a few others around the world. This?" He waved toward the precipice. "An appetizer, a bowl of wings, to a thirty-two-ounce Texas steak."

He slipped off his backpack and pulled out the long coil of rope. Opening a pocket, he fingered ultralight power cams, crampons, and a hammer.

"You didn't plan on a hike in Israel; you planned on climbing," Kat declared.

"Well, partially." He fasted the crampons to his hiking boots, shoved the cams into a cargo pocket and grasped the hammer in his right hand.

"What are you planning, Max?"

"We've got great cellular reception up here," he said. "When I get into the castle I'll call you and, with my video feed on, you can walk me to where you want. I'll be your marionette." He stood on his toes, raised his arms and wiggled his fingers as if he were suspended in air and held by strings of twine.

Kat laughed.

Max started to dance with hands raised and exaggerating the height of his leg kicks.

She laughed even harder.

Finally, she waved submission to the ache in her ribs and for him to stop. Once he did, she asked, "Are you certain about this?"

"You be the puppeteer; I'll be the puppet, and we'll turn the world on its head when we find this music."

"Okay, you win."

He grinned. She grinned back. And Max rushed off toward the pathway that led up the cliff.

The breeze turned into a wind as Max made his way up the path.

The trail quickly narrowed further and further still until it was less than a foot wide and he had to face the rock and cling to it, edging sideways.

Not so beautiful close-up, he thought, spitting dust out of his mouth.

Then he began preceding every step by slamming the pointed end of the hammer into the mountain and pulling himself along. Finally, the pathway disappeared for about twelve feet. Max peered up to see how much higher the castle proper was.

"Thirty, forty feet," he said to himself. "Easy peasy."

Max took a deep breath, tied down one end of his climbing rope and began the straight-up ascent—a foot or two at a time. The higher he rose, the harsher the wind.

Finally, he pulled himself up and over the edge of the cliff. He looked up at a stone wall that rose fifty feet and was capped by a tower.

He opened a cargo pocket and felt for his iPod. Amazing, he thought, in the midst of Jordan, up on a mountain, I've got reception. He dialed Kat and she answered, breathless in anticipation before the first ring ended.

"Max!" she said.

"A mountain goat at your service, professor."

She laughed.

"Let me show you where I am," he said and scanned his iPod slowly from left to right.

"If you look to your left, you should see what was the forecourt to the castle," she said.

He did and there it was—a flat, manmade court of hewn stone, half crumbled, half intact.

He turned the iPod to show the forecourt.

"Go to the forecourt and you'll find entrance stairs immediately inside the wall."

Max climbed over large and small stones that had disengaged from the castle walls and reached the forecourt. He looked to his right and a huge wooden gate hung limply by mammoth steel hinges. He squeezed inside and a steep flight of stairs rose to his right. They were in extraordinary condition for an eighteen-hundred-year-old abandoned structure.

Max hurried up the stairs and onto a yard. He turned the iPod toward himself and asked, "So exactly where do you think the music might be safeguarded?"

"The keep," Kat said.

"Of course," Max said. "The castle within the castle."

He looked beyond the yard and, indeed, a polygonal tower rose about two stories high. To its right was a cistern, probably full of water, he thought.

"In there?" he asked, pointing the iPod in that direction.

"Exactly!"

Max could sense the heightened expectation in Kat's voice.

"Go up the stairs, two flights," she said, "and, if I remember correctly, there'll be an entry at ten o'clock."

Max two-stepped up a couple dozen stairs to one plateau, then up another couple dozen stairs, and another flat area lay before him. He looked to his ten o'clock and, indeed, a very wide steel-plated door hung awry. Again he held up his iPod to show Kat where he was and stepped quickly to the door. With a heave, he pushed past the door.

He looked to his left and saw two stone-faced square structures, each with several tall slits in them that became narrower and narrower.

"The baileys!" he exclaimed and pointed the iPod for Kat. "Where they could fire their weapons out but the enemy had little chance of firing in and hitting them."

"Right," Kat said. "Look to your right."

Max did. Before him was a door that looked to be bronze. Eight feet wide and another eight feet high, it appeared almost untouched by time. He scanned the area around him. Time, wind, storms—the centuries had played havoc everywhere around this castle. Everywhere but here.

"That's the keep, Max."

Max again turned the iPod toward his face and asked, "Are you ready for this, Kat?"

Her face smiled back at him. "Sure am, soldier."

"Ah, it's Max the Marionette. Lead me on, professor."

"You'll have to go inside."

At that, Max suddenly had the terrible thought that the door would be locked from the inside and impenetrable from the outside. His heart sank for an instant at the thought of it.

He'd been taught plenty in his special-ops training, but picking locks wasn't one of those things and he had no C4 in his back pocket. Then he looked at the hinges. There were two, at two- and six-foot heights. He stepped in for a closer look. Pins. Simple pins. Well, simple if you considered ten-inch pins simple.

"What's up?" Kat asked.

Kat! He had forgotten her.

"Sorry. I forgot to 'aim' you." Max aimed his phone toward the hinges. "That's our way in; I'll take the door off its hinges."

"How?"

Max shrugged. "Maybe I've got something in my backpack that could do it."

He opened his backpack, looking for a strong, thick wire. Something, anything that he could use to push the pins out of the hinges. He pulled out everything, rummaging through the gear. Nothing.

Frustration had diminished determination. He started to shove his gear back into the backpack and noticed how well-formed his backpack was. Then his moment at the LL Bean store flashed before him.

"This is not a soft pack, sir," the clerk had said. "It's made with heavy-duty wire ribs to prevent being crushed."

Max slipped his Ranger Assault knife into his hand and cut the canvas along the rim of his backpack.

"Aha!" he exclaimed.

"What is it?" Kat asked.

"Our way into the keep."

"Great!"

Max cut out the wire rib, about three feet of it.

"Too much is better than not enough," he said with a laugh.

He set his phone on the ground, pointing it toward the door so Kat could see. Then he stepped to the door and, with the pointed end of his climbing ax, hammered at the pin. It didn't budge. Again he hammered it. Again, no movement.

"Lotion!" It was Kat.

"What?" he asked.

"Do you have any lotion of any sort? Doesn't need to be WD-40, just a lubricant.

Max's eyebrow rose. "My gun oil!" he said. "I may have left my gun at the border, but not my oil." He scrambled over to his backpack and found the gun oil in a tiny pocket.

He picked up his phone and held it in front of him. "You're brilliant, Kat."

He could see her green eyes sparkle and face light up.

"Thanks," she said, "but let's see if it works."

"It will. Guaranteed."

Two minutes later, he was proved correct. He poured the gun oil over both hinges, waited for it to work its magic, then hammered the lower pin. It moved easily and he took the heavy wire from his backpack and shoved it into the hinge, driving the pin up and out. The same trick worked on the top hinge and the heavy bronze door creaked. Max hefted his hammer, jammed it between the door and the wall and yanked at it with fierce strength. With a sudden lurch, the door groaned and moved outward.

Max stepped out of the way. While the lock held the door at the right side, the sheer weight of the door turned it cockeyed frontward and down.

Max picked up the phone. "Would you like to go inside with me, marionette master?"

"Sure would. Max, you'll need light when you go in. There should lamps and torches inside. Who knows if the oil has dried up for the lamps, but the torches ought to light."

"I've got a light," Max pulled a small CSI-type flashlight out of one cargo pocket, "and a match." He pulled a matchbox out of another and showed them both to Kat.

"What do you *not* have inside a pocket somewhere?" she asked with a laugh.

"MacGyver," he said, "was a hero of mine growing up."

"I thought it must be Ike or Patton."

"Well, them, too," Max grinned. "Let's go. And we'll record this for posterity." He touch-padded the phone a couple of times and the video function began.

Holding the flashlight in one hand and the phone in the other, Max slipped into the castle keep.

"First, find a lamp or torch," Kat said.

Max looked to his right and spotted a torch cradled on the wall. He took it down and lit it. Flames shot up a foot high and illuminated the keep.

A domed ceiling rose to twenty feet high. The room was circular and Max guessed forty feet in diameter. "This is larger than I thought it would be," he said. "And it's all stone, no timber."

"They stopped building timber keeps in the 12th century," Kat said. "This was one of the first all-stone keeps in the world."

"Thanks, Doctor Katherine Cardova. So, the key question: where's the music?"

"You're welcome, Colonel Max Braxton," she said with a laugh. "Now walk me around. We're looking for something religious but not obvious."

"Shouldn't there be a bookcase, with a secret room behind it?" Max asked.

"I don't remember any mention of one."

There was no furniture, save a pulpit-looking stand at the far side of the room.

Max walked straight to it. "How about this?"

"Check it out for hidden drawers or chambers."

Max held the torch close to the stand, set the phone on the floor, knelt and felt all around it.

"Solid stone," he said. "I don't feel any latches, or knobs, or anything like that."

"What about the top?" Kat asked.

Max stood up and felt all around it.

"Nothing," he said, then hesitated. "Hold on."

Setting down the torch, he grabbed the edges of the top of the stand and pulled straight up. The top didn't move, but surprisingly the entire stand lifted slightly off the floor.

"What's this?" he said.

Kat, her face on the LED of Max's cell, asked, "What is what, Max?"

"Wait a sec." He bent down in a football lineman's stance and shouldered his weight into the podium. It slid several inches across the floor.

Max picked up the phone. "Kat, that stand is not solid stone. I think it's hollow. I'm moving it to see if something is hidden beneath it.

"Okay."

Setting down the phone and facing it toward him, again Max shouldered the podium and shoved it a full two feet along the floor.

Beneath it was an iron ring four inches in diameter, hooked into a floor stone. Max's neck hairs tingled. *This has to be extraordinary!*

He hustled to his backpack which he had dropped to the floor by the door. He grabbed his climbing hammer and rushed back to the ring. Hooking the narrow spiked hammerhead into the ring, he tugged hard. Up came the square of fieldstone.

Max heard Kat gasp. "What's there, Max?"

He swept the torch off the floor, held it above the hole and peered inside. A small scroll held together with crude twine lay alone in the hole. For a moment, he lost his breath. So *this* is what kept archeologists like Kat sifting through centuries of dirt. Far out!

He pulled out the scroll, half expecting a scorpion or other villainous creature to bite, and showed it to Kat. She cried out in joy.

"I'll bring it down," he said.

"No," Kat said. "Read it now. I can't wait."

Max untied the twine and opened the scroll. "It looks similar to Hebrew but not quite," he said.

"Show me."

"Let me go outside in the sunlight and you'll be able to see it better than in this place."

"Good idea."

Seconds later, Max stood outside the keep. A steady wind whipped across the castle. He set the scroll on the ground, placed small stones on the four corners to keep it from rolling up or blowing away, and held the phone above it.

"It's Aramaic," Kat said, identifying the pre-Hebrew language.

"I'm taking a photo as well as this video," Max said, then scrolled to that application and snapped two photographs before returning to video.

Then he turned the telephone back over the scroll.

"Can you read it?" Max asked.

"Oh, Lord," Kat said. "Max, it says one of the Crusaders was taking the music away—before the castle is captured by Saladin."

Max's shoulders sagged. "Oh, no! Where were they taking it?"

Just then Max heard a shriek and his connection to Kat went dead.

The hair on his neck bristled. Picking up the scroll, the cell phone, and his backpack, he raced through the castle, down the flight of stairs, over the boulders and to the edge of the plateau. Looking down, he spotted Kat. One man held her with her arms locked behind her. Another was bent over her backpack, pulling things out of it as if he were looking for something in particular.

Max hurriedly pulled the rope up the cliffside, hoping he could do so before the men spotted it. Once he had it all, he untied it from the boulder.

He pulled his pack over his shoulders, dropped the scroll and phone in a cargo pocket, slipped the hammer between his belt and back and rushed along the plateau, hauling the rope with him. When he reached a point from which he could repel down the mountainside and be out of sight of the two men, he knelt down.

Hurriedly he wrapped the rope around a large rock and tied a shortened version of a Blake's Hitch knot. Wrapping his left hand in a handkerchief and using his right as a guide, he pushed off the edge of the cliff and slid silently all the way down to the plateau on which Kat and the men stood, but around a bend in the cliff out of their sight.

Setting foot on the ground, he leaned down and slipped the crampons off his hiking boots.

He sidled along the edge of the cliff in the direction of Kat and the two men, then looked around the bend and spotted them. Max was close enough to see the rotten teeth, the anger etched on the speaker's bearded face.

The man was speaking loudly at Kat, but the words were muffled. The wind was blowing in another direction.

Were they aware Max was around? Did they think he was in the castle? Maybe they thought Kat was alone. Who in the world were they in the first place? From the same group that had shot Danny Arens on Dragot?

It took all the strength Max could muster not to rush them for mishandling Kat. But he recalled his SEAL commander's words: "Stay cool as ice, son."

Instead, he surveyed the scene. It was flat, barren rock where they stood. But if he could get ten feet below them and circle around, he figured he could surprise them.

Max turned and raced to the rim of the plateau, laid down and lifted himself downward several feet. Feeling a boulder below him with his toes, he let go of the edge of the cliff and looked around. He could get all the way to a spot behind Kat and the men, then climb up onto the plateau again.

He scrambled over several boulders to the best spot. There the plateau was only a few inches above his head. He pulled himself up enough to peek over the edge. The interrogator and Kat were face to face, Kat to Max's left. The second man was behind Kat, looking up and around the cliffs toward the castle.

The wind was blowing directly at Max now and he could tell the language was Arabic. Some of the words were muffled, but he could make out the gist of the interrogation.

"You were a consultant to Professor Arens."

Kat nodded.

"What do you know?"

Kat shrugged her shoulders.

"You've been to the Temple Faithful."

She mumbled something.

The man stepped in closer and slapped her face. "You're a collaborator!"

She stood firm and shook her head.

"You crossed the border with a man. Where is he?"

She raised her hands as if questioning Max's whereabouts herself.

"Is he up there? In the castle?"

Kat shrugged again.

He slapped her again.

Max again had to submerge the urge to charge the man.

"What are you two looking for?"

She mumbled something.

"What have you found?"

She shook her head.

"Is it music?"

Kat stood still.

The man leaned forward, almost nose-to-nose with her. "Tell us!" he screamed.

She remained unmoved. He slapped her again, harder this time, and it snapped her head toward Max. Did she notice him, looking over the ridge of the cliff? Quickly she turned back to face the man.

Max tightened his hands into fists and felt the adrenaline surge.

"Tell us or you will die right here—alone!"

Suddenly the second man pulled a rifle from beneath his robes and pointed it at Kat's head. Max was amazed that she didn't shriek, but stood her ground. This is some cool woman, he thought.

Max pulled his Ranger Assault knife from its holster on his hip and, with one swift, nimble lift, was over the top and on his feet.

"Not too soon!" he yelled. Startled, the man with the rifle turned toward him and when he did, Max flung his knife with ferocity. In a split second, the blade had found its mark, slicing into the gunman's right shoulder like into a soft melon.

The gunman screamed in pain, dropping his rifle and falling to his knees. The other man grabbed Kat and spun around toward Max. Suddenly he had a knife at Kat's throat.

"Move forward and she dies!" he said in Arabic.

Max caught Kat's eyes in his and said, "Don't be scared."

"Easy for *you* to say."

"Does this guy speak English?" Max said.

"Apparently not. I tried."

"Then when I say 'duck,' do so."

"Okay."

Max stared at the man and spoke in Arabic. "You don't want to hurt this harmless woman. She's an ant, less than an ant, a flea, not worth bloodying your blade, my friend."

The man chuckled and nodded. "A flea," he repeated.

"I'm unarmed. She's unarmed. You could use your friend's rifle and be done with us in a much less painful way—and not bloody your clothes in the meantime."

The man looked down at his friend who was writhing in pain and calling, "Ahmed! Ahmed!"

"Quiet," Ahmed said. "Shall I kill these infidels with my knife or your rifle, Hussein?"

"My rifle. It will be my revenge," Hussein said through clenched teeth. "Just get it done so I can get to a doctor!"

Ahmed dragged Kat the four or five feet to his friend and put away his knife at the same time he reached for the rifle.

"Duck!" Max said and Kat ducked and dove to the ground.

Max was in fast-forward motion, reaching behind him with his right hand and grasping the climbing hammer held tight by his belt. As Ahmed's hand touched the butt of the rifle, he noticed him rushing ahead and fumbled to pick up the weapon. Max gobbled up a yard with each stride. Ahmed picked up the barrel of the rifle with his left hand. Max closed in. Ahmed pushed the butt of the rifle to his shoulder. Max, now fifteen feet away, flung the hammer. As Ahmed's index finger reached for the trigger, the hammer struck him square in the chest.

The crack of the sternum was surprisingly loud, like an echo in a canyon. Ahmed crumpled to the ground, the rifle tumbling from his hands. He gasped for breath and pulled his body into a fetal position.

Hussein screamed, "No! Ahmed!" and tried to crawl toward his buddy. Max cut him off with a kick to the chin that sent him sprawling, unconscious.

He picked up the rifle and handed it to Kat. "Hold this on our pal Ahmed to make sure he doesn't get sassy, okay?"

Kat nodded and took the rifle.

Max hurried to the place thirty yards away where he had left his backpack, cut a long length of rope that was hanging from the cliff with his Swiss Army knife, and brought both, along with his crampons, with him back to the unconscious men. He tied both men's hands behind their backs and their ankles together. He reached into the backpack, pulled out a roll of duct tape, ripped off two pieces and put them over the men's mouths.

"That ought to keep them from complaining," he said.

Kat simply nodded.

Again he reached into his backpack and pulled out a tiny container of canned heat, opened it and lit it with a match. Stepping over to Hussein,

119

he frowned, ripped open the shirt where the knife stuck in and looked at Kat.

"When I pull the knife out of our friend's shoulder, put as much pressure on the wound as possible."

Kat set down the rifle and bent over next to Max. He slid the knife out and she pressed in on the wound, blood oozing through her fingers.

"Tell me if this is too much for you," Max said.

"I've delivered baby sheep and goats back home," she said.

Max laughed. "Well, okay then."

He wiped the blood from the blade of the knife on the man's shirt, then held the blade over the canned heat's blue flame for a minute. Then, kneeling over Hussein, he said, "Okay, let go."

When she did, Max held the knife blade to the wound and cauterized the bleeding.

Hussein awoke with a scream muffled by the tape. His eyes widened in horror, then closed again as he passed into unconsciousness.

"Check Ahmed for identification or a cell phone, and I'll examine Hussein here," he said.

Both pulled cell phones out of the men's pockets but no forms of identification.

"Makes you wonder how they got across the border," Max said.

"Maybe they didn't. Maybe they live here."

Max nodded, thought a moment, then went again to his backpack, peered inside and pulled out two Band-Aids.

"What—" Kat began.

Max held up a finger. "In lieu of a fingerprint kit, voilà!"

He took off the little plastic coverings to the Band-Aids and, one by one, pressed Ahmed's and Hussein's right forefingers onto each one.

"For our friends, the Israeli police," he said. "We can't take them back with us, but we can ID them."

"Don't you want to question them?" Kat asked.

"I don't know when they'll wake up and we have to create some distance before help shows up for them, so—guess not. But we can snap a couple photos to accompany their fingerprints."

"I'll do that," Kat said. She scrambled back to where the two men had accosted her, picked her phone up from the ground and checked it out.

"Still works!" she said. Walking back, she propped up Ahmed and snapped a photo, then did the same with Hussein.

"It would be good if I could push their mouths up into a smile," she said with a grin.

"You do have a funny side, don't you?" Max said. "But grins might not be in their DNA."

"Might not."

"Then let's head out of here before someone else dangerous shows up."

Kat stood up, put her hands on her hips and said, "Exactly what did you said you do?"

Max chuckled. "More on that later. Let's scoot out of here first."

In a half hour, they had returned their rental car and had easily checked back into Israel. They hurried to the Land Rover in a nearby parking lot, tossed in their gear and climbed into their seats.

Breathlessly, Kat said, "Can I see the scroll?" She had barely been able to contain herself all the way from the castle. Imagine this discovery!

Max handed the parchment to her.

Trying to keep her hands from trembling, she unrolled the scroll and held it taut. She could feel the familiar tickle of the hair on her neck at the anticipation.

How she loved Aramaic. Through over three thousand years the language mutated here and there—from place to place and dialect to dialect—always animated and succinct. The language both of the administration of empires and of divine worship, the language of Israel in the time of the Second Temple from 539 BC until the Temple's destruction in 70 AD. The language Jesus spoke. The books of Daniel and Ezra were largely written in Aramaic. Parts of the Dead Sea Scrolls, which she had been honored to study, were written in Jewish Aramaic with unique lettering that so closely resembled Hebrew.

She read down the brief message of the scroll, then turned to Max in the driver's seat. "They knew the castle was going to be overrun," she said. "They sent one of the Crusaders, Godfrey the Irish, to escape with the music to his homeland, to a newly built church in Dublin—St. Michan's."

"Why not to Rome?"

"I'd like to ask them that myself," Kat said with a shrug. "Perhaps they didn't fully trust Rome since they were in and out of favor with various Popes from when the Catholic Church endorsed them around 1120 AD until Pope Clement disbanded them in 1312 AD."

"Well, when exactly did Saladin overthrow Petra?"

"In 1188 AD."

"Who was the Pope then?"

Kat raised her eyebrows, caught his eyes in hers and asked with mock incredulity. "What! Do you think I'm a walking encyclopedia or something?"

"Well, aren't you?" Max grinned and raised his eyebrows, too.

"You're asking for the name of the Pope more than eight hundred years ago. If I know this answer, you'll give me what?" she asked.

"Give you?" Max hesitated. "How about bangers and mash in a Dublin pub?"

"Bangers and mash? You're on."

"Well?"

"It was Pope Clement the Third."

"You're sure."

"Yep. He's the one who persuaded King Henry the Second of England and King Philip the Second of France to finance the Third Crusade."

"You amaze me, professor."

"I just love good bangers and mash," she said with a grin. "Actually, I was blessed with a fine memory. Some might say 'photographic,' but I don't know what that means. I don't see photographs of things in my mind. I simply remember."

"Whatever your definition, I'm impressed."

"A gift from God while in my Mom's womb, I'd say."

Max cocked his head. "So," he said, "when do you want to go to Dublin?"

"How about—" Kat looked at her wristwatch and then back at him, "now?"

He laughed.

"Ovda Airport is about forty miles north of Eilat," she said.

"That's right! Maybe we could catch an Aer Lingus or British Air flight."

"Okay, soldier. Onward and upward." Kat knew her smile went from ear to ear. She could feel the adrenaline of a thrilling "find." Actually, the scroll she held in her hands was a quite a discovery in itself.

As Max drove away from the border, he flicked on the InSync in the Rover and when the application asked for a command, he said, "Call Dudi Danino."

When Danino's secretary connected them, the Israeli chief of police exclaimed, "Max!"

123

"Hello, Dudi. I have news," he said in Hebrew.

"I was about to call you with some news of my own. But go first, my friend."

Max really wanted to hear Dudi's information first but proceeded to tell him about the confrontation with the two terrorists.

"Kat took their photos and will send them to you from her phone," he said. "We've got their cell phones and fingerprints and will drop them off at your offices here in Eilat. Then we're heading to the airport to catch a flight to Ireland if we can."

"Ireland? What's there?"

"The prize, we hope."

"The prize. The music." Dudi's voice sounded different. Heightened? "So you found a clue in Petra?"

"Yes. My question is, how did those two goons know where we were?"

"I know the answer. It's one of my bits of news."

"Go ahead, Dudi. You're on speaker. Tell us your news."

"First of all, Doctor Arens is still unconscious but out of critical condition."

Kat raised a fist in exuberance and whispered, "Praise you, Lord."

"But now he's got a neighbor," Dudi said.

"Who's that?" Max asked.

"Gershon Zoref. We got a call from The Temple Faithful HQ last night. Zoref was found in his office nearly beaten to death."

Kat gasped and Max reached for her hand to comfort her, preparing for what came next.

"They rushed him to Hadassah and we've had him placed in the room next to Doctor Arens so we could have a protective detail on both of them.

"He's in serious condition. He was unconscious when Sub-Inspector

124

Pollard arrived at the hospital. But before he passed out, Zoref told his assistant what happened."

"And?" Max urged Dudi on; he loved his friend, but the man spoke in measured tones at all times, probably part of his training as an intelligence officer whose every word could be parsed by an intense Israeli and Palestinian media.

"And he told his assistant four Arab men busted into his office demanding to know the whereabouts of Doctor Cardova."

Kat gasped again.

"That's my second bit of news. Kat, our chief inspector for the Tel Aviv District—Jacob Ayalon—found a witness who was at the bar Sam Livingston went to. This witness overheard a very drunk Livingston boasting to a group of what he called 'very attentive' men about Danny Arens' discovery and mentioning the name of an American consultant."

"So somehow they figured out Kat would be in touch with Zoref?" Max asked.

"Makes sense. Who would be more interested in the discovery than The Third Temple people?"

There was a moment of silence, then Dudi continued, "We've found all the members of the dig and offered protection. Once they heard about Zoref, all five decided to return home—one to America, two to England, one to Holland and one to Puerto Rico."

"Sounds like you've got the bases covered," Max said.

"Bases covered?" Dudi asked.

"It's a American baseball term." Max chuckled. "You've got all the angles covered, Dudi."

"Commander?" Kat asked.

"Yes."

"Will you have someone keep us informed about Gershon's condition? I feel horrible."

125

"Of course. Meanwhile, please let me know where you are and, when you return, I'll have you met with an escort at the airport."

"Where is the police station here in Eilat?" Max asked.

"Drive past the little Eilat Airport, not Ovda but the one downtown. Then take your first left-hand turn and the station's on your left."

"Easy enough. Talk to you later, Dudi."

When Max and Kat walked into the Eilat police station, they found out Danino had called ahead. An inspector met them at the front desk and promised to get the Arabs' phones and fingerprints directly to headquarters in Jerusalem.

"What are the odds the two men can be arrested in Petra?" Max asked in Hebrew.

The inspector chuckled. "What are the odds of winning one of your big American lotteries?"

"I get the picture." Max shrugged. "The word 'friend' in the Middle East, even concerning Jordan, is a relative term."

"With many variations and hues," the inspector said.

"Thank you, Inspector," Max said and shook his hand.

"Thank you, sir. And, ma'am." He took Kat's hand—a little too warmly for Max's liking. Then Max caught himself. Who was he to be possessive, anyhow? He looked at his watch. He'd known her all of fifty-one hours.

Chapter Nine

A minute later they were driving north toward Ovda Airport.

Kat pulled out her cell phone, went online to get the Ovda phone number and called.

A woman answered and Kat asked in Hebrew about flights to Dublin.

"There's an Aer Lingus flight leaving in one hour," she said. "The next flight out is tomorrow—on British Air."

"Thank you," Kat said. She looked sadly at Max. "Too bad we weren't a little closer. An Aer Lingus takes off in an hour. We'll have to wait for a British Air tomorrow."

Max peeked over at her as he accelerated. "Wait?" he asked. "We're in the desert, Doctor Cardova. Buckle up and hold on."

In thirty minutes they pulled into the Hertz parking lot and Max gave orders to ship his camping gear to the company's private storage area outside Ben Gurion Airport in Tel Aviv, where he had rented the vehicle.

He flipped the man at the counter the Rover's keys and he and Kat headed toward Ovda Airport next door, hustling as best they could while carrying large duffel bags.

Max turned to Kat as they hustled toward the building. "You feel like someone's looking over you?"

She sounded surprised at his question. "Who? God?"

"No." He pointed at the gigantic window above the forty-yard-wide entry doors. "It looks like a mammoth eye peering at you."

Kat appeared disappointed at his answer. Max shrugged and they rushed ahead.

The building was low to the desert ground, modern and efficient-looking.

"Second-busiest airport in Israel," Kat said.

"You've been here before?"

"I've flown here a couple of times from Europe," Kat said. "Follow me." And she hurried off, seemingly oblivious to the weight of her duffel bag.

Max caught up to her and said, "Let me take this off your hands." He grabbed the duffel bag and hustled to keep up her pace.

Within a minute, they had reached the Aer Lingus counter.

"Omigosh!" Kat said, looking at the Departures board. "It's on time and leaving in fifteen minutes."

They were three people deep in the line. Max and Kat heard the boarding call over the din of people—spoken in Hebrew, then repeated in English. "Boarding Aer Lingus, flight 1202. Gate 16. All business-class boarding now."

Max stepped to the front of the line and turned to face the people.

"Hello, folks," he said in English. "Is anyone here in an absolute rush? Because my friend and I need to get on a plane that is boarding right now, if indeed it has any seats."

Everyone shook their heads and, in unison, said, "Go right ahead."

"Thank you, thank you!" he said and Kat hurried to his side.

The Aer Lingus lady at the counter had heard Max and said, "We have two first-class seats remaining. That's all."

"We'll take them." Max handed her a credit card and identification.

"We just have two carry-ons."

The lady was quick, giving them their tickets within one minute.

Kat turned to the people in line. "Thank you all *so* much!"

Off they raced through the terminal and reached a single line brooding its way through metal detectors.

"Boarding Aer Lingus, flight 1202, Gate 16," came the announcement. "All coach seats boarding now."

Max looked at his wristwatch. "What time does it depart?"

"Ten minutes," Kat said.

Max looked over the heads of the crowd toward the Gates, hoping 16 would be close. The first one? Gate 1.

As Max and Kat raced away a heavyset man wearing a Muslim taqiyah on his head bullied through the Aer Lingus line, pushing people aside.

"Hey!" a young European-looking man objected. His mouth shut quickly when the man flashed him a menacing look.

Reaching the counter, he asked the Aer Lingus clerk in Arabic, "Those two. Where are they heading?"

The girl hesitated.

"Where did they go?!" He leaned over the counter, anger lining his mouth.

"Ireland, sir. Ireland," she responded in Hebrew.

"When does the flight leave?"

"Right now."

The man turned, snarled at the couple at the head of the line, shoved past the European man with a dangerously high elbow and stepped toward another man who had followed him in.

"Aer Lingus to Ireland. Boarding now," he said in Arabic.

"A dagger dug deeply will make sure he never flies anywhere, Aashif—except to the depths of hell," his companion snarled.

Aashif put a thumb and index finger to his chin. He scanned the terminal, noting that several armed Israeli IDF soldiers were stationed around the bank of airline counters, watching the crowd.

"Yes," he said. "Very good, Yashim. But it must be done while they are in line. Once they get past the security screener, we can't get to them."

He pointed toward a bank of ATMs and added, "I will cause a commotion over there. When I do, you will do the deed."

Yashim nodded and hurried toward the line where Max and Kat stood.

As Aashif strode to the ATMs, he thought how good Allah was to have them here, casing the airport for a planned bombing at the exact time this man and woman arrived. Allah be blessed!

Patience was something ingrained in officers' training. Max had learned the lesson in college; lived it in jungles, deserts, and assorted other military theaters; even taught it to officers-in-training. Rush, and you cause more problems than you solve. Rush in the wrong circumstances and you could end up dead, or worse, cause others to die. Rushing had lost wars that otherwise would have been won.

Controlled breathing helps manage anxiety, nervousness, apprehension, worry. Max gulped in deep breaths.

"You okay?" Kat asked.

"Coping," he said. "Patience has always been my short suit. You know they say life in the military is 'hurry up and wait.' True, but I've never overcome my shortcoming. You'd think this, waiting in line at an airport, would be easier than at the mess hall, or in the battlefield. But in a way, here is worse."

Yashim pushed his way through the crowd, his eyes keenly on the big American and the red-headed woman. *No shame*, he thought. *None of these Western women have any shame, walking around in public with their heads uncovered. Killing this woman will be my gift to Allah. That is, after gutting the swine beside her.*

His hand went to the dagger at his side. He'd killed before, with this dagger. Yashim had even named it Al-Thar, meaning "vengeance," for the weapon had indeed inflicted much retribution.

"Why not do the same thing you did back at the Aer Lingus counter?" Kat asked Max.

He looked at the long line and back at his watch.

"Eight minutes and counting," he said. "Listen, you're much prettier. You'd have better luck with a big line like this. I'll hold our place in line here in case they cold-shoulder you. But the odds are in your favor, professor."

Kat smiled and shrugged, then hurried to the metal detectors and turned.

"Hello, folks," she said loud enough to be heard. "Our flight leaves in, oh, six minutes. Can we possibly move to the front?"

Responses varied from groans to "of courses."

Aashif reached the ATM machines. His plan was easy: Pretend one of the machines wasn't working and start kicking the contraption and screaming in protest. That would draw the attention of the soldiers— enough so that none of them would notice the killing in their midst.

When the Americans collapsed, people would think the cause was a heart attack, a swooning for the woman. Such a tragedy, they'd say before scurrying off to their lives. *Ha! Tragedy indeed. The tragedy would be if these two infidels discovered the Jews' music so the Third Temple offenders could trespass and build on Islam's holy ground.*

Aashif looked through the crowd for Yashim. There he was, no more than ten feet from the American. The woman wasn't there? Oh, well, this would be an easy kill. Aashif wished he had given the assignment to himself. *Ah, the pleasure.*

Yashim stepped around one last couple and was at the end of the line. The American man was just ahead, within two arms' lengths.

There was a familiar taste in Yashim's mouth, the coppery taste when he was about to avenge his people's mistreatment. The taste was bitter yet, to his spirit, as sweet as honey from his grandfather's honeycombs.

Just then, having gotten approval from the people at the front of the line, Kat waved to Max and he hurried to her side, lugging their duffel bags.

Quickly they moved through the detector. Max breathed easy, thinking how they could have been stopped interminably if he had not left his knives with his camping gear.

Aashif was a moment away from hammering at the ATM when he noticed the American rush forward. He cursed in Arabic and waved frantically to Yashim.

They had to regroup. Suddenly fear shivered through his mind. He would have to report failure to Mumim. First, Hussein and Ahmed had fallen short, even been overcome by these two. Now, he and Yashim. He lowered his head and shook it, dejected and, more than that, afraid. His ears felt as hot as a mouthful of radishes.

Yashim had seen his gestures and was hurrying in his direction.

"Three minutes," Max announced as they looked down the terminal. "Gate Sixteen."

Ahead and to their left was Gate 2.

"I'm a runner," Kat said. "Let's run and I'll try to keep up with you."

With duffel bags on each arm, Max dashed ahead.

Would the flight leave without two first-class customers checking in? He'd seen it firsthand—heck, experienced it himself, in Philly, when he was so close to the airplane he could have thrown a football and hit the darn thing. No, he wasn't going to slow down and test Aer Lingus' attitude in that regard. As opposed to the Irish's famous "I'll-see-you-soon-and-I-don't-wear-a-watch" thinking, Aer Lingus was famous for promptness.

Max could run miles with forty pounds on his back, but a large duffel bag on each arm presented a tougher test, especially wielding them to avoid collisions in the busy terminal.

They hustled past Gates 6 and 7.

At this point, Max didn't check his watch. After all his missions, whose success or failure depended largely on perfect timing between six and eight men, he could feel the countdown in his head.

Two minutes and ten seconds.

Then Gates 8 and 9. *Hard to believe this building is so long!*

Gates 10 and 11 went by.

133

One minute and forty seconds.

Suddenly an IDF soldier stepped out from behind a post right in front of them and Max slammed into him. Both men were knocked backward and Kat's duffel bag fell to the floor. Max hurried to pick it up, but the soldier, a young man with suspicion etched on his face, pulled his rifle from off his shoulder and stood in his way.

"Let's see your bag," he said in Hebrew.

"No time, soldier. Flight to catch," Max replied.

The soldier stood firm. Then Max leaned forward and whispered something in the soldier's ear. Without hesitation, the soldier pulled back his rifle, saluted Max and stepped aside.

A minute and ten seconds.

Max got back in stride.

Sixty seconds, fifty-five seconds.

Thirty seconds later, Kat pulled up beside him and pointed ahead and to the left. "Right up there."

That was good. He was down to seventeen seconds.

Sliding around a family outside Gate 14, hugging their goodbyes on another flight, Max and Kat raced toward Gate 16.

The gate attendant, thirty feet away, was nearing the door to the runway.

"Wait!" Max said.

Kat held their two tickets high in her right hand and waved them. "Two for first class!" she called.

The attendant, a pleasant-looking young woman, smiled.

"You didn't have to run," she said with a beautiful Irish lilt as Max and Kat pulled up in front of her. "Front desk told us you were on your way."

Max and Kat exchanged looks and burst out laughing.

Aashif looked up at Departures and scanned the board.

When Yashim stood before him, Aashif said, "There's a British Air flight to Ireland, but it's not until tomorrow."

"And we'd never find them," Yashim said.

"We have operatives in Ireland," Aashif said. "We're everywhere. Like Allah. And we are his avengers."

He pulled a cell phone from his pocket and punched in a number.

A moment later, "Mumim."

Aashif lowered his voice. "We've lost them, my commander."

At Mumim's response, he involuntarily flinched his shoulders and winced. Maybe he would delay his return to Jerusalem. The Negev looked good right now.

Chapter Ten

Max stashed their duffel bags in the overhead bin, looked at Kat and smiled. "We made it, professor."

"Thanks to you carrying my bag."

"Thanks to you getting us past that line."

"Thanks to God, I'd say. You know, it's not like LaGuardia or Reagan International. I'll bet Ovda only has a flight to Ireland once a day."

"And we got it," Max said.

"Like I said, I give God the credit. We got here just in time, not a second to spare. That's not coincidence; that's a God-incidence."

"God-incidence," Max repeated, mulling the word over in his mind.

After they settled into their seats and the Boeing 737 had taken off, Kat turned to Max and said, "Two hours and I haven't thanked you for saving my life."

"No thanks necessary."

"My parents and friends—and, at least, a few students—would disagree."

Max grinned. "In that case, you're welcome." He looked intently at her and added, "You looked pretty calm being manhandled by those guys, but you must have been frightened."

"Out of my mind." A tear worked its way out of the corner of her eye. Kat dried her cheek and drew a deep breath. "But I knew I couldn't let you know."

She shrugged and added: "When that steel blade touched my neck, I nearly fainted. I think my knees wobbled."

"That's normal," Max said.

"Really?" Kat chuckled. "I think it was the stench from his sweat that kept me standing. Talk about BO!"

"Ha!" Max said. "Now you're making light of the situation. I know what it's like to be scared."

"I highly doubt that."

"It's true. In this case, I was scared of losing you."

"Afraid of losing me?" Kat's look was full of tease.

"Well, you are my charge."

"Oh." The word leaked disappointment.

The two fell into silence as the airplane taxied down the tarmac and lifted off, the midafternoon sun glinting off the window at Kat's right.

As the plane leveled off, Kat turned again toward Max.

"I have to admit," she said, "certain thoughts flashed through my mind back there at the castle."

"Thoughts of mortality?"

"Well, that, too. But more so of despair. The first time he slapped me in the face, my thought wasn't of the pain. I rued I'd never get to find the music, hold the paper in my hands, watch and behold as the Christian and Jewish world embraced the worship and as the Third Temple Faithful incorporated the music into their synagogue."

Max was taken aback. "Looking at death, that's what you thought of?"

Kat nodded agreement, then chuckled and said, "Now the *second* time he slapped me, I tried to slap him back, but my hands were being held by the other guy. That really miffed me."

"Did you wonder where I was?"

"Sure did. Where was my hero? Actually, the longer they took with me, the better I felt about the possibility of you rescuing me."

"Even though they were armed and I wasn't?"

Kat lowered her head but raised her eyes to his. "Well, you *are* a SEAL-Ranger type, right? Making weapons out of thin air—"

"This 'thin air' was actually mountain-climbing gear."

"I stand corrected."

The smile she flashed seemed to light up the airplane's cabin. At least, it seemed that way to Max.

The flight attendant, a beautiful dark-skinned young lady, offered drinks and a light snack. Max and Kat devoured the snack and opted for water.

They were flying over Italy when Kat turned and asked, "Are you as excited as I am?"

"As excited as you? I wouldn't say so since this is your field, not mine," he said. "But since joining the Marines to serve my country, I've thrived on adventure. It powers my life. Well, partly. I also like the idea of being in shape, of facing new challenges—ones that require training and skills not found at your neighborhood health club or gym. There's nothing like rappelling out of a helicopter a hundred feet off the ground amidst gunfire or scuba-diving deep into the harbor of an enemy and taking out a boat loaded with explosives intended for an American aircraft carrier. Nothing."

"Adrenaline rush," Kat said.

"Some say it's addictive," he said. "I guess I'd agree."

"Are you?"

"Addicted?" Max shrugged. "Maybe. I might have figured that out if I'd continued on my hiking trip through Israel. A trip of introspection as well as relaxation and inspiration, planning out my book. But," he winked at her, "then you came along."

Kat chuckled. "I guess I did."

"In spades."

"Yes, in spades, though I never meant to."

"Think my arrival was fate? Like your God-incidence?"

Kat pondered the question, then slowly nodded. "I guess I'd have to say so."

Max crossed his arms and looked at her seriously. "Doctor Cardova, I believe, from what I've seen, you, yourself might have an addiction."

"Really? To what?"

"Adventure."

She shook her head. "You don't know me that well."

"Oh?" He locked her eyes in his. "Just look how you jumped on this chase. I think I know you—enough."

"Enough for what?"

"Enough to assess an extraordinary character. You've got enough initials after your name you could rest at home on your laurels and not gallivant around the world."

Kat shrugged. "I'm an oddity among most of my colleagues—a creature tied to the past but intent to live in the present. My field assistants, at least, some of them, appear to have that same trait. We learn from history, and the more we discover and uncover, the more we all learn.

"Besides," she looked at him with a playful twinkle in her eyes, "you know what Tolstoy said about an ordinary life."

"No, what?"

Kat spoke dramatically, "Ivan Ilych's life had been most simple and most ordinary and, therefore, most terrible."

Max chuckled. "How true." He thought a moment, then asked, "You want to know my Tolstoy quote?"

"Probably has to do with warfare," she said.

"Yep. Care to guess?"

"No."

"Okay, then: 'The most powerful warriors are patience and time.'"

"Patience and time," Kat repeated. "Or lack of patience and not enough time."

"Those two men back in Petra," Max said, "do you think they and the rest of the terrorists have patience and time?"

"I think they don't care for patience and they're trying to condense time, win the world as fast as possible—"

"To hasten the Mahdi's return," Max finished.

"Yes. Conquer the world, then welcome their messiah. Endgame. Checkmate."

"And there are a few million more just like those two. If ten percent of the Muslims in the world agree with holy jihad—which studies show is true—there are sixteen million who'd like to kill Westerners and Jews, not just prevent us from discovering Jewish and Christian artifacts."

Kat wrapped her arms around her shoulders and shivered. "That's a scary thought."

Max closed his eyes and remembered the quote was driven home by his War College instructor. "From the beginning, men used God to justify the unjustifiable."

"Salman, Rushdie," Kat said. "From *True Satanic Verses*."

"Correct, professor." Max nodded.

"'Human beings are never more frightening than when they're convinced beyond doubt they're right,'" Kat said.

"Aha," Max said, "from Laurens Van der Post in *The Lost World of the Kalahari*."

"My learned friend!" Kat trilled.

"At your service." He bowed.

"Here's another. This also has to do with those who are convinced they're right. You get this one and you get a special reward," she teased.

There was a glint in Max's eyes. "Fire away."

"'They would not find me changed from him they knew—only more sure of all I thought was true.'"

"A poet, obviously."

"Oh-oh."

"Oh-oh, you say. So you don't want me to get this right."

Kat didn't respond, but a smile curled her lips.

Max pondered the brief list of poets with whom he was familiar. A short list indeed. Poetry was not his forte, nor one of his aspirations. He guessed, "Carl Sandburg?"

"Sandburg? You're a Sandburg fan?"

"Well, I'm impressed with his life: firefighter, milkman, ice harvester. He was probably somehow related to Jack London."

Kat joined him in a chuckle, then honed in on his eyes. "Ah, I was right. It's the firefighter, the savior-type, that enamors you—"

Max shrugged, at this point not at all surprised at this lady's discernment.

"So, was Sandburg right? And do I get my prize?" he asked.

"No, the answer is Robert Frost, and you don't."

Max snapped his fingers in mock frustration. "What *was* the prize?"

"A kiss—on the cheek."

"On the cheek, eh?" He smiled. "And do I get another chance?"

"Perhaps. Maybe. We'll see. I don't give them away."

"Precious as diamonds, eh? Even if it's on the cheek?"

She simply smiled.

"Okay," he said, "I have a quote for you with a prize if you get it right."

"The prize?"

142

"We'll see."

"Maybe I don't want it."

Then you can refuse."

"Go ahead then."

"'Principles are what make a boy into a man.'"

Kat thought for a moment, then answered, "Mark Twain."

"Sorry. And, yes, I *am* sorry."

"So who is it?"

"The Rifleman."

"Chuck Connors!"

"None other."

"Not fair!"

Max simply grinned.

Just then, the stunning flight attendant stepped up to them and, with a winning smile, offered hot face towels.

Max returned the smile and waved a no-thanks, but Kat said, "That, I'll take. Thanks!" She splayed her fingertips and spread the towel across them, saying, "I need this."

With that, she laid her head back and covered her eyes with the moist warmth.

Chapter Eleven

Dublin, Ireland, is not a tall city as cities go. She sits alongside the Irish Sea at the mouth of the River Liffey, which some of the world's most beautiful bridges span, seeming to smile wide for tourists' cameras.

Dublin's history is laden with conquests and defeats, internal strife and even terrorism. When the Irish speak of "trouble" it usually begins with a capital "T" as in The Troubles.

Some thirty or forty years of bombings, shootings, and undefused hatreds, The Troubles supposedly ended with the Belfast Good Friday Agreement of 1998. Actually spawned four centuries earlier when England conquered the entire island of Ireland, The Troubles pitted Catholic against Protestant and spilled over from Northern Ireland into the Republic of Ireland.

Mainly Catholic nationalists wanting freedom from British rule did battle—deadly clashes—with mainly Protestant unionists wanting to remain within the United Kingdom.

The anti-British Irish Republican Army and the pro-Brit Ulster Volunteer Force were the flames that burned hottest and the triggers that pulled quickest.

Adding an odd element to this conflict was Dublin's Old English community which was predominantly Roman Catholic and—though pleased with disarmament of the native Irish—fumed about the Protestant Reformation having alienated them.

But lost on most observers around the world as The Troubles blasted through the international news in the late 20th century was something sinister taking root on the Emerald Isle.

A Muslim community had planted feet in Dublin. The Dublin Islamic Society was formed in 1959 and built its first mosque in 1976. Leaders in Saudi Arabia and Kuwait had fostered this growth. A Muslim had even been elected to the Irish Parliament in 1992—many years before America's first Muslim congressman.

From first glance and even second look, all was peaceful. Indeed, most all Muslims are a nonviolent people. But dark hearts invade many religions—as witnessed through the Catholic and Protestant gunmen who roamed the island. And now, more than a half-century later, darkness gripped some of the hearts in Dublin's Muslim community.

Several of those dark hearts had given their imam oaths to religious jihad—holy war. And one of them had received a call from Israel five hours before Max and Kat's airplane rolled along the tarmac of Dublin Airport on the northern outskirts of the city.

"Moosajee," the caller said in Arabic, "this is your leader. I call directly to you because of a dire thing."

Moosajee instantly straightened his back, as if standing before a general inspecting his troops. "Yes, Commander. What can I do? What do you want? Anything."

The commander described Max and Kat, related their Aer Lingus flight and time of arrival, and said firmly: "I want them dead. Kill them someplace quietly. But kill them. I want a photograph of their dead bodies."

146

Moosajee asked no questions. Whys and hows and wherefores did not exist in the language between the commander and anyone—anyone.

"Yes, my commander," he said.

"And Moosajee, take more than two of you. This man is dangerous, very dangerous. I'm told if the world of men were a forest this man would be the sycamore."

Moosajee gulped. True, he had learned hand-to-hand combat in a training camp in North Africa. He had trained in the making of bombs. But he had never faced death in mortal combat.

Fear trickled up his spine. Then he thought, I will have a gun. This Braxton fellow, coming off a plane, will not. Perhaps I can do this alone and get all the credit.

As soon as this thought passed his mind, he remembered: Whys and hows and wherefores did not exist in the language between the commander and anyone—anyone. No, Mumim Maloof, the commander of the newest and greatest Muslim terror group Salah al-Din Brigades, had done bodily harm to more than one of his own inner circle.

Soon, Moosajee called his right-hand man, Ali Wasem, and a lieutenant, Basam Tahan, a Brit born Brian Folsem, and they laid their plan.

As the Boeing 737 flew over the Irish Sea, Kat sipped a drink of 7-Up and looked at Max. "You haven't mentioned Ireland in the litany of countries you've been in," she said. "Have you been there?"

"Not officially," he said with a grin.

"Oh, boy, here we go again. You've been there unofficially then."

Max cocked his head and smiled.

"You're an easy read, soldier," she said.

"Only when I want to be easily read."

She laughed. "So you don't mind my reading you."

"Not at all."

"So you were in Ireland in an unofficial capacity."

He nodded.

"As a consultant?"

"More than that."

"As a combatant?"

"I can't say."

"Was it to do with Muslims or the IRA?"

"Guess."

"Muslims."

He shook his head.

"The New IRA?"

He nodded.

"How long ago?"

"Years."

"Are they still lurking around street corners?"

"Some are still training along with other terror groups in Africa."

"In league with one another?"

"Not really. Just in training together. They share tactics but vastly different goals."

Just then, the pilot spoke over the intercom, "Please prepare for landing. In ten minutes, we will begin our descent. Ahead are clear skies, a soft wind, a warm stout, a ballad sung with a pleasant lilt and everything else you might expect in the Land of the Leprechauns."

Max and Kat shared a laugh with the others in business class.

Max looked at Kat and said, "Too bad we're not here on vacation."

"That would be nice," she said. "But the hunt is on, as Sherlock Holmes would say."

"A Holmes fan, are you?"

"Isn't everyone?"

"I see you as a Miss Marple aficionado."

"Her, too. And are you also a Hercule Poirot fan?"

"Poirot, Marple, Holmes, Campion, Lord Peter Wimsey, Moss, Lewis. Most anyone British. Doesn't have to be an Agatha Christie character."

"Aha, Kat said. "Then I see us as Tommy and Tuppence."

"If we're Tommy and Tuppence, I get to kiss you sometime today."

Kat grinned. "Don't count your chickens, soldier."

Max shrugged. "Okay, boss."

"With Tommy and Tuppence, there's no boss. They're a team."

"Are you this contrary with your students?"

Kat's answer was a smile.

"Anyhow," Max said, "I'll bet you wear hats just as well as Tuppence."

"You joke."

"Fasten your seatbelts, please," said the flight attendant who had been especially pleasant to Max the entire trip. "Can I help you, sir?" She smiled and bent toward him.

Max met her brown-eyed gaze and smiled back. "I think I can handle it. But thank you."

Kat elbowed him.

Max turned to her. "As I recall, both Tommy and Tuppence were a bit flirty, weren't they?"

Kat had to agree.

A moment later, the airplane began its final descent to a smooth landing at Dublin Airport.

Max and Kat were quickly off the plane with duffel bags in hand, Kat flashed a VIP card at Thrifty Car Rental and, at 5:19 p.m., they were on the road.

What they did not notice when they disembarked the airplane were two dark-skinned men leaning against a column near Gate 6. Those two men followed them outside the terminal to the Thrifty car lot, then hopped into a black van driven by a third man. As Max drove toward M1, then followed traffic the six miles into city center, Kat went online with her iPhone and called up information on the church.

"This is one cool place, St. Michan's," she said. "It was built in 1065—"

"Hey, just twenty-three years before our Crusader escaped Israel and sailed here," Max said.

"That's right. And it was reconstructed in 1686," Kat said, reading on. "Handel composed his Messiah on its organ. And in its basement are vaults that contain a number of mummified remains. Since the walls of the vaults are limestone, the air has been kept dry and created ideal conditions for preservation. They say Bram Stoker of Dracula fame visited the vaults."

"Weird, but I always picture Bram Stoker as looking like Dracula, cape and all," Max said.

"Strange. Me too." Kat shivered.

"Just who are these remains?"

"There's a 400-year-old nun, the legendary Shears brothers who took part in the 1798 rebellion, several highly decorated coffins of the Earls of Leitrim and," she hesitated, "wait for it. Wait for it—and our crusader who, at six-foot-six, was one extraordinarily tall man for his day."

"So, are you thinking our crusader is in these vaults?"

Kat nodded.

"Fantastic!"

"You bet!"

They drove on for a few minutes when Max glanced at Kat and asked, "Have you ever hefted one of their swords?"

Kat shook her head.

"They're made of high-carbon steel. You have to be in pretty good shape to fight with one of those—"

"Hey," Kat interjected while reading her iPhone. "Some of these caskets are open!"

"Really? Is our crusader's open?"

"Not only open ... local legend says if you shake his hand you get good luck."

"So our crusader is a local celebrity?" Max asked.

"Appears so, though they don't seem to know he's Godfrey the Irish."

"Maybe he's not."

"Maybe, but I'd give you odds."

Max thought a bit, then said, "Guess not. And I think I'll let you deal with shaking Godfrey's hand." He laughed.

"Old dead bones?" she said. "I have no problem with that. Make you squeamish, do they?"

"The thought of them does." Max stole a peek at her. "Boy, if looks don't deceive."

She chuckled. "As often as not, my students who are big rugged football players or wrestlers are the squeamish ones, while the young ladies from the big city are like granite at the sight of ancient bones."

As they approached a bridge over the River Liffey, Kat directed Max to turn right onto Church Street. A minute later, she said, "Take the next left before we get to St. Michan's. I think we should park the next block over and get to the church through its lawns."

Suddenly Kat held up a hand. "Oh, no!"

"What?"

"Visiting hours closed at 4:45. It's 5:32."

"Visiting hours at a church?"

"Hey, besides a vicar, they have a curator and a tour guide."

"Whoa!" Max said. "Well, maybe you could flash your credentials and they'd let you in."

Chapter 12

Max found a convenient parking spot on the street and they hurried along a path meandering through a well-manicured lawn toward St. Michan's. With a tall castle-like steeple rising from its front, the church loomed high and stood shoulder-to-shoulder with the glass-walled, six-story Kings Building to their left and a long, narrow, four-story apartment building to their right.

The path ended at a large blue curved door entering the sanctuary. Max knocked. There was no answer. He knocked again. No answer. He tried the handle of the door—locked.

"Maybe we'll have to wait until tomorrow," Kat said.

"Could you sleep?" he asked.

She thought for a moment. "It would be tough."

Max looked to his left. A narrow path led along the wall which ended in ten feet. He took Kat's hand and headed there. Turning the corner, they saw an alcove to the church with a separate door.

"Maybe that's the office," Kat said.

They hastened ahead and knocked on the door. This time, it opened— to a diminutive man Max could swear was the look-alike child of Barry Fitzgerald, who played little Irish vicars in more than one movie. And, if Max's memory served him well, Fitzgerald was born and died in Dublin.

The man's accent certainly matched his look as he peered up at them.

"Oh, me." The words escaped the man's lips as if they were air forced from a paper bag.

"Sir," Max said, "my name is Max Braxton, but more importantly," he gestured toward Kat, "this is Doctor Katherine Cardova, a famous archeologist and Yale University professor."

"Oh, me." The little man's eyes grew wide. "An archeologist? From Yale?"

Kat nodded and put her hand out to shake his.

He took her hand and said, "I forget myself. I'm Seamus O'Donnell, the curator here. Come in. Come in."

He waved them into the room, obviously the church office with desks and filing cabinets and an oversized fax machine and photocopier.

"Mister O'Donnell—" Kat began.

"Seamus," he interrupted.

"Seamus, I realize it's beyond your tour hours—"

"Beyond? For you, dear lady? No, no, no."

"You see," she said, "we're on a very important mission and must see your crusader."

"The Irish!" Seamus said with a whistle.

"Actually, we think he was known as Godfrey the Irish," Kat said.

"Godfrey? Aha! I've secretly called him Godfrey for thirty-three years! I had no clue. Just seemed right for him. Sometimes I talk to him, trying to get him to tell me his story. But—" He threw up his arms.

"Dead men tend not to talk," Max said.

"But we think he can tell us a story," Kat said.

"Yes?" Seamus said. "And what might the story be?"

"We think he may have secreted the music of the Psalms here to prevent its destruction at the hands of Suliman, who was invading Petra."

"The music of the Psalms?!" Seamus said with a raised eyebrow.

154

Kat nodded.

"Extraordinary!" Seamus threw his shoulders back, obviously exhilarated. His face burst into a grin. "Thrilling!"

"The Crusaders were keeping it hidden and protected in a castle in Petra," Kat said.

"Why hide such a treasure?" Seamus threw up his hands. "A blessing for the entire world."

Kat shrugged, then added, "But, of course, no one knew until just a couple of days ago when an archeologist friend of mine discovered a mention of the music at a dig in Israel."

Seamus shook his head in wonderment. "And the music might be here? At St. Michan's?"

"We think the music came here with Godfrey in 1088," Max said.

Kat reached into a bag she carried over her shoulder and pulled out the scroll. "This tells us Godfrey left Petra for this church. He must have lived here before joining the Crusades."

"Where would the music be? Where would it be?" Seamus said to himself as he took the scroll and carefully rolled the document over in his hands before opening it. He looked skyward. "Oh, where would the music be? Where?"

"Can we see Godfrey?" Kat asked.

"Of course. Of course." Seamus took off at a fast walk and motioned with his arm. "Follow me. Follow me."

He led them through a door out of the offices, into the church proper and across behind the rear pews. Max noticed magnificent burgundy-colored pipes rise from an organ behind the pulpit.

Speaking as he went, Seamus said, "'Michan' is of unknown origin, possibly Danish, though I argue that Michan was an Irish martyr and confessor and probably a native of Dublin. His name is listed in the Martyrology of Christ Church."

Max thought of a classmate growing up who had to talk when he was nervous. Talk, talk, talk. Max wondered if this was a malady shared by Seamus O'Donnell. He had probably kissed the Blarney Stone. Fate sealed.

Seamus led them down the far wall toward the pulpit, then opened a side door. "Here. Here," he said.

Max and Kat followed his lead into a smaller room, where Seamus opened a door leading down a long flight of stairs. Grabbing a large flashlight, he hustled down a couple of dozen stone steps tight against the outside stone wall.

The air became cool and dry.

"We've undergone construction and reconstruction since the church was first built," Seamus said, "but the crypts have not changed. No, the crypts have not changed."

They turned left at the bottom of the stairs. Almost immediately to their right, a crypt or alcove contained eight caskets; two stacks of three laid atop one another and another stack of two. The caskets were ornate, hand-carved.

"The famous Shears brothers," Seamus announced with a wave of the hand. He reached up and lit a torch set in a hinge on the wall. The next crypt contained four more caskets: one a dark mahogany, another a bright-red color, and two others various shades of green.

"Here and in the next vault," Seamus said, "are various Earls of Leitrim." He lit another torch on the wall.

"Fascinating," Kat said.

"We've many famous people here," Seamus said, walking along, "but here is our Crusader and two neighbors." With a flourish, he motioned toward three mahogany caskets, side by side, their lids open. Mummies, appearing like leather tightened around bones, lay before them. The mummy on the left lay on its side.

156

"His feet had to be cut off so he could fit in the casket," Seamus said. "They cut them off."

On the right, the mummy faced further right as if distracted by a noise.

In the center, lay the remains of a very tall person. His casket indeed was custom-built for his size, for he remained in one piece. On the wall behind him, hung on some sort of manikin, were the cloak, chain armor, breastplate, helmet and shield, along with a knife in a scabbard, a massive broadsword with a Crusader's crest fitted into its handle, and a three-and-a-half-foot-high shield, also with the Crusader's crest.

Max got a chill.

"Man, look at *that*," he enthused.

"Straight out of the early Middle Ages," Kat said.

"Early?" Max asked.

"Yes, the Dark Ages were from 476 to 1066 AD, the Middle Ages from then until 1500. This is early Middle Ages since Godfrey came here in 1088."

"Our legend," said Seamus, "is that if you touch Godfrey's hand, you get good luck."

"What if you touch his sword?" Max asked.

"I've never. I've never," Seamus said.

"May I?" Max asked.

"I—I suppose so—suppose so," Seamus stuttered.

First, Max stepped forward and leaned down, touching Godfrey's hand. "That's for good luck," he said.

Then he stepped to the head of the coffin, careful not to disturb the other mummy's casket, and took hold of the broadsword. "And this is for—"

Suddenly, Kat interrupted, "What's that?"

Max looked at her and noticed she was listening intently.

"I heard something on the stairway. People, I think."

"No one should be in here now," Seamus said. "The church is obviously closed. Closed!"

Max's danger barometer—the tiny hairs on the back of his neck—stood up and he leaned closer to the manikin, slipping the knife from its scabbard.

He stepped back next to Kat and Seamus, all three of them intent on the stairway about twenty feet away.

Just then, two men stepped down to the basement floor and rounded the corner. The first thing Max noticed was the men's handguns—one the frightening-looking Desert Eagle Blowback, the other sleek gunmetal Colt Delta Elite. These guys were loaded for killing.

Bullets exploded around them as Max grabbed Kat's shoulder and pulled her behind him into the vault. Seamus copied their every move, sidestepping between the caskets of Godfrey and the neighbor to his left.

"No hope. You have no hope!" one of the men hollered with a thick accent. "Allah be blessed, you will all die here and now!"

"Hand me Godfrey's shield, will you, Seamus?" Max said. "And Kat, pass me his sword."

Max peered around the wall and bullets splattered the barrier a couple of feet away. Judging the distance of the misses, Max thought, They're trained but not professionals.

Kat handed him the sword at the same time Seamus, struggling against the weight of the shield, passed it to him.

"Is there back way out of here?" Max asked.

"Yes," Seamus said., "A tunnel leads outside the church through a doorway hidden in some bushes. But the only way to get there is along this corridor. This corridor."

"So there's no other way out but through these men," Max said firmly.

At the bottom of the stairway, Moosajee turned to Ali beside him and Basam, standing on the bottom-most step, and said, "These three will be our gift to Commander Mumim and to Allah. We will be famous to our comrades everywhere. Be brave."

Ali and Basam nodded agreement.

"Side by side we walk forward slowly, weapons ready, firing only when we see the infidels," Moosajee ordered.

Basam stepped down and took his place to Moosajee's left, with Ali to their leader's right. At Moosajee's command, they began a slow, deliberate walk.

Roman and Crusader shields were two sizes. Small ones, easy to wield and run with; and scutums, large enough for the wielder to take shelter behind for protection from barrages of arrows. As Max hefted Godfrey's shield, he thanked God it was a scutum.

He slipped his right arm through a brace in the back of the shield and raised the armor off the ground edging toward the end of the vault's wall. These Crusaders were a rugged lot, he thought to himself as he hefted the scutum.

Suddenly, Kat grabbed his elbow. Their eyes locked and she whispered, "Please be careful, Max."

"Careful," he repeated. "Yes."

"I mean, really be careful," she said, fright obvious in her eyes.

"Really careful," he said with a smile. "Grab Godfrey's chain mail and wrap it around you. But first—"

"Yes?"

"First, touch his hand for good luck." He winked and turned back

159

toward the corridor.

Max leaned the giant broadsword against the wall of the vault and tested the weight of the knife in his right hand. By the sound of their steps, he guessed the terrorists were about ten feet away.

Counting down to himself—three, two, one—he stepped out into the corridor, ready to throw his knife. He was startled to see three men before him and in a split second, reasoned the leader of three men must be the one in the middle.

He whipped the knife at the gunman in the center at the same time the muzzles of their guns flashed. Max heard the man cry out in pain. He ducked behind his shield and bullets bounced off the heavy metal. He swiftly leaned left to grab the broadsword, then sprinted forward to catch the men by surprise. Never would they expect such an offensive move from an undermanned adversary.

More bullets pinged off his shield. After taking three steps, Max straightened and looked over the armor. He was close enough to swing the sword and he did, ferociously slicing into the left arm of the man to his right. Indeed, as warm blood splattered onto his hand, he thought he may have severed the arm.

With his comrade clutching his arm in agony and his leader already sprawled on the ground, the gunman to Max's left turned and began to race away.

Max dropped his shield and broadsword and took off in pursuit.

Five long strides later, he dove at the man's legs and brought him down like a sack of potatoes. The memory of a game-saving tackle he made in his middle linebacker days at The Citadel flashed before him. The man's handgun clambered along the stone floor in front of them and Max flipped him belly-down. Ripping the man's keffiyeh from his head, Max tightly tied his hands behind him.

Standing up, Max spoke down at the man. "My advice? Play dead."

He turned to see the other men on the ground writhing in pain and shrieking curses at him. The knife he'd thrown had hit the leader in the shoulder directly above the heart. The man was breathing with difficulty and screaming, after all. Blood gushed from the other man's arm, which hung to the ground from where he was lying.

Kat and Seamus had come out from the vault and, each with a handgun they'd scooped off the ground, stood over the men.

Kat looked down at the three, then at Max, and said, "This is so far out of my comfort zone, and yet, here I am, holding a pistol on three terrorists."

"You dazzle me," he said.

"Look who's talking" was her retort.

"But I always loved Annie Oakley."

"I'll call an ambulance," Seamus said, "but there's no signal down here." He handed Max the handgun and hustled toward the stairway.

Max leaned down to the man with the injured arm, ripped a length of cloth from the man's shirt and tied it tightly around his upper arm, trying to cut off the flow of blood.

He looked up at Kat. "This is no good. He'll bleed out if they don't get here quickly—like right now."

As he spoke, the man passed out. Max slapped him in the face but to no avail.

Max turned his attention to the leader. "I think you said something about us all dying today, to Allah's glory."

The man looked away.

"You suppose Allah's not so happy with you right now?"

The man did not respond.

"What's your name?" Max asked.

The man turned and spat at him.

"So, your name is 'Spit'?" Max asked in Arabic.

The man turned his face from Max's.

"Who sent you?" Max asked again in Arabic.

The man winced in pain and shook his head.

"How did they know we were here?" Max asked.

The man cursed at him.

Max looked at Kat. "Why don't you go up and see how Seamus is doing? I'll watch over these guys."

"No—" Kat shook her head, but then noticed his expression. "Yeah, okay. Good idea."

She turned and hurried down the corridor and up the stairs.

Max turned back to the leader and knelt, sticking his face just inches away, and said calmly, "I suppose you got a phone call from Petra or Israel this afternoon."

Within three minutes, two ambulances arrived at St. Michan's. Several emergency medical technicians swarmed down to the crypts, carrying two stretchers and following Seamus and Kat.

Max had hauled the gunman whom he had wrestled to the ground over next to his comrades and now stood over the three of them.

First, pointing to the leader and then to his comrades, Max said to the medics, "This is Moosajee Issa. His badly injured friend here, who may lose his arm if you don't hurry, is Ali Wasem, and this coward and traitor to his country is Basam Tahan, known to his betrayed mom and dad as Brian Folsem, recruited at his local mosque. They're members of Dublin's cell of Salah al-Din Brigades, a heap of dung on the earth as are all Muslim terrorist groups."

Max looked at the three. Moosajee snarled back. Writhing in pain Ali removed his hands from his shoulder and placed his palms tight against his ears. Anger twisted Folsem's lips, surely upset that he couldn't finish

162

this job for Allah.

As the paramedics went to work on Ali and the others, Max stepped up to Kat's side. "Moosajee here got a call this afternoon from his commander." He held Moosajee's cell phone for Kat and Seamus to see.

"How did you—?" Kat started.

Max cut her off, saying, "He told me other stuff but not his commander's name, only that the guy's in Jerusalem."

Disbelief in her eyes, Kat pointed to Moosajee and said, "That man there, who wouldn't tell you his name, revealed this information to you?"

"Yeah, he and Basam—or Brian, if you will."

Kat simply shook her head and exhaled deeply.

"Kat," Max said, "should I have not done all I could to get that information?"

"Torture?" she asked.

"Did I say I tortured them?"

Just then two Dublin police officers came around the corner, their eyes widening as they surveyed the crowded calamity in front of them.

Seamus walked up to Max and Kat and, with a wide grin, said, "This is the most action we've seen here—ever. It's usually so tranquil! Isn't it wonderful? Wonderful?"

Max and Kat could only gaze at him with their mouths open.

Two hours later, with the grandfather clock in the St. Michan's office ticking toward nine o'clock, the police left. With Max, Kat and Seamus were the vicar, Peter Keogh, and the parish administrator, Robert Condell, whom Seamus had called to join them.

Max walked to a kitchenette at the opposite corner of the room from the entry door to get water for Kat and him.

Suddenly, the door opened and in came three very serious men looking all the world like James Bond and a couple of other 00s.

"Max!" The taller of the three men walked directly to Max with a large hand outstretched. "When I heard you were in town, causing trouble, I knew I had to be here."

Max shook the man's hand. "Chris."

Max turned to the others in the room and said, "Folks, this is Christopher Hollingsworth of MI5."

"It's MI6 now," Hollingsworth said. "Made the move a year ago along the river from Thames House to Vauxhall Cross."

"If MI6 focuses on foreign threats, shouldn't MI5 be here instead?" Max asked.

"We cross paths often," Hollingsworth said. "Like your Homeland Security and CIA, it can be a messy cross-dressing kind of operation—paranoia and all. But I think the guys you took down tonight are linked overseas. Therefore, you get MI6.

"And these," Hollingsworth waved toward the men with him, "are Agents Stone and Lawrence."

"Well, I'm glad you're here," Max said. He introduced everyone, then turned to Hollingsworth and said, "I'm assisting Doctor Cardova in a very important archeological mission, but our pals from Salah al-Din Brigades have tried both in Petra and here to stop us."

"Kill us, you mean," Kat said with force.

Max shrugged.

"Agent Hollingsworth," she said, "if not for some ancient armor stuck away in a vault downstairs, and Max's, ah, particular skills, we'd be dead right now."

"I understand, Doctor Cardova. I'm aware of Max's 'particular skills,' although I must say I've never seen him wield a broadsword." Hollingsworth smiled at Max.

"Like a very long shillelagh with a sharp edge," Max said with a grin.

"I wish I'd been there to witness it," Hollingsworth said.

"You probably would have laughed yourself silly, seeing me behind that shield."

"It was no laughing matter for Seamus and me," Kat scolded.

"Right." Max felt sufficiently reprimanded.

He passed a cell phone to Hollingsworth. "I was going to have the Israeli police check this out, but you'll do."

The question was obvious in Hollingsworth's look.

Max explained: "This belongs to the leader of our friends heading for the hospital. Could be some important contacts in there. Foolish of him to carry his cell with him on an operation."

"Probably thought the operation wouldn't be a problem. Should have known better."

Hollingsworth looked around the room and asked, "So what's this 'mission' you're on, Max?"

Seamus stood up from his chair and interrupted, "As the curator of St. Michan's, I think I can answer for you, Mr. Hollingsworth. The mission Mr. Braxton and Doctor Cardova are here on is a task from God, I might say. From God. And it involves one of our most famous residents—our Crusader, whom we now know as Godfrey the Irish."

Kat filled them in on the search for the music.

"You'd think people would be praising God for the possibility of this music, not killing one another," said Keogh, the vicar.

Kat explained why the Muslim community, especially the zealots, would do anything to prevent the music's discovery.

"Does anyone here have a clue about where this music could be?" Max asked. "And, indeed, if such a thing could still be here?"

The men all shook their heads.

"Then, can we go back down to the crypts?" Kat asked.

Seamus sought and got approval from Keogh.

Nearly leaping from his chair, Seamus said, "I'll lead the way. Lead the way."

All five of them walked down the stairway, Seamus holding a torch high as they had descended to the basement and walked past the vaults.

When they reached the Crusader, Kat turned to Max, "So, soldier, if you were the Crusader where would you leave something so valuable?"

Max turned to Seamus and asked, "Did Godfrey know he was going to die?"

"He died of pneumonia," Seamus said. "It probably took awhile."

"And so," Kat said, "he would have made preparations for the music's safety. But where?"

"Have you ever examined his casket?" Max asked.

Seamus thought for a moment and shook his head. Max turned to Keogh and Condell. They both shook their heads.

"You think it's in the casket with him?" Kat asked.

Max shrugged. Looking at Keogh, he asked, "Mind if we look more closely?"

"Not at all. Not if the music's here or Godfrey will reveal a clue."

Max and Kat stepped to either side of the coffin.

"Do you find this a bit creepy?" Max asked her, bending over Godfrey.

She grinned. "Sometimes an archeologist is a kissing cousin to a pathologist."

"A morbid thought."

Max and Kat felt all around the inside of the casket, even under the mummy, moving Godfrey ever so slightly.

"Nothing," Max declared.

"What about under the casket?" Hollingsworth asked.

"But why—?" Condell asked.

Max noticed Kat had put a finger to her lips. A familiar pose. He could see the thoughts whirling. He waited for the process to culminate.

Abruptly, she turned to him and declared, "The sword of the spirit."

Max shook his head. "What?"

"The sword of the spirit," Keogh said. "Saint Paul wrote to the Christians in Ephesus they needed to daily 'put on the full armor of God.'"

"That being," Seamus said, "the belt of truth, the breastplate of righteousness—"

"The shield of faith, the helmet of salvation—" Keogh said.

"And the sword of the Spirit, which is the word of God," Kat finished. Her gaze narrowed on Max. "Check the scabbard that held Godfrey's sword."

Max stepped to the back of Godfrey's casket and disconnected the scabbard from where it hung off the manikin. He peered inside then asked for a torch so he could see deep into the sheath.

Hollingsworth passed him a torch and Max held up the light. "Empty," he said.

He handed the torch back to Hollingsworth and passed the scabbard to Kat. "It's your party, doc. Any other ideas?"

Again, Kat assumed the pose.

"The sword itself?" Seamus asked. "Maybe hidden behind the Crusader crest."

The sword lay nearby, where Max had left it when fighting the gunmen. Max picked the weapon up and looked closely at the crest, then pried the crest gently with the knife.

"No," he determined.

Kat whirled to face Seamus and Keogh. "Did Godfrey have a Bible?"

"Why, yes!" Seamus said. "Yes, indeed!"

"The sword of the Spirit, *which is the word of God*," she quoted.

"Follow me. Follow me." Seamus waved his arm and hurried past the MI6 agents. Back up the stairs they all went, and into the office. Seamus stopped at his desk, knelt to the bottom right-hand drawer, rifled through papers, found a tiny wooden box and pulled out an ancient key. Holding it up for everyone to see, he stood, then hustled into the church's nave. "This way. This way."

Pointing to the front left corner of the nave, Seamus said, "There. There."

As they all rushed to keep up with the curator, Keogh turned to the others and explained, "We keep the Crusader's Bible locked and under cover on top of a pedestal up front."

Kat daily ran five miles or more with her dog, Tuck, when in the States. But the anticipation, combined with the exertion, seemed to make her heart skip a beat. As an archeologist, she had discovered proof of the existence of King David—whom naysayers had declared a myth; she had inspected the Qumran Caves' precious writings. But this ... This was what she lived for!

Seven people all stood in a circle around Seamus, waiting for him to open the sealed, see-through container. When he did, he turned to Kat, handed her two plastic gloves and offered the Bible to her to scrutinize.

She only wished her parents were here with her instead of necessarily being kept in the dark about the entire situation. She thought too of her twin sister, Kaitlin, and wondered for the thousandth time if our loved ones could somehow look down upon us from Heaven. The anticipated pain in her stomach came a second later and she held back a groan.

Finally, pulling on the plastic gloves, Kat leaned over the Bible. The book was the size of an atlas—bulky, substantial—leather—black and ornate. A cross adorned its cover. She felt the cross and found the symbol was embossed. Quite something for its era.

She carefully opened the Bible. "Old English," she said, "meaning the printing was sometime between the mid-5th and mid-12th centuries. Since Godfrey came here in 1188, it dates to his lifetime."

"I hate Old English," Max muttered. "*Beowulf.* Yecht."

She grinned up at him. Was this his one weakness, a dislike for Old English and *Beowulf*? Ha! She shook her head. "Think of it as not just related to Old Frisian and Low German, Max," she said. "Think on the fact its grammar is in many ways related to classical Latin—I know you must love Latin—and it is closer to German and Icelandic than modern English."

"Oh, that helps," he harrumphed. "Icelandic too. I do Hebrew, Arabic, Russian, French, Spanish and, to a lesser degree, English."

Kat chuckled, but she could sense the tenseness in the air. She could almost feel the hair on her head stand on end. Seamus, beside her, was breathing loudly while she doubted Keogh had breathed at all in the last minute. The MI6 agents? She didn't know. They were stealth people. Inscrutable.

Max walked around the pedestal and stood behind her. He put a hand to her shoulder and urged, "Go on, Kat, find us the music or a clue to where it is."

She carefully leafed through the Bible. Its pages were remarkably "limber." There were no loose papers. She examined the front and back covers, hoping to discover a slit or hidden sleeve. None.

She took a deep breath. *Kat. Kat. Think!*

"Ephesians!" The words burst out of her.

She quickly found the New Testament book, *The Epistle of Paul the Apostle to the Ephesians.*

She looked up at Keogh. "Where is that armor scripture, vicar?"

"Chapter six, verse eleven."

She turned two pages and there, in the half-page space where the chapter ended, was a note written in Old English.

"Oh, me. Oh, me!" Seamus exclaimed.

Keogh caught his breath.

"What does it say?" Max asked.

Kat felt as if all the oxygen had left her body like putting a pin in a balloon. She sighed, "The music's not here. Godfrey writes he was dying and was giving the music to a comrade, another Crusader, from Wales. This Crusader was taking the music to St. David's and the Cathedral Close, in Pembrokeshire, Wales."

"Named after the patron saint of Wales," Keogh said.

Kat shrugged and turned to face Max. "So the search goes on."

He grinned—an encouraging look that fortified her to stare discouragement in the face and go on.

Hollingsworth spoke up. "Doctor Cardova. Max. We need to stay in contact with you. Who knows what we'll turn up with these three terrorists today?"

"We can't stay and wait," Kat said, looking deeply into Hollingworth's eyes. "You understand, don't you?"

He nodded, then said, "You understand this is not a personal matter anymore. These men invaded an Irish church, trying to kill innocent Irishmen as well as you two Americans. We'll take this to the limit."

"Whatever you need us for, we'll do," Kat promised. "But can't we leave the country?"

Hollingsworth exchanged a look with Max, receiving his friend's assurances, then nodded with obvious reluctance. "Okay."

Kat gave him her cell phone number and Max followed suit.

Kat carefully placed Godfrey's Bible on the pedestal and turned her gaze on Seamus and then Keogh and Candell. "You realize this Bible is now a more precious artifact than anyone could have imagined."

"Yes," Keogh said. "I will immediately check with the church fathers to see what we should do."

"And we'll keep such an artifact fully protected," Seamus promised. "Fully protected."

"The rest of the story is yet to be written," Kat said.

"Our prayers will go with you morning and night," Keogh promised.

"Morning and night," Seamus repeated. He stepped forward and gave Kat a bear hug. Amazing strength for a little leprechaun, she thought whimsically as she tried to draw a breath.

As everyone left the church, Max asked Hollingsworth, "So how do we get to Wales? Ferry?"

Hollingsworth looked at his watch—nearly ten o'clock. "Yeah, but there won't be any running tonight. When you go, make sure to take the fast ferry, not the slow one. You'll get there in two hours."

"Any suggestions on where to stay overnight tonight?"

"There are several hotels near the ferry. Try The Gibson. It's right in Point Village and looks out over Dublin Port. It will be the lap of luxury for you, Max. Not at all what you're used to."

"I don't always sleep in the mud and the woods," Max said.

Hollingsworth chuckled. "Then, I don't know you." He looked at Kat and asked, "Who *is* this guy?"

She shrugged. "I'm just finding that out myself."

Before they separated, Hollingsworth took Max aside, away from the others.

"Listen, my friend, I don't like the idea of you fighting these jokers with broadswords—as good as you might be with them." He reached beneath the hem of his trousers and pulled out a snub-nosed pistol.

"You don't—" Max objected.

"Yes, I do. Remember Belfast?"

Max nodded.

"Then you know I do. Take this."

Max obliged, slipping the handgun into a cargo pocket.

Thick evergreen bushes lined the wall of St. Michan's office door as it looked out on the expansive lawn where the eight people gathered. Behind the bushes squatted a young man, no more than eighteen years old, listening intently.

He had hidden there since his leader, his father, and the white guy who'd converted to Islam, all from the Dublin cell, had gone into the church, armed to kill the infidels from America. He had waited expectantly for them to return in a matter of minutes, prepared to receive grand praise for their success. After those minutes passed, he had hunkered down anxiously as emergency medical technicians and then police arrived, scurrying by him through the church door.

His anxiety had grown along with the pain of his discomfort as the vicar and another man arrived, followed in short order by three men in dark suits, all appearing very dangerous. What had happened to his father? Being where he was—outdoors and far from the underground vaults—he had not heard any gunfire. But all the commotion meant bad news; of that much he was certain.

He had thought of his mother and the idea of needing to assume headship of the house. What would the imam expect then? His imam, who demanded warriors of Mohammed to not be submissive but actually do battle for Allah.

When the EMTs rushed out through the church door pushing gurneys, the young man had nearly stood, then caught his indiscretion and knelt, still trying to spot if one of the injured was his father. He detect. Then his emotions flew high, dove low, and hovered in between when his father, handcuffed with his arms behind him, walked out the door with a police officer on either side of him.

The young man had nearly cried out "Baba!" but caught himself. Had his father and the others killed both Americans, or just one American? Or had they failed completely? How could they fail? How could they if they were doing the will of Allah?

As he had pondered this great question, several others stepped outside the church, including a woman and a broad-shouldered man.

He heard their plans and determined to gain glory for himself. He would contact the commander, Mumim Maloof, himself and tell him of the Americans' plans. Where his father and his comrades had failed, he would, at least, regain some of their lost respect. He could hold his head high. His mother could be proud, just as his aunt in Palestine was proud of the boy's cousin who had died a martyr's death, blowing up a bar mitzvah in the Jewish Quarter of the Old City. His aunt and uncle had even been given a small fortune by Hamas for their heroic son's actions.

Chapter 13

Max and Kat had checked into The Gibson, a luxurious hotel whose pool and gymnasium Max would have liked to take full advantage of—if only he were not exhausted from a day that had begun at 6 a.m. and taken them from the sands of Jordan to the emerald green of Ireland.

Kat had reserved two seats on the Dublin Fast Ferry, called the Jonathan Swift, departing the next morning at 11:50 and arriving at 1:39 p.m. in Holyhead, a point of land in Anglesey in North Wales.

Max had ordered room service for him and Kat, who was in a room down the hall. She should be arriving any minute.

He checked his watch. Ten o'clock, which meant it was midnight in Israel. Which meant Dudi was awake and maybe in his office. That was because Dudi, bearing the weight of keeping his beloved country safe, never slept.

Max called Dudi.

"How's Doctor Arens."

"They've given him enough blood to handle a legion of competitive bicyclists," Dudi said, chuckling at his own joke. "His vitals remain stable, but he's still unconscious."

"I'll tell Kat," Max said and proceeded to fill Dudi in on what had happened since they left Petra.

"You waste no time, my friend," Dudi joked.

"Doctor Cardova wastes no time," Max rejoined.

"Doctor Cardova is a dedicated, as well as beautiful, person."

"You noticed."

"That and the chemistry between you."

Max leaned back in the sofa, a smile curling his lips. He was good at reading body language but sometimes Kat was a difficult book to decipher. Dudi confirmed what Max had hoped.

"Now for *my* news," Dudi said. "The men you, ah, neutralized in Petra—"

"Uh-huh."

"They're Ahmed Salem, who, I'm afraid, is quite dead and Hussein Kattan. They have both been in and out of Israeli jails. Even with blood on their hands, our government set them free, along with a couple hundred of their comrades in arms, in exchange for two Israeli soldiers who were being held hostage."

"How's Kattan doing?" Max asked.

"He's alive, but in a Jordanian hospital, and our friends there are not being cooperative in allowing us access."

"A shame," Max said. "Who knows what information we could extract from him."

"On the other hand," Dudi said, "their cell phones have given us some of their contacts around the country."

"They didn't use burn phones?"

"Foolish, huh?"

"Not always known for wisdom," Max agreed.

"That's it from here," Dudi said. "Anything else we should discuss?"

"As a matter of fact," Max said, "it occurred to me that since this Islamist group has people here in Dublin, they must have them in a lot of places. MI6 is on the scene here and is digging into the attack. Perhaps you should contact the secret service folks in the countries where the other members of Danny Arens' dig returned."

"Excellent thought. I'm on the case," Dudi said. "As for you: Be careful. And take care of that lady of yours."

When he hung up the phone, Max's thoughts went to Dudi's mention of the chemistry between Kat and him. He had not felt this way about a woman since the first months of his marriage. That was before his job took over, before he mustered the nerve to kill another human being, before he began the long trek into booze, before he saved his wife from further torment by allowing her a divorce.

He was on better footing now. He had conquered the doubts and anguish. Bad men, men who beheaded and burned to death innocents, even children, simply to push their religious agendas, men who had no shame about their hatred—these men deserved a dark corner in hell. And he was not now averse to giving them a nudge into that abyss.

Chapter 14

Max and Kat arose at seven in the morning, both having needed the long rest.

After showering, Max called Kat's room phone. "Breakfast downstairs?" he asked when she picked up.

"Sure. Now?"

"Yep."

They met at the elevators and rode down together.

A minute later, they were in an airy dining room with square slate-top tables. Max ordered espresso, steak, and two eggs over easy; Kat—decaf and hot oatmeal cereal with seven-grain toast.

"So," Max said, stretching out the word, "what do we know about St. David's."

"That's the 'editorial we' asking, right?" Kat said with a smile.

"Unless it's about the history of warfare, I leave all historical subjects at your lovely feet," he said and stole a peek below the table.

"I think you passed the history test pretty well the other day when we were swapping quotes, soldier," Kat said, her grin widening. "And keep my feet out of the conversation."

Max shrugged.

"The original St. David's Cathedral," she said, "was plundered, burned, and destroyed by the Vikings in 1087. The Normans then built the cathedral we're going to see. The church contains a number of relics besides the remains of St. David. Pilgrims, including several kings, visited St. David's over the early years. I recall one thing because it was so unusual: A Pope—Calixtus the Second, I think—decreed that two pilgrimages to St. David's were equivalent to one pilgrimage to Rome."

"Maybe we should skip St. David's and head straight to the Vatican. Kill two birds with one stone," Max joked.

Kat laughed. "We may end up in Rome at that."

"Are you soothsaying?"

"I am neither a prophet nor the daughter of a prophet," she said demurely.

"You must be disappointed the music wasn't at Petra, then not in Dublin," Max said.

"If an archeologist doesn't have patience to the nth degree, they're in the wrong field. "We dig and dig and dig some more. We feather-dust with a whisk. We blow cool breath over ancient ruins. We carefully sift and then—then—well, then sometimes find nothing."

"Disappointing," Max said.

"Yes, but we keep on going, not giving up because—because maybe tomorrow, or maybe the next day, or the next week we will discover something that will change what we know or think we know about our past and how we got to where we are—culturally, socially and theologically. The theological part? That's mostly why I do it."

"Are you saying a discovery is like a shot of endorphins?"

"Adrenaline and endorphins."

"Okay. Then I was correct with what I said about you and adventure the other day," Max grinned while putting his hand on hers. "Unlike other Midwest farm girls who'd just as soon plant a field with corn and reap a harvest, you'd rather harvest something else."

"An odd way to put it, but I guess so."

Max and Kat stood above deck as the Jonathan Swift backed off the dock at Dublin Port. Kat checked her watch. "Eleven fifty-two. Just two minutes late," she said.

"Well, you know the Irish and time," Max said. "It's good to see the ferry does adhere more closely to its promises—"

Kat folded her arms. "Unlike you."

She had obviously taken him aback. "What do you mean?" he asked.

"I didn't get my bangers and mash in a Dublin pub."

"It was late."

"I'm just saying—"

Max noticed the obvious twinkle in her eye and cocked his head. "Okay, professor. You're on. When this is all over, we'll return to Dublin and the bangers and mash are on me."

That sounded pretty good to her. "Agreed."

Kat leaned back and wondered at her own actions, how she had trusted this man so quickly—so very out of character for her. Ever since she trusted Dan, an old boyfriend, to drive her twin sister home from a high school dance while she stayed behind with the cleanup committee.

She hadn't realized Dan had been drinking and the next thing she knew, word came back to the school there had been an accident. Dan had wrapped his car around a tree. Her sister, Kaitlin, was dead on arrival at the local hospital.

Kat never trusted Dan again. Hadn't trusted most people—unless, of course, they earned it. To some degree, under certain circumstances, she found she didn't fully trust herself.

And forget about forgiveness. As far as Dan was concerned, she could forget but not forgive. As for herself, she could neither forget nor forgive. And though her parents had been totally supportive and comforting, she sometimes wondered if they, deep in their hearts, forgave her.

She fought off a tear while shutting down the memories, then looked up at the man beside her. *Can I truly trust him? Absolutely. He is not Dan. Categorically not Dan.*

She extended her hand and Max engulfed it in his. Still struggling to manage her feelings, she asked, "And when we go, can I take you to one of my favorite places?"

"Where's that?"

"A castle in Adare that's now a hotel."

"And Adare is where?"

"Western Ireland, near the coast. A pretty little village with thatched roofs, tidy stores, a beautiful church. It dates from the time of the Norman conquest." She hesitated for a moment, then continued, "And, in large letters around the castle and just below the top of the wall are the words 'Except the Lord buildeth the house, they labor in vain who build it.'"

There we go again with the God stuff, Max thought. He shook his head slowly, mulling over the significance, tumbling his God experiences over in his mind. He knew he, not God, was the one who had closed the door of communication.

Finally, he said, "Then we obviously need to go there. Is there golf?"

"Yes, a Robert Trent Jones Senior course is next to the castle and Lahinch is a short drive away."

"Then I'm definitely there with you."

"You golf?"

Max read skepticism in the question.

"What military man doesn't?" he replied.

"I never made the connection between golf and the military."

"There are a ton of military courses," Max said.

"Then we'll play Lahinch," Kat said.

"Are you good?"

"No, but I hit it straight."

"I do believe you *are* a straight shooter," Max said. "Probably the straightest shooter I've met in a long time."

She smiled at him and the look made his ears tingle. Max noticed they still stood there hand in hand. This feels good, he thought, then switched hands, so they could turn to look back on Dublin as the city grew smaller in the distance.

"What a sight," he said. "British armies sailing ashore probably had this view."

Kat followed his gaze. "My thoughts were on the namesake of the ferry," she said. "Jonathan Swift."

"*Gulliver's Travels*," Max said and chuckled. "I read the book as a kid and had nightmares for a week."

Kat laughed.

"You laugh. I never read him again," Max said.

"Really?"

"Really."

"I don't picture you ever being scared, not after what I've witnessed."

"Fear is part of a soldier's battle armor."

"His armor ought to be faith."

"Well—at least for believers."

"Fear and faith are contradictory," she said.

"Counterintuitive maybe, but isn't there a scripture somewhere about the fear of God is the beginning of wisdom?"

"Yes, but that's 'a righteous and worshipful' fear of God, not a fear of man. Fear and faith are not equal, Max. Fear is an emotion. Faith

183

is a rock, a cornerstone, and the power of God. Fear robs you. Faith strengthens you."

Max turned squarely to face her. "You sure you didn't miss your calling? As a preacher?"

Her expression twisted into one of pain. "Not after what my Dad went through. But that's a tale for another time. You're changing the subject."

Max grimaced. She'd caught him.

He hemmed a bit, then said, "The fear I was talking about *is* fear of God. It's fear of what will happen if you die on that spot at that time. That's why there are so many foxhole prayers. Guys who have never believed suddenly think, 'Uh-oh, what if He's really out there? I'd better pray—just in case.'"

"Well, then, if fear *does* lead you to faith, fear's good," Kat said.

Max shrugged, admitting defeat. He could not win against this lady.

An hour into the ferry ride, Kat said, "Look how grand is the Irish Sea and yet it's but a speck of creation, a tiny fragment of even the earth. How majestic God must be!"

Max simply nodded.

"My, what a wake this ferry leaves behind."

"We're zipping along at about forty knots," Max said.

"Which is?"

"About forty-five miles per hour, take or leave a few yards."

"Then we'd better get below decks to the restaurant for lunch before it's too late."

Moments later, Kat was stunned as they descended the wide staircase. The scene was like walking into a grand ballroom at a five-star resort. Knee-high-to-ceiling windows ran the full length of the dining area.

She looked up at Max, catching a gaze from his big brown eyes. "Glad we chose Club class?" she asked.

He scanned the room and smiled back at her. "Classy place for a classy lady."

She grinned, then looked down at what she was wearing. The outfit was the best of what she could cram into a duffel bag, but still was khaki pants, a three-quarter-sleeve white blouse, and white sneakers. Her mismatched socks were out of sight. Max was in blue jeans and a bright red polo shirt, his chest and arm muscles bulging.

"You think we might be underdressed?" she asked.

"I think when women see you, they'll be jealous and when men see you, they'll, well—" He left the sentence unfinished.

She knew the complement left her blushing. She lowered her head to disguise the fact. Indeed, the women in the room would not be looking at her at all, but at the tall, handsome, broad-shouldered man at her side. If she was sure of anything in the world, it was this.

They seated themselves side-by-side at the one empty table they could find along the windows. A round, four-person setting with a white tablecloth.

A waiter placed menus on their table and, upon first glance, Kat exclaimed, "Bangers and Mash!"

Max laughed. "Okay, I'll simply pay up sooner than expected."

An eyebrow raised. "This isn't Dublin, soldier."

Max shrugged. "So, what would you like?"

"Bangers and mash now and bangers and mash later, in Dublin. No reneging allowed."

"You're a double-dipper."

"No, I'm a double lover—of bangers and mash."

Max laughed. "I caught the hesitation."

Kat smiled back at him. "I *am* a double lover. I love animals, certain

185

foods, certain localities, certain books—and certain people."

Max held up his right hand. "I counted five loves. So you're a cinco-lover, more than twice a double lover."

"Now you're being silly."

"It's a trait I sometimes resort to when overwhelmed."

"I doubt you're ever 'overwhelmed.'" She held up her fingers to form quotation marks.

"I'm afraid *you* overwhelm me," he said.

She read honesty in his eyes. It startled her.

"Me?" she asked. "Why?"

"Besides your obvious intelligence and beauty, you've twice escaped attempts on your life in the last twenty-four hours or so; you've seen one of your friends nearly murdered; and yet you're undeterred, even steadfast, in your quest. Those reactions, coming from a non-military person, are quite something in my view. And once in a very great while, I feel overwhelmed by the character of a person."

Tears formed in Kat's eyes as she looked up at this man, this hero who had twice saved her life and now he was complimenting her. She swiped at those tears and was trying to form a response when the waiter returned to take their order.

Saved by the bell.

As they compared notes on other ferry rides each had taken, Max had an odd feeling someone was watching them. Trying not to give away his intentions, he slowly looked around, scouting the room. To no effect.

A minute later, as Max leaned forward to ask Kat a question, an older couple appeared beside him. The man—tall, athletic, in his mid-60s, Max guessed—smiled at them and asked, "I wonder if my wife and I could join you. There seem to be no other empty seats with a view—and we do love this crossing. That is if you don't mind and we're not interfering."

Max looked at Kat, who nodded approval. And within ten minutes, they were fast friends with Carl and Betty Sampson. Carl was a retired lawyer who had finished his career as counsel general of the Welsh Government. Betty, short and slender with short-cut graying hair, was a former concert pianist who was now giving private lessons.

When Betty revealed she was the worship leader at their Anglican church in St. David's, Max asked, "St. David's? As in the St. David's Cathedral?"

"We live not more than four kilometers from the cathedral," she said.

Max glanced at Kat. His unspoken question, *God-incidence?*

She nodded assent.

The waiter arrived, and after he had taken the Sampsons' orders, Max said to Carl, "I thought the Welsh were under British rule, but you mentioned working for the Welsh Government."

"Like the Scottish Government," Carl said, "the Queen appoints our First Minister, who in turn appoints ten ministers and deputy ministers, but the Welsh National Assembly is elected by the people. The Counsel General is nominated by the First Minister and approved by the National Assembly."

"Then we're especially honored to meet you," Kat said.

Carl grinned shyly. "Well, I'm retired now, entirely devoted to my wife and my God."

Max's ears perked up, and Carl obviously noticed. "I'm studying to enter the Anglican clergy," he answered the unasked question. "Never too late."

Betty looked at Max and then Kat. "And, may I ask, are you on vacation?"

Max laughed and "hardly" escaped his lips.

Kat looked up at him. The question in her eyes was, "Should we reveal what we're up to? Maybe this God-incidence is to serve a purpose."

"I trust your judgment," he whispered to her.

Kat returned Betty's gaze, exhaled, then said, "We're searching for the lost music of the Psalms."

Betty's eyes went wide and she gasped. She turned quickly to her husband, "Can you imagine that, Carl? The original music? If I could only play that music! If the choir could sing to that score! Oh, my Lord, my Lord!"

Kat, sitting next to Betty, put her hand on the woman's wrist, then slowly told a brief version of their search.

"This," Betty said, "is extraordinary news. You *do* realize you're in Wales where every man, woman, and child is born to sing."

"Really?" Max said.

"Truly," Carl said. "That old movie, *How Green Is My Valley*, with Roddy McDowall, was true. For centuries, the men coming out of the mines have sung *a cappella*—"

"Great and difficult songs," Betty said. "And when we have hymn fests, thousands turn out to raise their voices."

"Not only that, but Wales is where the 1903 revival began—"

"And spread across the world, even to the United States," Betty said.

"The worship and prayer would go on all night and into the early hours of the morning," Carl said.

"Miners became better workers—"

"And prayed together."

"Feuds, quarreling, bickering—it all stopped—"

"Dead as a frozen herring," Carl finished.

They all chuckled.

"Yes, you're in God's country," Betty said. "We may have slip-slided away from where we were in those revival times, but the Lord can rekindle embers in the fireplace. And how better to resuscitate believers than with His original music? Oh, my!"

Max looked back and forth as the two spoke, amused by their oneness, feeling the odd man out.

"You know," Carl said, "the revival was so powerful that all around Wales, the pubs closed."

"Really?" Kat asked, a look of astonishment crossing her face.

"Some businesses closed for awhile," Betty said. "Their owners and employees were always at church."

"The worst sinners got saved," Carl added.

"The worst cheats."

"The worst womanizers."

"You didn't hear cursing in public anymore," Betty said.

"No taking the Lord's name in vain."

"It must have been bliss." Betty sighed deeply. "Oh, to play the organ or piano at a time like that!"

"*Another* time like that," Carl said.

Max glanced at Kat to see her reaction. Her shoulders relaxed, her lips slightly parted, she seemed in a place of calm and peace.

Silence reigned for a minute, then Carl said, "You do realize if you find this music in Wales, the manuscript could be considered 'national treasure,' with our government mandated to retain it in Wales."

"Now, dear," Betty said, "you needn't always be wearing your lawyer's hat."

Carl shrugged, but Kat nodded agreement, then looked at Betty and said, "Many countries have the same laws."

"But that being said, how can we help?" Carl asked.

"Well, since you live nearby St. David's, perhaps we can follow you there—" Max said.

"And also recommend a place to stay overnight," Kat said.

"Stay?" Betty said. "My dear, you'll stay with us."

"It's a big old house, so empty since our children grew up and left it echoes our footsteps," Carl said.

"Carl," Max said, "thank you for your hospitality. And we'd love to stay with you. But you must know danger has dogged us every step of the way."

"Max saved my life at Petra," Kat said, "and my life as well as the curator's at St. Michan's just yesterday. Three gunmen tried to kill us, but Max disarmed them, and the police now have them in custody."

Obviously startled, Carl blurted out, "Max did what?"

At the same moment, Betty's hand shot out to grab Kat's. "Why? Who?"

"There are Islamic extremists who do not want us to find this music," Kat said.

"But— but it's a treasure for the world!" Betty exclaimed.

"But it also would be the cherry on top of the birthday cake for the people planning to build the Jews' Third Temple on Jerusalem's Temple Mount," Max said.

"Aha!" Carl said. "So that's the rub."

"The rub and more," Max said. "For the Muslims, it's to-die-for. So, again, thank you for your offer, but—"

"But nothing, my boy," Carl interjected. "Listen, if you left those men in the hands of the police in Ireland, no way are they getting out of jail anytime soon. Besides, even if there were others over there, how would they know where you went from Dublin? And they certainly wouldn't be aware of any connection between you two and us—"

"And besides," Betty said, "if need be, my dear husband is a crack shot."

Carl lowered his head and shook it.

"Don't you be so humble," Betty scolded him. She looked at Max and declared, "My Carl was a silver medalist in the Olympics. Twice."

"Really?" Max was impressed.

"The fifty-meter rifle 3-positions," she said.

"Twenty years ago," Carl objected.

"And sixteen years ago," Betty said.

"3-Positions?" Kat asked.

"That's prone, standing, and kneeling," Carl explained.

"So, in effect, you're saying we should stay with you because Carl could join me in our protection," Max said. "You're actually volunteering to make your house a possible shooting ground and for yourselves to be, ah, collateral damage in our defense."

Betty hesitated, looking a bit confused for a moment, then stiffened her back and nodded agreement.

"Sounds safer than putting a lot of people in harm's way in a hotel," Carl said.

"I can tell you must have been an extremely good lawyer," Kat said.

"Oh, he was, he was," Betty said.

"But you barely know us. Why would you put yourselves possibly in danger?" Kat asked.

Before they could answer, Max looked at Carl and said, "You served in the military."

"Right."

"You were infantry."

"The Welch 160 Brigade. How'd you know?"

Kat interjected, "Your ring."

191

Carl lifted his eyes to meet hers, then glanced down at a ring on his right ring finger, which contained a blazing red crest with a dagger. A smile slowly filled his face and he looked at Max, "That ring was my Dad's."

"The 160 Brigade's 53rd Division," Max said, "is famous for heroics in the Battle of the Bulge."

"His stories of the war encouraged me to also join the infantry," Carl said. He showed Max a crooked grin. "I thought you were telepathic or something."

"I wish," Max said with a laugh. "Just observant. And, by offering two strangers protection, I think you inherited some very special genes."

Carl smiled, then asked, "Well, son, what do you say? Stay with us or put up at the Wolfscastle Country Hotel? I've got a security system; they don't. I've got weapons; they don't. We're Christians and would love to help. I don't know about their religion, but I doubt they'd bear arms with you."

Max turned to Kat and they locked eyes.

Kat broke the silence. "They're right. No one knows where we are."

"No one except our friends at MI6," Max said.

"Right. And they're not telling anyone."

They both looked at their new friends.

"Okay," Kat said, "we'd love to stay with you."

"Count us as your guests," Max echoed.

As they approached the landfall at Anglesey, North Wales, Max, Kat, Carl and Betty all stood at the railing above deck.

Carl pointed to a very tall, sparkling white lighthouse with whitewashed walls and a long barracks-like building set precariously along a tall cliff at the end of a long promontory overlooking the Irish Strait.

"Holy Head Lighthouse," he said. "One of our enduring landmarks."

Under a slight breeze, several small sailboats whistled along, silently circling around the harbor, while a tall ship, jet-black hull glistening in the sun, headed past them out to sea.

"What a sight!" Kat exclaimed.

A long, low seawall stretched out in a slow curl into the strait to meet them. As they approached the ferry dock, Max sidled closer to Kat and said in hushed tones, "I'm not wholly at ease about staying with the Sampsons."

"Paranoia does not fit you," she said. "Remember, there's no way the bad guys would know where we are, or where we're heading, or where we're staying overnight. Heck, we didn't know the Sampsons until lunchtime."

Max shrugged but could not shed the uneasy feeling.

Carl and Betty disembarked with them at the tail end of a long train of passengers.

"We'd be happy to chauffeur you around," Carl said.

"Thank you, but no," Max said. "We don't yet know our destination from here. Just in case the trail gets more complicated, we'll rent a vehicle and not bother you about any more than you've already chewed off."

Carl nodded approval of the plan and added, "Hertz has the monopoly here. They're very good."

They all walked down a long ramp and another hundred yards or so down the wharf.

As they stepped out onto an ocean-side street, Max felt an ominous chill. He quickly scanned the street and the crowd of people to his right, then straight ahead, then to his left, then behind him.

"Anything wrong?" Kat asked.

Max hesitated. "No. No. Just a feeling."

Kat's right eyebrow rose in question.

"The feeling you get when there's enemy about."

Carl and Betty had noticed they were trailing behind and stopped to wait.

"Max, would you rather just sprint to St. David's, then race out of town too fast for anyone to catch up?" Kat asked.

"You're jesting."

"I don't know. Maybe we should trust your instincts. You're the soldier here. I'm just a dirt girl."

He looked down at her beautiful green eyes. "Oh, dear professor, you're much, much more than 'just a dirt girl.'"

She laughed lightheartedly, then stepped back. "Okay, I'm with you. We rent the car and go straight to the cathedral." She looked at her watch: 1:50 p.m.

Turning to the Sampsons, she asked, "How far is St. David's from here?"

Carl checked his wristwatch. "We'll be home by four o'clock—maybe sooner."

"Can we go straight to the cathedral?"

"Why not to our place for dinner first?" Betty said. "It won't get dark until nine o'clock tonight. We can freshen up, then go together to St. David's."

"Yes. Not only does Betty play the organ there, but I know the Dean well," Carl said. "The Right Reverend David de Swinssey—formerly 'Davey.' He and I've been friends since childhood. I'll call and arrange for us all to get inside. David will be especially thrilled to let you in, Kat."

On the ride to Pembrokeshire, the land rolled like small waves of the sea, with a dune-like swale racing to the sky here and there. To their right, through the fields and scattered woods they caught glimpses of the Irish Sea, a faded blue. Low stone walls partitioned the land in small and large squares and rectangles. Some fields were a deeper green than others, making it look like a patchwork quilt.

As they drew closer to St. David's, Caerfai Bay came into sight. Steep cliffs rose up from both ends of the bay, giving the impression of open arms welcoming home seafarers. Finally, they rode into an ancient village with mostly two-story shops tight upon one another, brightly painted houses, some with thatched roofs, and bright-faced people, some with shocks of red hair.

"I could live here," Kat said in a soft whisper. "I wish you could be the passenger and me the driver so you could absorb all this."

Max slowed down and looked around, then chuckled. "It does look like a fantasy village."

"Like in *The Quiet Man*," Kat said.

"John Wayne and Maureen O'Hara," Max said with a laugh. "My mom and dad used to watch it every St. Patrick's Day."

"You're joking," Kat said. She felt like he had been reading her diary from her youth.

He glanced at her. "No kidding."

"Yeah. My parents would turn on that video religiously." She remembered it vividly, she and Kaitlin cuddling with Mom and Dad on the living-room couch.

"Did they wear green when they watched it?" Max teased.

Kat landed a firm jab to his shoulder. "I'm serious. This is a beautiful village."

"Do you see a cathedral anywhere?" Max asked.

Kat scanned above the rooftops all around. "Nope. Must be inland a bit."

In front of them, Carl and Betty led the way. To the south side of the village, they drove and hugged the sea. Soon, they turned right and angled down a long, crushed rock driveway. Well-groomed lawns fled away on both sides. To the left was what appeared to be a golf putting green, with sand bunkers on either side and a pin sticking out of a cup near the center.

Kat pointed. "Hey, maybe we don't have to go to Lahinch to play!"

Max followed her finger and grinned broadly. "Carl's a man after my own heart," he declared.

To the right a wide swath of wildflowers ran alongside the drive all the way to the house, looking remarkably kempt for an unkempt garden.

The house was not simply "a house." Fronted by the driveway circling around a flash of red and yellow flowers, the striking two-story, brick, neo-Tudor practically breathed elegance and tidiness. Front and slightly off-center was a Tudor arch with straight sides meeting in a point and a round-arched door set back in a shallow entryway. Tall, multiple-paned casement windows—four-in-a-row—on either side of the entry gave the house symmetry. Second-floor windows resembled those on the first floor and were directly above them, but the roofline to the right side matched the Tudor arch in the entry. A massive brick chimney rose up the left side of the building. Steeply pitched roofs fell to the front and sides, with a four-paned gable peeking out of the front roof, evidence of a third-floor attic.

Max pointed to that top gable and said, "I'll bet Carl's den is on the first floor and that's where his hideaway is."

The Sampsons' car crunched to a stop, leaving enough room for Max to pull in behind them and still be in front of the entryway.

Carl nearly flew out of his Lexus and hustled to greet them. "I'm so sorry. Betty told me I should have meandered slowly through our village so you could soak up the ambiance." His waved his hand to emphasize "ambiance."

Max and Kat laughed lightly and shook their heads.

"It's beautiful," Kat said. "Like a postcard."

"And so is your home," Max said, looking up at the architecture.

"But we didn't see the cathedral," Kat said.

Betty had stepped out of their vehicle and pointed vaguely back toward the village. "It's in sort of a swale behind the village, not easily seen as you drive through town, or from this angle—"

"But hard to miss from any other," Carl added.

"Why don't we all unpack, freshen up a bit, have a sip of tea and a biscuit—though it's past tea-time—," Betty said.

"And I'll prepare the way for us all to investigate St. David's," Carl said. "Think of it! The treasure!"

Suddenly the front door opened and a fiftyish redheaded lady hurried out the short walkway to the drive.

"Mr. Sampson. Missus. Welcome home!" she said.

Carol turned to Max and Kat and said, "Meet our housekeeper, Valerie. Val, this is Mr. Braxton and Doctor Cardova."

"Pleased to meet you," Valerie said with a bow.

Minutes later, they had taken their luggage to second-floor bedrooms and were situated in a large sitting area. Wide windows looked out over a stone-floored deck and a close-cut back lawn slipping down to a seawall and the Irish Sea not more than thirty yards beyond the house. A long dock into the sea served as mooring for what Kat guessed was a forty-foot sailboat.

Looking closely, she turned to Betty. "Are those straw targets I see out on the dock?"

Betty laughed. "That's our competition."

"What do you mean?"

Carl answered. "Betty mentioned I'm a marksman. Well, she's quite the archer."

"So," Betty said, "we set up the targets as a contest."

"Betty uses her bow and arrows and fires away from twenty-five or thirty-five meters and I shoot with a handgun from fifty or sixty meters and we compare who hits the bulls-eye the most. She usually wins, I must admit."

They all chuckled.

Valerie served tea and Carl turned to Kat. "I just got off the phone with the Right Reverend and he's excited for your visit."

"Thanks for breaking the ice," Kat said.

"St. David's is a huge cathedral," Betty said. "Do you have a clue as to where to look for the music?"

"None whatsoever," Kat said, "except maybe somewhere in relation to worship."

"Like their famous organ?" Carl said.

"Oh, it's magnificent," Betty said. "It's a Henry Willis dating back to the late 1800s and rebuilt a couple of times since then."

"Maybe the music's hidden in the organ or the pipes," Max offered.

"I wouldn't say so," Betty said. "Anything in the pipes would gargle the sound. Besides, the organ was dismantled in the late 1990s and rebuilt and now has four manuals and fifty-four stops."

"I remember when the bishop rededicated it," Carl said. "I think it was in 2000."

"Yes," Betty said, "because I remember the scare about the new millennium and the disaster that was supposed to happen. But it didn't."

"So," Kat said, "what you're saying is if the music were hidden in the organ these folks would have made the discovery then."

"In which case," Max said, "they would have told the world."

"We're forgetting," Kat said, "the music was brought here back in the 13th century."

There were moans all around and, seemingly in synchrony, they sipped their tea.

"That's a beautiful boat you have," Max said, pointing toward the dock.

"That's our Valiant Cutter," Carl said.

"We sailed a lot when the kids were with us," Betty said.

"Not so much now," Carl said. "I'm spending more time on the golf course, or our golf holes right here, and less on the sea nowadays."

"I noticed your putting green," Max said.

"Green?" Betty chuckled. "He has three of them."

"And a dozen tees scattered around," Carl said. "You can play eighteen distinct holes and then play another eighteen and, if you want, another eighteen and none of them will be the same."

Max's eyes lit up. "I love the idea."

"Well, we may not know where to begin at the cathedral," Betty said, "but what's keeping us?"

"One biscuit and one last sip of tea," Carl said.

Chapter 15

Within fifteen minutes, they all climbed out of the Sampsons' Lexus into a parking lot that led onto a walkway to St. David's Cathedral.

Beside them was a long hillside replete with beautiful yellow flowers. Before them was a mammoth stone structure with the classic square bell tower in the middle and a long wing on either side. Clocks on the two sides they could see revealed the time to be just past five o'clock.

Several tourists roamed the grounds, some snapping photographs and with good reason.

"Magnificent," Kat breathed.

Thirty-foot-high, stained-glass, arched, mullioned windows adorned every ten feet of the lower level of both wings. Above them was an upper row with smaller arched windows.

Fronting the steeple and protruding from the rest of the structure, Max guessed, was probably the sanctuary, which stood square with a pitched tin roof, gold-rimmed, arched windows, and peaked at the front corners.

When Kat grabbed Max's hand and looked up at him with a wide smile of expectation, a deep warmth flowed over him. At the same time, he could not control a sense of menace nearby. He looked all around but spotted nothing the least bit threatening.

A group of Japanese people, some with long-lensed cameras hanging from their necks and others with hand-sized cameras in their grasp, walked by in a gaggle. They strode down a walkway toward the cathedral. The walkway led to an arched entryway on the left wing of the cathedral. A path branched off to the right up a slight incline to the front entrance, but Carl and Betty led Max and Kat straight ahead into the left wing.

Waiting to greet them inside the door was a very tall, very thin man—Max guessed four inches taller than his own six-foot-two. He was dressed in a tweed sport coat, open-collared white shirt, and trousers. Not priest-like at all.

Carl introduced Max and Kat to the Right Reverend David de Swinssey, and the dean of St. David's quickly said, "Just call me David."

Upon taking Kat's hand, he said, "I am truly honored, Doctor Cardova. I subscribe to *Biblical Archaeology* magazine and just finished reading a feature story about your dig up in the Dan region of Israel. Fascinating."

"It was a wonderful find," Kat said. "The Discovery Channel has filmed a documentary on the dig."

Max knew his look at Kat showed he was startled. She had not mentioned anything about Dan or the documentary.

She returned his gaze and said, "It's a long story. Has to do with the Rub El Hizb, which Muslims use as a sort of coat of arms. Our dig proves the symbol was created by the Syrian King Hazael and used to signify 'terror for victory's sake'—a pejorative they obviously wouldn't want the world to know about."

"Of course, not everyone pays attention to *Biblical Archaeology*," David said.

"But they do the Discovery Channel," Carl added.

"You'll be famous!" Betty said.

Kat simply shrugged and looked way up at David. "If we find the music of the Psalms, it will be a treasure for all Christendom, not to mention the Jewish faith."

"When Carl called," David said, "I got to thinking. We know about a young Crusader, who came home to Pembrokeshire after visiting Ireland in the early 13th century. His name was Anéislis Bòideach. He was active in our church and even left us with his diary. I'm afraid no one I know has ever read the manuscript, but we hold it as an artifact of that time in our history. It's usually kept under glass, but—" He reached inside his sport coat and pulled out a small leather book, along with plastic gloves. "Can you read Gaelic?"

"No," Kat said, "but may I see the book?"

He handed it to her, along with the gloves. She pulled on the gloves and quickly leafed through the book. The pages were yellowed with age, the ink faded to varying degrees, but nevertheless readable. "He has dates from 1224 through 1277," she said. "You'd have to guess that if he came here in his twenties, he must have died in his seventies or eighties."

She passed the book back to David, "Can you read Gaelic?"

He nodded.

"Then, would you do the honors of reading us the last couple entries? They would be the ones most likely to give us a clue."

"My pleasure," David said. Opening the book, he began: "'July sixteen, the Year of Our Lord Twelve Hundred and Seventy-seven. The day of my birth lies two days hence, but I will not live to celebrate. I am about to leave this earth for a better place, prepared for me by my Lord and Savior. He awaits me and I look forward to meeting Him. The two tasks I have been given worthy of mention in this life have been fighting for His Holy Land and, in these past thirty-four years, keeping His original, sacred music to accompany the Psalms.

"'As Godfrey the Irish imparted to me when I was a much younger man, Christians have been ordered—first by decree of King David who foresaw the need, then, I understand, by decree of our Lord's brethren who were leaders of the early church—to hold this music until the Jewish people build a Third Temple on the Temple Mount in Jerusalem. The Holy Spirit revealed to King David that two temples would be built and both destroyed, but when a third temple was built, his music was to be unveiled to be used in praise and worship at the temple's dedication and thereafter. At some point, the Crusaders took over the task of the music's safekeeping."

David raised his eyes and scanned the group attentively listening. He breathed deeply and continued: "My death now looms. And with the troops of England's King Edward the 1st about to conquer Pembrokeshire as they have Anglesey, Clwyd, and Gwynedd—all to defeat Llewellyn-ap-Graffyd, the prince of Gwynedd—I am loathe to give up my mission.

"'I know many in this world, namely the hordes of Islamic warriors overrunning much of Europe and the Middle East, would stop at nothing to prevent the music's disclosure if they knew of its existence. I have been able to keep my word and, until two days ago, felt like Caleb of the Bible when he was eighty yet felt himself as strong as at forty. But I did not foresee this quick death coming, this intense fever sapping my strength, and no man stands at my bedside to hear of my mission. So whoever reads these words, please carry on my task. To find this treasure of God, think: "Ancient instrument." God save you if you find the music yet do not protect such a treasure until the Third Temple!'"

Suddenly Betty exclaimed, "Aha!"

"What?" Carl asked.

"The ancient instruments—"

"The ones stored in the west wing of the cathedral?" David asked.

"Yes!" Betty looked straight at Kat. "Once St. David's Cathedral was deemed worthy of pilgrimages, the church began providing the finest of instruments for worship. Organs were evolving into complex instruments. They also used guitars and citterns, lutes, shawms the precursor to the oboe), recorders—"

"What Betty is saying," Carl said, "is St. David's became a sort of repository for these Middle Age instruments."

"I've been trying to raise money for years to restore them and show them to the public," David said. "At the very least, we should have them refurbished."

"Wood loses moisture and oils through oxidation even though varnish or lacquer does help protection," Betty said. "At the same time, dirt exacerbates the deterioration process, so the instruments should be kept clean. I'm afraid little of this had been done here."

"God knows there are enough tourists in and out of this cathedral and many of them would love to view these instruments—even if they were not restored," Carl said.

"Dear, David and the others have enough to do over here," Betty said.

"True, true."

David simply shrugged, then said, "It's true. I have failed in this regard—as a musician like Betty can attest. So, Doctor Cardova, is our store of ancient instruments where you'd like to start your search?"

At the question, Kat suddenly felt a chill—the good kind. "Absolutely."

David turned on his heels, waved for them to follow him and took off at a quick, long-legged pace.

Kat looked about her as they hustled through a cavernous room and into the sanctuary. The space was striking. Heavy wooden benches the hue of gold dominated the room, looking toward the pulpit. Carvings of saints peered out from eight feet high behind the pulpit. Above them in an alcove, a set of magnificent silver organ pipes rose toward the ceiling, their tops hidden by a series of five circular golden caps.

Carved woodworks adorned the ceiling and there was a series of three wide arches from the back to the front of the sanctuary on both sides.

Kat sighed deeply. *Oh, to be able to pray here!*

Through the sanctuary they went, and through another wide door into the right wing of the cathedral. They walked through a black wrought-iron gate and entered a long corridor with arch after arch on their right. High at the end of the corridor was a circular glass window in the shape of a many-petaled flower.

All of a sudden, the Dean stopped, spun to the right, walked about thirty feet and entered a stairway leading up a long flight of stairs.

At the top, he turned to see Kat and the others were still with him. Kat turned to look with him. Max was at her heel, Carl and Betty behind him. Excitement was etched on all their faces.

Another corridor went in both directions and David turned to the left, again heading toward the far end of the cathedral. When they reached the end, David stopped and pulled a ring of old-fashioned church keys off his belt. Finding the one he wanted, he slipped the tip and bit into a keyhole of a large, arched heavy oak door.

Pushing the door open, he waved them all inside.

Sunlight from a high window filtered into the room, revealing swirling dust in the air and lighting up a number of instruments.

Betty gasped and pointed. "Oh, Carl, look! I think that may date to the 12th century, just before our friend the Crusader came here."

They all stepped between chests and chairs piled upon one another.

"This is a hybrid between the hydraulis and the organ!" Betty declared, unable to control her enthusiasm.

"Hydraulis?" Max asked.

"About 200 BC, Ctesibius of Alexandria, a musician and engineer, built the first pipe organ, which he called the hydraulis because he used water pressure to create the wind supply. Over the centuries, the hydraulis evolved into the more complex organ capable of producing different timbers. You know how anthropologists keep trying to find the missing link between apes and humans—which they never will, by the way?"

Max nodded.

"Well, as organs go, this is a missing link!"

"And you say this was developed in the 12th century?" Kat asked.

Betty nodded.

"Then perhaps the music is hidden somewhere inside," Carl said.

David stepped around the instrument and lifted the top nearly the same way as a grand piano. All five people stood and squatted around the contraption. Max pulled a penlight from the back pocket of his jeans and scooted underneath.

Ten minutes later, they all threw up their hands. Nothing.

"Ancient instrument. Ancient instrument," Kat repeated. "Betty, why don't you look around and see what else might qualify?"

Betty smiled. "My pleasure, my dear."

All eyes were on Betty as she slowly traversed the room. She ambled lithely, with the moves of a dancer.

"Oh, my!" she exclaimed. "Remember the shawm I mentioned, Kat? This is one—the ancestor of the oboe."

Indeed, the shawm appeared like a bassoon, with a curl at the top but much wider at the end of the horn.

"In case the music is hidden inside, you should have the honors, Kat."

Kat acquiesced, stepping in and lifting the instrument from the stand on which it sat.

Max handed her his penlight and she twisted off the reed piece, then shone the light into the instrument from both ends.

She looked up, disappointment on her face. "No luck."

"Okay, dear. Okay," Betty said. "There's more to see."

She continued ambling around the room. She pointed toward several recorders of different sizes. None of them looked large enough to hold much of anything.

"Perhaps this cittern?" she said, pointing to an instrument that appeared to be a cross between a guitar and mandolin, with a lovely tear-shaped body.

Again Kat stepped close and peered inside the body with Max's penlight.

She shook her head. "Nothing."

Betty put her hands on her hips and slowly scanned the room.

Carl and the others all followed her direction to an organ-shaped instrument in the back-right corner.

All of a sudden something caught her eye. Her gaze focused on the far back corner where an instrument rested on a small table.

"Is that a, a—" she stopped herself and rushed past boxes and a set of varied sized tambourines.

"Yes!" she exclaimed, picking up the instrument. "It's a gittern. I'm sure it is!"

She stretched her arms out before her and admired the instrument. Made of maple, the piece was small, pear-shaped and stringed, except the strings all hung deteriorated. The circular hole to the body was capped with a finely crafted wooden piece with tiny Celtic designs.

"Gittern?" Kat asked.

"I think there're only two of these still known to exist!" Betty said, her voice dripping with admiration.

"Are you sure?" David asked, stepping closer for a better look. "This would be only the third?!"

"I believe so," Betty said. "The gittern was quill-plucked. Before the guitar, before the lute, this is what minstrels and musicians used. Very popular. Pretty, isn't it?"

"A museum piece!" Kat said. "So our search will indeed bear fruit."

"The question is," Max said, "is there anything inside?"

"Well, let's see," Betty said and handed the gittern to Kat. She held the instrument gingerly, like a newborn baby. "I won't drop this," she said quietly. Then, setting it on a nearby table, she flicked on the penlight and tried to look inside. But the cap to the hole stopped her.

"Actually," Betty said, "the cap was made separately, then slipped over the opening. We should be able to lift and gently prying it off."

"May I?" David said, offering a hand.

Kat passed the gittern to the dean and he pulled out a pen knife. "I'll be ever so careful, but if I do cause harm, the result will be on me, not one of you good folks."

Slowly, gently, he placed the blade to the cap. He added pressure, then added some more. And after a few moments, "Aha! It moved!" he announced.

All eyes were on his fingers as he continued to tenderly add leverage to the knife to pry off the lid. Finally, one side came up and David grabbed and dislodged the lid between a thumb and forefinger.

He set the gittern back on the table and Kat gazed inside. A puff of breath escaped her and she reached her thumb, index and middle fingers inside. Pulling out a very small scroll, her shoulders hung and she shook her head.

"It's definitely not the music," Max said, "but what is it, Kat?"

After so many digs, Kat was used to disappointment, but this was more a conundrum because, though it was not the music, she did indeed probably have another clue in front of her. She just wished this moment were the end of the search, not another step in the journey.

Still wearing the plastic gloves, she gently untied a strand of coarse string keeping the scroll curled tightly. When she did, the scroll unrolled only partially.

"It's old, brittle," she said. "Written in Latin—by a very intelligent person, it appears."

"Can you translate ?" Carl asked.

Kat peered at the scroll and began: "Whoever discovers this, know I have indeed taken up the mission of the noble Welch Crusader Anéislis Bòideach and will protect King David's music of the Psalms with my life, or until the Third Temple is built in the Holy City.

"My plans are to take this music to our headquarters so that it might always be under the protection of our Order.

"Signed, Jacques de Molay, Pauperes commilitones Christi Templique Solomonici"

"Jacques de Molay?!" David asked.

"The martyred Grand Master of the Knights Templar," Max said softly.

"Yes." Kat nodded.

"Oh, my," Betty whispered. "So where would he have taken it?"

Kat looked at her and shrugged. "We'll have to research to find out where de Molay went from here, where the Templars' headquarters were at the time."

"Well, if he kept the music to his death, he was burned on a cross, right?" Max asked.

"Yes, in Paris," David said. "A very sad chapter for the Catholic Church, and one for which we have long needed repentance." He closed his eyes, as if recalling a memory, then added, "Dieu sait qui a tort et a pëché. Il va bientot arriver malheur à ceux qui nous ont condamnés à mort."

"You lost me," Carl said.

"Those were de Molay's last words," David said. "The Templars' existence had been closely tied to the Crusades and when the Holy Land was lost, rumors abounded. The Templars were charged with apostasy, heresy, obscene rituals, fraud—you name it. King Philip the Fourth of France, deeply in debt to the Order, took advantage, had the Knights arrested, tortured into false confessions and then burned at the stake.

"And to the church's shame, Pope Clement the Fifth disbanded the Order in 1312. Before being burned to death along with Geoffroi de Charney, who was the Grand Master of Normandy for the Knights Templar, de Molay purportedly said of the king and the Pope, '*God* knows who is wrong and has sinned. Soon a calamity will occur to those who have condemned us to death.'"

"Did a calamity occur?" Max asked.

"A month later, Pope Clement died, and before the end of the year, King Philip died in a hunting accident."

"Whoa!" Carl exclaimed. "Prophetic!"

"Well, I did say 'purportedly," David said, "Maybe someone fabricated that quote afterward.'

"If he did say so, talk about a condemnation," Betty said.

Kat felt all eyes then turn upon her. She was deep in thought. She looked back down at the scroll.

De Molay had written: "My plans are to take this music to our headquarters so that the treasure might always be under the protection of our Order."

Where did the music end up? Certainly de Molay would not have taken such an object with his personal effects to his death in Paris. Or would he?

She looked up at Max and then the others. "Research," she said. "Research and a good guess."

"Let's first try prayer," David said.

In a circle they joined hands and, with her eyes closed, Kat wondered how Max was responding to this impulsive action.

David led the prayer, asking for wisdom and discernment, for God's guidance and open doors, for correct passage but closed ones when Kat headed in the wrong direction.

With "amens" all around, Kat, Max, Carl, and Betty thanked David and left him holding the scroll. With help from the bishop and, perhaps, Rome, he would determine what would happen with this information.

"Looks like you'll *have* to stay with us tonight," Carl grinned. "Like you said, Kat: research."

After they arrived back at the Sampson estate, Valerie served all four a delicious duck à l'orange with asparagus baked potato.

Afterward, Carl told Valerie to take off the weekend and enjoy her grandchildren. Then Max and Kat followed Carl and Betty into the den, each carrying a mug of hot coffee.

Max looked around. The three inner walls were of rich, carved walnut and the outside wall was filled with knee-to-ceiling windows looking out to the sea, glistening with the yellows and reds of the setting sun. On the wall before him, a floor-to-ceiling bookcase was filled with hardcover books, a spacious fireplace centered the wall to the right, but Max's attention was drawn to the wall immediately to his left.

Two large display cases hugged the wall. The first showed off an impressive collection of rifles and pistols, both ancient and modern.

Carl followed Max's eye and his face lit up. "My collection!" he said.

"I'm impressed."

Carl pointed. "This is my Pensby School Full Bore Rifle. This next one's the Whisper, trimmed down from the Predator, designed for noise reduction, which the neighbors like, I'm sure. But check the over-the-barrel design. Nifty, huh?"

Max smiled assent.

"And here's my custom-built John Bowkett. Such fine quality and efficient moderators. But maybe my favorite—and as an American, you can appreciate this." He pointed to a long rifle at the far right. "The quintessential frontier gun from America: the Marlin Lever-Action Big Bore."

Carl stuck his hand underneath a side table and pulled out a small key. He used it to open the cabinet, then took the Marlin from its place. Passing the gun to Max, he said, "Heft that."

The rifle was heavy. Max admired the workmanship. "You can almost feel the history," he said.

"If it's history you like, take a look at this!" Carl reached into the case, pulled out a handgun and swapped firearms with Max.

"A Colt .45," Max said. "The Peacekeeper. I can feel the inner Texas Ranger right now." He aimed the revolver toward the fireplace and put on his best Lone Ranger voice. "Okay, Jesse, Frank, time for you James boys to stop the outlawin'."

"Are they hiding in the fireplace?" Kat joked.

Betty and Carl chuckled and Max flashed Kat a crooked smile.

A moment later, Carl handed Max another handgun and asked, "And how about this one?"

"A Smith and Wesson 1917," Max said. "My dad used one of these. Willed her to me when he died."

"Served well in World War I, and you see them even today on the firing range," Carl said. He pointed to a square six-foot-high cabinet.

"I've got the ammo right here."

Kat stepped past the two men toward the other case. The cabinet contained three bows, a leather quiver of arrows, and a crossbow with a sheaf of tiny crossbow bolts.

"And what do we have here? Robin Hood's arsenal?" she asked.

"Carl has his collection; I have mine," Betty said.

She pointed to one. "This is my new favorite, perhaps because it's called the Insanity CPX so you can 'unleash the insanity.' Scary, huh?"

Max and Carl set the firearms back in the showcase and stepped up next to the women. To Max, the Insanity looked like coiled girders on a bridge. Black with red accents.

"As stable and recoilless a bow as I've ever shot," Betty said. She pointed and said, "The long stabilizer is great for target shooting and I love the Hitman 5 sight when zooming in on the bulls-eye—"

"Which she hits more often than not," Carl said. "I'm *so* envious."

Betty pointed to another bow and said, "This is my limited edition Silverado. My favorite feature is I can relax the string for adjustments."

"And it's sexy, too," Carl said.

"Not usual to see black powder-coated risers, brown components, and camouflage limbs," Betty said.

"What I'm admiring," Kat said, "is the crossbow. Our soldier here," she eyed Max, "probably is proficient in crossbows."

Max grinned and shook his head. "Never used one."

"Well, I have," Kat said.

Max's eyes widened in surprise.

"Once," she said. "In England. At a Medieval celebration. The guy who was giving a demonstration showed me how to shoot one. I'm afraid I missed the target completely."

"It takes practice," Betty said. "I think you'd love this one. A Darton FireForce. So easy. Darton makes great compound bows, so I picked

214

one up. I'll have to show you before you leave."

Max looked at Carl, "You mentioned Betty and you competing. How do you compete with a handgun against a bow?"

"Shall we show them?" Carl asked Betty.

"Of course." Betty opened the showcase, removed the Insanity CPX and a sheath of arrows, then handed the Darton FireForce to Kat. "Might as well have you shoot a few, too," she said.

Kat grinned broadly and took hold of the crossbow.

Holding the Colt .45 in one hand and a box of ammunition in the other, Carl led the way into the entryway and back through the living room, then out through veranda doors. Across the lawn, they walked toward the dock, where two sizeable targets were set up on stands—a thick bale of straw behind each target and one in front of the other. The boat floated languidly beyond them and to the left.

They arrived at a spot on the lawn where two small, red wooden pins four feet apart, stuck about a foot high out of the earth. There they stopped.

"This spot," Betty said, "is forty feet from the first of two targets and sixty feet from the second one."

"She shoots at the front target and I shoot at the rear one," Carl said.

"If we miss, so what?" Betty said. "The bullet or arrow goes into the water. Far from the boat."

"But we seldom miss," Carl said.

"Only when you distract me," Betty giggled.

"Ha! Distraction, thy name is Betty Sampson."

"Once you tickled me when I fired and the arrow stuck in the prow of the boat."

"A mere ding. No problem. I counted the cost before I carried out my plan."

"Pshaw!" Betty said. "Stop fooling and let's show these two a bit of competition."

Carl loaded his Colt .45 and motioned to her. "Ladies first."

Betty stood sideways to the target, set her arrow in place and turned to Kat. "Notice my stance, the feet set under my shoulders, the angle of my left and right elbows and how I'm holding the arrow with the tips of my thumb and index and middle fingers. You want to aim down the shaft of the arrow and simply release the pressure on the arrow."

She turned, aimed and released. Pfft! The arrow fled toward the target and pinged into the bull's-eye.

Carl took his stand next to where Betty stood, held up the pistol, supporting his right wrist with his left hand, aimed and fired. Almost immediately a tiny British flag rose above the target.

Max laughed and asked, "What's that?"

"We can't see where the bullet landed from this distance," Carl said, "so we have an electronic sensor in the target. If I hit the bull's-eye, the British flag rises. If I hit the first ring, it's solid blue; second ring, solid yellow; fourth ring, purple; fifth ring, black."

"My dear," Betty said, "I don't recall you ever getting yellow, purple, or black. Those flags probably don't even work, they've been unused for so long."

"Impressive," Max said.

Betty gestured for Kat to come to her side. "Now let's see you shoot the FireForce, my dear."

Kat stood beside Betty and placed the crossbow on its stirrup on the ground, put her left foot through the stirrup and pulled the bowstring to the cocking mechanism.

"There, do you hear the popping noise?" Betty asked.

Kat nodded.

"The pop means it's secure. Now put your bolt—it's not an arrow but a bolt—in that little groove so that one of the fletchings—" Betty pointed to the feathers, "is resting in the groove and the end of the bolt is against the string."

Kat followed directions.

"Are the automatic and manual safeties on?"

Kat checked and nodded.

"You're right handed?"

Kat nodded.

"Then, place your left arm below and along the crossbow for stability. You should really have something here to set the crossbow on, but we don't, so be extra firm in securing the foregrip with that arm."

Kat nodded.

"Now place the butt against your right shoulder and place your finger on the trigger."

Kat did so.

"Now take sight on the target, release the safety and apply even pressure with your finger to pull the trigger."

Kat took aim, pulled the trigger and the bolt zipped through the air, slithering into the first ring outside the bull's-eye.

"Fabulous!"" Betty exclaimed. "You're a natural!"

The four friends spent the next half hour firing away at the targets until dusk fell so they went inside the house and back to the den where they replaced the weapons.

Max turned to Kat and asked, "Just where are we going tomorrow, professor?"

Kat looked at the large oak desk on the opposite wall and asked, "May I use your computer?"

While the men talked about guns, golf, and warfare, Kat searched for information on de Molay and the Knights Templar with Betty looking over her shoulder.

217

One snippet of the men's conversation Kat overheard was Carl asking Max about special-operations units "taking out" a leader of an enemy in a non-war situation.

Max's response: "If a black-ops unit is loaned to our CIA, the operation is not considered 'military,' so an assassination does not then violate the Geneva Convention."

That raised an eyebrow and Kat wondered if he had been part of such operations. After a brief moment and reviewing their short history together—*Probably so.*

A half-hour into their search, Kat and Betty stepped away from the desk. Max noticed and asked, "So we have an answer?"

"We're going back to Israel," Kat said. "Atlit, to be specific."

A quizzical look overtook Max's face. "Did you say Atlit?"

"Yes."

"A-t-l-i-t?"

"Yes." She furrowed her brows and cocked her head. "You're familiar?

"Familiar? I trained there."

"Trained? As in military trained?"

"It's a drill area for the IDF Naval Commandos, and I was with a couple of SEAL teams who spent about a month there a few years ago."

"So you're saying this old castle is a naval training base."

"It's actually a little promontory on the Mediterranean a few miles south of Haifa and the castle sits on the tip of the headland."

"Archeologists and anthropologists know about it," Kat said, "because Atlit Yam was a submerged Neolithic village off the coast and gave us the earliest evidence for an agro-pastoral-marine subsistence system in the eastern Mediterranean."

"What's its connection to the Crusaders and to de Molay?" Carl asked.

"The Knights Templar were forced to move their headquarters to other cities in northern Israel, like Acre on the northern edge of Haifa Bay in the late 1200s," Kat said. "At this time de Molay had become Grand Master."

"Once they lost Tortosa as a stronghold, Atlit Castle became their final outpost in the Holy Land. Atlit was never overtaken, but when all else around it was, the Crusaders simply abandoned the castle in 1291."

"So," Betty said, "de Molay was there at the time?"

"It's a good guess," Kat said. "There was a twenty-year period after de Molay went overseas—to the East—in 1270 when little is known about his activities."

"Makes sense he would have been at the Crusaders' last outpost," Max said.

"What's the castle like now, Max?" Carl asked.

"It was badly destroyed by an earthquake a couple hundred years ago. I tell you, no one would have ever conquered the place. It was the crowning achievement in Crusader military architecture, being supplied by ship and with two outer walls. The outer wall was about twenty feet high and ten feet thick and the inner wall forty feet high and sixteen feet thick. You can still see remnants of them."

Max paused, then looked at Kat and asked, "So back to another destroyed castle we go?"

Kat shrugged. "My fate. Doesn't have to be yours."

"Beats writing a book," Max smiled.

"Especially since your computer's back in Israel, right, Mr. Author?"

"In a backpack in Jerusalem."

"What an adventure!" Betty said. "Can't we go, too?" She cast a forlorn look at Carl.

"I'm afraid we'd be intruding on Max and Kat," Carl said.

"In a perfect world, we'd love to have you along," Kat said. "But

219

like you've heard, danger has trailed us from the beginning."

"If we can ever do anything—anything for you two, please let us know," Carl said.

"We *do* have an invitation to come back and play some golf, right?" Max said with a grin.

"Any time for as long a time as you'd like," Betty said.

"Then you're on," Max and Kat responded simultaneously.

Three hours later, everyone had gone to bed in second-floor bedrooms. Carl and Betty lay beside each other trading thoughts about their guests.

"I *love* those two!" Betty said.

"They're like kindred spirits, aren't they?" Carl asked.

"Mm-hmm."

"He's from Texas, you know," Carl said.

"And she's from the Nebraska. In the Midwest, right?"

"Mm-hmm."

"She's so inquisitive," Betty said. "I know she lives a spellbinding life, but I couldn't find out much because she was more interested in us, asking about our children and grandchildren, wondering if I grew up in the city or country, how you and I met—"

"And I have so many questions to ask Max," Carl said. "He was fascinated about my golf course and how I designed and built the greens, and about our boat, if we get to sail her into the ocean or up to Scotland—"

There was silence for a minute, then Betty asked, "Don't you wish we could go with them to search for the music?"

"An adventure of a lifetime."

"Yes."

220

"I'd love to."

"Can you imagine anyone trying to stop such a wonderful thing?"

"Betty, you've seen the spirit here in Wales and in Great Britain for years. The Islamists will stop at nothing. They send their children off strapped with bombs on their chests to blow up innocents and looking for a twenty-five-thousand-dollar payday for their 'gift to Allah.'"

Suddenly they heard a sound, "Blip-blip-blip … Blip-blip-blip." It came from both the front door downstairs and a tiny security console on Carl's bedside table.

He leaped out of bed. Pulling on a pair of jeans, he looked sharply at Betty. "I'll check this out, but get dressed in case you have to get Kat and go to the attic safe room."

Betty hustled out of bed and was slipping on a robe as Carl slipped into the hallway and into what appeared to be a closet. Before him on a shelf set at chest height were four ten-inch-diameter monitors. He scanned across them: nothing, nothing, nothing …

"Aha!" he said aloud. Four silhouettes were hurrying along the dock past the boat and the targets and two more were climbing up onto the dock from what appeared to be a high-speed inflatable motor boat. They all shouldered weapons.

He stepped out of the closet. "Armed men! Six of them. Hurry along and—" he hesitated.

Betty caught his hesitation. "Yes?"

"I love you, sweetie."

She smiled back at him and turned to run.

"Betty!"

Again she stopped and turned.

"Remember the revolver and ammunition."

Max had fallen asleep as soon as his head hit the pillow. These last few days had been long and exhausting though exhilarating. When he'd said his goodnights to Kat, he'd noticed the normal sparkle in her eyes wasn't quite the diamond-like shine he was used to seeing.

"I don't know if I can sleep, I'm so excited," she had said, but he guessed she was in la-la-land already.

Just as he was about to fall into REM sleep, an urgent rapping at his bedroom door awakened him. He bolted upright. "Yes!"

Carl poked his head in the doorway.

"Our alarm system's gone off and there are six men on the dock."

Kat and Betty were talking excitedly down the hall.

"Someone stealing your boat, maybe?"

"No. They're running toward the house and it looks like they're heavily armed."

Max slipped his feet, sockless, into sneakers and, dressed only in pajama shorts, hurried to the door.

Carl opened the door wide and held out a rifle for Max to take.

"AR-15?" Max said. "Easy. Accurate. Boy, you come armed."

"Amen, brother." Carl held up an SAK. "Simple but effective."

"What about the women?" Max asked.

"They're heading to a safe room in the attic." Carl hesitated, then asked, "How do you want to handle this?"

"Some would say, 'Let them come to us,' but we don't know what they might have for weapons. If grenades, that would be suicide. I say, be aggressive."

"What do you think their plan is?"

"If they know what they're doing, they're setting up a perimeter. But they don't know the layout of your house. You do. Did you notice if they were wearing night-vision gear?"

"It didn't appear so. I saw no head gear."

"Well, that's probably out of their league. Keep the lights off."

They both raced down the staircase to the ground floor.

Max said, "I'll go toward the den—"

Just then they heard glass breaking in the living room.

"They're coming in through the patio doors," Carl said.

"I'll take those guys," Max said. He pointed toward the kitchen at the rear corner of the house which contained a door to the back. "If they come that way, they're all yours."

"What about the den?"

"That'll be my territory, too." Max looked at Carl in the dim glow of a nightlight. "Be calm and shoot straight, my friend."

Dressed in summer-weight pajamas, Kat followed Betty to the end of the second-floor hallway. There, a steep flight of stairs rose to the right. At the top of the stairs, Betty opened a door and ushered Kat inside.

"In here, my dear," she said. "Our safe room."

She flicked on a light switch and an overhead light came on as well as a small lamp on a table.

When they were inside, Betty turned, slammed two dead bolt locks into place near the doorknob and a bolt above the door.

Kat looked around. There were no windows. It was sparse. Two chairs. A card table. A telephone on a stand.

Betty hurried to the telephone and picked it up. Eyes wide, she looked at Kat. "It's dead."

"And our cell phones are downstairs," Kat said. "But doesn't your alarm alert a security company, or the local constabulary?"

"Yes, but here in Pembrokeshire, our police department keeps a skeleton staff in the middle of the night. We might have one officer in St. David's and the nearest other station is in Haverfordwest, a distance away."

"So our two men are taking on a half dozen armed terrorists," Kat said.

Fright filled Betty's face and her shoulders slumped. The word, "Yes," barely escaped her lips.

Chapter 16

As Carl rushed toward the kitchen, Max stepped quickly to the wide archway entering the living room. The AK-47 felt comfortable in his grip—like an old friend who'd saved his life more than once.

He heard a scratching noise, like someone cutting glass. Another spoke in hushed tones, in English. "Jabir! Hurry up! You make too much noise!"

"I'm hurrying, Hosni. Shut up."

Max peeked around the corner. Moonlight shone partial light on the lawn behind the house, exposing the silhouette of one man, his hand through a hole in the patio door, unlatching the lock. In a moment, the man was pushing the patio door open, a rifle butt tight against his shoulder.

Max couldn't see the man's comrade or comrades. Max stepped into the room and unleashed a torrent of bullets, slicing through the man inside and spraying glass into the rear deck. Leaping forward, he rolled behind the sofa, with the rifle tucked close to his waist.

Bullets splatted around him from two rifles. Some bullets ricocheted off the hardwood floor; others were swallowed up by the sofa.

At the same time, an exchange of gunfire sounded from the kitchen. Carl's SAK and an AK-47, like the two AK-47s firing at him right now.

We're on equal terms.

The sound of windows breaking reached him from the front-left corner of the house. *The dining room? Didn't these guys synchronize their watches?*

Max crawled to the edge of the sofa, lifted the AK-47 and sprayed bullets through the patio doors. A scream of pain followed. There were more gunshots from the kitchen. But he had to head off whoever was coming through the front windows.

He spun back to the other side of the sofa, then sprinted to the door. Gunfire lit up the room behind him.

At the doorway, he turned to the left and hugged the wall with his back. Someone was indeed coming through a dining-room window. Max sprinted past the stairway to the wide door of the dining room.

More gunfire lit up the kitchen. Carl had a true fight on his hands.

Max dove to the floor with his weapon at the ready. A silhouette. Max sprayed bullets at it and the silhouette slumped to the floor.

Through the window, he spotted another figure, but the man backed away into the darkness.

In the attic, Kat and Betty held hands and anxiously prayed through the noises of the battle.

"Carl and I've been through a lot," Betty said. "He was in a horrible car accident that took months of recuperation and rehabilitation. My breast cancer took one operation and months of chemotherapy and radiation. But I've never been so scared."

"I think it's always worse for the loved ones *not* involved—whether it's war, something like this, or some sort of catastrophe," Kat said. She wondered if she had spoken her last words to Max. If so, what were they? 'Goodnight'? Big deal. She had so much more to share.

Betty interrupted her thoughts. "I feel my prayers aren't enough. I feel helpless and I despise that word—"

"And the feeling," Kat agreed.

More gunfire exploded downstairs and they both flinched.

Noise from the living room got Max to his feet, running back. When he reached the doorway, bullets splintered the door frame around him. He peeked into the room. There was a large mirror on the right-side wall. A figure, moving like the person he had wounded, slipped across the mirror. He was right next to the doorway! Max dropped to his knees, then dove through the doorway and pulled the trigger, sending a salvo of bullets into the gunman.

He scanned the room. No one else. Where had the third man gone? A volley of bullets sounded from the other back corner of the house.

Max jumped to his feet and rushed toward the kitchen. At the doorway, he spotted Carl hunched down below a cooking island.

"You all right?" he asked.

Carl nodded, then hand-signaled. There was one man down, another in the room.

Max checked the kitchen, its pots hanging from the ceiling, a mega-refrigerator shining on the back wall, a double stove beside it, and a double-sink to the other side.

He signaled he would rush into the left and for Carl to go to the right. Three fingers, two fingers, one—both men moved quickly, with trigger fingers ready. The gunman had gone.

"I've got two down in the den and one down in the dining room," Max said. "You've got one down here. That's only four of the six. I saw one disappear into the night out the front, and this guy went out this back door.

"We've gotta go get them," Carl said.

"First, we need more ammo. I've about used up my thirty-round clip."

Carl led the way back to the den, where he opened the cabinet containing the ammunition. Max grabbed two thirty-round clips and Carl took three ten-rounders.

"Okay," Max said. "We go out the patio doors from the living room and do a counterclockwise sweep around the house."

Carl nodded approval.

Max led the way outside onto the patio. He looked down at himself and chuckled. Never, ever had he fought a battle dressed only in pajama shorts and sneakers. He was glad the shorts were black. But if he died tonight, he certainly wouldn't go out looking like a great warrior.

Clouds had momentarily covered the half moon but now swept aside so moonlight again cast faint light into the darkness around them. Max turned left. The back-left corner of the house was fifteen feet away. He dashed straight there, with Carl a step behind, and peered around the corner.

He spotted no movement. A broad willow tree stood about thirty feet away.

"I'm sure they're waiting for us," Max whispered. "Follow me." He sprang for the tree as bullets thudded the ground around him. He saw the fire out of the barrels of two rifles—one from what appeared to be a low brick wall, the other from a mammoth bush near the driveway turnaround.

Putting a hand out against the tree to break the force of his rush, he turned and pressed his back against the willow.

Carl drew up beside him and squatted down. "I'm hit!" he gasped.

"Where?!"

"My left thigh." He groaned in pain.

228

"Let me see."

Carl pulled his hand away from the wound. They were on the western or shadow side of the willow. Once his eyes adjusted to the dark, Max could see the blood covering Carl's hand.

"Lie back with your knees above your head," he ordered.

Carl lay down and winced.

Max reached over his head and grabbed hold of a thin branch of the willow tree. Bullets split branches around him as he snapped off a length about two feet long.

"Our constable must be nearby by now," Carl grunted.

"Can't rely on that," Max said. He straightened out the branch like a rope and knelt next to Carl.

"Grit your teeth. This may hurt," he said.

Carl did so as Max tightened the branch around his thigh just above the bullet wound. The willow's super flexibility allowed him to tie it into a knot.

"Keep your leg up and lay here," Max said. "I'll handle these guys."

"Godspeed," Carl said.

Max nodded, then stood and turned his attention to the gunmen.

He peered around the tree at the brick wall, which was at one o'clock, and wondered if the gunmen had changed positions. Impossible to tell. Looking to ten o'clock where the bush stood, he could barely make out the gunman sixty to sixty-five feet away. The man was kneeling in a firing position.

To Max's left was the left-front corner of the house. If he went there, he would be exposed to the man behind the stone wall.

"Look out!" Carl hollered.

Max spun around and spotted a figure not forty feet away. One of the gunmen had gone around behind them. Just as a bullet hit the tree beside him, he pulled the trigger and a volley of lead sent the gunman to the ground.

Max looked down to Carl and gave him the thumbs-up.

One left—the man behind the bush.

"I'll head directly away," Max said, "trying to keep the tree between him and me, then circle around behind him."

"Good strategy, but watch out. There's a tiny mud pond in that direction."

"Mud pond?"

"Yes."

Max looked at his white upper body and legs and sprouted an idea.

He bent and took off his sneakers. Grasping them in his right hand, he threw them to his left, then spun to his right and sprinted away. The gunman fired at the sneakers.

Max raced away, jumped over the prone gunman and dove behind a hedgerow. There he saw the pond Carl had mentioned, the little bit of water in it reflecting moonlight. Setting down his AK-47, he stepped to the edge ol and sat down in the pool. He expected chilly, but instead the water was invitingly warm. With two hands, he slathered mud all over his body and face. Now, this was more like the battlefield.

A memory flashed of a black-ops mission in Kosovo when he went black-face on a full-moon night and Jackson, a black comrade, cracked a joke about Max trying to copy his buddy's "natural" good looks. He smiled at the thought and, for the moment, wished Jackson were here with him now. But, hey, Carl had fought admirably.

In a minute, he sprang to his feet and, bent over, looked through the hedges. Clouds again stole the moonlight, but he thought he spotted a figure behind the same bush; the man hadn't moved.

Bent over, Max raced along behind the hedgerow to his right until he reached the driveway. Again he peered through the hedgerow.

The man had shifted in Max's direction, obviously trying to get an angle to fire at Carl.

Between Max and the gunman was the golf green he and Kat had seen when they first arrived. A deep sand bunker curved around part of the green directly ahead of him, about thirty feet away. If he could get there, he could get a good shot at the gunman while staying hidden by the edge of the putting green. Holding the AK-47 tight to his chest, Max sprinted for the bunker and dove. Quickly rising up on his knees, he looked over the apron of the green. The gunman was slowly walking toward the tree, his rifle at his shoulder.

Max rested his weapon's barrel on the ground for support, aimed and pulled the trigger. Jammed! *Must be sand from the bunker.*

He looked up and saw the man was about twenty feet from the tree and closing. In a few steps, he would be upon Carl and, well—.

Max fought off fear for his friend's life and looked about him. A seven-foot-high flagstick in the green's cup was the only thing of substance he could see.

He stood and rushed to the flagstick, pulled the flag off to prevent drag, then gripped the pole about two feet from its bottom like a javelin. He looked up. The gunman was now close to the willow.

Max hefted the flagstick and felt that much of its weight, thankfully, was at the bottom by his hands. Taking a deep breath, he raced toward the gunman and, just as the man was about to round the tree, let the flagstick fly with a mighty heave.

Max shot a prayer heavenward as the "javelin" whistled through the air.

Hey!" he yelled, and the gunman turned in his direction just in time for the missile to penetrate his chest. The man's AK-47 fired a volley of bullets into the air as he crumpled to the ground.

The attack was over. Max hurried to the tree, stepped around the trunk and looked at Carl. "Six down, probably all dead," he reported.

Carl looked him up and down and chuckled. "Boy, are you a sight to behold!"

Max looked at his own mud-covered torso in the moonlight and laughed.

"Let's get back inside and find out where in the world the police are," Carl said.

"And order an ambulance for you," Max said.

"It's a through-and-through, I think," Carl said.

"Let's hope so. Especially if we're going to be golfing anytime soon."

Carl chuckled, then winced. "Don't make me laugh. Help me inside and we'll let the ladies know we're okay."

Max leaned down and grabbed Carl, pulling him to his feet. Carl strapped his SAK over his left shoulder, wrapped his right arm around Max's neck and they both walked slowly toward the back of the house.

Shortly, they turned the left-rear corner of the house and took several steps toward the kitchen door. Max was about to help Carl up the first stair when they heard two sounds—"pfft, pfft"—and a shriek of pain.

"What the—?" Carl began.

Max unwrapped Carl's arm and turned in the direction of the scream. Then Betty called out, "Don't worry, guys. It's just us women, helping clean up the mess from those noisy houseguests."

Kat's giggle trilled out of the darkness.

Light came on in the living room, sending a glow onto the deck, and Betty and Kat stepped into it, Betty in a blue housecoat, Kat in brilliant green pajamas.

Kat pointed toward the sea. Max looked in that direction and saw the shape of a man on the ground. He was groaning loudly. "They left a man behind, probably to drive the get-away boat," she said.

"But he was aiming a rifle right at you two when you came around the corner," Betty said.

"Betty went high and I went low," Kat said. "I think we both struck our targets."

Both women sported wide smiles as Betty held up her Insanity bow and Kat gripped the FireForce crossbow.

"What's that expression?" Betty asked.

"Girls rule!" Kat answered.

Max shook his head. "They certainly do."

"Thank you, ladies." Carl bowed low, then winced in pain.

Betty set down her bow and rushed to Carl's side.

Kat gazed at Max and said, "Is that a new look for you, soldier? The man's version of Victoria's Secret at the Mud Bowl?"

Max laughed. "I've actually never done this before."

"I'm surprised."

A police siren sounded nearby as if it were coming down the street.

"Will you call 911 and ask for an ambulance?" Max said to Kat. "I'll check on your, ah, target out here."

He took off toward the felled gunman and found him with a crossbow bolt embedded in his hip and an arrow lodged in his shoulder. The man was writhing on the ground, groaning and alternately trying to grab the hip and then the shoulder. He spotted Max and tried to reach for his rifle, which had fallen a good four feet away.

"My advice?" Max said. "Stay down. No seventy-two virgins awaiting you today, pal, just a cozy little Welsh cell. And you know what?"

"What?" the man managed to say through gritted teeth.

"It was two *women* who took you down, big guy."

The man cursed.

Max reached down and spun the man to his feet, then wrapped his arms behind him. Gripping the man's wrist in his right hand, he pushed him toward the house, the arrows sticking out of him like loose strands of hay from a scarecrow.

233

Seconds later, a police vehicle, lights flashing, screeched into the driveway and an officer jumped out.

Max, who had stepped inside the house and put on one of Carl's overcoats, and Kat met the officer, Max, now with Carl's rifle strapped over his left shoulder in case some other gunmen appeared.

Obviously wary of the appearance of two strangers, one with his face and arms covered with mud, the officer put his right hand on the handle of his service revolver and asked, "Where are the Sampsons?"

"Carl's injured, Betty's with him in the house and an ambulance is on the way," Max said. "Meanwhile, we have one terrorist tied up and needing medical attention as well, but there are a half dozen other bodies around the property. I don't think they'll need any attention at all—except from a coroner, perhaps."

Max and Kat led the officer through the front door and found Betty at work on Carl's leg. She had cut the leg off his pants to expose his wound and was dabbing on antiseptic with a cotton swab.

Carl flinched, gritting his teeth. "Too bad we don't have any whiskey in the house," he said. "That might help."

Betty chuckled. "A whiskey after all these years might just knock you out, husband of mine."

Carl grimaced. "Okay, but that sounds like a good idea, too." He looked at Max. "I gave up the stuff sixteen years ago when I met the Lord. Not only have I not had a drop since, we don't even keep it in the house."

"An infantryman like you? You don't need anything but a bullet to bite down on, do you?"

Carl laughed, then looked at the officer. "Hello, Tom. You've met our houseguests, Max Braxton and Doctor Kat Cardova. Max, Kat, this is Constable Tom Allen."

They all shook hands.

"And this fellow over here," Carl said, pointing to the corner of the room, "is the lone survivor of a group of men who invaded our home intent on killing us."

Constable Allen looked at the miserable specimen on the floor. His hands and feet were tied together behind him and a handkerchief was tied around his mouth.

"I had to shut him up," Max said. "All he would say was curse words and we have two ladies in the house."

Allen nodded. "I think I'll need some help," he said. Grabbing his radio, he clicked a button and said, "This is Constable Allen. Call in Inspector Davies and two off-duties, please, and ask Haverfordwest Station to send us any help they can spare. We've got six dead and one in custody from a home invasion at Sir Carl Sampson's house."

Max caught Carl's eye and asked, "Sir?"

Carl shrugged. "I don't like to advertise it. You discover true friends when you don't."

Sirens sounded in the distance, drawing closer.

Soon, three EMTs rushed to the house, Kat opened the door for them and they stepped quickly to Carl's side. None seemed to pay much attention to the man tied up on the floor with two feathered shafts sticking out of his hip and arm.

Chapter 17

While the ambulance whisked Carl to Withybush General Hospital in Haverfordwest, with Betty on board as well, Max and Kat stayed behind to answer questions from Constable Allen. Max took a few minutes to shower off the mud, and when he dressed and returned downstairs, there was a new twist to the investigation. Inspector Donna Davies had arrived and the inquisition began.

Probably because they were guests in Sir Carl's home, Allen had shown deference. Davies, not so much.

Police officers and a forensics team were inside and outdoors, investigating the scene, inspecting the dead bodies, photographing everything possible from multiple angles, and basically gathering evidence.

With all that action about them, the atmosphere in the living room was tempered.

Davies apparently worked alone. A tall blonde lady in her 40s, she looked a cross of Helen Mirren and Emma Thompson—totally in charge but elusively pretty. Dressed in a dark-gray, pin-striped pants suit, she spoke in staccato—short words and curt sentences. For Max, it was like listening to a female Jim Rome, the American sports radio jock.

"Who are they, anyway?"

"Islamic terrorists?"

"Here in St. David's?"

"Why after you?"

"What're you doing here?"

"AK-47, huh?"

"Got a license for that?"

"You killed before?"

"You a trained killer, sir?"

"Where were you, ma'am?"

"Doctor of what?"

"Forget the explanation."

"You house guests?"

"The Sampsons. They long-time friends?"

Her longest question: "Did you give these men a chance to throw down their weapons and surrender before gunning them down?"

Max and Kat had divulged their personal information, their meeting the Sampsons, the search upon which they had embarked, the fact they had been followed by danger, the Sampsons' alarm going off, and the monitor picking up a group of armed men bound for the house in the middle of the night.

Max finally narrowed his gaze on Davies, aka Mirren-Thompson, and said, "Why not call MI6's Christopher Hollingsworth, who right now is in Dublin, and ask him?"

Davies scoffed. "MI6? MI6!? You think a bit of good looks and a nifty little call to MI6 is going to get you out of this mess you've wrought? It's like Dodge City here. Talk about an American cowboy!"

"I'm not a cowboy," Max said. "Well, actually, I rode broncos as a kid." He smirked at Kat, noticed Davies wasn't smiling, so he put on a straight face. "But really, MI6 is investigating an attack in Dublin, where three gunmen tried to kill us—"

"That's right," Kat said. "We're the victims here, Inspector. Those men came armed to murder us."

"Hey," Max said, "doesn't the fact that Sir Carl and his wife were under attack too have any impact here?"

Davies took a step back and peered at Max, then Kat. Putting hands to hips, she squared her shoulders and, with piercing eyes, said, "Lords, sirs, dukes, princes, or paupers, I could give a spit. (That was Helen Mirren.) If you were Sean Connery or Harrison Ford, well, then, we could hop atop a horse and ride off together hand-in-hand into the sunset and let the credits tell the story of what happened here. (That was Emma Thompson). "I'll talk to the Sampsons at the hospital once I'm done with you two. Got it?" (That was Inspector Davies.)

"At least, call Agent Hollingsworth," Kat pleaded.

Davies puckered her lips, then a self-assured smile curled them. "And I suppose you have Hollingsworth's personal phone number handy, right?"

"As a matter of fact, I do," Max said.

Davies' eyes went wide and a look of massive disappointment covered her face. "You do?"

"In my cell phone in one of the guest bedrooms upstairs," Max said, pointing up.

"Which room is that?"

"Turn right at the top of the stairs, first door on the left."

Davies looked at Kat. "I suppose that's your room, too, Doctor?"

Kat shook her head. "Mr. Braxton and I are unattached. He's my—"

"Bodyguard?" Davies finished.

"No," Kat said. She looked directly at Max. "He's my partner."

Max felt like Kat had reached over, taken his hand in hers and pledged undying friendship. Now that was a nice warm feeling.

Raising an eyebrow, Max looked at Davies. Her shoulders sagged just a tad. He caught her eyes with his. There was Emma Thompson, interested, intrigued, and yet—

Davies turned to Constable Allen. "Bring back Mr. Braxton's cell and let's dial up this Agent Hollingsworth."

Allen nodded and hustled off.

After a few moments of silence, she turned to Kat. "So you dig dirt."

Kat smiled back at the slight. "And teach."

"Teach schoolkids about digging dirt?"

"They're Yale University students and much of it is about ancient cultures, signs, and symbols, what drove the people in those cultures. How and why we ended up where we are today."

Davies nodded. "And it's all in the dirt."

"You'd be surprised," Kat said with a grin. It was obvious to Max she was not going to let this woman of authority get her on edge or defensive.

"And you're the one who fired the crossbow." It was a statement.

Kat shrugged. "Well, I did fire a crossbow once before. Crossbows, bows-and-arrows, catapults, they're all part of warfare, and warfare isn't new to the 21st century. It goes back to those times that I dig up—'in the dirt,' as you say. Men have been fighting men since before Father Abraham's time."

Davies nodded again. "So today wasn't the first crossbow experience for you."

"No."

"Shooting a man. That come naturally?"

"I didn't have time to think about it."

"No?"

"No."

"Haven't considered it before?"

240

"Inspector, that man whom Betty and I wounded was pointing a rifle at Max and Carl—"

Constable Lewis came into the room at that moment, holding up a cell phone. "Found it," he announced.

He handed the phone to Davies.

"Check the contacts list," Max said, "It's alphabetical and you'll find Agent Hollingsworth there."

Davies clicked a couple of times, then started scrolling.

"Dudi Danino!" she exclaimed and peered at Max. "Israel's police commissioner?"

"An old friend," Max said.

More scrolling. "Alfred Fisher, FM? Does that mean 'field marshal?'" She turned a sharp look on Max.

"Yes."

"FM of where?"

"The Special Air Service Regiment of the Australian Army."

"Hmm." Davies looked back down at the cell and scrolled.

Suddenly she looked up with brow raised. "Justin Gruden? The head of the German Bundesnachrichtendienst?"

Max nodded and looked at Kat, explaining, "Their foreign intelligence agency. Justin actually helped mediate secret negotiations between Israel and Hezbollah for a prisoner swap."

"You involved?" Davies asked.

"Oh, no."

"Hmm." Davies continued to scroll though now it was apparent she was simply trolling, on a fact-finding mission about Max's friends and colleagues. Max felt uncomfortable about her gaining this amount of information.

"May I?" he asked and leaned forward, reaching for the cell. "I can find Hollingsworth and make the call."

Davies swung away from his reach. "Stand your ground, Mr. Braxton," she said and continued.

"Pierre Jacquier?!" Davies' eyes widened again and she looked at Max in disbelief.

"Now you've gone by the H's," Max said. "Hollingsworth comes before Jacquier. Please make the call, Inspector."

"Max," Kat said, "who's Pierre Jacquier?"

"He's the general in charge of the French Deuxième Bureau, which is involved in military intelligence."

"Did I miss Daniel Craig's name?" Davies snickered.

"Double-o-seven?" Max answered, playing it straight. "Never met the man."

"Imagine that," Davies said, then turned her attention back to the cell phone and pressed a name on the display. A moment later, she turned and walked away from them. After several minute's conversation, she returned and announced, "Agent Hollingsworth is catching an MI6 helicopter here as soon as he can get dressed and to MI6 HQ, where they have a helipad. He asked that we not take you into custody—either of you."

Kat looked up at Max, relief spreading across her mouth, and her left hand shot out to grab his.

Davies eyed Max. "Mr. Braxton, you must be a 'bad man.' Obviously, these six dead men scattered around the Sampsons' home would testify to that if they could. But I hope you're heading elsewhere and aren't planning to return here anytime soon."

Max shrugged and offered a crooked smile. "Sir Carl and I *are* planning to play a little golf sometime."

Davies lowered her head and shook it, then looked up and narrowed her eyes at his. "Then, please, let me know so I can take a vacation somewhere— the Lakes Region perhaps, or some place further. Spain, maybe."

"I hear the Costa Dorada is beautiful," Max said with a smirk.

Davies raised an eyebrow, let out a deep breath and handed Max his cell phone.

She turned her attention to Constable Lewis and said, "Let's see what the technicians have found out." She took two steps toward the shattered patio doors, then looked back over her shoulder and said dismissively, "You two are free to go. I'm sure, Mr. Braxton, that your pal from MI6 knows how to reach you."

Max looked at Kat, then back at Davies and said, "Thank you, Inspector."

Kat grabbed his elbow. "Shouldn't we get to the hospital and see how Carl is doing?"

"Sure," he said. "Our rental has a GPS. I'm sure it will lead us there."

It was five o'clock before Max and Kat arrived at Withybush General Hospital, a sprawling, three-story, modern structure. As Max parked the car, Kat looked around. The odd looking scene appeared to be asleep. With dawn an hour away, darkness enveloped the area and a handful of vehicles were interspersed throughout the visitors' parking lot. Street lights here and there glowed dimly. No one strolled the walkways.

When they entered the hospital, the reception area was empty. Kat had to ring an old-fashioned bell to attract help to the reception desk and find out where Carl was.

A very tired-looking young woman ambled down a long corridor and directed them to a transition room between emergency treatment and inpatient care.

When they arrived at the room, Betty motioned toward her sleeping husband and said, "They're just monitoring his vitals. The bullet went right through and missed the muscle altogether. So they sewed him up and gave him Vicodin. He's been sound asleep for an hour."

Kat placed a comforting hand on Betty's arm. "I'm so, so sorry we brought this attack on you," she said.

"No, no, no, dear." Betty shook her head and looked Kat in the eyes. "How could anyone have guessed those men would find you at our home? How in the world would they have tracked your travel on the ferry and then driving down to St. David's—especially without any of us noticing?"

"That's on me," Max said. "Of all people, I should have noticed. My guess is there is a source in the Dublin Police Department or MI6 or maybe even the Israeli police force. Either that or someone overheard us telling our MI6 friends where we were going.

"We were standing outside St. Michan's when that conversation took place," Kat said.

Max nodded, thinking it through, then said, "If St. David's were mentioned, it would have been easy to figure out we'd take the ferry. And if that's the case, someone could have been waiting for our arrival at Holyhead."

"But with all those passengers," Kat said, "how would they know what we look like?"

"A simple Google search would show a photo of you," Max said, "but I'm nowhere on the Internet—unless they hacked into a military site and any mention of me would be Top Secret."

"Oh, dear, dear," Betty said, patting Kat on the shoulder. "Have you not looked in the mirror, you two? One terrorist calls another: 'Mohammed, they're taking the ferry to Holyhead.' The other says, 'Okay, Mustaf, how do I recognize them?' Mustaf says, 'One's tall, dark, very handsome, rugged and could play the part of James Bond.'"

"There's that James Bond thing again," Kat said, elbowing Max and smirking.

Betty continued, "'And the woman?' Mohammed asks. To which Mustaf replies, 'A gorgeous redhead with green eyes who the men will all be swooning over as she walks down the gangplank.'"

"Betty," Max said, "you're the friend to have if anyone needs a boost of self-confidence."

"Or pride," Kat said.

"Pride?" Max asked.

"The pride from being called a James Bond."

"Or 'a dazzling redhead.'"

"Touché."

Max pointed toward Carl. "There's your James Bond, Miss Moneypenny. That's one brave man."

Betty beamed.

"He is," she said, "but usually before Parliament or in the bailey, not with bullets whistling all about."

"Well, when he knocked on my door, he didn't flinch about confronting those gunmen."

"He figures our home is his castle and you're our guests."

Kat wondered at the good fortune of befriending the Sampsons on board the ferry, then the memory of a few hours ago crashed in. She looked up at Max and said, "It was scary for us up there in the safe room. We could hear the bullets but had no idea if you were all right."

"We prayed," Betty said. "That usually settles my nerves, but not tonight."

"If you hadn't felt *un*settled, Carl and I could well be dead right now," Max said. "Thank God for anxiety."

"And for Betty's sure aim with her bow-and-arrow," Kat said with a wide smile.

"And you and that crossbow, Kat. And having only shot the thing once before last night!" Betty said.

A feeling of triumph washed over Kat and for the first time, she felt in awe of what had transpired.

She gazed at Betty. "You're so right. I can easily see you hitting that man, but what were the odds I would, too?"

Betty reached for a Gideon Bible laying on top of the bedside table. "I'm sure there are lots of explanations in here. I think you two have to look upon your search with new eyes. To see what you're doing as a mission—an assignment God has laid square in your laps."

Kat was caught short. "Why us?"

"Why not?"

Kat glanced at Max. He cocked his head and shrugged a *maybe*.

Max was returning to Carl's room, his hands filled with three coffees from a machine in the visitors' waiting area when the Marine Corps Hymn erupted on his cell phone.

Setting down the coffees, he pulled the phone from a pocket and Christopher Hollingsworth's face appeared.

"Max, we're at the Sampsons' house. Where are you?"

"Kat and I are at Withybush General Hospital in Haverfordwest. We'll get out of here and head back to you."

"Good. You'll want to know what we found out."

Ending the call, Max stepped into the hospital room. Carl was still asleep. Kat and Betty sat in straight-backed chairs chatting about senior colleges or some such thing. It sounded like Betty wanted to go on a dig with Kat somewhere.

He handed each of them a coffee. "I hope I got the orders right."

"As long as it's caffeine," Kat said.

"And hot," Betty said. "Anyone notice it's cool in here?"

"All I can say is the liquid is caffeine and certainly hot," Max said, shaking his left hand which had borne most of the heat from the cups.

Catching Kat's eye, he said, "We've gotta go. Agent Hollingsworth is waiting for us back at Carl and Betty's."

Kat rose out of her chair to go and Betty said, "As soon as Carl wakes up we'll be along as well."

"In an age of space travel, hospitals act at the speed of horseback," Max said with a chuckle. "We'll hope yours in Wales is a bit quicker in releasing patients."

Betty smiled up at him. "Sometimes the 'Sir' before your name can work minor miracles. I'm sure Carl wants to see you before you have to leave. But our house is yours until then."

Kat and Max both hugged her and went on their way.

Halfway on their drive westward back to St. David's, Max received a phone call. He checked the LED. It was Dudi Danino.

"Commissioner!" Max answered.

"Max, I've got news on three fronts."

Max punched the SPEAKER button and placed the phone between him and Kat.

"Fire away, Dudi," he said.

"I've got news about Doctor Arens and Gershon Zoref of the Temple Faithful; about the gunmen you took down at Dragot and Petra; and about the terrorists who are gunning for the people involved in the dig."

Max heard a rustling of papers, then Dudi said, "First, Doctor Arens awoke a few hours ago and is expected to fully recover while Zoref is out of critical condition. They're both thrilled about your search, but we've told them and anyone else to keep mum. The less anyone knows, the better. I've issued a command: there is to be absolutely no mention of the music to the media, family, friends, no one. Doctor Arens is ecstatic you've taken charge, Doctor Cardova."

Max looked at Kat, who sported a wide grin.

"Second, the man you took down at Dragot? The one you called Abu?"

"Yeah."

"His name is Nail Jabari. He and your two pals from Petra—Ahmed Tuma and Dawud Khouri—are all associated with a new terror group, Salah al-Din Brigades. It's named for Salah al-Din, the Sultan of Egypt and Syria who captured Jerusalem in 1187 and defended it during the Third Crusade from 1189 to 1192."

"Interesting choice of names," Max said. He glanced at Kat, who simply frowned.

"Jabari isn't talking and, no, Max, I can't leave him alone with you for a minute. You know how our courts bend over backward to protect these terrorists."

Max shrugged agreement.

"The head of Salah al-Din Brigades is a man named Mumim Maloof, a long-time terrorist whom we released from jail back in the nineties. He's been at the head of his class for awhile—from burning down a yeshiva school in Jaffa with the students and faculty in it to blowing up a bus on Ben Yehuda Street here in Jerusalem—and now has taken his 'rightful place' starting this group."

Kat winced and Max pulled off the road into a small parking lot. He grabbed her hand in his.

"This is the man who's after us?" Kat said.

Max raised and dropped his shoulders briefly. "That's the truth of it. Do you want to still go on or cut the bait?"

"I can not stop," she said, determination in her eyes.

"Then we will not." He squeezed her hand in reassurance and she squeezed his back.

Max looked back at the phone and said, "Sounds like this Maloof is cut right out of the cloth of Yasser Arafat. Got a wheelchair-bound Jew? Push him off the cruise liner into the ocean."

"Right down to Arafat's black heart," Dudi said. "Cross him and you're dead, no matter what blood you bleed—Arab or Jewish."

"You mentioned the others involved in the dig?" Kat asked.

Dudi breathed heavily on the other end of the call. "I can't fathom how such a new organization has such reach but listen to this," Dudi began. "One of them, Robert Goode of Tallahassee, Florida, was run down and killed in a hit-and-run accident outside his home yesterday. Another one, Susanne Paradis, was shot in the chest last night while shopping and is in critical condition at a hospital in Nantes, France."

Kat added her second hand to the grip she had on Max's. Tears started to flow. He handed a handkerchief to her. She took the cloth and dabbed at the corners of her eyes, but the tears didn't stop.

"We've contacted two others who went home: Baruti Aguda in Port Elizabeth, South Africa, and Arndt Brauer in Stuttgart, Germany," Dudi continued, "as well as Germany's SGS-9 and France's DCRG counter-terrorism authorities. Both agreed to provide protection."

Max shook his head. "Hard to believe this new organization would have cells in so many places. "Think of it. Ireland, Wales, France, America."

"We believe they're working hand-in-glove with ISIS, al-Qaeda and others of the same ilk," Dudi said. "Armed Islamic Group has been terrorizing people in France for more than thirty years and Islamic Jihad Group and others have been wrecking havoc in Germany."

A look of amazement crossed Kat's face. "These terrorists have no line they won't cross, do they?"

"Little old ladies, babies, newlyweds, old folks, it doesn't matter," Max said. He turned his attention to the phone. "You're looking for Maloof?"

"Correct, but he's staying well-hidden."

"We might eventually have to lure him out of his cave," Max said.

"Max," Dudi said, "what happened to your vacation? Your hiking trip to clear your mind for your book? Enjoying Israel for a few weeks?"

"It'll wait."

"Are you volunteering again?"

Kat shot Max a look—one that asked, "Volunteering *again*?"

"I may have to," he replied.

There was silence for a moment, then Dudi added, "There's one more thing."

"What's that?" Max asked

"The Livingston fellow—the one who was involved in the dig and got killed in Tel Aviv?"

"Yes?"

"Livingston had been in contact—for some time—with a number here in Jerusalem connected with YHVY Alpha YHVY Omega."

"God is the Alpha and the Omega," Max translated.

"Right."

"What's that?"

"An ultra-orthodox Jewish group."

"What do you know about them?"

"Very little, I'm afraid to say. We've tried to infiltrate them, but with absolutely no luck. They sniff out an undercover person like a hound does a fox. They may be a branch of Neturei Karta."

"Neturei—"

"Karta," Dudi finished. "They're religious Jews who believe the return of Jewish sovereignty to the historic land of Israel is integral to humanity's redemption and Messiah's coming. But they say our sovereignty is supposed to be under God's ultimate kingship, operating according to the Torah.

"They've opposed Israel's creation every step of the way. They've even stood with our enemies—from Arafat to Abbas to Ahmadinejad. By doing so, they're really serving the purposes of anti-Semitic propagandists everywhere."

"Oh, great." Max sighed. "So, do you think Livingston was an anti-Semite and when Doctor Arens found the music he contacted this Alpha-and-Omega group so they could stop him?"

"I can't yet say, but I'll keep you informed."

"Okay, Dudi. Thanks for keeping us in the loop on all this. But I have one more question for you."

"Yes?"

"Is there any possibility at all someone in your office could be sending information to these people?"

Dudi coughed out, "Never!" He hesitated and asked, "Why do you ask?"

Max told him about last night's attack.

"Only ears I trust explicitly have any knowledge of your whereabouts, or your mission," Dudi said. "If there is a leak, it's not from my headquarters, Max."

Max sighed and shared a look with Kat, then said, "Okay, Dudi. Thank you for all your help."

"Anything for you, Max. By the way, the PM sends his regards and asked me to keep him apprised of everything. And, Max, I trust *his* inner circle as well."

"Please tell him I look forward to seeing him again."

"Will do."

"Right now we're off to visit with MI6."

"These people are everywhere, Max. Watch your back."

"Later." Max clicked off the phone and looked at Kat. The sun had risen while they were speaking to Dudi and he could see her eyes were

251

red from crying.

She managed to say, "The PM sends his regards? As in the Prime Minister?"

"He's more than a Prime Minister to me," Max said. "He's a close friend."

Kat simply shook her head and smiled.

"We first met on a mission to recover two Israeli soldiers being held hostage. He was a commander with the Sayeret Matkal, the General Staff Reconnaissance Unit, which is a special forces unit of the IDF. Since I spoke Hebrew and Arabic and the mission involved both SEAL- and Ranger-type operations, they brought me on board."

Max grinned and added, "We certainly went different paths. I'm still a soldier and he's the Prime Minister of Israel."

"Israel is, by necessity, a military country," Kat said. "It makes sense having military experience carries more weight in politics there."

"The US Congress has just over one hundred men and women who are veterans," Max said. "That's fewer than one out of five. That's one reason I'm writing my book. More credentials, more qualifications to do the one thing the federal government is charged with doing: keep Americans safe."

"Preach on, soldier. I'm the choir," Kat said, her mouth firm, her face serious.

With the sun low in the sky, the sight around the Sampson house was much less daunting than when Max and Kat had left. Flashing police and ambulance lights in the daylight were less menacing than the middle of the night, but when they entered the driveway, there was a new focal point: a sleek black helicopter with the British Military Intelligence seal of a lion and a horse back-to-back and covered with a crown.

Kat had been napping since Dudi's phone call. Max tapped her on the shoulder and, pointing to the unmarked black whirlybird, said, "Our friends from MI6."

He pulled around a white van marked *Pembroke District Forensics* and parked the vehicle.

At the moment they stepped out of the vehicle, Christopher Hollingsworth exited the house, followed by Agents Stone and Lawrence.

Bookends usually come in twos, not threes, Max thought as he watched the three men. It was the same with American Secret Service; you could always tell them apart from the rest of humanity. Short-cropped hair. Tall. Virile. Broad-shouldered. Athletic-looking. Expressionless.

"If you can tell when two Mormons are coming to your door, you can do the same with these guys," Max said to Kat.

She chuckled.

"Well, Hollingsworth might have shattered the mold," Max allowed, but he felt this a minor one-person concession.

Hollingsworth broke a smile as he approached them. With a sweeping motion of a hand, he said, "You leave carnage wherever you go, Max."

"Can't help it. We had messy overnight guests."

"And how did you end up staying with Sir Carl and his wife?"

"A lovely couple. We met them on the ferry and struck up a friendship."

"Thought you'd bring some excitement into their lives, did you?"

"Chris, we had no—"

"Sort of a 'Welcome to my world of fun and guns.'"

"But we had no clue anyone would know—"

"'Sir Carl, we'd love to have a sleep-over, and just to prove our gratitude we'll have some pals over to liven it up.'"

"Chris, how would those men know we were here? Heck, we didn't know ourselves, not until we were nearing the end of the voyage."

Hollingsworth put his hand on his hips. "My guess?" he said, "Someone—a lookout probably for the guys who came after you in the crypts—followed you from St. Michan's."

"Or there's a leak in MI6." Max's gaze wandered to Agents Stone and Lawrence.

"Don't even think it," Hollingsworth cut him off. "I trust my men with my life."

"It's Doctor Cardova's and the Sampsons' lives I'm concerned with."

"Do you trust me, Max?"

Max didn't have to think this over. He and Hollingsworth had shared a life-or-death experience with one another. "Of course."

"Then trust my judgment about my men."

"If you say. But if someone followed us, he was a great tail. I didn't notice anyone. I'm afraid I was off my guard. Won't happen again."

Hollingsworth caught Max's eyes in his. "You did most of our work for us back there in Dublin. Those three gunmen were who they told you and they belong to a cell of a group called Salah al-Din Brigades."

"That's exactly what Dudi Danino just told us about the guys who attacked Kat in Petra," Max said. "They're like ISIS. We need a smack-down of these guys."

"Looks like you've had a good beginning," Hollingsworth said, spinning a slow look around.

"Do you have anything new?" Kat asked.

"The big guy in the St. Michan's crypt, Moosajee Issa, is the head of the Dublin cell. The local imam preaches death to the infidels—in other words, everyone but Muslims—overthrow of satanic governments, et cetera. He's clearly locked in as a supporter if not a member.

"Issa received a call on his cell phone from Israel at the same time you were on your flight from Petra to Dublin."

"Let me guess," Max said. "The call was from a burn phone."

"You're right. Not traceable, except we know what we knew."

"What?"

"The guy who pulls the strings is based in Israel."

Max and Kat walked the agents through what had transpired in the attack, taking them from the living room into the kitchen, then around the house behind the willow tree.

"Really, Max, using the branch of a willow tree as a tourniquet?" Hollingsworth shook his head in amusement. "Didn't you have a belt or something?"

"I was dressed in pajama shorts and nothing else," Max said with a shrug. "*Mater atrium necessitas.*"

Hollingsworth returned a vague expression.

"Necessity is the mother of invention," Kat interpreted. "Your friend's showing off, Agent Hollingsworth."

Hollingsworth smiled at Kat. "It's good you're around. This fellow needs some good education."

"Ha!" Max said. "And that comment coming from a Royal Military Academy alum."

"So, you nailed the terrorist with a crossbow?" Hollingsworth said to Kat, a look of awe on his face.

"Ma'am," Agent Lawrence cut in, "you get my award for best take-down of the year."

Kat grinned. "Why, thank you, agent. But Betty Sampson's arrow did most of the damage."

"Well, then, you can share the prize with Mrs. Sampson."

It was apparently Agent Stone's turn to come out of his shell. "I have a renewed respect for Sir Carl," he said. "For my taste, he was a bit too much of a stickler for regulations when he was counsel general of the Welsh Government. But after tonight? From what you've explained, Colonel, I'd take him on my team any day."

"So would I, Agent Stone," Max said.

"Listen, Max," Hollingsworth said, "what are your immediate plans and what can we do?"

"I haven't slept since—well, Dublin," Max said. "Neither has Doctor Cardova. So I think we should catch a few hours. And then—"

He looked at Kat for an answer.

"We're Israel-bound," she said.

"What's the best way to do that?" Max asked Hollingsworth.

A cell phone rang in Hollingsworth's holster, and he held up his index finger, motioning to wait a minute. When he turned the phone off, he said, "I'd take you with the copter right now to the airport at Cardiff. But the call was our director. We have an incident—one that demands we get back to Dublin ASAP."

"Anything to do with all this?"

"Don't think so. I'll let you know."

"Thanks again, Chris."

"What're friends for? Look me up when you get back to Ireland," Hollingsworth said. "As for now, the best way back to Israel? They've shut down the old airfield at Withybush in Haverfordwest. I'd catch a train at the station here, ride the rails to London and fly out of Heathrow."

Mumim Maloof got the word of the latest failed attack on Max and Kat from his lieutenant, Zafar Haik. Haik immediately ducked away from the lamp thrown at him.

"Must I do this myself?!" Maloof hollered. "Hamas and ISIS give us hundreds of thousands of dollars to train these men. We pay them to do a simple job and what is this? Is it not bad enough two of our warriors could not kill these Americans in Petra, then three others couldn't do the job in Dublin, then seven—*seven*—can't get it done in Wales?"

He kicked the leg of a chair. "Morons! All morons! If we didn't give their families twenty thousand dollars a year for them keeping quiet, they'd probably be spilling everything they know!"

Haik shrunk back from the onslaught.

"Get me Widad," Maloof ordered. "We will end this now."

"Widad is in America, Commander," Haik said, "embedded in our consulate there, gathering information for the attacks in Washington, DC."

"Do you think I don't know that!?"

Haik raised his eyes to look at Maloof. The Commander was often angry, sometimes livid, but this? What Haik saw on Maloof's face he had not seen before. He thought for a moment if he were within arm's reach of the Commander he would be dead by now—strangled, or his neck snapped, probably.

"We can spare him for a few days. A couple of days and Widad can take care of these two Americans."

"Yes, sir. I'm sure you're right."

Maloof peered at his lieutenant. "Listen, Haik, the quicker we deal with the Americans, the less will be known the world over. Snap off the head before the mouth can speak." He snapped his finger and thumb loudly. "Most important is to take out these Americans, to stop their search dead. The police have shut down the dig at Dragot for fear of us. Threats work. Terror works. Look how the United Nations voted to recognize Palestine as a state, immediately after we bombed Israel incessantly. Yes, for sure, terror works! And someday we will rule the world—Allah will rule the world—because of it."

Maloof crossed his arms. That normally signaled his rage had calmed. Haik took the cue and said, "I will contact Widad, Commander."

Chapter 18

The police and forensic crews had left. The Sampson's maid, Valerie, had heard the news and returned. Max and Kat found her, armed with a broom, dustpan, and vacuum cleaner, cleaning up the mess in the house. They joined in the clean-up.

Then, exhausted, they had gone to their bedrooms and caught some sleep. The last three days had reminded Max of a particularly grueling surveillance detail where he had laid under the desert floor tracking the maneuvers of a terrorist training camp for a raid.

The lack of sleep was similar on both missions, though he had to admit the heat was worse then, and he certainly didn't have a beautiful companion in the desert hole. Nope, Corporal Morris, a New England farm boy and a fine Ranger, but he certainly was no "looker," he laughed to himself. The poor kid couldn't get a date in a palm grove.

In the mid-afternoon, he heard a vehicle pull into the driveway and car doors shut. Then the vehicle left.

Max yawned, stretched, then pushed himself out of bed and dressed.

When he stepped out into the second-floor hallway, Kat was coming out of her room as well.

"Nice nap?" he asked.

She smiled a "yes."

They walked down the staircase and reached the bottom at the same moment Valerie opened the front door and Carl and Betty came through, Carl using a cane.

"Our guests!" Carl announced, looking excited they were still in the house. "And Valerie. You're supposed to be away." He hobbled to Max. Max extended his hand, but Carl walked past it and embraced him.

Beside them, Kat and Betty hugged.

"I'm starved," Carl said. "They didn't feed me anything edible in that place."

"They just wanted to get you out of there," Betty said. "National health's not such a great thing and the 'sir' thing didn't even help."

"No, it's not—and it didn't." Carl chuckled.

"I'll fix something up for you in a jiffy," Valerie said.

But Betty would have none of the idea. "Valerie, you get yourself away and take the day off like we planned."

"But—"

"But nothing, dear. Thank you for coming back." She looked around. "You've cleaned up well."

Valerie smiled and nodded toward Max and Kat. "With a lot of help. And I called Jacobs Glass and Coventry Carpentry. They'll both be over tomorrow."

"Excellent," Carl said and motioned with his arm. "Now go."

Betty announced: "Let's go down to The Farmers Arms and have a little food."

"If we do, there'll be lots of people surrounding you with questions you'll have to answer about last night," Max said.

"The Prime Minister called this morning," Kat said. "Asked how you were doing."

"Word spreads," Carl said.

Betty laughed. "Great Britain's a tiny country, darling. When a knight gets involved in a shootout, you'd better believe the police and MI6 let the PM know.."

Carl hesitated for a moment, then straightened his shoulders. "I haven't had a good story to tell at the pub in ages. I don't mind going center stage."

"Seems like our cue to catch the next train to London," Max said.

"No, please, be our guests," Betty said.

"Yes, yes," Carl said. "You need to relax for a few hours in the midst of this great adventure of yours. And St. David's is the perfect place to do so. Stay tonight and take the train tomorrow."

Max shrugged and looked at Kat. She smiled and nodded approval. "This *has* been a race, and I could use a pit stop, so to speak."

They heard a vehicle coming up the drive. Max leaned to his right to look out the window running full-length alongside the front door. "A black SUV with British government plates," he said. "Here comes your security, folks."

Moments later, Carl welcomed six men in black into the house.

The first man through the door, a tall red-head, held up a badge. "Special Police Force, South Wales. I'm Lieutenant Terfel," he proclaimed.

Maloof eyed Haik as the young man stepped behind Maloof's desk, reached to the bottom drawer and pulled out a satellite phone, which was the Salah al-Din Brigades' full-security phone.

He dialed a number. After a half-dozen rings, a voice answered. Haik put the phone on SPEAKER.

"Salam," the voice said in Arabic.

"Aleichem salam," Haik said. "The Commander wishes to speak to you,

261

Widad."

"I'm honored."

Haik held out the satellite phone to the Commander.

Maloof grabbed it. "Salam, Saa-hebi."

"Aleichem salam, my Commander," Widad said. "To what do I owe this honor?"

"I need you here," Maloof said.

"But, Commander, I've nearly completed plans. The ripe time to carry them out is close at hand."

"What I have you to do will take no time at all."

"Then can't another do it?"

"All have failed me," Maloof said. "I trust only you or myself to finish this."

"Finish what?"

"Kill two Americans."

"Cannot Gadiel do it?"

"No. I want *you*." Maloof cursed, then said, "This American! This American took down our two best men in Jordan. They had rifles and he? He had a knife and climbing hammer. One's dead and one's in critical condition in Al Ahli Hospital in Amman."

A moan came over the airwaves.

"Three of our best in Ireland had him and the woman trapped in a church basement in Dublin, and he conquered them using a sword, a dagger, and his fists."

A growl emitted from Widad.

"We sent our lieutenant in charge of Great Britain and six others—all trained in al-Qaeda camps in North Africa and Mali—and this man, along with a Brit, killed all but one of them, this time with weapons of their own. And there they captured one of ours. His orders, of course, are to take his own life as soon as possible."

"What do you know of this infidel American?" Widad asked.

"We can find out nothing. It is as if he is a ghost with no past. He is swine but a formidable swine. From our source, it appears he has ways to quickly make our men give up information."

Maloof heard Widad grumble. It was an angry noise.

"A torturer," Widad said.

"We don't know how, torture or not—but they sing to him like babies crying in their cribs."

The grumble was now a roar.

Maloof was certain he could hear Widad crack his knuckles, a sign his quick temper had already prepared him for the task.

A moment of silence followed.

"I must return here to Washington very soon," Widad said. "We kill the Republicans in Congress in six days—the seventeenth of the month. We're planting the bombs in four days and I'm leading that mission."

"Then prepare to leave," Maloof said. "We're tracking down the Americans. We have reason to believe they will be leaving Wales. We have people in St. David's, where this last attack took place, to spot and track them. And we have watchmen in Cardiff. Wherever that flight might be, we don't know."

"Unless I hear from you otherwise, I will fly to London," Widad said. "Then, at least, I will be near their heels. Don't worry, Commander. This I will do with pleasure, for the vengeance of my brethren." The voice was low, even, under control. Widad exuded confidence. Maloof smiled and hung up.

Lieutenant Terfel arranged for three officers to accompany Max, Kat, and the Sampsons into town while he secured the house and property

263

with the others in his detail. "We'll have to do something about that patio door," he said, pointing to the broken timberwork.

"The carpenter's coming tomorrow," Carl said.

Terfel looked around. "Given the broken windows and patio door, bullet holes in the walls, and furniture shredded by bullets, I'd say he can't come too soon."

"Oh, my couch!" Betty cried, walking into the living room. "And my pictures of the kids!"

Carl walked to her side and wrapped his arm around her shoulders. "We'll get it all back to right, sweetie. Don't worry."

Betty looked at him with a pained expression.

"You called the kids from the hospital?" he asked.

"Yes. Áedán wanted to fly home from Cambridge and Sophie, well, she's already on her way.

"No!"

"Yes, and you know there's no dissuading our girl."

"But we don't need her to interrupt her work."

"In her eyes, we always need her."

Carl shook his head. "Good thing she's the boss there, that's all I can say."

He looked at Terfel. "Do you mind if we go now? You can do what you need to do and we can get some nourishment."

Terfel nodded approval. "My men will be with you but will try to be invisible, to not interfere with your night."

"Fine," Carl said, then, looking the men over from head to foot, said, "I'd suggest removing your ties and looking 'pub-worthy,' gentlemen."

Max tossed car keys to one of them. "Probably a good idea for you to take our rental rather than the police vehicle."

They all left the house. Max, Kat, Carl, and Betty piled into the Sampsons' Lexus. The officers followed suit in Max's rental.

Under a blue sky that seemed to camouflage the chaos of the last fifteen hours, Betty drove into the quiet little city of St. David's.

Kat observed as they drove past stone houses and shops, some painted red or light blue or pale yellow, all seemingly in ideal repair. What a fine place! It was almost surreal, comparing this serenity to the experience the four of them had just experienced—from facing death to Carl being shot, and they had all walked away alive.

Betty parked in a little lot, and Kat and Max followed Betty and Carl on his crutches along a narrow brick sidewalk. In the distance were pasturelands, but here the sidewalk sloped downhill to a series of interconnected buildings. They reached a long white-stone, two-story building with two entrances.

Kat noticed the three officers, now looking less official, trailed them at a discreet distance, chatting amongst themselves like three blokes dropping by their local pub.

On the sidewalk, a three-foot-high placard with an array of colors declared: "Darts at 8 Tonight!"

Eight feet off the ground, between the doorways, hung a small sign announcing they had reached "The Farmers Arms." In the foreground of the sign was a black-faced ewe, in the background St. David's Cathedral and between the two, the blade of a scythe.

Being an expert in symbols, Kat smiled. The pub had captured the significant characteristics of St. David's to which they wanted their clientele to relate. Some day, perhaps, in a break between her archeological digs into the far past, she might do a study of modern semiology.

They stepped into the pub, an elongated room filled with long wooden tables and chairs. The dinner crowd obviously hadn't arrived yet, but several couples and foursomes were scattered around.

A streamer with tiny Welsh flags—a red dragon in front of a bottom half of emerald green and top half of white—was hung across the room, a foot or so below the wooden rafters. On the rear wall, a small chalkboard announced the week's specials: Beef and Yorkshire pudding, lamb shank, monkfish, and fish-and-triple-cooked chips.

At ease on his crutches, Carl led them through the large room toward a corner where there was a narrow corridor. A small sign with an arrow said, "The Glue Pot. "

"In here's the *real* pub, where the locals gather," Carl said, motioning for them to walk on. Inside, a fiddler was fiddling, a mandolin player was mandolining, and a pretty young girl was singing a soft, lilting song.

Rich dark wood made the room seem smaller. A bar ran along the right-side wall and a handful of men and women sat at bar stools drinking beer and ale.

Betty turned to Kat and said, "Must be warming up for the evening."

The bartender, a wide, jolly-looking man with a flamboyant mustache, noticed them enter and announced, "Our local hero: Sir Carl Sampson!"

All faces turned to look and three cheers reached the rafters.

Carl raised a crutch in acknowledgment.

"Thank you, Dylan, but the real heroes here are heroines." Placing a crutch in the crux of his arm, Carl waved toward Kat and Betty. "These ladies, armed merely with bow and crossbow, saved the men's lives at the end of it all."

The pub broke out into cheers and the girl at the microphone began singing, "For they are jolly good ladies, for they are jolly good ladies—"

Everyone joined in and finished, "for they are jolly good ladies and so say all of us!"

Kat couldn't help but beam and noticed that Betty did as well.

"I know you do not imbibe, Sir Carl," Dylan said, "so, in your honor, it's a round of non-alcoholic ale on the house." Another round of cheers rose up. The sound apparently was heard out in the main room and several people tussled with one another to squeeze through the tight hall into the pub.

Seeing them, Dylan said, "Drinks on the house in honor of Sir Carl and Lady Betty!"

When yet another round of cheers erupted, Kat grinned and looked up at Max. The message her eyes told him was "*This* is what draws people to Wales!"

The next hour was spent with Sir Carl mesmerizing a standing-room-only room with the tale of the harrowing night at the Sampson estate.

When he was done, questions flew and Kat noticed his answers had people shaking with excitement.

Kat leaned into Max, who stood beside her. "With a fine storyteller, vicarious living takes on a whole new dimension," she said.

Max grinned. "I'd say he has the Welsh equivalent of the Irish power of persuasion."

Standing in a corner, trying to be as inconspicuous as possible, stood two men—one slight of stature, the other beefy—highly attentive to what Sir Carl was saying. Each one wore a glare. This crowd was cheering the death of their comrades! Both were thinking, *Infidels! They should all die!* Both wished they had a bomb strapped to their chest at that very moment so they could pull a cord and kill all these heathen and, at the second of explosion, soar into Paradise where a bevy of virgins awaited them.

The beefy man, proud of his newfound faith and knowing that Allah approved deception when it was for His cause and the deceived were pagans, held a glass of Murphy's Stout in one hand, a cell phone in another.

He texted: "Found them!"

Moments later, the response flashed on his phone: "Keep track. Discover where they're going. Let us know."

He looked at his comrade and said in hushed tones, "Keep watch. That's all they want, Abdul. Keep watch and see where the Americans are going."

"Of course, Taweel," his friend whispered. "Widad The Assassin has been called in. He will deal with them. He may even behead them as a lesson for what they have done to our brethren."

Taweel grunted and turned his attention back to Max and Kat and the Sampsons. Women killers? They should be heavy with child, cooking for their families, knitting clothing! He wanted to spit out his irritation.

With pats on their backs from all their well-wishers, Carl, Betty, Max, and Kat made their way out a back door and onto a patio where tables were set for people wanting to dine outdoors.

More than a dozen others followed them out. Each table seated four people so the four new friends could have a bit of private conversation.

Max noticed the three officers took a table as did the two Arab-looking men who seemed to be hunters in search of game and didn't appear to be friends with anyone else in the pub. He made sure to sit in a position to keep an eye on them.

Carl pointed into the distance. "See the view of the cathedral from here.

The sun was hurrying toward the horizon and seemed to enshroud the cathedral in a hazy purple color.

"It's beautiful from any angle," Kat said.

Everyone agreed.

After a few moments to admire the view, Max asked, "What do you recommend from the menu?"

"The beef and Yorkshire pudding's to die for," Carl said. "Oops, that may have been a badly timed remark."

Max chuckled.

Betty tossed Carl a mock look of anger. "Carl Sampson, mind your sensitivity."

Carl shrugged.

"What do you recommend, Betty?" Kat asked.

"Hands-down, it's the fish-and-chips," she said. "They're the best in Pembrokeshire and that you can smell the sea while you eat the fish certainly helps."

They all ordered—the men choosing the beef and the women the fish-and-chips—and enjoyed their meals, but an uneasy feeling haunted Max.

As they sipped on mugs of coffee, Kat noticed and asked, "Is something wrong, Max?"

"Can't say," he responded. "Carl, do you recognize the two men seated over near the door to the pub?"

Carl pretended to look for the waitress, spotted the men and turned to Max. "Never seen them before."

"You, Betty?"

Betty, seated so she was looking at the men, quickly shook her head.

"Excuse me for a moment," Max said. He stood up and Kat grabbed his elbow.

"Please don't do anything dangerous," she pleaded.

"Not me," he said. "Just going to the men's room."

Max shot her a wide smile which seemed to relieve her, then stepped off toward the pub. As he approached the door, he scratched his nose, using it as a way to check out the two mysterious men. The burly one was in his early thirties, the skinny one a bit younger. The hefty one sported a full beard, the thin one wore a scruff. The beefy one looked angry, the scrawny one appeared ill-at-ease. The closer Max got to them, the more uncomfortable the thin one appeared.

As he drew next to them, he coughed loudly. The little guy jumped in his seat. This was fishier than what was in the fish-and-chips.

Max stepped into the pub.

Taweel, trying hard not to look at the American, wondered where he was going, then guessed he was headed to the men's restroom.

He turned to Abdul and said, "So Widad is called for the mission and he will get the glory. His family will get the honor. What of my glory? What of my family's honor?"

"Your time will come," Abdul said.

"Not soon enough," Taweel shot back and rose out of his chair.

Abdul reached for his arm, but Taweel pulled away.

Max pushed open the men's room door immediately to the right. There was no one inside. Seeing spare rolls of toilet paper on a shelf, he grabbed one, then swept his belt out of his trousers while walking to the center of three urinal stalls. There he stood and waited.

After a moment, the door swung open and in stepped Taweel. Max stood rod-straight and pretended to read the bulletin board in front of him. The latest scores and standings of the Wales Rugby League, along with a feature story on St. David's own fly-half, Fane Gibbons.

Max watched peripherally as Taweel glanced his way and entered the room. He was six steps away—as well as a mile when it came to hand-to-hand combat.

Max squeezed his left hand inside the roll of toilet paper, grasped his belt in his right hand and drew a deep breath. Taweel took one step in Max's

270

direction as if heading toward a urinal, then another step, and another. Max turned his head just enough to see out of the corner of his eye. He noticed as Taweel reached his right hand behind his waist. When Taweel made a hasty move, Max spun around to face him, obviously surprising him.

Taweel held a serrated hunter's knife, its blade about six inches long, in front of him. Max looked in Taweel's eyes and read determination mixed with fear.

Taweel's face then twisted into a mask of hate, and he stepped directly at Max and slashed at him. Max blocked the knife with the toilet paper, then snapped the belt like a whip, smacking Taweel's hand so hard, he dropped the knife to the floor.

Taweel bent down to retrieve the weapon and Max lifted a knee that caught him squarely on the nose. A nauseating "crack" announced he had broken the nose and blood spouting from Taweel's nostrils punctuated the fact. Taweel's head snapped back and he landed on his buttocks. He was clearly in a daze.

Max kicked the knife across the floor into a stall. With one swift move, he spun around behind Taweel. He grabbed one hand and then the other and yanked Taweel's arms behind his back. Swiftly, he curled his belt around Taweel's wrists—three, four, five times—then tied it off in a knot.

Just then the door opened. Max looked up and Abdul walked in. When the skinny man saw what had happened, his eyes went wide and he twirled around to rush back out the door. But Max did a half-turn and kicked sideways, catching the man on the side of his head and crashing him into the door. He fell instantly to the ground.

Someone started pushing at the door but met the resistance of Abdul's moaning body. Max pulled Abdul out of the way. In the doorway stood the biggest of the three plainclothes policemen, his nameplate announcing he was Ian Maddock.

Maddock knelt beside Abdul, showed him a badge, then asked, "Going somewhere?"

Groggy, Abdul shook his head. "Guess not," he said.

Maddock looked over Abdul's head to where Max stood in front of the slumped-over Taweel.

"Sergeant Maddock here," he identified himself. "I'd say I've got clean-up duty, Mr. Braxton."

"That would be very kind of you, sergeant," Max said.

Maddock pushed Abdul against a wall and handcuffed him. Holding Abdul with one hand, he went out the door and called to his fellow officers.

As he did, Max walked up close to Abdul and asked, "You're with Salah al-Din Brigades, am I right?"

Abdul did not respond, but reading his eyes, Max knew he was indeed connected to the terror group.

Somehow word of the action spread around the tavern and out in the patio and a crowd started to gather.

"Police!" Maddock declared. "Stand aside. Please stand aside!"

Max stepped back and allowed the officers to do their duty. Another officer came in, handcuffed Taweel and tossed Max his belt. Then he and Maddock took Taweel and Abdul into custody, through The Glue Pot, the front room and outside, while the third officer stayed behind.

By then, Kat, Carl, and Betty had joined the people crowded in a circle by the patio door. Max smiled and waved to them.

The officer who was left behind looked at Carl and asked, "Sir, can I catch a ride with you when you return home? Seems my seat in the squad car is taken by a couple louts looking for trouble."

Max exited the men's room to a volley of cheers—the bartender, Dylan, obviously feeling chipper about the excitement, offered another round on the house.

Max, Kat, Carl, and Betty returned to their seats and ordered another mug of hot coffee.

"Can't take you anywhere, can I?" Kat said to Max with a smile. "Who were those guys?"

"I spotted them when we sat down. I think, folks, the men who attacked us at the house weren't the only ones wanting us dead. That big brute had a knife and intended to carve me up."

"Didn't work out for him," Carl deadpanned.

"Nope, but I was at an advantage."

Carl looked surprised. "What was that?"

"Looking at him reminded me of the words of the Happy Warrior: 'Who, doomed to go in company with pain, and fear and bloodshed, miserable train! Turns his necessity to glorious gain.'" Max paused, then added, "This man, in mortal fear, was neglecting that trepidation in order to gain glory for himself."

"I've always thought, in combat, fear is weakness," Carl said.

"There's fear and there's healthy fear," Max said. "The kind you give in to can kill you, or, perhaps, save you."

"Well," Betty interjected, "I fear I haven't slept in—" she checked her wristwatch, "well, I don't remember. And here I am drinking coffee. Thank the Lord it's decaffeinated."

"I hear you, dear," Carl said. "Let's head home."

Carl removed a credit card from his wallet and lifted it toward their waitress, but she raised her hands. "Oh, no, Sir Carl, tonight's meal for your party is on the house. Dylan wanted to thank you for—how did he say it?" She squared her shoulders and raised up on her toes to a new height, then continued in a deep voice, "for 'bringing honor to the entire community of St. David's.'"

273

Carl smiled broadly. "Well, then," he said, "please take this as a tip, my dear, for being so helpful tonight." He handed her a large-denomination bill.

On their way through The Glue Pot, Carl personally thanked Dylan, whom he told Max and Kat was The Farmers Arms' owner as well as bartender.

Once on their way home, Max turned to Kat, who sat between him and the officer in the back seat. "I think we ought to head out tonight," he said. "It appears the longer we're here, the more danger we're putting Carl and Betty in."

Carl turned in his seat, "No!"

"I'm afraid he's right, Carl," Kat said.

"But—" Betty began.

"We've brought you nothing but trouble," Max said. "Not the way to treat friends."

"Well, the 'trouble' was more excitement than we've had in ages," Carl said.

Kat brought her iPhone to life and went on-line. In a moment she looked up and said, "There's an eleven-o'clock train out of St. David's, arriving in London at ten tomorrow morning."

Max looked at his wristwatch. It was 8:48.

"Plenty of time," he said. "We can grab our things at the Sampsons', but I don't know about the rental car."

"We can take care of that," Carl said.

Betty added, "We'll drive you to the train station tonight and handle your rental tomorrow."

"But—" Kat started.

"But nothing, dear," Betty said. "Let us do our part in your wonderful mission to find David's music. We *will* benefit from it, after all."

Betty had settled the matter.

Chapter 19

Max, Kat, Carl, and Betty all stood at the Ariva Train Station in Haverfordwest. Besides the three officers standing nearby, keeping a watch out, only a handful of people shared the station with them. The train to Cardiff and then London idled on the tracks, waiting for the few travelers to board.

Max smiled broadly at Carl and Betty, sure they would be eternal friends. He shook Carl's hand and hugged Betty. "Thanks for taking care of our rental car— a huge help."

"No problem," Betty said.

"You're our lifesavers—in more ways than one," Max added.

"Goes both ways," Carl said.

"But the ladies *do* rule, don't they?" Betty said with a smirk, wrapping an arm around Kat.

"Oh, yes," Kat said. After a pause, she added, "You know, there's a lot of evidence the women warriors of the Amazon were not a myth at all."

"Ever the professor," Max deadpanned.

"I know if I were choosing up teams to go to battle with, after Max, I'd pick you two ladies," Carl said. "You and your ancient weapons."

A whistle sounded and "All aboard!" came the call from a conductor a few feet away.

Max grabbed Kat's duffel bag as well as his own and stepped toward the train steps.

"Give us a ring when you can come for a stay," Carl said.

"And plan for the visit to be awhile, too," Betty said, "not just some overnight pass-through."

Max waited for Kat as she gave Carl and Betty one last embrace. When she held Betty tight, Max noticed her whisper something into Betty's ear.

When Kat scooted up the steps to join him, Max asked, "What's your secret with Betty?"

Kat flashed a demure smile. "It's called a secret for a reason, soldier. Let's just say, we have a plan."

Moments later, as they settled into their seats, Max checked his wristwatch: 10:58 p.m. and the departure time was 11:00.

"Gotta love trains in the UK and Europe," Max said.

"They'd *better* be on-time," Kat said. "This train takes us into Paddington Station. We have to catch another from there to Heathrow, which takes twenty or thirty minutes if I remember correctly. And I've booked us on a flight from Heathrow to Tel Aviv at twelve-thirty."

"Efficiency, thy name is Katherine Cardova," Max said.

"Efficiency, thy name is Colleen O'Hara Cardova, my mother. I learned from the best."

"O'Hara, eh? So that's where you get the red hair—a bit of the Irish."

Kat nodded.

"I'd like to meet your Mom."

"You'd have to travel to the Midwest."

"Then we could go down to Dallas and visit my mother."

"Is this an editorial 'we'?" Kat tilted her head and sported a mischievous look.

Max caught her eyes in his. "Not since Patty Littleton in the fifth grade has any girl been good enough for me, in my mother's eyes," Max said.

"And not since Larry Burkett in the third grade has any boy been good enough for me, in my dad's eyes," Kat countered.

"Then you have a two-grade advantage over me."

"You jest. I grew up on a farm—I've always been two years more mature than my classmates."

"I grew up on a ranch—I've always been three years the elder to my classmates."

Kat crossed her arms. Max could see the wheels churning. Finally, she said, "I believe you're older than me."

"I'm sure. Forty-two beats you by six or eight years."

Kat chuckled. "You won't get my age from me that easily."

A couple of hours later, Max was having difficulty sleeping. Sitting in the aisle seat, he could stretch his long legs but he couldn't get his mind to shut down from the peppering of questions —about these assailants, the music, the danger this girl beside him faced. He looked at his watch. 1:25 a.m. There was a long way to go. He turned to look out the window and noticed Kat was awake and tears flowed down her cheek.

He touched her forearm. "What is it?"

She shook her head and waved her hand. "Nothing."

"Do you want to talk about it?"

"I can't." She hesitated, then added, "I'm okay. Truly."

Max nodded but said, "You don't need a degree in body language to decipher tears, Kat."

She swiped, double-palmed at the tears at the corner of her eyes.

277

Finally, she said, "Memories. Memories that sometimes bring nightmares."

"Whoa! Kat, I'm familiar with nightmares. I had to go through psychiatric debriefing for a time when nightmares plagued me every night—after one very bad mission went very wrong and I lost two close friends."

Kat sniffed and looked at him, her eyes flickering against the tears. "Really?"

"Really. Certainly helps to talk about it."

She turned her body toward him and began, quietly, "Nearly costing Betty and Carl their lives brought back my worst memory—the one point in my life I doubted God and hated myself."

Max remained silent, knowing to simply let the story flow.

"I was seventeen and a junior in high school. My twin sister, Kaitlin, and I went to a dance together, as singles."

Surprised, Max couldn't help but blurt out, "You have a twin sister?"

Tears suddenly flowed more freely, and Kat gulped for air. Wanting to kick himself, Max put an arm around her shoulders.

A young couple two seats ahead of them and on the other side of the aisle apparently heard Kat's weeping and turned around, concerned. Max motioned that everything was okay.

A minute later, Kat could continue. "I *had* one. Twin sister and best friend. I was always the straight-laced one and Kaitlin the wild one." She stopped a laughed lightly, wiping away a tear. "But we were close— oh, so close."

Kat told Max about staying behind to clean up, about asking her old boyfriend to drive Kaitlin home, about hearing of the accident.

"If not for me, Kait would still be alive today," she said.

"You're shouldering full blame," he objected.

She nodded.

"Not sharing a drop of it with the boy," he said.

"He would have been alone in that car if not for me."

"If you had superhuman foresight."

"He'd been drinking. I didn't recognize that."

"Nor did Kaitlin, apparently."

She shot him a look of anguish.

"Have you asked God for forgiveness?"

"God. Kait. My parents."

"And?"

"God and my parents forgave me."

"But you didn't and haven't."

A fresh swell of tears.

"Have you thought that by not forgiving yourself, you were putting yourself in a higher position than God?"

She looked at him, startled. "No!"

"I'm far from being an expert, Kat, but isn't this how Christianity works. It's God, Jesus Christ, the Holy Spirit up here," he held above his head, "and all us creatures down here." He held a hand at chest level.

She nodded and bowed her head, put her hands together and rested her chin on them, her eyes closed.

Max dared not push any further; not now. He just waited for her to process her emotions.

A couple of minutes ticked by, seeming like hours. Max felt like he was in a hospital room, waiting for a beloved and injured friend to wake up from a coma.

Finally, Kat chuckled and sat up straight, looking at him. Then she lifted her left leg over her right knee and pulled up the leg of her slacks to expose a purple and yellow striped sock. She pointed, then set her leg back down and lifted her right leg over her left knee, exposing a dark-blue sock with tiny red stars.

279

She wiped another tear from her cheek and sniffled. "I'm sure you've noticed," she said.

Max nodded and raised an eyebrow, expecting an explanation.

"This is my constant reminder of my sister," Kat said. "It was her trademark. That and wearing mismatched pajama tops and bottoms."

Max laughed.

"I wear them now so whenever I look down at them, I remember Kait, how I loved her, how I miss her still."

"Now I understand," Max said. He thought for a moment, then added, "But, Kat, doesn't wearing those socks continue to make you pick at a terrible scab? Doesn't the mismatch hold your attention to something you can't forgive yourself for? That is until you do?"

Kat's eyes flashed. Anger? Pique? A "don't-judge-me" look? Max held his breath.

Kat didn't answer. Instead, she said, "I need some sleep," and turned her head toward the window and the darkness beyond.

A half-hour later, lights started appearing along the landscape, and the train began to slow. They must be in Cardiff, Max thought. He turned to look out the window. Kat was still sleeping.

When the train stopped, she opened her eyes, looked outside and pointed. Lit up by streetlights and little else was a great hulking structure.

"Millennium Stadium. Opened back in 2000, therefore, the name."

"Great soccer there, probably."

"And rugby."

As passengers got off and others stepped onto the train, Max said, "I'm sorry, Kat, if I was too personal with you, if I infringed in any way."

She shook her head. "I opened up. I asked for it, Max. You gave good advice. Great advice. I know God forgives. What you said about me putting myself in His place? That stung, but I thought about your point before I went to sleep and I know you are right. Nevertheless, I can't focus on this right now. I'm going to have to take time alone with God soon and give Him this burden of guilt and allow Him to remove the pain and heal me."

A vision of his friend Vic, dying in Max's arms, flashed, along with his mind's continued needling he could have saved his comrade's life if only his reflexes had been quicker when the sniper first fired on them. Had he forgiven himself, like he'd told Kat she should forgive herself? No, he'd simply driven those thoughts into a dark abyss somewhere in the back of his mind. The memory was like a Jack-in-the-box; Jacks popped out at the most unexpected moments, none of them ever welcomed.

After just a few minutes, the train began chugging along, then quickened its pace. Soon they were whizzing past a small downtown area and were quickly on the outskirts.

Kat was still tired, but thankful she had had the talk with Max. That a person who had slipped softly off the path of Christ could direct her toward Him, at once discouraged her about her own walk but encouraged her Max was a lot closer to the Truth than he thought.

Suddenly he raised an eyebrow and, in a Scottish brogue said, "Well, it was nice to see Cardiff, eh, lassie?"

She smiled. "That's Scottish."

"Can't do Welsh," he said.

"You might have noticed when they speak English, they sound exactly like someone from the Northeast—Maine perhaps."

"I did notice."

Just then a conductor walked by.

"Everything all right, folks?" he asked.

Kat looked at Max and said, "See? Sounds just like a Mainer."

He held up his hands. "I can't argue, professor. Never been there."

"Too bad," she said and then turned to the conductor. "We're doing fine. I was just thinking about my one visit to Cardiff."

"I hope she treated you with utmost hospitality," he said.

"It *is* actually a pretty little city. Takes you back a couple centuries—" she said.

Max obviously sensed her hesitation and asked, "Is there a 'but'?"

"Well, I was in a nice little bed-and-breakfast in the center of town, right near Centre Church where they had the revival back in the early 1900s Carl and Betty were talking about—"

"Yes?"

"A Saturday night and I was kept awake deep into the night by police sirens. I looked out the window once and they were filling paddy wagons with rowdy people."

"That's true," the conductor said. "Happens all the time."

"I'd never even seen a paddy wagon, except in the movies," Kat said.

"Cardiff is my hometown," the conductor said, "and I've heard stories about the great Welsh revival. Yet here we are, just over a hundred years later, and we're back in the same boat: drunken revelry and sin."

After a moment's pause, he asked, "You two are American?"

"Yes," they responded.

"I love America. Got family over there. They all tell me they want to come home to the old country where they won't be taxed to death. I tell 'em, 'You're taxed everywhere—even for the Internet now, eh? Come home for the love.'" He smiled and started to walk on. "Have a good trip, folks. Let me know if there's anything I can do for you."

Widad Said shut the window shade to keep the early-morning sun out of his eyes and sat rigidly in his first-class seat, trying to avoid contact with the man next to him. The man was not just a Westerner but a cowboy like the murderer George W. Bush, judging by the hat he had worn into the airplane. Widad did not even want to exchange pleasantries with this man.

In fact, the disgust he had been building for one of the targets of his assassination, this Max Braxton, he now transferred to this man sitting next to him. The woman? Cardova? She was simply an afterthought, an easy mark. But indeed, he might just kill this man for practice—that is if Widad disembarked in London in time to catch his connecting flight to Tel Aviv.

Widad scratched his beard and smiled to himself. He pictured walking into a restroom behind this man and, well, strangling him to death. Widad had no "weapon." His hands were a weapon and they were deadly enough. Deadly enough for a cowboy. Deadly enough for an infidel. He had proven that enough times.

To be sure, it was this effectiveness that had won Widad the right to first-class travel wherever he went. He had earned the privilege. Wasn't he the Master Assassin? Wasn't he the one they always called when the task was too difficult for anyone else—and perhaps even for the Commander himself?

Widad puffed out his sizable chest. Ever since he was a boy and saw his father cut down by an Israeli bullet, he had wanted to make a difference for his people.

In the wake of his father's death, as a child, he had helped lift mortar shells into the hands of the men firing them. He prayed to Allah that each shell would kill a Jewish family—especially a Jewish soldier and his or her family.

He had listened well in school when his teachers told him and his classmates the best way to die was as a martyr, killing Jewish swine.

283

When they told him the Jews wanted to kill the Prophet Mohammed, he listened.

When they told him the Jews wanted to kill his Muslim brothers and sisters, he listened—and fumed.

When they told him to curse the Jews and pray, "Oh, God, destroy the Jews," he did so—with vehemence.

When taught to praise the feda'i (guerillas) and the shahid (suicide martyr), he did so—with gusto.

When his older brother painted a mural of Muslims stomping a Jew into the ground, he added the red blood to the artwork.

As his friends walked into their schools, he was the child who read over the loud speaker: "The sound of stones is the sound of anger. Little hands are carrying stones to challenge aggression. His blood is calling for a holy war."

Widad was cheered on by his mother and other adults as a model for other boys to follow.

As a ten-year-old, he was featured in a video that went viral over the Internet in the Muslim world. In the garb of a Fatah fighter, he declared, "Heroes of Gaza, you were victorious; you were not defeated when you forced the enemy to withdraw in humiliation. You were victorious; you were not defeated when you refused to surrender to the accursed Jews. Judgment Day will not come until the Muslims fight the Jews, and the Muslims will kill them, and the Jews will hide behind stones and trees. And the Holy Quran tells us the stones and the trees will call out: 'Oh Muslim, O servant of Allah, there is a Jew behind me. Come and kill him—except for the gharqad tree, which is the tree of the Jews."

In seventh grade, when taught the poem, "The Shahid," he read the words: "I see my death and I rush toward it." But he had hesitated and thought *Why die when I could continue killing?*

His favorite game as a teenager was called "Jews and Arabs." The Jews were actually bags filled with hay, and the Arabs were in the streets shooting at the Jews and throwing stones and bombs at them. It was all good practice for real life—and fast fun, to boot.

He hung photographs of suicide bombers on his bedroom walls as his heroes. But he aspired not to kill just once and, therefore, kill himself, but to do even better, to kill again and again. "Why just once?" he asked.

In September 2001, when An-Najach University in Nablus held a celebration of the suicide bombing of the Sbarro restaurant in Jerusalem, which killed many Jews, Widad was there, smiling with his friends and neighbors.

He remembered picking up what was supposed to be the entrails of a Jew and screaming, "If I starve, I will eat the flesh of my usurpers! Beware of my hunger and my rage!"

His declaration drew cheers from all around him, and he had reveled in it. And yet again he wondered, *why be a suicide bomber and die with the Jews? Why not live and continue killing?*

When Yasser Arafat said, "If anyone is growing weary, let him stay home and send me his children," Widad, fatherless, set himself free to join the cause of freedom from the Jewish pigs.

When Arafat said, "The child holding the stone and facing the tank, is he not the greatest message to the world? When that hero becomes a Shahid and dies for Allah?" Widad thought *Not a stone but an anti-tank rocket launcher, I'll hold.*

When Arafat said, "The new generals are our boys," Widad took the statement to heart. He would become a great leader.

When an infidel pointed out to him as a teenager that his hero Arafat had pilfered millions of dollars from the Palestinian cause and stored it in a personal French bank account, the claim did not dissuade him. In fact, he sought revenge for the statement by killing the man's son. The boy was his first offering up to Allah.

When taught to hold a rifle in order to kill Jews, he learned and excelled at firing it.

Then, when an Arab neighbor said he thought the Palestinians should continue the fine businesses left behind by the Jews who had been forced by the Israeli government from their homes in Gush Katif in Gaza in 2005, Widad nodded as if considering the idea. Then he swiftly beat the fellow within an inch of his life. The man never uttered such treason again.

He had trained in the "summer camps" funded by the United States and United Nations, who thought they were times of games and swimming. In fact, they were camps for paramilitary training and Widad learned his lessons well—better than any other.

His was the head upon which the honors were laid. And his were the shoulders upon which Hamas called to bring vengeance on the little Satan, Israel, the big Satan, America, and the rest of the infidel world who did not submit to Islam.

So, here he sat, in first class next to this cowboy. Widad noticed the man wore a wedding ring, which meant he was spawning more of the same. He growled, which drew the man's attention.

Widad checked his wristwatch. Would they land in London in time for Widad to snuff out this man? Then it occurred to him if he did so, he could very well spoil his mission. Someone might find the dead body, the police would be called in and they might shut down departing flights to question travelers and hold them all until they found the killer.

He turned his gaze on the man and asked, "Where are you from?"

"Oklahoma."

"I'd guessed Texas."

"Nope. From Nebraska, living in Oklahoma.

"You're a cowboy?"

The man laughed, then caught himself short. "Well, you could say that. I raise cattle—all-natural, grain-fed, premium Angus beef. Here." The man reached in his coat pocket and passed him his business card.

Widad looked it over and smiled. The card announced the farm was a family operation. He pocketed it. Some day he might just take a vacation to Lindsay, Oklahoma, and have some fun with an infidel and his children.

Exactly at ten o'clock, the train pulled into Paddington Station, a large, bustling place. As Max looked out the window, he was reminded of Central Station in New York City. In New York City, of course, people absolutely *raced* at breakneck pace from one train to another or onto the streets. Here they merely *rushed*.

"This is an example of 'the London minute,'" he said with a chuckle.

"Exactly twice that of a New York minute," Kat said.

Max and Kat grabbed their bags and hurried off the train.

"You seem to know where you're going," Max said. "I'll follow you."

In a few minutes, they were on an express train to Heathrow, Kat settled into a seat and Max clinging to a vertical bar.

"Fifteen minutes and we're at Heathrow—Terminals One and Three," Kat said.

"Which terminal is ours?"

"Terminal One."

Max checked his watch. 10:09 a.m. Would they ever have time to spare when connecting to plane or train rides?

Widad disembarked from the airplane, scowling one last time at his cowboy neighbor, who was walking away in the opposite direction as quickly as his feet would carry him. Widad had to get to the far end of Terminal 5 and catch a people-carrier to Terminal 1. He had a seat aboard KLM Royal Dutch Airlines Flight number KL0462, departing at 12:34 p.m., hopping to Amsterdam in half an hour, then on to Tel Aviv, a four-and-a-half-hour trip that would drop him at Ben-Gurion International Airport in Tel Aviv at 7:40 p.m.

At first, he had fumed he was losing so much time from his most important mission ever to assassinate this irritating American man and woman. But then he thought of the pain this man had caused his comrades and the pleasure he would derive from watching his last breath before departing this earth for hell.

He walked at a brisk pace to the monorail, which would carry him to Terminal 3, then on to Terminal 1 in this interminable airport. In a quick twelve minutes, along with a crowd of other people babbling in various languages, he set foot in Terminal 1—a large, square structure lined with various shops on three walls and the check-in lines on the fourth. He glanced at his watch. Two hours to flitter away. How he hated wasted time—the one thing you could never recover. Once it was gone, it was gone—pfft!

He decided to make the best of his wait. Spotting a small Harrods store dropped right in the middle of the terminal, he smiled. Harrods might be an old British establishment but the store's heritage was one with which he could relate. Maybe he could find something for his nephew or nieces.

He sauntered toward a display of Paddington Bears.

Jostled about by an army of travelers scurrying in myriad directions, Max and Kat stepped off the train. It was 10:24 a.m. They had to hurry through the check-in line, then reach the departure gate in time for

British Air's Flight 153, leaving at 11:30 a.m. on its non-stop, five-hour flight.

On their way, Kat slowed down at the Paddington bear display and thought about a twelve-year-old niece in Lincoln, Nebraska, then decided a stuffed bear might be too "young" for her. Besides, they needed to hurry, so she picked up her pace and caught up to Max.

Widad held a bear in one hand and a toy train engine in another, thinking through his purchase when a beautiful redhead caught his attention. With high cheekbones, long neck, and athletic body, she was striking.

He thought evil things for a few moments, but then the woman disappeared in the crowd, apparently hurrying to the side of a broad-shouldered man with close-cropped hair. Lucky creep, Widad thought.

For a moment, his mind fled to the last time he was in a "gentleman's club," which broke the commands of the Koran unless—a big unless—the visit was done for the cause of Allah. And when a Muslim warrior was in a foreign land, he had to look like he was not a Muslim at all—how easier to accomplish this than to drink and womanize? Indeed, the enterprise was a delightful pastime, though he would never admit so to his imam.

Widad grabbed a second bear, placed the bears and the engine in a basket, then picked a colorful scarf for his sister-in-law to wear when she was in her home with her family and thus not covering her face.

Only three people were ahead of Max and Kat at the British Airways ticket counter—obviously a fluke in time, Kat thought. She held her credit card and passport tightly to her chest and fidgeted.

"We could pull what we did in Israel," Max said.

"That was a once-in-a-lifetime, soldier," she said, and with piercing eyes added, "Besides, we can't always take advantage of people's goodwill, can we?"

"Lesson learned, professor."

The cashier had bagged Widad's gifts and he had wandered a few feet when his cell phone rang.

"Widad Said," he answered in Arabic.

"Where are you?" barked the Commander.

Widad straightened up and looked around for a place of solitude, then headed toward a little coffee shop called Caffè Nero. A sign read "Handcrafted Italian coffee." Only four or five people were inside. Must be bad coffee, he thought. Besides, how do you "craft" coffee, anyhow?

He walked in and sat on a bar stool at a tiny, empty table. Turning his face away from the ordering counter, he said, "I am at Heathrow, Commander, waiting for my flight to Tel Aviv. Should that still be my destination?"

"We don't know. We've lost them."

Widad cursed. "Then I should head back to New York and not waste any of my time on this mission."

"First, come to Tel Aviv. I will meet you at our headquarters there and we can go over your plans for the American Congress."

"But—"

Maloof cut him off. "I just secured the woman's photo. I'm sending it to you. But we have only descriptions of Braxton from our men in Petra."

"But if I'm returning to New York, I don't need photos," Widad objected.

290

In a moment, a photograph appeared on his cell phone and he lost his breath. *The woman! The redheaded beauty!*

Widad felt he couldn't speak quickly enough. "The man—Braxton," he said. "What did our warriors say of him?"

"Strong, tall, brawny, fierce. You'd think he was Superman listening to these fools."

Widad's eyes went wide. "I saw them!"

"You what?"

"I just saw them, not more than ten minutes ago, Commander!"

"Then go! Find them, Widad. Kill them if you can. If you can't, then find out where they're going. Whatever you do, stay with them. You're back on mission!"

Kat grabbed the tickets from the British Air clerk, handed Max his and led the way to the security line. Several people were ahead of them, but the line was moving smoothly.

"It helps having only carry-ons, doesn't it?" Max said.

Kat nodded. "I've discovered when I'm going on a dig, if I have a lot of stuff to take, I simply FedEx my things ahead a week before. Wherever I go, FedEx goes and my stuff is always there waiting for me."

"Brilliant."

"Thanks."

"If only the military could do that."

"Send weapons FedEx?"

He chuckled. "Sure. Imagine with me, Kat." He waved a hand upward as if showing off a marquee. "FedEx rules the world!"

She giggled.

"Think what a feather in the cap for FedEx," Max said. "But it would then behoove them to perpetrate wars—something akin to William Randolph Hearst and the Spanish-American War."

"Remember the Maine," Kat said.

"Exactly."

"Then—" she paused for effect, "it would *not* be a good idea for FedEx to handle the logistics."

Max hesitated, squinted half his face as if in discomfort, then answered, "All great ideas have some wrinkles to iron out."

Kat shook her head and laughed softly.

"Is 'general' the next step up for you?" she asked with a grin.

Max nodded then said, "But a fighting man never makes general and continues in mortal combat."

"Which means."

"If offered; I refuse. If cajoled; I consider acquiescing. If the President asks, I *must* accept. But the current President would never ask me."

"Why?"

"Well, I should qualify the statement in that once my book's published, he'll never do it."

"Ah." Kat wondered whose feet he was going to step on, whose feet he *could* step on as a member of the military. Then again, he didn't seem like a man who would *not* do what he thought was right even if it meant his career would suffer.

Widad dashed across the great hall of Terminal 1, retracing his steps to Harrods and followed the direction the redhead had gone. The fact he had left his gifts behind at the café occurred to him, but he flicked the forgotten gifts aside as vastly unimportant. His path took him to the British Air counters.

Even in a crowd like this, the couple ought to stand out. Braxton was bigger than most. The girl was taller than most women and that red hair was eye-catching. He looked up and down the several lines of travelers. They were not there.

Widad cursed. He felt the rush of adrenaline he always experienced when he was on the hunt. He spun around and slowly scanned the terminal. He thought of reconnoitering the hall slowly, *If they're here, they'll still be here; but if they're heading toward a gate I won't catch them unless—*

He took off at a sprint toward the hallway to the gates, then dug his heels in when he reached the security line.

He looked up and down the long line. They were not there. But looking down the hall, he noticed Braxton and the woman walking jauntily away. They seemed to be laughing. He gripped his fists tightly. He'd wipe those smirks off their faces.

He took his place in line.

Ten minutes after Max and Kat arrived at Gate 8, the call in the terminal went out for all those in seats fifteen to twenty of British Air's flight to Tel Aviv to board.

"What are we?" Max asked, looking at his ticket.

"First class." Kat beamed. "I figure I owe you for putting your life at risk."

"Then we can go now because they've called first class."

"Right, soldier."

"You're my favorite traveling partner," Max said. And he meant it.

Widad slapped his hands together in frustration. Here he stood at

293

Gate 8. And there they were, about to walk down the gangway to their airplane.

He growled and ground his teeth. Then a slow smile overtook his face, starting at his chin, and he looked up at the gate's destination board. "Tel Aviv."

For a moment he was wistful. *That's another thing that's going to change. Ben Gurion International Airport will in time be called Yasser Arafat International Airport—as soon as we overthrow the Jews.*

He pulled his cell phone out of a pocket and punched numbers.

A moment later he said, "The bad news is that I just missed them."

"The good news?" the Commander asked.

"They're heading home—to Palestine. British Air flight BA0163. They're arriving in four hours and fifty-five minutes."

Widad heard a snicker on the other end of the line, then the question, "What about you?"

"I'm booked on KLM, departing at—" Widad looked at his ticket. "Oh, no!"

He turned off the phone and sprinted for his life to get to Gate 14.

As he ran, he prayed. *Thank you, Allah, for leading me to these swine who must die. It must be your doing that, in all the world, they would cross my path. I will find them. I will catch them and do your will with them. Allah Akbar!*

Despite the air-conditioned terminal, Widad felt perspiration on his forehead and underarms. He slipped off the lightweight jacket he had been wearing and kept running. *This is a far cry from heading an operation to blow up half of Congress—from reconnoitering and planning and this and that ad nauseam.*

This, he thought, was invigorating. He was meant for the field, not the office. He was meant as a warrior, not a planner. He was meant to carry Allah's vengeful sword of death.

Widad reached the gate just as a KLM employee was shutting the door to the gangway.

"Stop!" he ordered. "Open the door!"

"But—" the girl interjected.

"No buts!"

She must have read the intensity on his face and feared it. Many did. With dispatch, she opened the door. As he swept past her, he heard her radioing ahead, "One more passenger, Irene. Please do not argue."

Chapter 20

As their plane began its final descent over the Mediterranean toward the Ben Gurion landing strip, Max nudged the napping Kat.

"We're homebound, Doc."

She rubbed the sleep from her eyes, then looked out the window. The sun was setting behind them to the west, yet they could see dusk envelope the land straight ahead to the east—a surreal sight.

"I love coming into Tel Aviv," Kat said. "There's always a sense of excitement."

"Well, there's bound to be that for us, methinks."

Kat looked up at him. "I can't wait to hit the ground and get to Atlit."

Max checked his wristwatch. "It's eight o'clock and Shabbat, Friday evening. I think we wait until tomorrow and see if we can even access that training zone."

Kat shrugged back her disappointment.

Ben Gurion International Airport is low and looks diminutive compared to the larger airports of the world—especially since so many people fly in and out of the Holy Land. Finding someone at Ben Gurion is an easy task. Similarly, if one wants to arrive *incognito*, good luck.

That reality was not lost on Khaled Tannous and Zafar Haik, who stood in the wide entryway to the airport whose windows looked out upon the tarmac. They could see every person disembarking from the arriving planes, descending the gangplanks, some of them bending to kiss the ground, and walking the fifty or eighty yards to the terminal to make their way through the check-in. Once the new arrivals were inside, Khaled and Zafar could see them proceed through the lines, show their passports, answer the questions presented them, then walk right past the two men to the exit.

"Is this our easiest mission ever, Zafar?" Khaled said in Arabic with a grin. "If only we could just gun down these two infidels when they—" He interrupted himself and pointed. "Is that them?"

Zafar followed his direction and nodded, "That's her, at least. We still are guessing he's the man our comrades in Petra described."

Khaled pulled a cell phone from his pocket and punched in a number. A moment later he announced in hushed tones, "They're here."

The voice said, "Stick to our plan. The Assassin is en route, arriving in two hours. I will personally be there to greet him."

"Yes, Commander."

Bags in hand, Max and Kat walked across the tarmac behind a handful of other first-class passengers. Max looked inside the building. Not many people obviously waiting for friends and family, business associates.

Two Arabs grabbed his attention. They seemed to be looking directly at Kat and him, following their footsteps. They appeared to be in their late twenties, poorly shaven, badly dressed, like Arafat on a particularly bad day.

Max turned to look at Kat to his right but continued his pace. "Say, Doc, check out the two Arab fellows not far from the door inside."

Kat looked in that direction.

"The two who could use a visit to Goodwill for a change of clothes?" she asked.

"Right."

"They're watching us," she said hoarsely.

"I do believe you're right."

She averted her eyes back to Max. "How would anyone know we were landing on this flight?"

"Maybe they're watching all the flights."

"But how would anyone know we were on any flight at all?"

Max inched a hand to his cell phone and pulled it out of a pocket, then with as little motion as possible, zoomed the photo lens to its highest magnification, then aimed and snapped a photograph of the two.

As they reached the entry door for passengers, Max said, "I called Commissioner Danino to let him know."

"Certainly he's not a leak."

"Certainly not," Max said. "Pay no attention to those two."

"What if they're armed?"

"Trust me."

"I do trust you, but—"

Right then, Max spotted a police officer motioning to them to the left of the half-dozen side-by-side glass-encased booths that were check-in lines.

Max and Kat approached him.

"Colonel Braxton, Doctor Cardova," he said, "Commissioner Danino sent me to pick you up. I'm Inspector Stas Halevi. I've taken over the investigation that began at Dragot."

Halevi shook their hands, then indicated they follow him past the

299

check-in booths.

As they followed Halevi, Max glanced back over his shoulder to see the two Arab men. They were gone.

Down a side corridor they went, then out a back door. Immediately outside the door, a police cruiser awaited them. Halevi stepped in the front passenger door, Max and Kat piled into the rear seat with their duffel bags, and the car tore out of the parking lot and headed westward into Tel Aviv.

"Where are we heading, Inspector?" Kat asked.

"We're meeting with the commissioner, who's waiting for us in our Tel Aviv headquarters."

Max leaned forward and asked, "Did you happen to notice a couple of suspicious Arab men inside the terminal?"

Halevi shook his head and asked. "Why?"

"They seemed to be watching us in particular," Kat said.

"And when we started past the check-in line with you, I looked and they were gone," Max said.

"Perhaps they were waiting for someone on your flight," Halevi offered.

"I have an uneasy feeling about them," Max said.

As they rode into the city, Max turned every couple of minutes to see if they were being followed. Darkness had overtaken the dusk, which made ascertain a tail difficult. In twenty minutes, the driver turned onto Salame Street and a minute later pulled over to the side. A sign in front of a modern building declared "Tel Aviv District Head Quarters for the Israeli Police."

Halevi led the way after they climbed out of the vehicle. An elevator took them to the third floor, and Halevi strode across the hall and into a small room dominated by a long conference table. Dudi Danino sat at the head of the table, with two men to his right and a man and woman to his left. When the door opened and Halevi, Max, and Kat stepped inside, Dudi stood and approached them.

He walked right past Max's extended hand and bear-hugged him.

"Max, Max, Max. I've been following your exploits," he said in English. "Yours and—" he stepped back and nodded toward Kat, "Doctor Cardova's, that is. Your quest is no longer a secret in some circles though I must say the media has not caught wind yet. Gershon Zoref has agreed to keep mum about the music—for now. And though you seem to have made waves wherever you've gone, the focus of your search has pretty much been like a shadow within a shadow.

"Good," Max said.

"Agreed," Dudi said. "But I wanted to talk with you and Doctor Cardova as soon as you returned, so we can fill you in on our investigation and remain on the same page and perhaps prepare to protect you better while you're here."

Dudi motioned for them to take seats, then stood at the head of the table.

"I want you to meet our team," he started.

Immediately to his left, he said, "MI6 Chief of Station Mary Proctor—"

Max and Kat nodded toward her.

"Next is Shabak agent Reuven Hofi." Looking at Kat, Dudi added, "You'd know Shabak as Shin Bet, our national security agency."

Max stood and extended his hand. "Hello, Reuv. Nice to see you again."

"My pleasure, Max," Hofi said, "although I'd prefer our reunion be under different circumstances."

"Amen to that."

Dudi nodded to his right. "This is Jacob Ayalon, our chief inspector for the Tel Aviv-Yafo District."

Max nodded.

"And, Max, you know David Dagan, our communications director."

"Sure do," Max said. "Shalom, David."

"Shalom aleichem," Dagan said and, extending a hand to Kat, added, "Glad to meet you, too, Doctor. Of course, I've read about your work here in Israel in the past."

"Nice to meet you," Kat returned.

"Tell us what you've learned, will you?" Dudi asked, nodding to MI6's Proctor.

Proctor looked at Max and Kat. "Agent Hollingsworth had the great fortune, Max, to follow your footsteps in both Dublin and Wales. I say, Colonel, please remain on England's good side, will you?" She chuckled and Max returned a smile.

"What we've discovered is this: Salah al-Din Brigade has emerged out of nowhere to be a prominent player nearly on a global basis—even as quickly as did ISIS. Much of the rise with the help of al-Qaeda, who helps fund them, train them and, obviously, incite them—although they probably don't require much outside incitement. They were there at Dragot. They were there at Petra. They were there in Dublin. They were there in St. David's. They are probably on the watch for your return to Israel—"

"I think so," Max said. "We noticed two suspicious Arabs watching us when we walked into Ben Gurion."

He held up his cell phone and showed the photo he had taken at the airport.

"Well done!" Proctor said.

"Share that photo with everyone here and we'll find those two and bring them in for questioning," Dudi said.

Max passed his cell to Proctor and after she copied the photo, she passed the cell around to the others.

"Did they follow you here?" Dudi asked Halevi.

"Not sure, but we don't think so. I'd think we got out of the airport in such a hurry they couldn't catch up to us."

"But they could guess where we were headed," Max said. "What I'd like to know is how they seem to find us wherever we go—Petra, Dublin, Wales. They're like leeches on our backs."

"Like I said," Proctor cut in, "they've either set up cells in all sorts of places or have al-Qaeda- and ISIS-type connections around the world. I'm not surprised they found you in Dublin. There's been an active anti-West Muslim presence there for decades. But Wales is a bit of a revelation. We've seen some signs around Cardiff, but nothing concrete."

"Anything you can penetrate with an informant?" Dudi asked.

"No. Not yet anyhow. They are very tight-knit, very afraid of someone getting into their ranks and exposing them and their plans."

"What have you found out from the men who came after us in Dublin and Wales?" Kat asked.

"We're still trying to get them to talk, and we've only had a couple of days, Doctor Cardova," Proctor said. "You two have been on a rocket ship as time goes, and investigations like these take time."

"You must have discovered something," Max said.

"Agent Hollingsworth and his men found their cell's headquarters in Dublin. Actually the apartment of—um," she looked at a file in front of her, "Moosajee Issa. He's the one you wounded with a knife in his left shoulder, Colonel. Shortly before the attack in the church, he received a phone call from a number here in Israel that was bounced off a tower in the new city of Jerusalem.

"Neither he nor his two buddies are talking, except to continually spit out your name in curses."

"My name?"

"Well, they call you 'the American swine.'"

"Nice to be loved," Max said with a grin.

"What about the men in St. David's?" Kat asked.

"They were all deftly dispatched, I'm told, except the last one you took down, Max, and the one Doctor Cardova and Mrs. Sampson wounded with—" Proctor laughed, "a bow and arrow and a crossbow."

She looked at Kat and smiled with a shake of her head as if impressed.

"When Agent Hollingsworth shared his information with me," Proctor said, "I must say he related the news with great exuberance and admiration—for all of you, including Sir Carl."

Proctor locked her eyes on Max. "And the golf flagstick? That was a work of art."

"Flagstick?" Dudi asked.

"A story for another day," Max said.

"Well, if you're not telling the story, your pal Hollingsworth is doing so for you—probably in every pub he walks into," Proctor said. "And he's a golfer, so I'm sure he'll turn the tale into some kind of a joke at some point." She smiled.

"You've got to tell us, Max," Dudi insisted.

Max related a short version of the harrowing story—everyone got a chuckle out of it.

Dudi turned to Halevi. "Fill everyone in, Inspector."

"First of all, our men injured at Dragot have recovered and both are back on duty. At the same time, Danny Arens's recovering well and Gershon Zoref is still hospitalized, but in much better condition. And both are 'round-the-clock under police protection.

"Second, the two men who attacked Doctor Cardova at Petra, of whom you sent us photos and fingerprints—and I love the Band-Aid fingerprints, Colonel—they're believed to be connected to the Brigades.

The one who survived remains in Jordan, and we can't touch him to interrogate him even though we've officially communicated with the Jordanians. In fact, they want *you* in *their* jail."

"Not unexpected," Max deadpanned.

"No. But the man you captured at Dragot? We've connected him to a bus bombing on Ben Yehuda Street in Jerusalem last year and an attack on a family in the Golan Heights earlier last spring."

"Sounds like a sweet guy," Max said.

"Just like his buddies," Halevi said.

Looking down at notes he had scrawled on lined paper, Halevi continued, "In the midst of all of this, they've been attacking people involved in the dig who've returned to their homelands."

"But why kill these people from the dig?" Kat asked. "They didn't do anything bad. They caused no harm."

"I imagine to prevent word from spreading about the music," Dudi said.

"Fat chance of that *now*," Max said.

"Perhaps they'll call off the dogs," Dudi said. "But we can't anticipate that happening."

Dudi turned to Reuven Hofi, the Shin Bet agent. "First, Max," Reuven said, "I want you to know the team at HQ sends its regards."

"I'll drop in and catch up with everyone before going home," Max said.

Reuven stood and walked to a large Smartboard on the wall facing Dudi.

"The Salah al-Din Brigades," Reuven said. Pointing to a map of the world, with pinpoints in various spots, he continued, "Newly minted, they're nevertheless well-funded, well-trained and have cells around the world. Indonesia, the Philippines, Europe, the UK, America. We think they have plans for various kinds of attacks from here to the States."

Max winced and asked, "Who, exactly, is in charge of this group anyhow?"

"Mumim Muhammed Maloof." Reuven clicked a button on a remote-control device in his hand and a photo appeared on the Smartboard.

Maloof was a rugged man about forty or forty-five years old, Max guessed. He looked fearsome. Pictured in desert camouflage, wearing an army green beret, he held an AK-47 in his right hand and rested his left hand on a grenade belt. His attire was well-worn and Maloof wore the uniform comfortably. He appeared to be posing for a poster or posterity.

"Looks like a recruitment ad," Kat said.

"Oh, his face has been used for 'the cause.'" Reuven said. "From a childhood star to an intifada warrior as a teenager when he trained with al-Qaeda and even helped his imam recruit suicide bombers, to a quick rise through the ranks. Then, about three years ago, he stepped out and started the Brigades. He's been leaving a pile of bodies wherever he put his thumb for most of his life. And we're sure he has been the one pulling the strings to thwart the dig—and now your search for the music, Doctor Cardova—from Dragot to Wales."

"Can't you arrest him and stop the madness?" Kat asked.

"Easier said than done," Reuven said. "He's under the protection of Palestinian authorities and deeply embedded in Ramallah. We think we've pinpointed his headquarters, but it's right in the midst of a populated neighborhood, which you know is standard operating procedure for these terror groups."

"Can't use a drone?" Max asked.

"The way America's State Department and the rest of the world are treating us?" Dudi said. "Hostility is a tame description."

"If Maloof strays far from his nest—and if we're fortunate enough to detect him when he does—then we might be able to take him out with a drone," Reuven said. "And, unlike ISIS, al-Qaeda, Hamas, and the others, if we were to take Maloof out, the Brigades would most likely die on the vine for lack of leadership. They're spread wide but as thin as a pane of glass. There's only one man among them we know of who might assume leadership. Which brings me to this—"

Reuven clicked the remote and Maloof's photo was replaced by another.

"Meet Widad Said, lovingly called the Assassin," he said. "He is the Brigade's key weapon, and—" he paused, "he's right now on a plane to Ben Gurion from Washington, D.C. by way of London and Amsterdam."

The photo was a passport shot, head and shoulders. While most people might smile or, at least, fake serenity when posing for a passport photo, Said sported what Max could best describe as a sneer, which seemed to fit his face perfectly, for the right-sided sneer counterbalanced a left-sided scar from his cheekbone to his chin.

"As you can see," Reuven said, "he apparently got too close to the action when glass exploded in one of his bombs—perhaps in a test, perhaps in one carried out somewhere, probably Israel. This is the only photo we have of him. His passport says he's from a village in the West Bank, but he seems to have no home."

"You say he's on a plane here?" Max asked.

"Scheduled to arrive in—" he checked his wristwatch, "thirty-four minutes. He caught a plane out early this morning, had stop-overs in London and Amsterdam, then on to Israel."

"London? When was that?" Kat asked.

"Oh, about six or seven hours ago."

Max could see Kat figuring the time, just as he was. They could have been strolling the very same Heathrow terminal with Said.

"Why do you ask?" Reuven said.

"Oh, no reason."

"Well," Reuven said, "we think his arrival so near yours might not be a coincidence."

"How's that?" Max asked.

Reuven narrowed his eyes on him and Max suddenly knew the reason, answering himself, "He's coming after Kat and me."

"It's a guess," Reuven said. "But our supposition is he's coming because their other people have failed at the mission—miserably, I might add. You've mortified them. I'm sure Maloof hates humiliation—unless he's the one bringing the dishonor."

Suddenly Kat's hand flew to Max's and she held on tightly.

"Don't worry, Doctor Cardova," Dudi said. "We'll have you protected. We'll have Said under heavy surveillance the moment his feet hit the ground."

"So, your search has brought you all the way back to Israel?" This came from Mary Proctor, the MI6 chief of station.

"Atlit, to be exact," Kat answered.

Proctor looked quizzical.

"It's a castle south of Haifa."

"In fact," Max added, "it's now a military training facility. And—" he looked at Dudi, "we'll need permission to get inside to look for the music."

"The PM said to give you whatever help you need, and I'm sure that extends to the military. I'll give them a call. Will tomorrow do?"

Max looked at Kat, who nodded assent.

"What are your plans for tonight?" Dudi asked.

"Dan Panorama Hotel," Kat said.

Dudi's eyebrow raised.

"Girl lives in style," Max said.

"Not on *my* budget," she objected. "The room is complimentary. I once led a dig financed by the Dan Hotels company. They treat me well."

Widad Said stepped onto the tarmac at Ben Gurion International Airport. As he approached the terminal, he looked through the windows and spotted Najil Ali, a young man he had trained in the fine art of bomb-making.

He had half-expected Mumim, but that would have meant suicide or, at least, capture for the Commander.

Widad hurried inside, a duffel bag under his arm. He was traveling light and had left his clothes behind at the Palestinian embassy in Washington. This little adventure wouldn't take long.

Inside, he went through the check-in line, winked at the security camera he knew was focused on him, then met Najil.

He handed Najil his bag and asked in Arabic, "Is our evasion plan in place?"

"Yes, sir."

Najil held the door open for him as they left the terminal. A black sedan sped up to the sidewalk and they jumped inside—Widad in the front passenger seat, Nijal behind him.

"Off!" he ordered the driver. "But do not lose them!"

The sedan sped out of the airport exit.

Widad turned in his seat and saw the black SUV in pursuit. He growled and showed his teeth in a wicked smile.

"Make the call," he said.

Nijal held up a cell phone and announced, "We'll be there in ten minutes."

Widad looked over at the driver, a young man he did not recognize.

"You trained for this?" Widad asked.

The young man nodded.

"Are you good?"

"The best."

"You're over-confident."

"Yes."

"Brash."

"Yes."

"That's good."

They tore down the Ayalon North highway and, in a few minutes, exited onto Kibbutz Galuyot Road. Widad turned the rearview mirror so he could watch behind them. The men in the black SUV were doing their job well.

A couple minutes later, they turned onto Allenby. They were getting closer. Kiryat Hamelacha. Their sanctuary. He had even grown to endure, without disgust, the graffiti on the neighborhood's buildings.

He turned to Nijal and asked, "Time?"

Nijal turned his wrist to catch a streetlight and check the time. "They'll be ready, sir."

Widad growled and rubbed his hands together.

Half a minute later, their car suddenly turned left and the driver laid rubber on the asphalt as they raced down a quiet street.

Widad looked to his left and right and saw dark figures behind a large dumpster on his one side and the edge of a building on the other.

Back to the mirror, he saw the SUV skid around the corner trying to catch up.

"Three—two—one!" Nijal announced.

Kaboom! An explosion, then a fireball, lit the street behind them. Widad turned in his seat just in time to see the SUV tilt on its side and sail a good five feet into the air.

Widad's driver pulled over the car and stopped.

Widad stepped out and looked down the street, then turned and slipped back in his seat.

"Well done!" he howled. "Well done!"

Minutes later, an older woman burst into the Police Headquarters conference room.

"I'm sorry, sir," she said, wide-eyed and looking with anxiety at Dudi.

"It's all right, Martha. What is it?" Dudi asked.

"We've lost contact with the team following Widad Said!"

"Lost contact?" Dudi asked.

"Yes, and there are reports of a bomb in Kiryat Hamelacha."

"Kiryat Hamelacha," Max said. "That sounds familiar."

"It's in the south side of the city, where Sam Livingston was killed," Dudi said. "Now—"

"What can I do, sir?" Martha asked.

Dudi looked at Ayalon. "Jacob, you're the chief inspector for the Tel Aviv-Yafo District. You handle the hands-on. I'll observe. Keep me posted on everything. Everything you find out. But I'm coming with you to the scene now."

"But, sir—"

"But nothing! I may have lost two officers!"

Jacob turned to Martha and said, "Call in Oren and his team. Give them the lead."

Dudi looked at Hofi. "Reuven, you coming with me?"

"My men are downstairs," Reuven said. "We'll be right behind you."

"Mind if I tag along?" Proctor asked.

"Please do."

"How about us?" Max asked. "Can Doctor Cardova and I join you?"

Dudi hesitated, then said, "Not a good idea, Max. You're the ones we need protected, not put in harm's way."

Max turned to look at Kat. He read two conflicting emotions, fright and anger, that he had experienced himself in the midst of battle. He could tell she was fully absorbed in the fray.

"What do you say, Professor?" he asked.

"I say, let them take a shot at me and maybe we can end this thing."

Max cast a questioning look at Dudi.

"I have veto power here, young lady," Dudi said. "The location is a crime scene, and I need my men to do their job, which would be made all the more difficult with you there."

Kat hung her head. "I see what you mean, Commissioner. Sorry."

Dudi pointed to Martha. "Make sure Colonel Braxton and Doctor Cardova have an escorted ride to Dan Panorama Hotel and tell Peter and Zalman they're on protective detail."

Dudi peered at Max. "I know you don't like the idea, you feel you can take care of yourself. I know. But I'd die myself if something happened to you in my country, on my watch."

Max shook his head. "As you say, my friend."

"Oh, and by the way," Dudi said, "you'll find all your gear you sent to Jerusalem in the outer office."

With that, Dudi, Reuven, and Jacob rushed out the door, leaving Martha, Kat, and Max.

Max shrugged. "Guess we're going to the hotel."

"I'd say so."

Chapter 21

Kat and Max were able to get rooms side by side, and they ordered in a late dinner in Kat's room. Before the meal arrived, she pulled open the curtains before a patio door and looked out on a view of Haifa Bay, noticeable only by the glimmer of moonbeams off the water, sailboats, and inboard motor boats of various sizes.

"I must say, I don't know if I will be able to sleep tonight," she said. "I'm not used to violence. In my world, hostility, brutality, war—they all happened two thousand, four thousand years ago. I've always looked at war from a safe distance—in time if not space. I've seen the results of charioteer against battle ax or catapult versus fort. But I've never truly felt what those people must have felt. They had no phones to call home and say, 'Dear, I may be in my last battle. Give the kids a farewell kiss from Daddy.' They had no way to sense how their lives were to affect history. This is all new to me, Max."

"Well, in my world violence happened last month," Max said. "Maybe I'm *too* used to war. I'd love to see you through this danger and back to your non-violent life."

A vision of her and Max in the green at Yale University on some future September day flashed in her mind and she suddenly tingled all over. Looking up at his warm brown eyes, she managed, "That would be nice. But first, I must *must* find that music."

She felt a renewed determination. These evil people wanted to stop her. Well, she'd show them not to mess with her. A Yale professor, maybe, but mess with a Midwestern girl? No way.

"We'll hear from Dudi in the morning about getting into Atlit, I'm sure of it," Max said. "No matter how busy he is; he never fails to deliver on a promise."

"Tomorrow promises, then, to be a busy day," Kat said. "Just how big is this castle?"

"Enormous."

"Great," she said, not meaning that at all. "All of a sudden, I'm particularly sick of castles. How about a cave or something?"

Max chuckled.

At six o'clock sharp the next morning, Max's room phone rang. He answered and a familiar voice spoke.

"Max, it's Yosi Shoval."

"Yosi!" Max exclaimed. "How long has it been? Two years? Three?"

"Four since you sat at my Shabbat table, my friend."

"That was a night to enjoy."

"We must have a repeat. But first, I've been told you want my help."

"I do?"

"I'm commanding Atlit nowadays—the IDF Naval Commando training camp."

"Really? Congratulations!"

"Perhaps if I do you your favor, you can return the courtesy by leading another session on strategy?"

"Count it done."

"So, how soon can you get here?" Yosi asked. "It's Saturday—Shabbat—so there's no training. And I'll bet I can get the entire camp to volunteer to hunt for your treasure."

"Seriously?"

"You know I'm a—how do you say it—*pragmatist*? But I sense I can guess most of the men would be willing, especially if told the search is at the behest of a Medal of Valor soldier."

"I'll check with Doctor Cardova to make sure she doesn't mind a squadron of men on site, but my guess is she'll be thrilled for the help. When do you want us there?"

"There'll be a car waiting for you outside the lobby at o-seven-thirty."

"I'll call you right back to confirm."

Max hung up, dressed and went to Kat's room.

When he knocked, she called, "Come on in."

She looked stunning in khaki shorts and a green top matching her eyes to perfection, and, of course, mismatched socks, this time, solid emerald green on her left foot, scarlet-and-white striped on her right.

"Guess what," he said. "If you want the help, you may be able to get a few dozen soldier volunteers for the search."

"Wow!" Her eyes went wide and bright. "Of course."

"Room service will take too long. I'll run down and get us a couple of coffees and pastries. Be right back. They're picking us up at seven-thirty."

"Okay."

Max shut the door and hurried down the corridor to the elevators.

Five minutes later he was back, carrying a tray of coffee and pastries and knocking at Kat's door.

There was silence, then a timid, "Come in."

315

Something in Kat's response caused caution in Max's spirit. He set down the tray and reached to his hip for his Glock 23, which had been in the luggage Dudi had ordered delivered to him from Jerusalem.

He turned the doorknob one degree at a time until the door clicked open. He stepped to the side and pushed the door wider bit by bit with his right toe.

Quiet greeted him.

A couple stepped out of a room two doors down. Seeing him armed, they bristled and backed up. He motioned for them to get back in their room.

Then, he swiftly swung into the doorway, firearm raised and finger ready to pull the trigger. What he saw sent his heart into his throat. Kat was seated in a straight-back chair, her arms bound behind her and her feet lashed to the legs of the chair. A fierce-looking man stood behind her, holding a handgun to her head.

The scar from his cheekbone to his chin told Max he was Widad Said, the Assassin.

"Come in, close and lock the door," Said ordered in Arabic. His voice sounded like gears grinding on a Mack truck.

Max stepped inside and shut the door.

"Drop the gun and kick it toward me."

Max stooped, placed the Glock on the floor and toed the weapon about five feet in front of him.

"You two have been troublemakers here in my country."

"It's not 'your' country."

"I speak prophetically."

"You speak wishfully."

"I speak historically."

"You speak nonsense. The Jews have lived on this land for four thousand years. Your people? Not so long. Some pretenders, like Arafat, weren't even 'Palestinians' to begin with."

316

"You speak lies."

"You speak what your hate-filled schools taught you, which is fabrications."

"You dare argue with a man with a gun?"

"If they're to be my last words, I don't want them to be driven by some sort of appeasement of my enemy."

Said growled. "As I said, you have caused nothing but trouble. I could have waited in the lobby and killed you with ease."

"Why didn't you?"

"Because I want this woman to see you beg for your life, to be humiliated as you have disgraced my comrades in Petra and in Ireland and in Wales."

"You're well-informed—at least about the places if not the humiliation. Your pals lost in even fights. Indeed, they had the advantage in each case. Their disgrace was only in their defeat. And even now, you hold the advantage. Tying up and terrorizing an unarmed woman. Is that 'honorable' among Muslim men?"

"Women are chattel," Said spit out. "There is no terrorism, no binding with women."

"This woman," Max said, pointing to Kat, "is your superior in every way. Besides, this is about you and me. I'm the one who embarrassed your comrades. Kat here's just an innocent archeologist looking for a Jewish treasure. You're not getting her head. And I guarantee you'll never get mine, Said."

"You know my name."

"You come as advertised: a murderous bully and slaughterer of innocents. I guessed the rest. Liar. Coward—"

Said turned the barrel of his gun on Max. "Coward!? One more word—" he said. "One more word, and I'll kill you right now and send you to hell."

"Afraid not. I'm heading the other way."

Said scowled, then a wicked smile spread across his face. "I'd much rather behead you alive than dead." He looked at Kat and, with the barrel of his pistol, slipped her blouse off her shoulder. "Then I can have my way with this infidel woman before gutting her. Afterward, I can get back to my *real* work and finish my *real* mission."

"What's that? Blowing up more wedding parties and bar mitzvahs?"

"Wedding parties? Bar mitzvahs?" Said chortled. "More like Congressmen, not little mice."

At the mention of Congressmen, Max noticed Kat's eyebrows rise in astonishment. *Congressmen?* This was worse than just Kat's and his lives—much, much more was at stake.

Looking Said straight in the eyes, Max said, "If you're as good as all your Salah al-Din Brigades brethren think, you don't need that gun to kill a mere American or lowly woman. I should be easy prey for you, Said."

"I don't need the gun."

"Prove it."

Said hesitated.

"Prove you're not a *coward* and need a gun to kill an unarmed man."

Said noticeably tensed again at the word "coward."

"You've been a hero since you were a boy, Said—featured on Palestinian television as a brave Muslim. What would they think now if they saw you frightening a woman? If they saw you kill an unarmed man?"

"They would hail me as a great warrior."

"Truly?"

"Truly. Like they cheer when watching videos of beheadings. Like they cheered years ago when we cut off the head of the American Jew journalist Daniel Perle and those ninety Christians in Syria. Like they did when the Jew soldiers were thrown through a second-floor window and dragged through the streets of Ramallah. Like they did when the planes hit the Twin Towers. Like they did when—you get the idea."

"It's a shame, but I do. An entire group of people with no morals. But what about you? In your own heart, you'll know you feared losing an even-handed battle with an infidel. You'll know you were a sissy, a momma's boy, a wuss."

Said's shoulders shot back, loathing crossed his face, and he took three steps toward Max with gun raised. On Said's third step, Kat was able to twist her left ankle and foot just enough to trip him and cause him to stumble.

As Said fell forward, the gun exploded and a bullet tore into the floor beside Max.

Max rushed forward and kicked the gun from Said's grasp. He raised a knee toward Said's face, but the terrorist scrambled to his side, avoiding the blow. Said looked with angst for his gun, which was resting against the wall several feet beyond Kat.

Max bent and removed a knife from a sheath behind his ankle. Stepping between Said and Kat, he cut loose her left hand, gave her the knife and said, "Cut yourself loose, Kat."

Said had leaped to his feet and, just then, pulled his own knife on Max. He leaped forward, his knife aimed at Max's chest. Max thwarted the thrust with his right hand and smacked Said on the forehead with the palm of his left hand. Said staggered backward and to his right, his legs shoved against the bed.

Max turned to Kat, who was now cutting her legs free. "Get out," he ordered.

"No!" she said.

"Please!"

"No!"

319

"Call security."

"He ripped out the phone line."

"Then go to another room and call. Now!"

Kat handed him his knife, then squeezed between him and a bureau and headed to the door.

"No!" Said screamed and, suddenly, Max felt a searing pain in his upper right bicep. He knew immediately the cause was a knife strike.

He spun around to face Said, who had regained his balance and stood with feet spread apart and dark menace in his eyes. Blood dripped from the blade of his knife.

Max looked at him and laughed. "Do you scare people, Said?"

Said growled.

"Do people look at you and that scar and tremble at the thought of facing you in hand-to-hand combat?"

Said's face distorted and he moved forward with deliberation. They stood only three feet apart.

Max heard Kat open and shut the door and run down the hallway.

"You know what I think?" he said, standing on the balls of his feet, ready to shift in any direction. "I think you were in a knife fight and the great Widad Said lost. Am I not right, Allah's awesome warrior?"

"I *am* Allah's awesome warrior!" Said hissed. "And, no, I have never lost." Then eyeing the blood seeping into Max's shirt, "I see you bleed red. You're human."

"Never said I wasn't. But this little cut? Heck, my two-year-old nephew's caused more harm playing Tonka trucks with me."

Said, eyes red with hatred, thrust his knife at Max's chest. Max dodged to the right, slapped Said's wrist aside, then drove his left leg with force into the man's stomach.

The blow straightened up Said and sent him falling several steps backward as in slow motion. The waist-high HVAC shelf in front of the window stopped him.

"I think you were a damaged little boy, Said. One who grew into a pathetic adult bent on killing people he thinks wronged him in some way. I believe you could have become a decent human being but, by your own volition, you turned into a disgusting rodent. The 'Great Assassin'? Ha!"

The color of his face now matching his eyes, Said raised his knife and flung the weapon at Max. Max ducked and the knife pierced the wallboard wall behind him. Now Max held the knife. He paused.

"Now who's the coward?" Said asked. "You're armed; I'm not."

"You of all people now plead for an even fight?" Max guffawed.

The muscle below Said's right eye twitched. Max smiled and tossed his knife, the point piercing the carpeted floor halfway between them.

"Well then, my friend," Max said, his eyes locking with Said's, "you want some settlement with an 'unjust world'—the 'unjust world' being me? Take your best shot."

Said looked frantically around him, then grabbed a large lamp off a bedside stand. He pulled the electric cord out of its socket, tore off the lampshade and broke the light bulb on the head post. Turning, he pointed the jagged lamp at Max.

"I see how it is," Max said. "You always want the upper hand, but you'd better make quick work of me because Kat must have security en route by now."

Holding the lamp before him like an awkward, hulking sword, Said jabbed at Max. Max simply shook his head and, after the third jab, yanked the lamp from Said's hand and threw it onto the bed.

"Is this your best, Said? Really?"

Said growled and swung a right-handed haymaker at him. Max leaned back from his waist to avoid the fist.

Righting himself, Said then heaved a left-handed hook. Max turned at the hips and avoided the blow.

Said then switched to karate moves, delivering a front kick, followed by a reverse roundhouse heel kick. Max stepped aside the front kick and ducked below the roundhouse.

Righting himself, Said followed with a double kick and then a left-legged back kick. Again Max slid away from the blows.

"You exert a lot of energy," Max said. "Who was your teacher down there in the camps of Africa, anyway? Was it Fawzi Surur?"

No response.

"Jumah Yaseen?"

No response.

"Ahured Al Nubi?"

Max read a flash of recognition in Said's face.

"It was Al Nubi," Max declared.

Said did not deny it.

"Because, my friend, like his name Ahured implies, he's dead."

Said's eyes leveled on Max's and a frown wrinkled his forehead. "No!" gurgled from his throat.

"It's true," Max said. "I saw his body myself. I didn't kill him, but I was there for the last breaths of the nasty piece of human sludge."

Said charged at Max, who stepped to the side and, grabbing his shoulders, pushed him on his way to the ground.

"All pretense at finesse gone now?" Max asked with a shake of his head.

Said scrambled to his feet and snarled.

"I tell you, I was expecting more."

"You fear being close," Said challenged.

Max wasted no time. He stepped close and threw five quick jabs to the man's stomach, followed with a right uppercut that sent him sprawling to the floor. Quickly Max attacked and when Said kicked straight up at him, he spun enough to avoid the boot and crashed to the floor with his right elbow out and hammered the elbow into Said's solar plexus. The man coughed once and curled up into a ball, moaning in pain.

Max walked over to the wall and picked up Said's handgun.

Just then, the door lock clicked and the door swung open, revealing two IDF soldiers—a sergeant and a corporal—a hotel security man and Kat. Their eyes went wide when they saw Said in a fetal position on the floor, coughing and gasping for air.

Kat ran to Max and wrapped her arms around him. She smelled like rain water, a welcome relief. He held her tightly while keeping an eye on Said.

"The cavalry," Max said with a smile.

"The what?" the sergeant asked in Hebrew.

"Men on horseback coming to the rescue," Max said in Hebrew.

The men laughed and strode into the room.

The corporal looked at Max and asked, "Are you all right, sir?"

"Fine. Just fine," Max said. He waved toward Said and said to the soldiers and security man, "May I introduce you to Widad Said, the Great Assassin for the Salah al-Din Brigades."

"Great Assassin, eh?" said the sergeant, bending to grab Said by the elbow. "Well, come on, Great Assassin, we have a new home waiting for you."

The security official looked at Max's shoulder, where his shirt had been sliced and blood was seeping out. "Looks like you need some medical attention," he said in English.

"Ah, just a scratch," Max said. "I'm used to it. A little needle and thread will do."

The security man chuckled, then punched a button on a radio at his shoulder. "Get the house doctor to room four-o-nine," he ordered.

While the corporal handcuffed Said, the sergeant turned to Max and said, "I'm sorry, sir, that we weren't on hand to protect you. We were in a shift change downstairs."

"No problem. If you'd been closer, Said might have tried another time and been successful. I think your absence was," he paused, "a God-incidence."

In short order, four more IDF soldiers arrived and they carried off Said, trussed up like a Thanksgiving turkey.

Max turned to Kat. "I'm afraid the coffee outside your door is far from hot at this point. And now we have a military vehicle waiting to take us to Atlit. Had enough excitement yet?"

She looked up at him with a beautiful grin that completely belied the way the day had started.

"Does anything faze you?" she asked.

"Only a beautiful face," he said, and he put a hand to her cheek.

She stood up on her toes and he bent down until their lips met.

After a long kiss, Kat pulled back and peered at him. "How many times are you going to have to save my life?"

"Until I don't have to anymore."

Sitting on a couch in the hotel lobby, pretending to read the *Ha'aretz* newspaper and look like he belonged there, Najil Ali waited expectantly. One of his heroes, Widad Said, had ordered him to wait while he "did his business." Sitting in the lobby with Najil, Widad had spotted the infidel Braxton exit an elevator across the lobby and enter the room containing the continental breakfast buffet.

"That's the man I saw in Heathrow," Widad said. He leaped to his feet and hustled to get into the elevator going up. He would soon kill the man and his female companion.

Widad never failed—ever. And so Najil was confident he would soon see his mentor with a broad smile of contentment at a job well done. Then Najil could tell and retell the tale to his family and comrades in the fight for freedom.

Every time one of the elevators opened, he looked up, expectant. He checked his watch. This was taking longer than expected.

He had begun to worry a few minutes earlier when two IDF soldiers appeared from somewhere behind him, met a hotel security man and, after a brief conversation in hushed tones, hurried to the elevators.

Since then, he prayed to Allah. Trying to keep his mind entertained, to keep from creating bad thoughts, he had turned to the Local section of the newspaper. His hackles had gone up when he read the headline: "PM Approves More Housing in East Jerusalem."

He had cursed in Arabic, then put a hand to his mouth when he realized how loudly he had spoken.

And now he heard the elevator chime and looked above the paper and, despite the growing feeling of unease, hoped to rejoice with Widad. Instead, he caught his breath. Out stepped the security man and, behind him, the two soldiers flanked Widad. Widad's arms were behind him, obviously cuffed and controlled by the older of the two soldiers. His legs were cuffed together as well so he took only short duck-steps.

Najil began to rise, to jump to the salvation of his hero. Then Widad saw him and shook his head in warning. Najil sat back down and again put the paper in front of him. Looking around the newspaper, he watched as the soldiers pushed Widad into the back seat of a military vehicle.

Najil hurried to the windows and watched, aghast, as the vehicle pulled into traffic and disappeared in the direction of Salame Street, where the police headquarters was located.

Najil grabbed his cell phone and, fingers shaking and a dull thrumming in his head, punched in a number.

Chapter 22

Highway 2 is one of the busiest thoroughfares in Israel. The road was widened to six lanes in the 1990s, and for that Max was grateful because traffic was still too slow for his liking.

From Tel Aviv to Haifa was around sixty miles. They didn't have clear sailing until they reached Hadera, about halfway to Atlit.

Max and Kat sat in the back seat of a military SUV, with two armed IDF soldiers in the front seat. Another IDF vehicle escorted them from behind.

"You think this protection might be overkill?" Kat asked Max.

He shrugged. "Maybe. Maybe not. I like to think of *myself*, not the Israeli Defense Forces, as your protector. But hey, Dudi's in charge of people's protection in this country, and he and the IDF work closely a lot."

He looked at her with a crooked smile. "You feel more safe now?"

"With all deference to our friends in the front seat and in the car behind us, only because I'm with you, soldier. I don't know what I would have done without you. And I mean from the very beginning—in the parking lot at Tiberias."

Max grinned. "Well, protecting you certainly adds to my résumé."

He raised a hand in front of him as if writing a note. "Guardian of the famous Doctor Katherine O'Hara Cardova."

"I'd say 'Israeli Medal of Valor hero' would do the trick, no matter what job you'd be applying for."

"I'd say having a Yalie on one's side can win lots more jobs."

"Only if I were in the Skull and Bones."

Max chuckled. "Now you jest."

Kat simply raised her eyebrows. "A topic for another time—a far-in-the-future time."

She paused for a moment, then added, "You know, finding the music today would be a fine birthday present."

"For who?"

"For me."

"Wow! I didn't know. We'll double our efforts then."

Max's cell phone rang and he pulled it from a cargo pocket. "Yes."

"Max." It was Dudi Danino. "What are you—a magnet for murderers?"

Max grumbled and pushed the SPEAKER button. "Guess so, Dudi. My question is, how do these guys always seem to find us?"

"We're digging to find any leaks," Dudi said. "But my file on you and Doctor Cardova is growing thicker by the hour."

Max chuckled, noticed that Kat did not, and said, "Let's hope the file doesn't get any bulkier, okay?"

"Agreed. I'm told this guy was Widad Said."

"Well, he matches the photo you folks showed us and I doubt *two* men in this world could be as ugly."

"And the temperament," Kat added.

"That, too," Max said. "I hope you can grill him about Salah al-Din Brigades, Dudi."

"We shall."

"There's one other thing," Kat said. "When he thought he had us both dead, he mentioned something else—"

"He said he was about to get back to his *real* mission in life," Max said.

"Something about blowing up Congress," Kat said.

"He's been in the Palestinian embassy in Washington," Dudi said. "Probably planning an attack while he's been over there." He paused for a moment. "I'll get in touch with U.S. Homeland Security. They'll get all over the situation."

"You want any help with the interrogation, I'll be happy to lend a hand," Max said.

"We have ways—" Dudi began.

"I know. Use them."

"When will we see you again, Commissioner?" Kat asked.

"When you find the music, or get back to Jerusalem, whichever comes first."

Captain Yosi Shoval looked the ideal soldier. Six-foot tall, bronzed by the sun. Even in full military garb, his muscled torso and arms were obvious. But when he met Max and Kat's SUV and Max stepped out of the car, Yosi lost all the aura and bearing of his position. He was like a kid.

With fierce goodwill, he shook Max's hand, then grabbed him by the collars and pulled him into an embrace.

Kat looked around at the soldiers who had delivered them here and saw no looks of embarrassment. Instead, they were smiling.

Max released himself from the embrace and motioned toward Kat. "Doctor Kat Cardova," he announced in introduction. "Kat, this is a friend and newly minted captain, Yosi Shoval."

"Doctor Cardova." Yosi extended a hand and a full-toothed grin.

"Call me Kat."

"Then please call me Yosi. Many of the men here do. We're a very laid-back military."

Yosi stepped back and waved toward the camp. "Welcome to Atlit, Kat. I have one hundred and thirty-three soldiers here and it's Shabbat. Shabbat's not a work day, rather a relax-and-thank-God day. And what better way to thank God than look for one of His treasures?"

"I couldn't agree more," Kat replied.

"Now I haven't told them about your search, but we've already called everyone into the auditorium. Follow me."

Yosi spun on his heels and started down a walkway.

He turned to Max and said, "So I heard you might leave special ops to teach?"

"That's one option. I'm taking a little time to write a book I think needs to be written."

Yosi's interest was obviously piqued, and Max spent the next minute highlighting his thesis.

As they walked along, Kat looked about her. The military grounds lay almost entirely on a promontory. A sprawling castle—mostly in shambles with one tower rising above its largely crumbled walls obviously badly damaged by the 1837 earthquake—loomed beyond the building toward which they were heading.

True, this promontory nearly screamed, "Use me for fortification. I'll defend you from siege." A protected harbor lay south of the promontory. And any enemy would have to traverse a narrow neck of level, highly visible land in order to launch an attack. The only trees in the area were tight to the castle.

They walked through a door into a steel-beamed building and a room resembling a basketball court with long tables in perfect alignment. Surely, more than a hundred men sat waiting.

A huge screen to their left displayed an aerial photograph of the training camp.

Yosi motioned Kat into the room ahead of Max and him and said, "Kat, I thought if you divided the camp into fifty-yard-square segments and we could assign a certain number of soldiers to search each one would be the best method. So the map on the screen already has the demarcations.

"Excellent idea, Captain. Let me look the map over and decide which areas should get the most scrutiny."

Yosi handed her a laser pointer and Kat stepped up beside the screen. She had spoken to hundreds of sessions of Yale students, to a couple dozen conferences of archeologists and anthropologists around the world, to television reporters and documentary filmmakers interested in her digs, but never to a group of soldiers. *How do I grab their interest?*

Drawing a deep breath, she began in Hebrew, "I'm an American. But I know you and your people are God's people. He chose you from all others in the world. No one can wrest His acclamation from you. And He chose this land for you. Prophecy after prophecy in the Tanach declare so and, now, here you are. God's heart is here in Israel and to this place, the Messiah will come."

"Omain!" came the response from several soldiers.

"Many Israelis are excited about the idea of building The Third Temple on the Temple Mount. And so my friend, Doctor Danny Arens, was thrilled when, on an archeological dig a few days ago, he discovered a stone inscribed with information about King David's music—music that was to be played to the Psalms."

Kat noticed a collective drawing of breath.

She continued, "In fact, we've discovered the Ruach HaKodesh, the Spirit of God, had revealed to King David two Temples would be built and destroyed after his lifetime, but the music was to be kept in secret and in waiting for a Third Temple. Doctor Arens was attacked because of his discovery. Islamists do not want David's music found because the music would be the crowning treasure in a Third Temple. And, as you know, they will not easily allow a temple to be built on the Temple Mount where Israel has given them controlling authority.

Moans of agreement met her statement.

"But Doctor Arens' search did not stop."

Kat pointed toward Max, who was sitting with Yosi at the end of the front row. "Colonel Braxton and I have been following lead after lead to find this treasure, which will transform the world of worship—and hopefully the world itself. Our search has led us here, to Atlit. And we could dearly use your help trying to unearth this music."

The room erupted in cheers.

Smiling, Kat continued: "Our last discovery—in Wales—was that a leader of the Knights Templar, a man named Jacques de Molay, brought the music to Atlit Castle, the last stronghold of the Crusaders. Perhaps he hid the music in the castle keep, perhaps in the chapel, perhaps in his own living quarters, wherever that might be. But we are close to certain he brought the scrolls here."

A living "hum-m-m" began to vibrate through the soldiers. They were getting excited. Kat could feel in her spirit.

Yosi stood. "I can show you where the keep and chapel were located," he said in Hebrew, "but not where de Molay stayed."

Kat passed Yosi the laser light and he pointed a purple dot onto the decrepit tower. "The keep and chapel are both in there, halfway up or so, and that area is dangerous. If we go in there, we will have to be very, very cautious."

Max spoke up. "I'll go!"

"I'll go!" "I'll go!" "I'll go!" rang out throughout the room.

Kat was overtaken by the reaction. A tingle sped up her spine and she laughed.

Yosi turned to her and handed back the laser light.

Kat looked out at the soldiers. "Please, everyone who just volunteered, raise your hands."

Several dozen hands shot up.

"That doesn't leave many people to search the rest of the site for de Molay's rooms," she said.

She asked the soldiers with raised hands to count off, starting immediately to her right and going toward the back of the hall. When they were finished, she said, "The person with every fourth number, please stand up."

They stood.

"You'll go with Colonel Braxton to the tower."

There were moans from those not chosen.

"Please," Kat said, "this is a volunteer effort. Don't feel obligated to take part. We want everyone on board to help because of the desire of their heart, not an obligation."

Kat spent the next fifteen minutes assigning soldiers to different sections of the camp. Not a single one deferred from participation.

As the soldiers readied to begin their search, Yosi said, "Report any findings to me. Leave no stone unturned—literally."

"No objects unmoved," Max added.

"And make sure to put pressure on all the stones in the walls for hidden places," Kat said. "If you find papyrus of any kind, or flat stones with inscriptions, anything that looks ancient, please photograph your find and let the captain know."

Max stood up and turned to face the room. "All those going to the tower, follow me."

"Report back to mess hall at thirteen hundred," Yosi said. "Dismissed!"

The room was abuzz with talk as the soldiers dispersed.

Max looked at Kat. "You coming?"

"You couldn't stop me," she said.

Just then a soldier rushed through the door. "Is there a Doctor Cardova here?" he asked in Hebrew.

Kat raised her hand.

"This is for you," he said and handed her a large envelope. "Compliments of Commissioner Danino."

Opening the packet, her eyes widened.

"What is it?" Max asked.

Kat looked at the cover and leafed through the papers. "It's the report by C.N. Johns, a British archeologist. He was assigned to lead a major excavation of Atlit for the British Mandate Authorities from 1930 to 1934. I'll have to look through this for any clues."

"How did Dudi get that, I wonder?" Max said.

"From the Israeli Antiquities Authority, I'd imagine," Kat said. "I'm a bit surprised they haven't taken charge of our hunt since we're back in Israel."

"I'm to tell you," said the soldier who delivered the envelope, "that the Prime Minister himself ordered the Authority that you remain in control of the search. They are to stay hands-off—at least for now."

"Nice to have the main man on your side," Yosi said.

Kat pointed to Max. "His side, you mean."

"Well, then," Max said. "I'll leave you to Johns' report and take the crew to the tower."

Itching to get outdoors and into the hunt, wondering what Max was doing and if getting up into the keep and chapel was difficult, whether the stone steps had crumbled, and if the soldiers had to repel, Kat made herself sit in the hall and read.

My, this Johns guy was long-winded. Well, he did spend four years here. Might not be an eternity, but long enough to get a college degree or two. She reminded herself that one of her major attributes was patience.

As time passed, she felt a presence beside her, looked, and saw no one. She wondered for a moment if Kait had come to be with her as she approached what would be the major discovery of her life. That, she dismissed, as non-biblical. Could the presence be the Holy Spirit? Now *that* would be biblical.

She was not uncomfortable with whatever or whomever the presence was; indeed, she recalled her Dad often preaching on the Holy Spirit, including Jesus' declaration that when He departed, He would leave the Holy Spirit to serve as Comforter and Guide. Well, she certainly needed guidance right now!

After a couple of hours, she scanned by, then stopped at one sentence:

We did discover a paper in Room C-2 that was written
in the Year of Our Lord 1301. The paper mentioned
that Knights Templar Grand Master Jacques de Molay,
in search of solitude, bought a cottage on a hillock
overlooking the sea a half-mile south of the castle.

Kat shot out of her chair.

Max was half-hanging from a rope inside the castle tower. One foot had just given up its hold on a dilapidated stair; the other foot settled against the inside wall. Above him was a grappling hook; below him were the six men who had helped him scout the castle keep, finding nothing. The stairs going upward to the chapel another level higher had long since fallen into oblivion and so they were rappelling up to the chapel. Max was first in line.

Suddenly his cell phone rang. Grumbling in displeasure, he held up a "wait-a-minute" index finger to the men below him and pulled the phone out of a cargo pocket, cautious not to drop the device the sixty feet or so to the ground.

Determined to turn his angst on end, he decided on an out-of-character answer. "It's a glorious morning," he singsonged.

Kat laughed and after a moment's hesitation asked, "Any luck?"

"Not in the keep, m'lady. We're rappelling up to the chapel."

"Boy, you're in a mood," she said. "Hey, I may have a lead on the music, which might not be in the castle at all. Can you come back yourself and send the others on up to the chapel?"

Max craned his neck to look at the climb ahead of him, *Nuts, I wanted to check out this place. Then, again.* He answered, "Will do."

Max hiked double-time from the castle to the auditorium. Kat was waiting inside the door.

She held up the Johns report and waved the document in the air.

"Short trip!" she announced. "De Molay took a cabin just south of here in his last years before the Catholic church burned him slowly at the stake in 1314."

"Ouch! Slowly, huh?" The thought made Max cringe. Fire was one thing that scared him.

"My point," Kat said, "is that while the soldiers are searching the castle, we might hit paydirt at this cabin."

"And I think I know exactly where the location is," Yosi interjected. He walked up beside Kat. "There's an old recluse living there, hardly ever leaves the place. A real oddball."

"Sounds like an interesting visit even if we don't find anything,"

Max said.

"I'll get Sergeant First Class Bennett to drive us there," Yosi said.

Minutes later, the four of them were in a military vehicle heading south on a dirt road just east of Highway 2. Kat sat next to Max in the back seat, watching the scenery and trying to contain her enthusiasm. This could be just one more lead, perhaps a bad one. But she had a "feeling" and previous "feelings" had produced a bumper crop of discoveries.

This one, in particular, would be a thrill to share with her mom and dad, but she was not about to jinx the discovery by alerting them to the possibilities. Her dad had been disappointed enough, even by his former church members who fired him from his pastorate. Since then, she had avoided any and all instances that might do the same. She didn't want to be added to the list of those who had done so.

She shook her head to concentrate on the immediate. A partly cloudy sky hung over them. The Mediterranean rippled in the sunlight to their right. The craggy coastline reminded Kat of Massachusetts or Rhode Island.

Shortly, Yosi in the front passenger seat pointed to their right. "There's the cottage."

At the end of a long footpath about sixty or eighty yards off the road, a small Jerusalem-stone cottage stood on a knoll overlooking the sea. There were no trees around the structure, no shrubs, just a desolate building.

Kat noticed no power lines supplied electricity. And the pathway barely looked traveled upon.

Bennett pulled the vehicle to the side of the road and they all piled out and walked along the path.

"You sure someone lives here?" Max asked Yosi in Hebrew.

"Well, I haven't seen him in a couple of years. When the IDF was trying to buy more coastland near the castle, I led a party who approached him, but he gave us a ton of grief and refused to sell. In the end, the IDF thought it not worth the battle. I think they figured he'd die soon enough and they'd be able to buy the property then. He's old enough that he could die any day."

When they reached the cabin, Max stepped ahead and extended his hand to knock on the door. Before he could, the door opened. Standing every bit as tall as Max was an ancient man, wispy white hair hanging below his shoulders, a beard reaching to his chest. He wore a long white robe and held an ancient sword in his hand. Kat spotted the Knights Templar crest on the handle of the sword—the spitting image of Sir Godfrey's sword in Dublin.

The knight, for obviously he was a knight, looked Max over, peered past him at Yosi and Bennett, then locked his cloudy eyes on Kat. His brow tightened. He looked again at Max, from his head to his feet. Then again at Kat. One eye opened wide. Suddenly Kat felt an odd exhilaration.

Pointing to her, the knight said in French, "You, young damsel, and you," he motioned toward Max, "come in."

He pointed at Yosi and said in Hebrew, "You two may remain. I am *not* selling."

Kat looked at Yosi and shrugged. As she and Max squeezed past the knight, Yosi began to object, "But, sir—"

But the knight shut the door in his face.

Kat and Max took several steps inside and looked around the cottage, which was one great room, containing kitchen, living room, dining nook, and sleeping area.

Suddenly Kat's eyes stopped. She couldn't believe what she was seeing. She grabbed Max's left elbow and motioned with her eyes.

On the wall before them was a wide, open fireplace; above the fireplace, items that told a story. In the center was a painting of an old Crusader wearing a white robe embossed with a black cross and with a long, flowing white cape bearing a black cross on the side. Chain mail peeked out beneath the robes and black, pointed boots adorned his feet. He wore a leather belt off which hung an empty sword sheath and in his right hand he gripped the handle of the huge broadsword, whose blade was grounded.

To the left and right of the painting hung two shields, both square except that the bottom portions curved to a point. In the northwest and southeast quadrants of the shield on the right were a red cross on a white background. In the other two quadrants, a wide yellow strip cut diagonally across a royal-blue background.

The shield on the left was a deep blue with short vertical gold lines and, in the center, a large golden lion wearing a crown, standing on its hind legs and with red-tipped appendages.

"Grand Master Jacques de Molay." The declaration came in aristocratic French from the old knight, who now stood beside Kat and Max, looking admiringly up at the wall. He pointed to the right, "The de Molay coat of arms," then to the left, "and the coat of arms of my family's ancestral home, Franche-Comté in eastern France."

"Wonderful!" Kat exclaimed. She turned to him and extended her hand. "I'm Doctor Katherine Cardova, this is Max Braxton and we're here—"

"Looking for King David's music," the man finished.

Kat was taken aback. "You know?!"

"Of course, I know. The Holy Spirit showed me four days ago you would be coming soon—very soon."

A delightful shiver went up Kat's spine. Could this truly be happening—to her? To a Midwest farm girl? She had a sudden thought of the Bible scripture in which Queen Esther's Jewish uncle told her that perhaps she was in her royal position "for such a time as this." Was this time, for Kat, a Godincidence? An Esther time?

Resting his left hand on the handle of the sword and maintaining its tip on the wooden floor, the knight bowed deeply. "Archibald of Franche-Comté, at your service, madam, monsieur," he said.

"We're so honored to meet you," Kat said in French. "But are you saying you possess the music of the Psalms?"

"Yes, dear lady, yes." The words came quickly and with excitement. A toothy smile widened further, then his eyes narrowed in seriousness. "My family and the family of Jacques de Molay were close friends and both lived in Molay, a commune in Franche-Comté.

"Molay, Besançon, Belfort, Montbéliard—that whole region was Christianized by Saint Columbanus, who founded monasteries there. Centuries later, many of the young men joined the Crusades. Jacques and my ancestor, Jean-Baptiste Blanc, fought side by side for years and were as brothers in Christ.

"When the Pope ordered Jacques' execution, Jacques passed the mantle of safekeeping the music to Jean-Baptiste. My family has protected the music for eight hundred years in this very home, waiting for the Third Temple to be built. Then, in a vision, I saw you and your red hair, with a broad man at your side, come to my door."

His eyes widened, a look of victory mixed with mirth flooding his face. "And here you are, madam, as the Holy Spirit foretold!"

Kat could barely contain her anticipation. "Did the Holy Spirit tell you what to do with the music once I arrived?" she asked.

"Why, give the music to you, of course!"

Kat felt her knees go weak, a quiver wiggled down the back of her neck, and she looked at her hands. They were shaking. As much to steady herself as for joy, she grabbed Max's right hand with her left.

"You don't know—" she began.

"Oh, yes, I do," Archibald responded. "The inspiration of the music, knowing its importance, has driven me on for many decades. And guarding the music has been both blessing and burden to my family all these centuries—and to me through my eighty-nine years. Not until my great-grandfather's time did we see a path to the Third Temple. The day when Binyamin Ze'ev—Theodor Herzl—restored the Yiddish language and inspired Jews to begin returning to the Holy Land. That encouraged the last couple of generations of Templars to keep our faith.

"Then, in 1948, the prophecy of Jewish return to their land was fulfilled. And in 1967 when the Jews retook all of Jerusalem we became excited that a Third Temple was imminent. But, God forbid, then the Jews incredibly gave control of the Temple Mount to their enemies. We were bewildered, astonished."

Archibald threw up his hands in incredulity, then added, "But now, yes, now, you are here. So this wonderful symbol that God is forever faithful—The Third Temple—must be truly impending!"

"You imply other Templars besides you are well aware of the music," Max said.

"Why, yes, a handful of descendants of the last Knights Templar, who manned Atlit, or Pilgrims Castle. My wife, bless her soul, was barren and gave me no son to carry on. So each of the Templars, from time to time, has come and relieved me, temporarily, of my duties so I can put off the Templar garments, leave this cottage and, for a week or so, be a person of today's world. Each time they do, I grow less and less anxious to do so. The world has become so much like Sodom and Gomorrah and, outside Israel, so anti-Semitic. My homeland, France? Oy!" His hands flew up in disgust.

Surprised this man had such a grasp for what was happening around the world, Kat nodded in agreement and held tight to her fervor for the task at hand. Thankfully, Archibald straightened, turned to make eye-contact with Kat and said, "But, dear lady, to your task before you—and mine fulfilled."

He stepped around her and Max and approached a nook to the right of the fireplace. Nearly filling the alcove were a sturdy round acacia wood dining table, encircled by four ornate, high-backed acacia chairs, in whose backs were carved wide crosses. A hand-woven rug of myriad colors covered the floor beneath the table and chairs.

"Help me move these," Archibald said.

Kat, Max, and Archibald moved the furniture and rug. Kat had guessed what to expect and she was correct. Archibald bent low and pressed a particular spot on one of the wide floorboards. The board popped up about one inch, enough for him to pry his fingers beneath.

In an instant, the floorboard was up and Archibald was tugging on a thick iron ring beneath. A moment later, a circle of floorboards rose up. Archibald looked at Max and, in French, said, "I'll need your strength, young man. I'm afraid I'm not as stalwart as I used to be."

Max leaned down and, with a singular motion, lifted the floorboards and set them down beside him that revealed a circular stairway descending into darkness.

Grabbing a flashlight from a countertop, Archibald led them down the stairway to a depth of about eight feet where their feet landed on what felt like marble.

Archibald pointed the flashlight into the room, which was much smaller than the cottage above—perhaps eight-by-eight feet.

"Cool, dry and acid-free," Archibald announced.

Thinking of the hundreds of hours she had spent pouring through ancient manuscripts at Yale University's extraordinary Beinecke Rare Book and Manuscript Library, built especially for preservation, Kat muttered, "Well done—under the circumstances."

Archibald's light stopped upon a simple five-foot-high marble pedestal. On top of the pedestal was a rectangular box about eighteen-by-twelve inches wide and six inches high.

"Oh, my Lord and my God." The words escaped Kat's lips unbidden. Her heart skipped a beat in her excitement.

"The music," Archibald announced.

Kat gripped Max's hand with such force she must have hurt him, then pulled him along as she took several hesitant steps toward the treasure. She an explosive. She had to consciously keep her knees from buckling.

Archibald strode to the pedestal and looked down at the box. "Acacia wood. The music was first kept secure in the residential palace of Jewish kings from King David until the destruction of the First Temple, which was about four hundred and fifty years. That palace was in Ir David, the City of David below Jerusalem's Old City to the east."

A memory kicked in for Kat. "I remember a major archeological excavation at Ir David," she said. "Professor Ronny Reich of Haifa University oversaw the dig in 2007. They discovered many artifacts—seals, signets, papyrus documents—a magnificent find. But they found no music."

"No," Archibald said. "Once the First Temple was destroyed, then began the music's journey."

Kat could feel Max by her shoulder as she took three more steps and found herself beside Archibald, looking down at the box. Its top was quite unique. Like a modern-day cardboard box, it had two lids that folded and met at the middle.

A flat stone was inset into the center of each lid. An etching of a lion's head dominated one stone.

"The Lion of Judah," Kat exclaimed, pointing. "symbolizing King David's family, the Tribe of Judah. And with a crown of royalty atop the Aramaic letter 'D' denoting the Davidic kingship—the exact same etching as we saw at the dig atop Dragot."

She read aloud the small Hebraic letters beneath the lion: "King David, son of Jesse."

Shivers of excitement played on Kat's s in like fingers on a keyboard.

The other stone contained an etching of a scroll with a musical note in its center. She pointed and read the words: "Hold secure and secret until the Third Temple."

She looked at Max, "David must have known two temples would be built and destroyed. He had told Solomon to build the First Temple, but—"

"God knows," Archibald interjected. "He always knows."

Kat could barely contain her eagerness and blurted, "May I open the box?"

Archibald nodded approval.

She leaned in toward the box and gingerly reached forward. When her fingers were about a foot away, electricity prickled her fingertips. She snatched her hands away.

"The presence of the Spirit," Archibald said. "It's a *good* thing."

Kat glanced tentatively at Max. He shrugged. Big help, she thought wryly.

Again she reached toward the box, felt the tingle but continued regardless. When her fingers touched the wood, a powerful warmth spread along her hands, up her arms, and throughout her body.

"Oh, my!" she exclaimed.

She lifted the lids and looked inside. The box was full of scrolls, all with royal purple ribbons tied tight about them. She picked one up, felt heat emanating from inside, and gingerly examined the scroll.

344

A half-dollar-sized seal kept the scroll shut. A large Aramaic letter "D" filled the seal.

"It's King David's signet, right?" Kat asked, looking up at Archibald. He nodded agreement.

"These scrolls," she said, looking up at Max, "were sealed by rolling the signet seal across soft wet clay. The signet authenticates that what is within the scroll is genuine, and if the etching of the musical scroll on the box is true, then this *is* the music of the Psalms."

"We can't unseal any of them, can we?" Max asked, obviously knowing the answer.

Kat shook her head. "But we can deliver the music to the Israeli government and they can go ahead with the Third Temple plans, knowing they have the blessing of the God of Abraham, Isaac and Jacob—the God, who actually wrote the music and the Psalms through His servants, David and the other psalmists."

Archibald laid a soft hand on Kat's shoulder and asked, "May I carry the box out of here?"

"Of course."

A minute later they were upstairs at the front door.

Giant tears were running in rivulets down Archibald's cheeks. Kat felt remorse for him but exuberance for the world.

"May I ask you one question before we go?" she asked.

"Why, of course."

"You've kept yourselves secret. Why didn't your ancestors give the music to the Vatican to protect?"

"Pshaw!" Archibald spat out. "The Vatican?! The same ones who tortured our ancestors and burned them at the stake? Who falsely declared them heretics? Who wrongly executed de Molay and others? Who then confiscated all their land and treasure? The Vatican?!"

Kat shrugged. "I see."

"The Knights Templar had to go underground, where we continued to practice. But no one—no one," Archibald raised an angry fist, "knew until 2001—when a professor assigned to the Vatican's secret archives discovered the misfiled Chinon parchment—that Pope Clement had absolved the order of heresy. The church did not deem to reveal this to the world."

Kat thought hard on this, caught between this bit of information and the most incredible discovery of the last few centuries: the music in Archibald's grasp.

"A group of us who are heirs of the Knights Templar—now called the Association of the Sovereign Order of the Temple of Christ—sued Pope Benedict the Sixteenth in a Spanish court in 2008 for one hundred and fifty billion dollars for assets the Catholic Church seized seven hundred years ago."

"How did that go?" Max asked.

"Nowhere."

"What will you do now you don't have the music to protect?" Kat asked.

"I've thought of this for so long and especially over the last four days as I've awaited your arrival. The first thing I'll do is visit family in France. Second, pursue our lawsuit against the Vatican. They're so powerful. They think by simply ignoring us they can manipulate the courts of justice."

"Well—Godspeed," Kat said. "I hope we meet again."

Archibald bowed to her, then handed her the box.

"And Godspeed to you, dear redhead of God," he said with a puckish smile.

He turned to Max and shook his hand with one giant hand while gripping his elbow with the other.

"Guard this music with your life, won't you, my friend?"

"As long as the treasure is in our possession, I promise."

Chapter 23

Yosi and Bennett were waiting for them outside. Their eyes went wide at the sight of the box and Yosi hustled them into the Humvee.

Yosi radioed Atlit and called off the search, then turned to Max and Kat, who were seated in the back. "We're heading for Jerusalem right now. Going straight to Police Headquarters. Those are our orders," he said.

Max and Kat smiled at one another. Kat's expression reminded Max of the look of a schoolgirl about to play hooky.

Minutes later, the Humvee rumbled past a toll booth and along Route 6. They sped over a railway track as if nonexistent.

Probably guessing at their concern, Bennett turned, "No trains on the Sabbath. No worries."

"That's right," Max said, turning to Kat. "You found the music, fittingly, on a Sabbath as well as your birthday."

She smiled.

Suddenly, Max remembered the surprise. He glanced at his wristwatch. Just past two o'clock, so seven in the morning on the East Coast. He was almost too late. He dialed a number and when a woman answered, he asked, "Ready?"

"Ready."

"What are you doing?" Kat asked.

Max pressed SPEAKER and handed her the phone, certain she had no clue who was on the end of the line.

"Hello?" Kat said.

Her answer came quickly with three barks.

Kat's face lit up like a candle. "Tuck!"

"Bark."

Kat looked at Max and whispered, "Thank you."

Max smiled back at her, glad to read the delight in her face.

"Tuck, I miss you."

"Bark."

"I'm sorry, but I won't be able to get home when I planned."

A low growl.

Kat looked at Max and said, "He's displeased."

"So I can hear," Max said, trying to suppress a chuckle.

"No, seriously. He is not happy."

Max wiped the smile from his face.

"Tucky, I love you."

A reluctant bark.

"I will get home as soon as possible. Tell Auntie that, okay?"

Another growl, followed by two barks.

"I can see him wagging his tail," Kat said to Max.

Back to the phone, she said: "What a wonderful birthday present. Thank you, Tuck. You're the best boy in the whole wide world. Bye-bye."

Three barks.

A moment later, Alice was on the phone wishing Kat a happy birthday.

"All things are restored to their rightful order," Kat answered.

348

"Thanks so much, dear friend. I love you."

"You, too."

"I have fabulous news, Alice. But I have to wait to tell you. Soon, though, soon."

After the two had signed off, Kat handed Max his phone. "What a surprise!"

She wiped a tear about to fall from the corner of her left eye.

"A lady and her best friend being separated too long is unnatural," Max said.

Kat gripped his hand in hers. "I do appreciate what you did."

Max felt a warm calm and happiness.

"You must truly be ready to breathe a sigh of relief from all this," he asked.

She grinned but answered, "Not quite yet. Not until the music's out of our hands and into a vault at Israeli Antiquities."

"You mean you can't show the box to the world on television?"

Kat cocked her head. "That's possible, but think of the security problems."

"Hey, they protect the PM every hour of every day and most of the Arab world would like to see him dead."

"Well, they did reveal a lot of artifacts from the dig at the City of David. We'll see, but the revelation is their call; the treasure is theirs."

Max peered at the wooden box.

"The box is beautifully simple," he said.

"I agree."

"I wonder if the chalice is an extraordinarily expensive silver or gold vessel, or if it's simply clay."

"My guess is 'simple.' Remember where Jesus was born? Definitely no palace."

"Right."

He tentatively moved his right hand toward the box. A sharp current ran up his hand and he snapped his hand back. "So *that's* what you felt," he said.

"You get a shock?"

"More of an Aqua Velva slap."

"Aqua Velva? You're more old-fashioned than your age would imply."

"In many ways, yes."

He couldn't help smile—probably like a schoolboy—at the sparkle in her green eyes.

They both paused and watched the Israeli landscape fly by.

"Up to Jerusalem," Kat said. "No matter the direction you're approaching from, you always go 'up' to the Old City."

Max nodded, then said, "I suppose this means the speakers' circuit for you."

She frowned and after a pause said, "I imagine you're right, but the focus should be on the music—how the discovery will transform both temple and church worship. Besides, the 'team' found the music. You and me—and, most of all, Danny Arens. Without Danny, the search never begins. Without you, the search never concludes."

Max felt pride swell up within him, then fought back that pride.

"You might have taken longer," he said, "but you've got the grit and wisdom to have completed the quest alone, no doubt."

"You're too humble."

"Whatever you call me, I'm staying in the shadows on this one. Besides, I've got a book to write."

"Right. So once we get the music to Jerusalem, what are your immediate—"

Suddenly an explosion rocked the road about forty feet in front of them. Bennett slammed on the brakes. When the smoke cleared, two large, covered flatbed trucks formed a "V" in the road, blocking their advance.

Max heard a rumble of trucks and spun to look behind them. Two more covered flatbeds filled the road there as well and trees lined both sides of the highway. *No way out.*

A deep voice in Hebrew crackled through a loudspeaker: "Out of the Humvee with the music!"

"How would they know—?" Max began.

"Now or face destruction!" the voice demanded and several men piled out of the front flatbeds, all armed with rifles.

"Stay here and stay down," Max said to Kat.

He tapped Yosi on the shoulder. "Got a weapon for me?"

As Yosi began to answer, they heard a loud "hum-m-m" nearing them from two directions.

"Sounds like Apaches!" Max declared.

Yosi smiled broadly and passed him a TAVOR X95, saying, "Just in case, my friend."

Just then, two black Boeing AH-64 Apache gunships rose over the treetops. Menacing was the one word Max thought of. One Apache's nose pointed at the flatbeds in front of the Humvee, the other hovered over the flatbeds behind.

Suddenly, the Apache in front unleashed two AGM-114 Hellfire missiles. Instantly, the two flatbeds blocking the road in front blew up in balls of fire, the vehicles lifting several feet off the ground. The bodies standing nearby all flew into the air.

A moment later, the Apache behind the Humvee unleashed a barrage of 30-millimeter rounds from its M230 Chain Gun, surrounding the men in those two flatbeds with sure death if they were to leave the trucks.

A loud speaker from the Apache bellowed to life in Hebrew: "Stand down! Drop your weapons!"

The gunmen still standing near the two forward flatbeds all threw their rifles to the ground and laid down on their stomachs.

Peripherally, Max saw movement through the window beside him and turned to see the barrel of a rifle. However the gunman got there, Max didn't consider. His hand was already on the door handle and he thrust the door open with terrible force, crashing it into the gunman. The barrel flashed, a bullet broke the window, and Max felt a searing pain in his side. He was hit. Kat screamed. Max leaped out of his seat, blood gushing. The gunman had stumbled to Max's left and Max helped him on the way, driving his right fist into the man's jaw. He tumbled to the ground and Max ripped the rifle from his grasp.

Kat was already at his side. "Max! Max, are you all right?"

He turned to look at her and smiled crookedly. He put a hand to his side and felt sticky warm blood oozing out. The world started to blur into a brown haze and Kat's beautiful face began to fade. "Just a flesh wound," he managed to say. "Is the music—"

Before he could finish the sentence, Max passed out.

Several hours later, Max partially woke up. Groggy and with a throbbing pain in his side as well as his shoulder where Said had stabbed him. He tried to slowly open his eyes to lights clearly too bright and noises obviously too loud. He recalled his final moments of consciousness—saw the rifle fire, felt his fist crack the man on the jaw, saw Kat look at him with alarm—and immediately felt embarrassed. Big warrior, him. Boy, oh boy. How to impress the girl you love. Love?

His eyes shot open and the light sent a piercing pain to the back of his head. He shut his eyelids, squinting with the ache. Yes, love. *Forgot what it felt like, didn't you?*

"Leave me alone." The words spilled out of his mouth unrequested.

"What?" The voice was familiar. Indeed, Kat's voice.

Max raised an arm so that his hand would shield his eyes from the light, then slowly opened them.

Kat sat in a straight-back chair tight up against the bed.

"You're awake," she announced. "Did you say you want me to leave?"

"Want you to leave?"

"You just said, 'Leave me alone.'"

Max wondered if any of his other thoughts had expressed themselves in spoken words.

"Is that all I said?" he asked. His mouth felt loaded with cotton batting, his tongue like an oversized hotdog.

"Yes."

"Good. Then, I don't want you to leave. You're the most welcome sight I could imagine."

Kat grinned and reached out for his right hand.

"My hero," she announced.

"Hero? Heroes don't pass out from flesh wounds."

"Good thing you're not a doctor," she said with a grin. "Your 'flesh wound' barely missed your left kidney and drained you of a fair amount of blood."

He laughed but the action hurt so badly he stopped. "So I'll be in overnight, will I?"

Kat looked at her watch, then out the large window behind her. "Well, it's now eleven o'clock, so I'd say that's a good bet, soldier. And for a few more days, I'd guess.

"No, tomorrow at noon, I'm out of here."

"Tomorrow at noon, you'll be having your bandages changed."

All of a sudden Max thought of something much more important. "The music," he said. "Is the music okay?"

Kat nodded. "Safe and secure. Tonight experts are authenticating the discovery. One of them is Professor Yosef Garfinkel of Hebrew University, perhaps the foremost expert on the Protohistoric era of the Near East, which is the 10th century BC when King David lived. Professor Garfinkel once found what is believed to be the earliest Hebrew inscription ever discovered—written in ink on a pottery shard. If all goes well, tomorrow morning Dudi and the director of the Israeli Department of Antiquities will announce the discovery."

"You'll be there?"

"I'll be there."

"I want to be there, too. Not up front but in the crowd, cheering you on."

"You should be, but—" Kat rose and went to the door. She spoke to someone outside.

She walked back to Max. "Speaking of Dudi, he's been in and out of here since you arrived this afternoon. The PM has called twice. Yosi's been in and out. Reuven Hofi has checked in on you. Mary Proctor from MI6 came by. Heck, Chris Hollingsworth somehow got my phone number."

"You make me blush."

"You?"

Max paused. "Where, by the way, is 'here'?"

"The Shaare Zedek Medical Center."

"On the Jaffa Road just outside the Old City," Max said.

"You know this place?"

"Because they handle so many mass-casualty incidents, their trauma unit has become a model for emergency medicine for the world."

At that moment, Dudi entered the room. "Better still," he said in English, "Shaare Zedek means 'Gates of Justice' and justice is what we

354

received today."

Dudi stepped up to the bed and added, "Good to see you awake, my friend. You sustained quite an injury."

"Flesh wound," Max said. "Out of here tomorrow."

Dudi shook his head.

"Just watch," Max said. He pushed his elbows down on the bed, attempting to sit up, but a brilliant shard of pain stabbed at his side and he laid back down. After a moment, he muttered, "What 'justice' are you talking about, Chief?"

"Shall I count the ways?" Dudi spoke the words in mirth but their undertones told Max a different story.

"What's the matter, Dudi?" he asked.

"You recall you thought there was a leak that allowed the Salah al-Din Brigades to know where you and Kat were all the time?"

Max nodded.

"Well, we discovered two things. The Brigade didn't need our help. They had eyes on you when you crossed the border into Petra—obviously because the Jordanians are our quasi-friends at best. They had eyes on you in Dublin—a young man we captured in a home occupied by the cell leader. That young man revealed he contacted another cell in Wales. Well, they're everywhere in Israel now."

Dudi pulled a chair to him and sat down. "But in our investigation, we did indeed find a leak."

"Yes?" Max turned to look at Dudi but that was his left side where the bullet and knife had done their damage, and he winced.

Dudi stood and came to the other side of the bed, standing beside Kat. Then he continued, "We found ever since we investigated the scene at Professor Arens' assault, my secretary, Martha, was informing YHVY Alpha YHVY Omega—which means God is the Alpha and the Omega and is connected to Neturei Karta—of your search.

"Martha?!" Max asked in disbelief.

Dudi nodded, then shook his head. "Hard to believe." He looked at Kat and said, "My secretary for many years. Many."

"Off to jail for Martha," Max said.

"Yes."

"Neturei Karta," Max said. "That's the ultra-religious group."

"Yes."

"And so?"

"It was YHVY Alpha YHVY Omega that attacked you on the way here from Haifa."

Max went silent, deep in thought. After several moments, he looked at Kat. "But they're religious; they should want the music for worship more than anyone."

"They feel the Jews revitalized Israel on their own power and shouldn't even be here. Construction of a Third Temple—and with David's music? For them, that would be the ultimate wickedness."

Max could only shake his head in disbelief.

"There's more," Dudi said.

Max's eyebrows rose. "Yes?"

"Your buddy the Assassin, Widad Said. He's been living in Washington, DC, embedded as part of the Palestinian embassy. Odd, isn't it?"

"Hardly," Max said. "I'm sure he's not the only terrorist at foreign embassies."

"Well, our friends at Homeland Security have been doing some deep checking." Dudi paused a moment and smiled at Max. "You know, you must have been very important to the Brigades. They pulled him away from his mission in Washington to kill you."

"What mission?"

"He was days away from blowing up the Republican Caucus, Israel's longest and greatest supporters."

Chapter 24

Three days had transpired since the discovery of David's music of the Psalms was revealed to the world media.

Danny Arens had awoken from unconsciousness and could barely contain his exuberance over the news.

Kat had spent an entire morning with Danny, retelling her and Max's travails in finding the music. He had cheered her on, living the adventure vicariously and loving every minute of the tale.

When Danny recovered enough and when the Israeli Antiquities Authority reopened the site, she promised to join him in the dig at Dragot.

The media was comparing Kat to Gertrude Bell (who traveled in dangerous countries), Kathleen Kenyon (of Jericho excavation fame) and others. Kat had done her best to defer the credit to Danny, but he had explicitly declined, saying he had stumbled upon a clue but she had pursued the clue to resolution.

For two days, she had tried to reach her mom and dad and had discovered they were off at a camp on a lake in Iowa without any telephones or electricity.

Finally, when driving home, they had heard the news on the radio and pulled off the road to call her. They were proud, thrilled, and sounded almost breathless. Her dad said they wanted to catch the next plane to Israel. Her mom had blubbered some mangled expression of consent to the idea.

When they hung up, Kat thought of her sister. "Kait," she had breathed to herself. "The only missing piece to my celebration."

Sitting nearby, Max had overheard. "Your twin," he said.

Kat pushed back a tear. At that moment she understood because Kait had died, she had been twice driven to succeed, that whatever she ever accomplished in her career was done for both of them, that if truth be told, she owed a share of this wonderful victory to her sister.

She butchered an explanation of all this, but Max masterfully masked his understanding. She knew he was covering and loved him for the deception. *Loved*? Her eyes shot to Max and his warm brown eyes looked back as if he read her mind. *Did he? Could he?*

And now, escaping reporters and invitations to speak around the world, Kat and Max sat on two tree stumps off the Israeli National Trail, atop an observation point overlooking the Hula Valley northwest of the Sea of Galilee. The panoramic view of the forest behind them was extraordinary and so different than the scene in front of them—a valley squared off in various shades of green much like the countrysides of Ireland and England. Before them, a small campfire burned and every few minutes, Max would turn a pheasant on a spit over an open fire. The odor was pleasant and, Max thought, the company both exhilarating and ravishing.

He looked again at this lady before him and smiled at the sight of two matching socks, both midnight blue with bursting white stars. She had settled accounts. She had forgiven herself. She was no longer in grief, or, at least, the kind that always lingered and sometimes devastated.

Max was skimming through an article in the Jewish newspaper *Ha'aretz*. "They compare you to Doctor Nahman Avigad," he said.

"Now they've gotten carried away. That's absurd," Kat replied. "Doctor Avigad was one of the great figures in the history of Hebrew and Jewish epigraphy."

"Epigraphy?"

"Ancient inscriptions. That's the only comparison. Avigad discovered many seals—one belonging to Queen Jezebel—and the reporter must be comparing Avigad's seals to the lost music."

"No," Max said, "he's quoting another archeologist who is comparing the music to the Dead Sea Scrolls and the Rosetta Stone."

"Well, Avigad was deeply involved in exploration of the caves and the Dead Sea Scrolls as well as Masada and Beit She'arim, an ancient Jewish town east of Haifa. But I'm no Avigad."

"How about Pessah Bar-Adon and Howard Carter?" Max asked with a smile. "Do you like those comparisons better?"

"Bar-Adon? Carter?" Kat threw up her arms in dismay. "Carter discovered King Tut's tomb, for goodness sake. And Bar-Adon? He only discovered Nahal Mishmar, a hoard of hundreds of copper, bronze, ivory and stone decorated artifacts including scepters, crowns, tools, weapons—"

"In other words, less significant than David's music," Max said, his lips curling into a smile.

"My involvement was sheer God-incidence," Kat said. "He's the one who gets the credit in my book."

"This whole experience has clearly shown me God does exist and He rules over the affairs of men," Max said. "*And* he chose you as His instrument."

His statement appeared to have struck a chord with Kat. She leaned into him. "You mentioned God."

He nodded.

"That He does exist?"

He nodded.

"That He rules over the affairs of men?"

He nodded.

"You believe."

"I've always believed."

"But now you confess."

"Now I confess. He has saved our lives enough times and shown Himself in so many ways. Last night I awoke from a dream—a nightmare, really. I stepped around a wall of the castle at Atlit and Widad Said stood before me, a sawed-off shotgun pointed at my head."

Kat gulped.

"He screamed, 'Allahu Akbar' and was about to pull the trigger when a brilliant flash of light blinded him and a lightning bolt blasted the shotgun from his hands."

Kat's eyes widened, accompanied by a cheek-to-cheek smile.

"Said looked to the source of the light and asked, 'Allah?' Deep in the light, I could discern the outline of a man—not so handsome that he would attract attention, not muscular that he would command subservience, but a man with a face effused with a mixture of sadness and love. Like he was sad at Said's beliefs, but he still loved the man as his creation, like you would if your child had gone horribly bad.

"When Said asked if he was Allah, the man shook his head and said, 'Allah does not exist, Widad. I am Yeshua the Messiah.'"

Max reached and took hold of Kat's hand. "I fell to the ground, facedown and wept. For how long, I don't know, but when I finally stopped, I looked up and Said was gone but Jesus was still there. He reached down, pulled me to my feet and just smiled."

"Just smiled," Kat asked, her face aglow.

"Just smiled," Max said, "and then I woke up and confessed Him as my Lord and Savior."

"Your mom will be thrilled."

"She will."

"And you waited until now to tell this to me?" Kat looked in shock.

Max smiled. "You had other important matters to deal with. Your mom. Your dad. Your invitations."

"But nothing more important than this. Nothing!"

Kat threw her arms around his neck and hugged him, then kissed him firmly on the lips.

Max lit up. "Now that's a prize I didn't expect."

"Expect?" she enthused. "You've just made all this last week or so worthwhile."

Kat turned to her backpack and dug out her Bible. Opening the Scriptures, she reefed through the pages until she found her place.

"Listen to this and imagine if we had King David's music," she said and read:

"'We give thanks to you, O God. We give thanks for your Name is near. Men tell of your wonderful deeds.'"

"I imagine the music must be wonderful," Max said.

"That you confessed Christ is more, even more, beautiful to me," she said and a tear started down her cheek. Suddenly her eyebrows knit, she sniffed and then turned to look at the fire. She sharply pointed to the forgotten pheasant, and Max hurriedly turned the spit a quarter-turn.

"Have you had any contact with Yale?"

"You'd better believe it. Can you believe, they want to name a building after me."

"Really?"

Kat shrugged. "What can I say?"

"How about 'Okay and I'll take the corner suite for my office'?"

"I'm humbled in a way."

"How humbled?"

"First, I'm far too young for that kind of honor. Second, the glory is displaced. Like I've said, this hoopla should be all about the music."

"But people—the world—can relate to people better than to an inanimate object," Max said.

"I guess."

"Think of Einstein and the bomb. Einstein's as famous as the bomb. Alexander Graham Bell's fame is equal to the telephone. Thomas Edison's as well-known as electricity."

"I'm not Einstein, Bell or Edison—not by a long shot."

"You *do* get my point, though," Max said.

"Reluctantly."

"Well, there's nothing so wonderful as a reluctant hero."

"You're the reluctant hero. Your name hasn't been mentioned in any of this."

Max grinned. "Friends in high places can help in two ways: garner you a high profile or anonymity, whichever you choose. I choose anonymity."

"I think you might want to choose to put the veggies over the fire," Kat said, handing him a pot half-filled with peas and baby onions in water.

Max balanced the pot on three rocks over the fire.

"What about you? What's next?" Kat asked.

He held out his hands before him. "You see these?"

"They've protected me enough. I see them."

"My weapons of 'no mas' destruction," he said, wondering if she caught the reference to the Sugar Ray Leonard-Roberto Duran fight. "I'm laying them aside until I finish my book. Then I'll decide whether to reenlist, teach, or what."

Kat looked seriously at Max. "You remember our talks about Godincidences?"

"I do."

"Well, I think my meeting you was a God-incidence."

He chuckled. "I know you do, and so do I."

They leaned in toward one another, their lips close, her aroma dizzying.

Settling down on his stomach on a summit two hundred yards away, Mumim Maloof grunted with satisfaction. Peering into the sights of his 62mm Bora sniper rifle, secured upon a tripod, Mumim zoomed in on his targets—the two American pigs.

He had lost everything. Seeking all the glory for Salah al-Din Brigades by single-handedly ending the search for the cursed music— but failing in that attempt—Mumim had, in effect, brought doom to the Brigades. All of his warriors from Petra to Ireland and Wales had failed. Even Widad had failed. And his crowning glory, the attack in Washington, D., the home of the Big Satan, had been discovered and his men rounded up like so many sheep. And now Mumim found himself an outcast with ISIS, al-Qaeda, the Muslim Brotherhood, Hamas, Hezbollah—and all the others.

Yes, he had lost everything and now he would get his revenge. He turned his head and spit on the ground. Revenge felt good. The rest of his former comrades said the music had been revealed, so they should let go of retribution; there was nothing to gain and everything to lose if the archeologist woman were killed; that, if she were killed, she would be honored as a martyr and they would even lose hearts and minds of those left-wing Christians who supported the Palestinians, as if that could happen.

The Third Temple Faithful now had full support of their fellow Israelis and even most of the Western world. What was there to gain from this assassination?

"I'll show you what," Mumim mumbled and took aim. The crosshair was square on the back of the American man who had disgraced Mumim's men. The woman would be next, an easy target because she would be in shock at her dead friend's head exploding and his blood splattering all over her.

Squeeze easy, he thought to himself. Calm and easy.

As he began to tighten the muscle in his index finger, a rocket flashed, unannounced, out of the sky and blew Mumim and the summit on which he lay into darkness. There were no seventy-two virgins, no Allah smiling down at him, no chorus of "Hail, Hero" from fallen comrades.

In that instant when Mumim Maloof's spirit departed his body, he realized his spiritual life choice had been the wrong one. Only the total lack of light and the cold, dead numbness of despair and anguish awaited him.

An explosion on a hilltop to their west brought Max and Kat to their feet.

Max's cell phone rang in a cargo pocket and he pulled it out.

"Braxton," he said.

"Got him, Max." The voice was that of Dudi Danino. Max pictured his friend seated in a war room with an IDF general, Reuven Hofi of

Shin Bet and perhaps Mary Proctor of MI6.

"Good shootin', pilgrim," Max said, knowing immediately that the John Wayne reference was lost on Danino.

"You and Kat make good pigeons," Dudi said.

"Thanks. I'll tell her. But I'd much rather be the hawk next time, okay?"

"Agreed."

Max replaced his phone to his pocket and turned to Kat. "Success," he said. "We drew Maloof out here in the hills where no one else would be in danger; he took the bait, and a drone took him out."

She breathed a deep sigh of relief and fell against his chest, her arms around him.

After a long embrace, he stepped back, held her at arm's length and said, "So now we can get you back to civilization and your adoring fans."

"Who said I wanted to go back?" she said, her lips full and smiling. "Tuck's with his second-best friend. I'm with you. The world can wait."

— END —

About the Author

Having won wide acclaim for his first historical novel, *Midnight Rider for the Morning Star*, and for another historical novel, *True North: Tice's Story*, a Publishers Weekly Featured Book, Mark Alan Leslie has jumped into the realm of modern action/thrillers with this first of a series.

A longtime journalist and editor, Leslie has won five national magazine writing awards. A golf writer for twenty-five years, Leslie has compiled two golf-industry e-books, *Putting a Little Spin on It: The Design's the Thing!* And *Putting a Little Spin on It: The Grooming's the Thing!* based on his hundreds of interviews with luminaries like Arnold Palmer, Jack Nicklaus, Sam Snead, Gene Sarazen, Ben Crenshaw, Gary Player, Kathy Whitworth, and Patti Berg as well as scores of people famous within the world of golf.

Leslie was a newspaper editor for fifteen years and a magazine editor for twelve years before forming his own media-relations company, which operated for thirteen years before he dove full time into writing books.

Leslie lives in Maine with his wife, Loy. The couple has two grown sons and three granddaughters.